Ordinary

Times

D.L. LaRoche

Also by D.L. LaRoche

The Arkansas Rose (a novella)
What Price Charlie's Soul
Abducted
The Mortician and Other Love Stories

Ordinary
Times

****

ISBN 979-8-9856230-4-8

Stillwater Press

San Jose, CA

Thank You

I am indebted to beta readers who caught errors and provided ideas, which will enhance the readers' experience and helped produce a better book.

Thank you, Colleen Rae, traveler, adventurer, and five-time published novelist, Richard Scott, writer, teacher, and creative arts aficionado, and Stephanie LaRoche, avid reader and insightful daughter. I am also indebted to my critique group, Our Voices, membered by Maddie McEwen, Dick Yaeger, and Anne Visnick Sanders. Their critique and advice are sincerely appreciated.

Karen

VENTURA BOULEVARD AMBLES ALONG the lowest fold in the San Fernando Valley, the Hollywood Hills, and Santa Monica Mountains precipitously up to the left if heading westward and to the right a gradual slope up to the San Gabriel and Santa Susanna ranges.

Down the wide and well-traveled boulevard in 1956 were 19 miles of real estate brokers, steak houses, beer joints, furniture stores, and an astonishing assortment of bomb shelter sales and installation—huge green tanks stocked with canned goods and dried meats, ready for planting deep in your yard—family safety from acoustical shock and radiation guaranteed.

Overt announcements and subliminal fear of "mutual assured destruction" hovered and quietly shrouded most social events while "duck and cover" was taught to the children in school.

President Eisenhower was serving the last year of his first term. Nikita Khrushchev threatened from the United Socialist Soviet Republic. The two nations had enough ready nuclear warheads to kill all life on the planet—leaving only smoldering ash and radiation. Life in the late fifties was not as dear or carefully led as it was a decade earlier ... or nearly as joyous.

Book One-- The Porcelain Cat

One
The Bet

ALLURING, MYSTERIOUS, OFF-PUTTING, but a feast for the eyes of any man with a pair, the beautiful Lacey could be seen most weekends sunning by the pool of the New Paradise Apartments in Studio City, giving the patio a panache not otherwise present. She was always alone.

It was rumored among those who engaged in New Paradise gossip that many a fearless, naïve, young male had attempted a connection. Still, none had scored. She was seen to be untouchable, damaging to the libido, and those in the know kept their distance.

Like an abstract of Picasso, she lured an interest—a need to engage, express admiration—and some new to the scene might approach but immediately be dispatched, their egos flattened and in need of a stint on the couch with a beer.

She was Miss Lacey Haift, and she basked in the sun, looking down her slender nose into a magazine she held—

exclusive in her interests, oblivious to her surroundings—a porcelain cat.

THROUGH THE OPEN DOOR of apartment 116, Giles Anderson could see her clearly—her eyes roaming the pages of Vogue, gorgeous, comely, feminine, but reputed to be stone.

"So, thirty?" Giles said, draped casually over an armchair, his blue eyes twinkling, his grin in place.

"That's the bet ... thirty says you won't touch first base," Paul said, enjoying a wager he knew he was bound to win. He turned to his housemate. "C'mon Dalton, get in on this. Not even our visiting lothario has a chance—easy money, D."

"Not *our*, but *your* lotha ... eh, whatchamacallit," Dalton said, running his fingers through his black curly hair. "I want that fucking straight. He ain't nothin' to me, maybe a mooch, but yeah, I'll donate another twenty, I guess. It's a stupid fucking bet; how we gonna know who wins?"

"That's fifty," Paul said, looking over at Giles. "Fifty redeemable trusting in God say you can't get a date."

"He ain't likely to get a hello," Dalton grumbled. "Nobody does."

PAUL SMYTHE, A TALL, SLENDER, BLUE-EYED, blond-haired, emotionally balanced, and accommodating accountant worked at the Chevrolet plant in Van Nuys. Dalton Dobbs, a short, stout, brown-eyed, hot-tempered refrigeration technician, was employed by Campos Refrigeration in North Hollywood. They had been sharing the two-bedroom apartment at the New Paradise for almost two years when Giles Anderson (Giles with a hard 'G' as in gold or God, he oft reminded), a fraternity brother of Paul's from Kansas State, arrived and squatted. Essentially broke, no particular skills, Giles assumed a night-time residence on Dalton's couch.

As his welcome began to wear thin, promises were made: yes, he would find a job, and yes, he would find a bed, and yes, he would participate fully. The question in Dalton's mind was, "fucking when?"

GILES CONTEMPLATED HIS MEAGER FUNDS and compared them to the risk. She might be a little older than ordinarily aroused his interest, but fifty bucks would feed his anorectic wallet should he make it to first base. He checked the patio again. *One date... hmm.* Yes, the cash—and otherwise, not a rainbow in sight, much less the pot.

"She's the payoff." Paul laughed. "You get the fifty ... and think about this, bother Giles, you may get *her* in the bargain." He cocked his head toward the door, a lingering, dimming glow in his eyes—while he had never made the attempt, he had considered it, the lovely Lacey willingly in his arms. But Paul was pragmatic in real life, resisting maneuvers unlikely to succeed.

"She is appealing," Giles admitted with a turn, imagining the cash in his pocket and the cat on his arm, but the hill was jagged and steep according to Paradise mythology, and he couldn't afford to lose a dime.

Paul opened his wallet, put a crisp new twenty and ten on the coffee table, and looked to Dalton. Catching the look and its hint of authority, Dalton grubbed out a wadded twenty from his pocket and flattened it next to its more presentable kin.

3

"It's yours with an actual date," Paul said. "You ask, she nods, and you spend money." He laughed. "If anyone can break the barrier, it's you. And if you don't ... well, it'll have been one hell of an experience, and you're only out twenty."

"Twenty?" Dalton said with a flash of surprise, his fingers combing through his thick black hair. "You said the bet was fifty."

"We're giving him odds," Paul said. "He's not working, and we are. We can afford it, and obviously, he can't."

"Huh?" Dalton muttered, pulling an ear. "I fucking don't get that. I didn't agree to no odds." He shook his head.

"It doesn't matter, D, we're gonna win." Paul laughed. "And if we clean him out completely, he'll be drinking your beer. I know you wouldn't want that."

A PERFECT TAN set off her dark green eyes and flaxen hair cut in a page boy. Full lips framed a generous mouth, perfectly set in her narrow face. Giles allowed his eyes a slow inquisitive roam over her golden legs, softly reflecting the late-afternoon light. What might he encounter, he wondered, should he succeed?

He liked her proportions—tall for a girl and slender, a swimmer's long muscles, yet shapely as his ideal might be if he ever considered one. She'd be a prize, the gold, he thought, and it was plausible considering a series of earlier successes. His perennial grin broadened at the upcoming prospect, and he was taken with an urge to get started.

"Okay, I'm in." He reached into his wallet and pulled out a ten, a five, and five ones—three dollars remaining—and placed them next to the opposition. "How long do I have?"

"Take what you need," Paul said. "The money's not going anywhere ... maybe right in this drawer." He pulled out a small drawer in a side table and placed the bills under a book.

"Bullshit," Dalton exclaimed, plopping his muscular body into the chair that Giles had earlier abandoned. "There ought to be a fucking limit. I say we give him a week. After that, the money's ours."

"Two weeks," Giles said. "If I can't get it done in two, I'm not the right guy."

"That's it," Paul said, "two weeks. Now a change of view; we're supposed to see the real-estate guy today. He might have something to show us."

"Well," Dalton huffed, "what about the bottom feeder here? He'll need more than promises to cover his part of the rent." He turned to Giles. "You know, we're not carrying your ass anymore." He glanced at Paul yet not meeting his eyes. "Well, at least not much longer."

Giles walked again to the door for another look—Lacey in view on the patio.

"You needn't worry, pal," Giles said. "I'm coming into some money."

THE DEVELOPERS HADN'T WASTED an inch of land or much imagination when throwing up these apartments in the exploding San Fernando Valley of the fifties. The New Paradise, a triangular, two-story donut with a patio around a pool the size of a saucepan, continually boasted a 'no vacancy' sign as it housed those from east of the Sierra on the move toward personal riches—the waiting list longer than the one naming those on a lease.

Despite the gloom of international threat and tippy-toe messaging about nuclear holocaust—all present in 1956—the valley bustled excessively with business and pleasure as money changed hands. The takers got rich while the givers returned to their birth cities and farms, eyes burning with smog, tails dragging through the exhaust fumes. Film studios had rooted in Burbank and Studio City, with workers, writers, and actors nearby, and the exaggerations of Hollywood pervaded the valley and catalyzed the scene. Today, a party; tomorrow, perhaps the mushroom cloud.

"WE NEED A BIGGER PLACE if that loafing friend of yours is gonna stay," Dalton had said on the third afternoon after Giles' arrival. "I don't like him sacked out on my couch; it stinks up the room."

"Yeah, okay!" Paul said, having harbored a similar thought. "I don't notice the smell, but we'll do it. Maybe ask the guys upstairs, Nick and Dennis, to join us and rent a house. Talk to 'em, D. You're the eager one."

"Sure, I'll do it," Dalton had said, some leery of being used. *Another brilliant idea from smart Mr. Smythe that blue-collar Dalton gets to execute.* He had laughed then and punched Paul lightly on the shoulder.

**

TURNING BACK THE CLOCK about two years, Paul had stopped in at the Little Brown Hut on the "Boulevard." After racking and stacking big numbers for General Motors, a beer or two was not unusual, and the Hut was kind to his budget—

two bits a tall glass for Pabst. He liked the casual atmosphere and schmoozing with the bartender/owner, Slick Eddy, and occasionally a game of pool with Mitzi, Slick Eddy's Vargas-like wife. Later, the usual crowd would gather. On Sundays, the front shutters went up, which opened the place to a parking lot between the Hut and the Boulevard, where patio tables with umbrellas and chairs found a home for the day. Slick Eddie brought in jazz—local combos seeking an audience, and all afternoon great vibrations from talented musicians.

"How's work, Paul?" Slick Eddy said. "You busy now? I'm thinkin' it's hard to keep up … running them new beans to the bank. That hot new Chevy they got is a winner; maybe get me one someday." He smiled, and a dollop of spittle slid from the corner of his mouth that he wiped with his sleeve, the sleeve on his apron.

"I sure like that car," Slick Eddy said, "first V8. Maybe give this beer racket up and sell those babies. Whatcha think, Paul … me, sell cars?" He drew a Pabst, blew off the foam, and topped it. "I'm gonna dump this joint someday, ya know. Here's your beer."

"Why sell? You've always got a crowd in here, especially after six. Sundays, it must be a goldmine. Who are those guys in the blue shirts over there making that racket?"

"Don't really know, but a thirsty lot, and good for the cashbox here." He patted the register.

Paul had his second beer to his mouth when one of those blue shirts, squeezing into the bar with an empty pitcher, bumped against Paul, and the suds meant for his pallet ended up on his shirt.

"Uh, sorry pal, didn't mean to bump ya. We're cele-bratin' over there, and maybe I lost my balance." He grinned. "I see ya spillt some beer ... I sure as hell apologize. Hey, bar-keep, can ya fill this up?" He slid the pitcher over the mahog-any top.

"Accidents happen," Paul said. "What are you celebrat-ing?"

"Refrigeration. And we're fuckin' official now—certified technicians. After two fuckin' years of bein' frozen in that school, we are qualified—make your office so cold, freeze your cajones. Ha, so no juice for a fancy-assed woman like the one over there." He pointed at the foxy Mitzi talking to Eddy. He laughed and chugged the glass he'd just filled from the new pitcher.

"Well, I'm Paul Smythe, and that woman over there that you think could be juiced is Slick Eddy's wife, and you may also want to know he keeps a sawed-off behind the bar that I've seen him use. You gotta name?"

"I didn't mean nothin' by it for sure." He smiled big. "I'm Dalton Dobbs. I live across the valley ... way the hell over there." He pointed to the wall behind the shuffleboard. "With my parents, ya know, and that ain't so good these days. Oh, I like 'em okay, nice people, but ya know how it is with parents. You got parents?"

"Yeah," Paul smiled. "But not around here."

"Well, you understand then. Hey, you're kinda dry there, pal ... er Paul, lemme buy you one."

Stout Dalton from Blue Sky Tech and Paul, the slender MBA from Kansas State, spent an hour shooting the breeze when Paul remembered something he'd earlier heard that aroused his frugal mentality.

"You lived north across the Valley with your parents. That's a long haul from here. Where's your work, there or here?"

"Here. Right fuckin' here. Jus started with Campos Refrigeration a couple blocks over on Tujunga; see the shirt." He turned to display the Campos name in red across his back. "Ya mighta heard a' them. So, I'm lookin' to move, and the sooner, the better."

"Yeah." Paul laughed. "I got that. So what do you have in mind?"

"I dunno," Dalton said, gulping down a beer. "You lookin' for a roommate? Where do you park it when it ain't parked here?"

"I have a two-bedroom apartment not far from here—half dozen blocks down the boulevard, and I could be induced to split the rent. You know what they say ... that first split is best and better be the last."

"What the hell's that mean? I don't get it."

"Well, I suppose it means this." Paul rubbed his chin. "You save 50% of the rent for takin' on a roommate, and you're dealing with the quirks of one other person. If you add another, you save only an additional 17%, but you need to deal with another whole load of quirks. With four, you save 8% more but still another whole person to deal with. See what I mean? The cost-benefit reduces with each new roommate after one."

"Yeah, I've heard about that cost-benefit stuff, but ...." He smiled and held up his hand. "I'll take your word for it. I

9

was never too good at math, or any a' those hard courses, though I guess I got by okay ... liked shop, buildin' stuff."

Paul didn't pinch pennies, though he might be inclined to caress them a bit, especially if on their way out. He revered a value, and while informing Dalton about a roommate's advantage, he had convinced himself.

"Tell you what," Paul said. "If you're interested in pursuing this, let's meet tomorrow after work, say 5:30. We'll have a beer and go over to my place. See what you think. We can talk it over more then. That okay?"

"Sure," Dalton said. "That's an appealin' idea. Now, I gotta get back. Good to meet ya, Paul. See ya tomorrow."

**

"HELLO THERE," GILES SAID, putting into play his most charming manner. "You're Lacey, right? I see you out here on weekends. I'm Giles Anderson, Paul's friend." He nodded toward the apartment. "A Kansas boy from Lawrence. You a native here? Likely not; most of us are immigrants."

She didn't look up, not an eyelash flicker.

"Hmm ... I see you're involved. Good reading?" He grinned, his blues twinkling.

Not a movement from the cat, the sun bouncing off her shapely, golden legs.

"I'm not easily discouraged," he said, moving back a bit. "It's a Jayhawker trait. Can I buy you a beer?"

He held out four sweating cans of Lucky Lager hanging loose in their wet cardboard harness.

She turned the page of her *Vogue* without a sign he was there.

He noticed the clear polish on her manicured nails and the identical treatment on her feet.

"Lacey," he said. "I like that name. Has substance." His earlier assurance waned. "Sounds like a Wisconsin name. You from Wisconsin?"

Her eyes moved over the page at an unsuspicious speed.

Shit, she's actually reading.

"Look." He pulled up a chair, sat down, and leaned forward. "You seem like a nice person. What've you got against a little conversation? I'm not dangerous, you know   ...   no communicable disease, and nothing grimy that'll rub off." He chuckled and sipped from his Lucky. *This was not going to be easy.*

"C'mon, Lacey-perhaps-from-Wisconsin," he worked at minimizing frustration, "this is a friendly place, and the whole idea is to get acquainted. Let me open you a beer."

Not a twitch, not a breath out of rhythm—yes, the porcelain cat.

Giles leaned back in his chair, searching his mind for a new tactic. He rifled aimlessly through a newspaper he'd brought and had a long sip of his beer. He let his eyes wander to the weather report. Wonderful here, he thought, the opposite of Kansas and its summer heat, high humidity, black skies, and noisy storms, and twice for him when things turned green and quiet—the rampage of a tornado.

He liked what he saw in the Valley: hot and dry, birds of paradise in the planters, the glittering pool—like dancing rhinestones catching their hue from the sky. An especially high tide, the most that garnered a weather-related headline. Yes, he liked it here and stopped at 'Entertainment.'

"Lacey, do you like the theater?" he said. "The *Three Penny Opera* is opening at the Music Box on Friday. Care to go? Great show, I hear, the original 'Mack the Knife.' You do know Mack, doncha?"

He could hit Paul up for the tickets.

"How about this Saturday? I can pick you up at six, and we'll have time for a drink. I'll drive, of course ... if you have a car. Mine was stolen last year and what I have now is a junk-yard clunker—hardly the style for a lady perhaps from Wisconsin."

Giles laughed at his brashness and his fleeting twenty bucks as he turned to the sports section. Football this weekend would be more fun than an opera with her.

"I would like to get to know you," he said to a photo of the Rams' starting quarterback, Billy Wade—an obligatory last try. "Maybe we could start with exchanging nods."

He lowered the paper to see her reaction, but she had gone.

"Umm ... I see you're softening, Lacey." He opened a fresh Lucky.

His second encounter was unintentional. He'd gone out early to the parking lot to retrieve shaving gear tucked away in a box on the floor of his old Plymouth coupe. If he was going after that money in the side table drawer, he might better look his best. As he approached his car, he saw her. She sat in a sparkling new Thunderbird still in the carport—the car silent, she staring straight ahead at the wall.

"Something wrong?" he said, hopefully tempting a response.

No recognition of his presence.

"Nothing, huh? Then why are you sitting out here looking so bummed?"

He waited; rubbed a hand over his stubbled chin.

"Battery," she muttered, turning her head only slightly toward him.

"Ah, the woman speaks." He grinned, pulling up his beltless Levi's. "You wanna jump? Got the cables right here as I use 'em often."

"I'll call the Auto Club."

Well, she didn't say no.

"It's not a bother," he said. "Give me a couple, and I'll save you some time."

She looked up and nodded. Gorgeous eyes—dark, clear, wet, and nicely framed in her pageboy. She was a looker.

"Great car, by the way. Pop the hood; I'll be right back."

Her T-Bird was powdery-green and a brand-spanking-new '57. He pulled his Plymouth up, but not too close, and jumped the batteries. The T-bird's engine started with a mellow sound he admired—the classic twin pipes rumble.

His own selection was an older Jaguar 3.8 Salon, but that little beauty was another's now, and he had said his benediction. Today his wheels were attached to an ancient coupe he'd picked up for forty bucks—loose rods and a burning-oil stink that would put most people on a bus. The car was a band-aid until he banked a few dollars from a job he had yet to acquire—delayed because he didn't care much for looking.

"Okay ... Giles, is it?" she said. "You've saved me an ugly squabble this morning had I been late. Thank you."

She backed out of her space, turned toward the street, and stopped. There was the beginning of a smile in her eyes he hadn't seen before.

"I mean it, Giles, thank you," she said.

That was Tuesday of the first week of the bet.

PAUL AND DALTON, BOTH WITH JOBS, were gone by eight AM. Giles slept in, rose about ten after a half hour or so thinking about what sort of job he'd be willing to take. By noon, he was by the pool with a sandwich and beer, his nose in the sports section. Later he might doze, then a dip, and back in the chaise before the sun slid below the roof—maybe about five. It was an easy, if fruitless, life, but someone needed to establish that end of the scale. Oh, he would "buckle under"— get serious about moving his weight off Dalton's couch, just not today.

"Good evening, Giles," Lacey said while crossing the patio.

"Uh, hi." He turned toward her melodious voice. She was dressed to the nines and stunning. Coming in from work, he supposed, and he wondered where that might be and what she might do when there.

"I'm surprised you're not out. Friday's the night for howling, isn't it?" Her voice sharpened some, each word severed cleanly from its neighbors.

"Yeah ... how about you join me. We'll go down on the boulevard with the rest of the pack and—"

"Wrong girl." She threw back and kept moving.

"Que sera," he said as she approached the stairs. "I'm not really big on wildlife. Content to sit out here with my beer and feel the day fade away." He looked up as she began mounting the steps. "How about you, Lacey?" he yelled after her. "Got a cold one just inside the door and still offering."

He held up his beer. She stopped and turned, opened her mouth, then shut it.

"Oh, alright," she finally said. "Let me change. I'll have mine in a glass ... I guess I owe you that." She turned back up the remaining steps and was gone from his view.

She owes me? Ha ... A simple neighborly gesture, and she owes me? He should have left it behind at the battery jump, but there was the money and, deep in his all-to-often governing subconscious, a reputation he thought he might have.

He didn't see her pause at the railing in front of her apartment and look back as he eased his angular body up from the chaise and moved fluidly toward his apartment to retrieve a couple of cold ones. Lanky and muscular, an inch over six feet, he bore a steely look that complemented his angular features—straight nose, square jaw, prominent cheekbones, and perpetual grin. His hair was wiry, sun-blond, curly, and short. His eyes continuously sparkled as if they had an energy source of their own. For most of his time on this planet, enjoyment enveloped his psyche.

Two
Looking Up

"I SEE YOU'RE APPROACHING and poised to invade," Paul observed that night. "Even parted with one of your beers."

"Too early," Giles said, "you know about icebergs—most of it is out of sight."

"Well, if she's anything but a cold-ass bitch," Dalton growled, "she's had us all fucking fooled."

ON SUNDAY, AS GILES LOUNGED in the sun with the front-page news and its threats to humanity, Lacey approached.

"See here, Giles, I mix a passable margarita, and if you'll put on a shirt and knock on my door about six, you'll find an opportunity to try one. Don't bring the newspaper."

HE APPROACHED her apartment—second-floor corner. Through the doorway, he saw her at the counter, dressed in a loose-fitting lime green-on-green pants suit. *Chic ... and a knockout complement to her tan.* He glanced at his wrinkled khakis and sandaled feet, grimaced momentarily, shrugged, and pushed through the screen door, already ajar.

"Is it six?"

"Yes, come in ... oh, you are in. Well, sit over there, Giles, where it's comfortable. Margaritas are on their way."

"Right." He flopped into an extra-large, overstuffed white leather chair and let his eyes roam. The living room narrowed into a dining space and that into a small kitchen where she stood behind a counter. He noted the openness afforded and the evening sun that came in through the windows of all three rooms. Her apartment, with champagne carpets, light, sand-colored walls, a white leather loveseat, and two matching chairs, seemed larger, felt roomier, than the one he was sleeping in, and the sun through the west-facing windows enhanced its airy, modern ambiance.

Looking down from the living room window, the entire pool and patio were in view, yet her second-floor corner provided some privacy. Well, best-looking woman, best Paradise location, he thought—makes sense.

"I'm impressed, Lacey. You've created a home from a box and very classy. I like the acrylics—this Alvar you have. He's new to the coast, isn't he?"

She squeezed limes while he continued to take in the place.

"I have to say," Giles continued, "this is comfortable ... elegant to the eyes and easy on the frame." He laughed as he kicked off his sandals and stretched out his legs on a marble coffee table. "When do I move in?"

"Giles, do you like salt on your rim?" She glanced up from behind the counter.

"Sure," he said. "I'm big on spice."

"I suspect you're a bit more than seasoning," she said as she picked up a tray and walked in—a pitcher of margaritas, two salted-rim glasses, and an assortment of things on toothpicks that he didn't recognize and didn't ask.

"I want to repeat," she said, placing the tray on the table, "I did appreciate your being there with your cables. I hate being late, one thing piled on another." She sat in the matching chair opposite. "It was one of those days, several in a row for me, though you probably don't have many of those ... do you, Giles?"

He took it all in. Not often, he was a guest, less that he was served. He enjoyed the idea more than the reality, and it brought a grin to his face that matched the light in his eyes.

"Always available to help a distressed lady," he said, his grin morphing into a smile. "Tell me, what do you do that you're in such a hurry to do it?"

She looked away for a moment and then, with a shrug, "I'm a producer. Radio shows. It's a rat-race, a harried rat-race, and one of the reasons I so value my time." She smiled. "You do understand about time, Giles, its use and its wasting."

"Of course," he said, crossing his legs out in front and slumping back in his chair. "I'm fairly well acquainted with time, but I don't care much for rats—defensive, snarly little bunch, running in packs. You're not really a rat, are you, Lacey?" He grinned, "Stunning outfit, by the way. What shows do you produce, and what is this producing anyway?"

"What do you do, Giles?" she said.

"Well, I thought you were answering, but if you mean, how do I occupy myself, I watch time slipping away one day and returning the next. It's a demanding vocation.

19

Occasionally I'm encouraged to do something associated with remuneration, but ... You're quite beautiful, you know, there in front of the late sun coming in through the window. You should be in the shows you produce—dramas, of course."

"Of course. And what would you do when you might be doing it, Giles ... for that occasional remuneration you mention?"

"It's puzzling," he said. "I'm not well equipped; I have no skills, and I'm not enthusiastic about developing any—it's all quite demanding."

"My, you are ambitious." She laughed, "You must be one of those triple 'A' types—can't stop climbing but would be disappointed at reaching the top. Refill, Giles? We have the entire pitcher in front of us, and maybe by its end, you will have learned to relax."

"Sure, top me off," he said. "I'm beginning to come down. Helluva day out there in the sun, constantly bombarded with vitamin D." He pushed his glass toward her. "These *are* quite passable, Lacey. So how did you get into show biz?"

"Why, they just singled me out from among the many."

"Your friendly disposition, no doubt. And how did you come by all that charm? You know, you have a reputation, the most gregarious woman in Paradise."

She poured, stood, and walked to the window, let her eyes turn toward the outside, and again the late sun anointed her face. She was quiet there for a moment, then turned and held up her glass.

"Let's talk about you through this one."

"It seems we've been doing that," he said. "There's been nothing from you while I've been an open book, at least through the foreward."

"Do you eat?" she said, sitting down across from him

"Humm ... sure, I eat." He wiped his mouth with the back of his hand. "Look ... I'd ask you out, um, and I'm planning to, but I've heard a rumor that patrons, when finished, are expected to pay. Well, my ship is out there but hasn't yet entered the harbor, and while the invitation is here, it comes with a rain check."

She was quiet. She rose again, walked to the window, and again looked out. She seemed to be wandering in a place where he wasn't invited. He looked around at the paintings on the walls and ran his hands over the cool white leather of the chair.

"I've probably overstayed my drink ... I mean, what's a battery charge worth?" He rose and walked toward the door, noting her eyes were following. "Thanks, Lacey. I'll be going now. I would like to take you out—a date and a nice place." He chuckled. "I may have some money coming in. Can you make it on Saturday?"

"You remind me of someone." She turned to him. "It's incredible the similarity. Oh, not the looks so much but the whole damned picture you paint for me." Her eyes filled a little, and her hand went up with a napkin.

"Tell you what, Giles, I'll take *you* to dinner, and we'll call it closure ... eh, for the battery jump. It was important to me that you were there that morning. Okay?" She got up, walked to the kitchen, put her glass on the bar, and turned.

"Actually, I prefer it that way."

**

THE TAHITIAN ROOM, SHE SAID—a couple miles down Ventura Boulevard, served paper umbrellas in their drinks. She took them there on Saturday night, and she drove.

Under a porte-cochère, they left her car to a dark-eyed, obsequious kid in a white smock who bowed and smiled and assured them that her Thunderbird was beautiful and would be safe with him. She seemed unconcerned.

Inside they were met with a world of fountains, waterfalls dribbling over irregular stones and splashing in pools surrounded by palms. Screeching birds of stunning colors flitted among exotic smells; some roosted, heads tucked under their wings. Wrought iron railings delineated paths of flagstone and separated seatings perched on different levels. Servers wore colorful, shortened kimonos, and busmen Nehru-like jackets appliquéd with impressions of flora.

An incense fragrance mingled with an earthy smell of jungle while melodies from flutes and soft metal drums soothed attending ears and rounded the senses. Rows of rums behind the bar combined, after they were seated, into something called "Bahama Mamas," and it all very quickly became deliriously intoxicating. Infused with this ambiance, they talked and laughed through the night, often reaching out and touching hands.

"I'VE HAD A GLORIOUS TIME, Giles, simply wonderful," she said at her door.

"It has been terrific, Lacey, and thank you, but next time I pay ... a Kansas thing, you know." He smiled, his eyes twinkling as he looked into hers and reached for her shoulders.

She withdrew.

His hands slid slowly down her arms to her hands, squeezed them lightly, then turned and left.

"Goodnight, Giles," she said to the night.

**

"IT DOESN'T COUNT. You have to take *her* out for it to count," Dalton yelled from the bathroom. "That means that you gotta pay, shithead."

"The bet was on dates, no conditions," Giles said matter-of-factly. "And there was nothing about who was to pick up the tab. As I see it, this one should count for two because she asked me out."

"C'mon," Paul interjected. "We're gonna be late; we'll settle it later."

**

HORACE BLUNT bore a large bulbous nose on a pocked face with a heavy shadow of rusty-red beard. Full bushy sideburns made up for his male-pattern baldness—flaky at the crown of his head. A swarthy man in a sagging tweed jacket that would be selling Watkins salve and shoelaces door-to-door but for the Valley's real estate boom. He slouched in an old swivel chair of wood that squeaked with every movement, his oak desk sporting burns on the edges from lit cigars too long ignored. A single ashtray overflowed. Two cheap prints hung on the wall—prancing children and romping dogs yellowing from smoke. Horace's nose ran, and he sniffled and wiped, first removing a dead cigar that otherwise hung from his rubbery lips.

"I got us that single property that might suit you," he said. "Belongs to a guy named Sampson. He's movin' out 'cause he can't afford the mortgage right now—old studio guy, down on his luck but wanting good tenants, people that'll take care of the place, 'cause, he says, he's moving back in as soon as he lands fattens his wallet."

The clients, Dalton, Giles, and Paul, sat in wooden straight-backs facing Horace's desk—having days earlier followed the flashing red arrow out front that bellowed "Rentals" and obvious to anyone within half a mile of the place.

Horace's office was no larger than a single-car garage, a frame cottage tucked onto a narrow lot. It needed paint and someone to clean the windows.

"Well, his rates were cheapest around," explained Paul as his cohorts began quickly to judge by appearances.

"From the photos you have," Paul said, "we like the house. As I said last week, it's more than the three of us can afford, but a couple of friends at the apartments where we live might go in ... if the place is suitable to them."

Dalton, head down, was watching his twiddling thumbs—one way and then the other. He was there reluctantly, although he agreed with expansion if Giles was to continue his use of the couch and drink the beer in the fridge no matter to whom it belonged. In Dalton's mind, Giles was a bum, not interested at all in the house or the rent, had no money, no apparent paycheck prospects, and showed no interest in developing any. Still, it was his fucking presence that was causing the fucking disturbance. *How fucked up is that?*

Dalton liked it at the New Paradise, sharing the apartment with Paul, but was inclined to acquiesce to the move only and solely because with a house, Giles would get off his couch. Dalton abhorred the disarray—the blankets, dirty clothes, disgusting smells, and other such shit belonging to Giles left in the living room. *Fucking Giles, the cause of it all, and has done nothing toward a resolution.*

Outside the couch, which was emblematic of Dalton's dislikes about Giles, his other interest was rent. Would Paul see to that? Giles hadn't that pot to piss in. Bottom line in all of this was Giles and Paul were friends, and Paul was the reigning oracle—providing advice and declarations.

Horace had relit his cigar, and the noxious smell of new smoke from an old stogie brought Dalton back to the present. But he wasn't interested in the negotiations and was happy to sit blank-eyed and silent, letting Paul take the lead in dealing with Horace, nod or shake accordingly if signaled.

"I could might make it work," Horace said through the vacant side of his mouth, and looking them over with the tired bulging eyes of a man who slept in a recliner—cataracts beginning to blanket the whites. "But Sampson, short on cash, thinks it's a temporary condition and that he'll recover and move back in, so he don't wanna rent to no hooligans that'll ruin the place—especially not five of 'em." He stuck a finger in his ear, jostled it around, then leaned toward Paul, his stained tie dragging over the desk, picking up ashes and crumbs from an earlier cheese-filled Danish. "Now I'm not sayin' that's you

25

or nuthin', but ... well, it's his home, ya' see, and he plans to return when things get better." He sat back, rubbing his pudgy hands with their polished nails. "If he knew you—upstandin', educated, employed, etcetera, etcetera, it might be different."

"We might stand for a larger deposit," Paul offered, "or maybe post a bond. We'd be at no risk of losing either."

"Yeah, I s'pose I gotta try, maybe push a little harder, might work something out." Horace smiled, his prominent teeth the same colorcast as the prints on the wall. "You guys seem, umm ... maybe special. Sampson ... he might just go for it. Said he needs to move fast; the bank's on his back." A large fly buzzed Horace's nose, and he brushed at it but missed.

"You know it comes partially furnished," he said, "corner lot in North Hollywood. Beck Street is just off Lankersham there and takes you straight to the freeway—damned convenient if you're goin' into the city."

Paul rose from his chair and moved to the side of the desk.

"We'll go out and see it. If we like it, and you can persuade Mr. Sampson of our integrity and ... well, if you can make it work, Mr. Blunt, put in the needed effort, we could probably add a few bucks to your fee." Paul put a hand on the sloping tweed shoulder and gave it a nudge.

"It's gonna be tough," Horace said, swiveling back, pushing his heavy lips toward a smile, which caused a large ash to fall from his cigar and dribble down on his shirt. "But I'll work for ya, you know ... give it a try.

**

"HOW CAN YOU AFFORD a house, Giles?" Lacey asked, later in her apartment, having heard of the new lease while allowing the Tahitian experience to soften her view of Giles. *He is interesting, and I'm loathe to fault his looks.* "You're apparently impoverished and don't have a job."

It seemed the Tahitian excursion had also increased Giles' interest in Lacey, and while not cozy and warm, the challenge had become less from Giles' point of view. *We had rum-fun the other night ... there might be more. Love those legs.*

"I probably have a job," Giles said. "It's sort of a job. Well, I'd call it a job. I may be starting next week, and I think I'll like it—no clocks to punch and no regular hours. There's a fair amount of money involved, and my time will be my own ... most of it."

"Why, that's outstanding, Giles." She smiled. "Sort of, probably, maybe, and you think you'll like it." She laughed. "You're the hallmark of stability and precision, everything planned and predictable, right down to the decimal point. I'm certainly impressed. Tell me, Giles, now with a jingle in your pocket ... does it mean you'll be developing an amenable relationship with cashiers? And tell me, what will you do for this fair amount of money?"

He watched her. She seemed disturbed. Shit, she hardly knew him, and here she was taking a swipe. But damn, she was beautiful when fired up.

"I'll be an escort," he said.

"Well, that figures."

**

IT WASN'T A JOB in the ordinary sense. He had met an older couple at the Little Brown Hut, where he'd become a kind of regular. The Padgetts, Izsak and Anna, came in on Sundays for the jazz. They had opened up to him—their lives and home—because, they said, he was a likable fellow. They lived off the Boulevard, the foothills in Encino, and like most in that neighborhood, had, what seemed to Giles at the time, endless wealth.

Izsak, sixty or so and wheeled around in a chair, had taken a liking to Giles. With his younger wife Anna, they had hosted him for supper after the sessions a couple of times. Izsak enjoyed showing his art collection, and Giles had a genuine interest.

Elegant meals had been presented with simple but cultivated delicacy, not by Anna but by Rose. Rose and Arthur were live-ins over a stable out back that housed a Bentley and Jaguar roadster, and not the horses earlier there. Rose and Arthur performed the household chores, including outstanding culinary.

After twenty-odd years at the grind as a movie producer, Izsak had encountered what he came to call his "fortunate misfortune." A fall from a horse that preceded the Bentley had crushed nerves in his back, and his legs became useless appendages he dragged along "simply because they're attached," he was known to say.

The "fortunate" side of the fall came after the fall, as he was forced to shed the rigors of producing and could then begin writing. Screenplays had been a dream if a challenge he'd harbored for years but avoided due to the demands of movie-making—a reasoning he advanced as acceptable. But

28

as it turned out, his physical inactivity—most spent in his library with paper and pen—brought with it the opportunity to ponder and, with it, a big load of increasing guilt. His immobility and time spent with his muse displaced what he felt he owed Anna as husband and booster, and was now less able to give.

"GILES, MY BOY," Izsak said on a Sunday at the Hut during a break in the music. "You know we're quite fond of you. I like your spirit, your apparent willingness to explore with an easy accommodation of what you encounter, good or bad ... eh, so I suppose." His eyebrows arched. "Well, we needn't dig into that right now. Anyway, you've got something there I like, something special, I think. And by the way, that fondness I mentioned goes double for Anna." He nodded in her direction, sipped at his drink, and wiped his mouth with a napkin.

"Izzy, that's really not important," Anna said.

"Well, he is a—"

"Izsak ...."

"Okay, okay," Izsak said and turned back to Giles. "You know I have a problem with ambulation. I'm getting old in other ways as well and, I'm afraid, somewhat uninteresting."

"Izsak Padgett!" Anna interrupted. "That's simply not true. You're very interesting to me, Honey-pops, and you know that." She leaned over and kissed him. "I find him very exciting, Giles, such a lovely temperament and that wonder-filled brain. We'll see his name again when the credits roll; you watch."

"Enough of that," Izsak said. "Giles, the short of this is, Anna isn't. She isn't getting old, or incapable, or uninteresting." He put his hand on her thigh. "And she likes to be out among her acting friends, engaging them in their pursuits and the studio news. She has a lot of those friends. She's an actress herself, you know. Or maybe you didn't. No major roles yet, though the situation is promising and ... I'm straying off, I know, but she needs that exposure I'm unable to give."

Anna remained quiet through his speech. She changed her position, sipped her drink, and occasionally nodded. A waitress came by, raised her brow, and Anna nodded—refills around.

"Giles," Izsak said, "I'm offering ... well, we are offering a job here. I want you to take Anna out and around. Show her a time, as they say. She needs to show and mingle—good for her career. I, by the way, am happy at home in my library with my music, a measure of imagination, and a pen with which to record it." He drummed his fingers on the table. "Where in damnation are those drinks?

"Now, Giles, I'll make it worth your while, use of the cars and expenses, whatever she wants and is needed, and of course, you'll be paid. So, what do you say, Giles? It would be a great favor to me ... to both of us." He looked over at Anna, who, smiling, seemed to agree.

Giles pushed back in his chair. His grin widened. *Well, if this isn't the damnedest.* His hands went into his pockets, and he leaned back, the chair on its back two legs. He glanced over at Anna, her legs crossing and re-crossing, and now for the first time in his maleness view, seemed sexy. He judged her to be about 40, maybe plus a sliver, and well put together. She was fun with a great sense of humor—he'd never be bored.

"See here, Giles," Izsak broke the silence. "Anna's taken a liking as well. And maybe a bit of history will lend perspective. Long ago, when we were married, she in diapers, and I a full grown man, I promised her: if she was still with me when I became, well, let's say, a social non-performer, I would see to her life in other, eh, other sustainable ways. Now, perhaps earlier than originally predicted, I'm thinking ... eh, we're thinking that time has come."

Anna smiled at Giles and tugged at her skirt, a skirt covering legs that were taking on an additional shapeliness.

"So, what do you say, Giles? You'll be handsomely rewarded."

"Jesus, Izsak, you've caught me off-guard. I know this isn't Kansas, but—"

"That's a fact, Giles. It isn't, and that's one of the reasons you're perfect for this role. Yes, Kansas. One must trust a Kansan, all that Midwestern rearing." He smiled and took a sip from his scotch, glancing at Anna under his lowered lids.

"You think about it," Izsak said. "We're not talking romance, you understand, merely escorting, and you'll meet interesting people. Now ... you ask your questions if you like, then give us your answer. I'll start you out with $1,000 a month, in advance, plus all related expenses. My name will bring you credit most anyplace you're likely to go."

Giles sat back in his chair, crossed one leg over the other. He glanced around at the Sunday crowd as if someone were watching—some other Giles wanting to step up, thinking it foolish to wait.

The rent was coming due; there was his junker car. And he thought about the difficulty he might have with the typical job—the eight-to-five paradigm working for a clock, a lackey to Mr. Somebody Else. And if he hated a job, he hated more the pressure of needing one, and it was all coming due like a train down the tracks on time.

"Okay." He looked over at Anna, a stately woman with the looks of Lollobrigida—a longer and narrower nose. "Okay," he said. "Okay, I'll do it … sure, I'll do it for a while."

**

"IT'S PROBABLY NOT what you think," Giles said, lounging in the comfort of Lacey's white leather chair. The attractive owner had become a draw, and the location even more desirable because of its distance from Dalton.

"It doesn't matter what I think," Lacey snipped, a bit of flash in her eyes. "Well, I am amused, but no more than that. How do you like the San Miguel, Giles?"

"Yeah, the beer," he said, eyeing the label. "I wish I could afford to get used to it."

"You will, Giles."

"Listen," he said, "I want to take you to dinner tomorrow night. You free?"

"It was Louie," she said. "The guy at the liquor store recommended the beer. I told him I knew someone who loved the stuff, lived on it, in fact, and I wanted to impress him. He said, 'San Miguel.' It's from the Philippines, you know."

"I thought we'd go down to Hawley's on the Boulevard. Ever been there? It's my turn, you know." He grinned, eyes sparkling.

"They make it in a light and dark," she said. "Which do you prefer?"

"The meat's cured on a rack behind big windows of glass," he said. "You can see it as you walk in. Some is actually green. You select your steak from a palate of raw cuts brought in by the waiter. They scrape off the mold, of course. The lettuce is so cold and crisp, you'd think it was frozen, and the Roquefort comes straight from a cave. Well ... not sure I believe it, but that's what they say."

"Do you like the beer?"

Ordinary Times

Three
Knowing You

GILES TOOK LACEY'S HAND as they exited Hawley's. It wasn't the forced maneuver that ordinarily comes after gathering courage. It didn't cross his mind until after it happened, and he noted she didn't react. Well, that was something.

The night was balmy. Above the lights along the Boulevard, a few stars peeped through the gathering valley overcast. He turned them away from her car.

"Would you like to walk a little?" he said. "Seems like a night that invites it."

"Why Giles, under the beer and sports page are you a romantic?"

"Don't drum up any fanciful illusions, Lacey. It's a nice night. The meal was outstanding, and they say that walking settles the stomach."

"So now you're a health nut?"

"Jesus ... It's hard to get straight with you; I just thought we might talk. Here's a neutral environment, and I'd like to know more about you."

"Why?" she asked.

"It's what we do here on Earth; we're social creatures; we get acquainted. We share our thoughts and a little history, like where ya from. So, what brought you to California? We'll start with that."

"More like drove me away from Wisconsin," she said. "Anyway, I'd rather not talk about me. What about you, friend? Why are you here?"

His grin broadened; his eyes cast down. "Just bumming, I guess. Here was somewhere to go, and Paul had a couch ... well, as it turned out, Dalton had it. But no more than bumming."

"No more than bumming. Well, that figures too," she said to the night.

They ambled on in silence, each, it seemed, with thoughts apart from the other.

"Giles ...."

"Yeah?"

"Do you think they'll bomb us? Do you think we'll be here a year from now, walking the Boulevard, feeling the balm of a Valley night?"

"Huh? What are you talking about?"

"All those shelters, those huge green tanks for sale, up and down the Boulevard here. Someone thinks we need them. It's awful, you know—the thought of being incinerated. What do you think?"

"I'm not concerned, Lacey. Today is my time."

"You don't think about the future ... not even tomorrow?"

"Not much."

"But what if they do? What if some crazy—"

"You and I ... we have no control over what happens in the heads of those guys, those politicians that decide our fate based on some political ideology or maybe the next move in a game. So, if I can do nothing about it, I don't let it take my time. Those shelters you see ... they're useless against a nuclear attack—a way for some asshole to make money, preying on fears. Now, tonight ... what about a gelato? There's a place across the street down in the next block. Their Amaretto's terrific"

**

LACEY CAME IN FROM THE PARKING LOT about seven. Giles sat in his usual spot, watching his day do its predictable fade, his usual Lucky Lager in hand.

"Hi," she said. "Give me ten minutes and come up for a drink, if you like."

"Right," he said, shrugging and dropping his eyes to her very fine legs. "Yell down when you're ready."

"I DON'T CARRY LUCKY," she said from the kitchenette, "and you drank all the San Miguel. Can I interest you in a whiskey?"

"Humm, a whiskey .... Sure, bartender, single malt over rocks if you have something decent. I'll be relaxing here on my throne."

"That new job is elevating your taste." She laughed. "And it's not hurting your confidence either. How's it going, by the way?"

"Good," he said. "I'm enjoying her cultivated taste; the people she knows I've only seen on the screen, and I'm amazed at the energy—we're out several nights every week so far. You better make it a double."

"And you're becoming demanding." She spoke up from the bar.

"Maybe it's the polished shoes and high-tone rags I wear when employed."

"Oh, they're dressing you up. That must be a challenge."

"Lots of ice, Lacey. Ice seems to warm things up around here."

"So, you're not happy with the required attire?" she said. "Here, Giles, and please use a coaster."

"Okay ...." He put his feet up and his drink on a side table. "It's not that I'm unhappy, more that I'm not accustomed to the fineries. I've seldom worn a tie—once at a funeral, borrowed one of Dad's."

"Think of it as a costume, Giles, and you are the actor. It's done around here, you know, it's only a part you are playing, and off-stage you can be the old Giles, barefoot, shirtless, Lucky in hand." She pulled an apron from a hook, paused, and then replaced it. "They'll likely discover you ... it cannot be avoided as you're perfect for an option soon expiring that must be struck—a sequel to a Fairbanks film, no doubt."

"And what if I get used to the set?" he said. "My name on my chair, and you'll need an appointment to speak to me. I'll give you my agent's name, but she'll be busy, and you will need to arrange an appointment ... with her assistant or her assistant's assistant."

"I'll give up," she said. "I'm not fond of important men."

"Humm ... do you suppose when that comes, I'll switch to San Miguel?"

"I suspect, Giles, it will be champagne and only the best."

"Well then, let's nix the entire idea. I'm attached to Lucky Lager, and I may need to quit this job if champagne is in my future."

"Good plan," she said. "I like a man shy of ambition, who hasn't a notion of where he's going, hardly aware of where he has been."

He didn't respond. He was joking, playing along, while her tone was serious. She didn't know him, and her opinion didn't count.

"Like a nibble to go with your scotch?" she said and placed a tray of hors d'oeuvres on the counter. "Come over here, give them a try. It's a sharp cheese spread on wheat crackers with an olive in the center. Not lobster, of course, but even at that, you may like them."

The scotch did its work in time, and as the ambiance warmed, their talk became more conversational. He wasn't fond of the critical innuendo she continually provided, but adding the scotch made her a better choice than downstairs listening to Dalton complain.

"So," she said, "you went to school at Kansas State, where your father teaches math. You graduated cum-lower-than-laude. You're not especially motivated, but you're open to most anything. Am I getting this right? You're just a partially educated, agreeable bum?"

"You're close," he said, walking over to the counter. "It's the motivation thing. It's been a stranger to me, but I'm occasionally moved to act with the right stimulus—you, for example."

39

"Me? Now Giles, what about me could—"

"You're strikingly beautiful, you serve a mean cheese and crackers, and your warm, amiable personality cannot be beaten. The scotch isn't half bad, but the greatest of all, Lacey, is that you have every other man in the place afraid to talk to you ... which means, fair one, the field is clear, and all I need do is stroll across."

"Why ... why Giles," she began to glow. "You are incorrigible, but you do say such nice things. Won't you go on? I liked the first part best."

"More fuel, lovely lady; I'm running low." He motioned to his empty glass.

She poured for them both. "Is it possible you're beginning to grow on me?"

"It may happen," he said. "But I warn you, be wary. We may begin to enjoy one another, develop a relationship—my surprise, your utter astonishment, I imagine."

YES, SHE WOULD BE ASTONISHED. She moved into an inner space and watched. Giles produced a quiet grin when amused, which was most of the time, and she found she was growing to like it—a curious attraction that she couldn't explain and maybe didn't want to try. His grin lit up his eyes as they narrowed and made her feel he was farther away, taking her in from a distance. She toyed with the notion that the Giles she was talking with was merely a puppet and the Giles with the strings was behind a curtain and not actually available to her. She made it a mystery, tantalizing and cryptic—and she found that she preferred it to raising the curtain.

She also found him attractive though didn't know why. He had none of the qualities she had wanted in a man back when she wanted one—had things changed? Time had passed. Was she regaining a normal approach toward men, this man? Why? Certainly not because of his sheer lack of aspiration regarding anything she'd seen him encounter, even talk about. In truth, she had never met, could hardly imagine, a less ambitious man, and while he had mentioned her in glowing terms, he'd yet to make an advance—no actual encounter, no opportunity for promise.

To be fair, she hadn't known him that long or been that close. Was she jumping the gun? The doors had been closed for so long, had she lost touch? He was charming in an unusual way, perhaps, but she wasn't sure of herself. She watched him sip his scotch. He was appealing to look at, and as things progressed, if one could call it progression, she was beginning to laugh a little at life for the first time in years, so many years she dared not count.

SHE CAME AROUND to his side of the counter and planted a kiss on his cheek.

She smelled enticing, and he pulled her in, but she withdrew immediately, pushing against his chest.

"No, not that," she said with a touch of anger. "Let's be friends. You're the guy with the cables that gave me a jump—remember? We're having fun. I'd like to keep it that way." She pulled back, but her eyes were yearning, coming on strong.

"Humm," He gave her a look—curious at first, then soon disinterested; he put his drink on the bar and started toward the door. He wasn't upset but preferred not to waste his time.

41

She'd been difficult from the start, and he saw more complications coming up. He didn't need the money now, not that it wasn't his, but the hell with it.

"Wait! Hear me out," she said as she hurried after him. He stopped and turned toward her.

"It's like this," she said and hesitated. "It's ... okay, dammit, I'll tell you. When I get involved, I'm all the way, no reservations. I can't ... I don't play games with affection—spoon a little, then a little more, maybe take some back. I don't know how and I'm unwilling to learn. Foolish, perhaps, but that's how it is."

There was a need in her voice, in her posture. She had his attention, and he turned into her. She seemed to be pleading.

"It's been years, Giles, since ...." She choked up a bit. "Many years since any man has affected me this way."

Her eyes glazed over, heightening their emerald color. She was beautiful, he thought, as he listened.

"And Giles, I don't ... well, I won't be hurt. If we get closer, you'll expect closer yet, and then other things, and I'll be there, and then, in time, you'll leave. Alaska, Timbuktu. It's what you'll do. Well, I won't. I'm familiar with hurt, know it well, and it sets me back ... too far back." Her voice was firm at first, and then quietly, she began to sob.

"Dammit, I do like you, Giles, but I simply can't." She dabbed at her eyes with a napkin from the counter she'd been holding.

"Look." He put his hands on her arms and caught her eyes. "You must know by now that I'm not a serious guy. I enjoy life and like to have fun ... and for some crazy reason, I've

42

grown to like you. And yes, we can leave it at that, though it'd be a shame. You're a rare lady, Lacey, and maybe someday ..." *Her eyes, her dazzling eyes.* "... I know we could make that music together and without the adagio, but—" He stopped.

Where was he going? He could pick up the fifty and call it a day. She was something, though, and he was attracted, which made it more. But what? This was dangerous. This was walking on thin ice during a spring thaw. But then—

"Oh well, what the hell," he mumbled, backing away and taking her in. "We'll do what we do as it comes. Friends, huh? I won't push it." He walked to the bar and picked up his drink. "Good scotch. Now, what about some music, no violins. This conversation has risen beyond my intellectual ability."

"You are deplorable, Giles." She laughed, relieved, but not free of a nagging anxiety. Maybe friends is really not what she had in the back of her mind.

"Do you like Johnny Mathis?" she said.

"He's not my favorite."

"What do you like?" she said

"Any jazz," he said.

"I have a Brubeck album."

"Sure."

She stacked a few records on the spindle and flipped the switch. They looked at each other.

"Do you dance?" he said. "You could call in a chaperone."

"Okay, let's dance," she said. "And dammit, don't make fun of me." She put her arm on his shoulder, her hand on the back of his neck, and moved toward him.

**

THE NEXT MORNING while poaching eggs, Giles said, "The money is yours; I'm out of it."

"You're giving it up?" Dalton said. "It's fucking yours."

"Yep, I'm resigning—the king is down, and you can pick up the wager."

"I don't get it ... the great Valentino admits to a failure? Maybe that gigolo shit has reduced your romantic drive, your interest in cash." Dalton gave him a playful punch on the shoulder. Dalton was feeling better; maybe that Giles had an income and would soon buy a bed and stay off his couch was allowing a little humor into his life.

"Yeah," said Paul, "what's this all about? I thought you were well on your way into the rarified air of the corner boudoir." He glanced toward her apartment. "You're a shoddy disappointment, my man, and your reputation is wavering now." He pulled open the side table drawer, and the three stared ruefully at the money—a mouse in a trap under the sink.

"I thought this was yours," Paul continued, "that at last, Lacey had slipped out of her armor and beneath it was a whole human being." He reached into the drawer. "Here, Dalton, twenty of this is yours. If he's not laying claim, it's gotta be ours."

"Look, she's a nice lady," Giles said as he popped open a can of Lucky. "I have no idea where we might go, but I don't want it moving along on a bet." He sat down and sipped on his beer. "Somebody needs to watch the eggs, about two minutes to go," and he allowed the night before to return and the story she had finally told to re-run in his head.

YEARS AGO IN WISCONSIN, she had fallen for Charles McNaughton, a childhood crush and high school steady who had blossomed into manhood at an eastern university where he earned his JD. Upon his return, the Wisconsin Bar passed, she saw a new seriousness in his eyes, a confidence in his walk, and heard a melodious baritone voice. Embers from her earlier passion fanned into flame, and she found herself deeply in love.

Charles, too, seemed pleasantly surprised by what he encountered. The bobbysoxer he remembered wearing his class ring had become a beautiful and sensual lady—ripened into womanhood over the several years he was gone.

Both smitten, older, and freer to sample the gratification of their natural needs, they quickly reacquainted and beyond, and he soon proposed marriage and presented the diamond. Enraptured with their updated perspectives and anticipating the best, she set a date for them to marry, and he joyfully agreed.

The wedding was planned by her mother and three aunts, and guests were invited. Gifts arrived, and the traditional prenuptial parties were held with congratulations and rosy feelings around. The ceremony approached on a beautiful spring day, and Lacey was transformed with flowers and dress into a flushed and radiant bride—a glorious life with her only true love ahead.

Her proud father, having dropped thousands of dollars and shaken hundreds of hands, erupted in tears as he waited to walk her down the aisle—she, his only daughter, the younger of two children, and these days his primary interest in life. Friends and family, over two hundred in all, murmured with pleasure from the pews.

The best man was in place at the railing, and smiling maids and groomsmen stood in reception while the organist waited on a signal to begin the march. But, as it turned out, the groom had dashed during the overture prelude, presumably attending to something more urgent than wedding vows.

Not knowing and suspecting only the likely, that he had forgotten something necessary, they waited— the bride and father, five lovely bridesmaids, the best man, and four groomsmen, the parson and the organist playing and replaying the overture. They waited in front of the altar while the aura of joy leaked from the enterprise, and a murmuring chatter replaced it.

Lacey succumbed to an emotional change—her joy to curiosity as she conjured up reasons that might explain his absence ... that he'd be back momentarily. Curiosity soon turned into anger, and anger begat an emptiness as she detested learning what she didn't want to know—that despite her attempts at refusing the obvious, her dream was collapsing into an embarrassment of shame.

Her clock stopped. She surrendered to shock and fainted away, leaving the rest to deal with the awkward confusion. As witnesses left shaking their heads, a man came in from the side vestibule and whispered to the parson, who reddened and nodded. Charles McNaughton had left his tuxedo in the dressing room and taken his leave without explanation—destination apparently unknown.

In the fog-bound days that followed, she and her mother returned gifts and settled affairs. In less than a month, a devastated Lacey was on a train to Los Angeles—the long ride intended to restore her balance and return a modicum of dignity.

Her older brother, Ross, owned and operated an established dinner house in Santa Monica and had made recommendations to his better-connected friends. After a successful series of friendly interviews with the local PBS station, she went to work as an apprentice producer. The publicly funded station provided the environment she needed, and in time she recovered her confidence and more. Lacey never heard of McNaughton again but never was able to shake it—marooned for years in self-examination and a fear of relationships with men.

She wept uncontrollably as, in fits and starts, she told him her story—the first time, she said, she had ever gone through it with anyone else. He had held her until her convulsions subsided, then helped her onto her bed, covered her gently, and left.

GILES FINISHED HIS LUCKY, opened another and, on his way back to the chair, glanced through the window up at her apartment. The door was closed, and the blinds were drawn.

"These fucking eggs," Dalton said, "have been poached into stone."

Four

Two Women

ANNA PADGETT HADN'T BEEN CIRCULATING or out with a man for eons, it seemed, and her appetite thrived. Giles, as it turned out, had hired on as her nourishment, and she hungrily devoured him. He was outstanding in the role, she said often, and he heard no complaints. The Bentley was hard to park.

He fully enjoyed the classy restaurants and clubs, the glitzy people he met, the shows he otherwise mightn't have seen, the Padgett cars, and his upscale clothes from the best haberdasheries. But she was a handful, demanding and more than he had initially imagined. His time was hardly his own— on call like a doctor, he mused. On the other hand, he had grown quite fond of Izsak. Izsak's intellect offered a challenge, and Izsak's money felt comfortable in his pocket.

The adventures varied. She was a good-looking woman—statuesque to a fault, popular with her friends, and a wonderful sense of humor. There was no good reason to quit, he regularly concluded, and the question occasionally posed in mild exasperation with his frenetic life became less and less frequent as he grew into the role.

"Giles dear ... oh, you are beautiful tonight, and I adore that smart-looking jacket over jeans." She danced through the foyer. "You have such a lovely tan, Giles. Do you live on the sun?" He waited; there was going to be more.

"Listen closely, honey-pops; I want to go down on the strip tonight, and let's take the roadster, top down, of course." She twirled, her hands high in the air. "There's a club, The Onion, down on the boulevard. They have the nastiest comedians. Ooh, I just love their talk. Can we go? Can we go now, Giles, or must you confer with the puppeteer?" She did a pirouette, leaned in and kissed him.

"I have to say, Giles, I'm getting the better part of this deal." Izsak let out a chuckle as he spoke up, wheeling himself into the large foyer. "Do I sense a new object for her abundant affection? Be wary, Giles, head above water and all that ... and remember the law of unintended consequences as you keep the vast plains of Kansas morality in mind."

"You know I'm just playing Izzy, dear," Anna said coyly. "I *am* an actress, you know, if missing a script and an agent." She kissed him on top of his head. "I *do* need an agent, dear, and you did promise ... though it was a long time ago, and you might not remember," she teased.

"In good time," Izsak said. "Now go on and let me be."

"We're off, Izzy dear. Can we bring you anything?" She tossed over her shoulder on their way to the door, but Izsak had wheeled into his library.

THE ONION WAS CROWDED, and she seemed to know everyone, everywhere.

"Hey, Anna."

"Hi, Anna."

"Saw you last night at the concert, Anna."

"Who's the young man with you, Anna, your grandson? Now ... I shouldn't say that; I know he's a nephew."

"Do meet Giles, Sherman. He's a dear friend and fantastic lover. Are you jealous, Sherm? You should be, you know, as the boat has sailed, and anyone can see you're still on the dock. Toodle-oo, Sherm."

"Who the hell is Sherman?"

"Oh, just another nobody, Giles. No need for concern."

There were others: Chandler with his musical baritone, his smirk, and wiry top. She knew Curtis and Height, Lemon, and Lancaster, and one by one, they approached and acknowledged.

"Say, babe, I thought you were gonna be mine when Izsak gave up; wait'll I get my hands on that Hungarian scoundrel. He promised, you know." A jowled and gravelly voice in the dim, but Giles believed it was Matthau. There weren't many women there, and, as usual, Anna had command of the floor.

"Here, honey-pops," she handed him a fresh champagne. "Drink up; we're just getting started."

**

"Hi, HANDSOME, how's the escort service?" Lacey came bouncing in from the Paradise parking lot, Giles in his chaise with a beer. "Do you like being a gigolo? I know the pay is good as I see you now and then on your way out, and wow, have you learned how to dress."

51

Giles turned toward her and put the sports pages down.

"Haven't seen you for a while," she went on. "Are you earning your keep? There must be overtime pay for those nights when the sun kisses the moon bye-bye—a tough gig, I suppose, but I imagine you're up to it."

"Uh ...."

"Hot today," she said, "and a balmy evening approaching. A margarita might cool us off. Interested?"

"I guess, sure ..." surprised at her perkiness, not having seen her since the night of confession.

"Come up about seven; I have a new 'Mulligan at the Drift Inn' just for you, and I'll throw in something Mexican to satisfy a more health-driven appetite." Her face was lit up with a warming smile, and her eyes danced.

"About seven," he said. *Humm, that's a one-eighty ... wonder what's into her? Damn, that's a marvelous shape ... and she knows how to keep it to herself.*

He knocked, though the door and the drapes were open, the late yellowing sun shining through—the first time, he reckoned, in a couple of weeks.

"Come in, dummy. Don't stand on ceremony. We're closer now ... two close and warming friends sharing our lives and innermost secrets, although you've been silent with yours."

"Are you taking a new vitamin? I've not seen you so bouncy, so full of life and pleasantries."

"It's only that I'm warming up to you, friend—trusting and sharing."

"I think I liked the earlier, cooler, Lacey ... seemed a little safer."

"Do you always play it safe, Giles? Stay on the cooler side?"

"Served me well so far." His grin widened, eyes twinkled.

"Sure ... and good for you, considering your boundaries, but what about the heartbreaks and longing you leave in your wake?"

"Well, I see that as their responsibility. Now, where are those margaritas you promised?"

"Comin' right up, masa Giles. I see you're still demanding."

She beamed, leaving the rest of the room in shadow. This was a Lacey he hadn't witnessed before—a happiness child, presents under the tree.

He hadn't thought of her much since the night she spilled her big disappointment. It was too mysterious and complex for an amateur like him and better to leave the whole thing alone. He hoped she had tuned to the same station—the far left of the dial where the frequency was low, like right after the battery jump.

He preferred not getting further involved, and her "aloof" for him at this point was fine, that and a Lucky. He wondered a little why he'd come up—the bet was over. He had assumed the loss through the past week or so and had come to leave it that way. Life seemed okay without her, Anna filling the vacancy with aplomb. But then, what the hell ... margaritas had beckoned, and he'd roll with it, see what the night had to offer.

"Here ya go, Mr. Playboy," she sang, "and the tacos are right behind. You do like tacos, everybody does. Hot and spicy or plain with bunny chews? Which is it, Giles? What's it to be for you?"

"Uh, I like 'em hot, I guess. What's got into you? Did they give you the broadcasting station, or have you been smoking something illegal?"

"No smoke, Giles, just happy."

"You seem beyond happy ... ebullient. Is that it, ebullient?"

"I have something I want to share with you ... but later." She dropped the first tortilla into the sizzling oil. "And yes, ebullient, wonderfully ebullient."

AT THE SINK, one pitcher down, the tacos trying at indigestion, "I'm finished with it, Giles, the whole ugly mess." She washed, he dried and stacked, the put-away to wait until later. "After we talked that night ... I spoke, you listened as I relived that experience. My first time through that memory dredge with any attendance, and I'm glad it was you, by the way—nonjudgmental, couldn't care less—Giles, with a Lucky Lager in hand.

"Anyway, I spent a week with my brother in Santa Monica, went down to the pier every night, and stared across the Pacific" She went to the window and looked out. "And every night, Giles, it went on and on, and somewhere out there it met a sky full of stars and everything seemed huge and still and silent. But one night I realized it wasn't. It was all moving and changing and roaring with life. Everything was moving on, and every person, too, everyone but me. I was curled up in my cozy cocoon, protecting my story."

She caught his eyes and wouldn't let go, talking exclusively to him. He found it uncomfortable, felt imprisoned ... waiting for the Lacey with keys.

"Now, that really began to frighten me," she said. "That I could be left behind because I wanted to be comfortable, secure in my shell. Well, the gist is I have faced it, Giles, and now it's gone. I think it's gone; I don't need it anymore. That guy, McNaughton, had turned out a jerk, and I just happened to be there. Oh, scars ... there are always scars when you're badly hurt, even when it isn't your fault. Can't help that; just life, I guess, but I'm good now. I got a glimpse that night, the last night you were here, and now it's behind me, Giles, and I'm good."

He broke away. An exhaust report in the street, a splash from a jump in the pool, something he found allowed his distraction, and he grabbed it and held on.

"Giles!" she said, "Are you listening to me? Do you hear what I'm saying?" She moved over to him and put her hands on his collar, her lips next to his ear. "I want to ..." she whispered. "I want to lie down with you."

He wasn't ready, but her presence was overwhelming, her fragrance intoxicating, her words soliciting, and his mind was losing its temporal control. Instinctively he reached for her waist—a slender waist, he noticed again, and pulled her in closer. Feeling her lovely breasts on his chest, a trickle of sweat down his underarms, his thought and reason ceding entirely to his awakening hormones. Their eyes met, and she took his face in her hands, kissed him, and he joined her. It was a gentle kiss, a how-is-this-working kiss, and do we like

55

it? The answer seemed yes. They parted lips but continued to hold one another.

"You know," he said, "I'm not ..."

"Yes, I know, you're not a serious man."

She led him into the bedroom and sat him down on the bed. "Stay right here, Mr. not-a-serious-man; you must tell me your last name sometime." Back in the living room, she turned on the record player, and Johnny Mathis floated in with her return.

He pulled her down onto the bed and kissed her, a yes-we-do-like-it kiss—their mouths opened, and they explored.

"Wait," she said and got up from the bed.

He watched her disrobe, and as she removed piece by piece, he realized he had underestimated. And when she had revealed herself completely, she started on him. Kneeling on the bed, straddling him, moving slowly, his shirt removed, she kissed his shoulders, his chest, his stomach. She opened his pants and pulled them down, then his briefs, her body moving lightly against his, her breasts brushing over him. And she ran her lips over his body. "Umm, you taste like the rim of a margarita glass," and she moved farther down.

His hands were all over the golden smoothness of her—her face, her shoulders, her thighs—stroking, gently stroking, deliciously unhurried.

"You are magnificent, Giles," her whisper silky and wet, "but I want to go slowly. You will be patient with me, Giles ...."

"Umm," he replied.

He pulled her up to him, and they kissed again. More hungrily and eager. She moved up and over on top of him with knees spread on his sides, and they connected slowly, rapturously, knowingly, and ultimately explosively.

She stayed with him, and soon they went again. In the morning, he awoke before her, dressed, spent a moment taking her in, kissed her forehead, and left. He knew nothing else to do.

**

"GILES, THAT YOU?" Izsak spoke up from his library, late afternoon, the week waning. "Come in for a minute. Sit, and let's talk. You know where the bar is."

Giles mixed a scotch and plopped into a chair near Izsak. He took a sip and set his drink on the table. "What's up?"

Izsak turned. "Haven't seen much of you lately—oh, a glance now and then as you whisk my wife off to pleasure and joy ... though reports are good. Anna is delighted with the exposure she gets, but how are you doing with this ... let's call it our arrangement. I have to say, Giles, you are giving me time. I have a third rewrite, perhaps the last, well underway. I like the way it's evolving, and an agent I know claims interest. I hope you are profiting as well."

Izsak sat relaxed, a reading lamp on, his manuscript in a notebook, cigars in a silver box. There were pens in a cup and reference books on a small table within reach. His crutches—he never used them—leaned against an arm of the chair he sat in, the wheelchair less than an arm-reach away. A waltz played softly—Johann Straus.

"I now have an opportunity to get to the crux of my new life," he said, "my creative, most private enjoyment. It's not as lucrative as producing but not as demanding either ... and God knows I don't need the money."

A thoughtful man, Izsak had stretched during earlier years and tasted all in his view, but recently now, and nearly exclusively, had been distracted with worrying over the needs of Anna. While he adored Anna and accepted his obligation, his awakening muse, fitfully present now, was all he had left of personal fulfillment, and he treasured the time to be with them ... it ... her. Giles gave that to him.

"So, are you profiting, Giles?"

"I'm learning on the job." Giles chuckled. "And because of you, my horizons are broadening, and I'm picking up on a fancier life." He shook his head. "How am I doing? I hear no complaints. It'll end, though, and I need to be ready."

"Ha ... We may all go up in Soviet smoke before that happens. The powers that be are warning us, scaring the shit out of believers, and we can't do a fucking thing about any of it. The bastards are playing games with our lives and a culture centuries in the making. It's a travesty, Giles. We put this country together, put those fucks in their jobs, yet we are less than pawns on their board—spectators, Giles, awaiting the game's end without a say in the play. Nowhere at any time have we been so helpless with regard to our fate. All we can do is look away.

"But now, Giles, let me get to my point. Anna says you're terrific, that you fit in well wherever you go, and that makes her life more enjoyable. She likes your nonchalance, the sa-voir-faire you easily exhibit, and that you don't seem intimi-dated by her high and mighty friends—some of them

58

verifiable shits. And importantly, she circulates in the crowd that can help her succeed with her acting objectives.

"I thought, originally, that could be awkward, you younger with that Kansas naiveté I'd imagined … convinced myself to believe." He chuckled. "Giles, top me off, will you please? But to my surprise … surprise and pleasure, she assures me you're a natural, that you float along on that smarmy bunch as if you're one, and her friends adore you." He grinned. "Her lady friends, in particular.

"You've done more than expected. You have assisted Anna in establishing herself, as a shoehorn assists a foot if you accept the analogy."

"Yes, I am your assessment, Mr. Padgett. I'm learning the moves and the language. I'll be a well-polished gigolo in no time at all, with a brilliant career in front of me. Ladies … open your purses." Giles chuckled quietly. *What the fuck am I doing here … and why? Well, I know why.* He got up and moved to the library bar with Izsak's empty glass.

"Umm. Of course, you're right," Izsak spoke up. "It won't prepare you for scientific discovery, and you won't win a Nobel, but here's the thing …. Pour one for yourself while you're there. This hobnob galivanting will increase your confidence with people, a skill you can use most anywhere, and you're gathering a knowledge of life—some stories there if you ever decide to write. I know … I know this arrangement cuts into your life, especially the late-night hours. I'd guess you've become a second Giles of sorts—made your adjustments."

"Here ya go, fresh from the aging barrels in Scotland."

"And…" Izsak took a cigar and offered one to Giles, who declined but passed the lighter under Izsak's until it glowed a bright red. "...here's another thing. Now that I've seen you in action, so to speak—got good reports, I'm bumping your salary one hundred percent. That's two thousand a month. Expenses will remain the same, all covered. You see, good fellow, we want you happy ... and to stick it out for a while."

"Izsak, Izsak ... that isn't necessary. Christ, I'd feel like Dillinger taking that."

Izsak laughed. "You're much smoother than Dillinger, my friend ... moreover, he got his from banks using threats of flying lead. I suppose it's a surprise, but don't let it bother you as it's no bother of mine and I assure you ... you perform a favor that is worth it to me and even more to Anna. You give more than your time, you're invested ... and, Anna says, deserving." He winked with the "deserving."

Giles rubbed his hand across his chin and heard the bristling whisper. *It does take my time—usually the best part of the day. I'm a fucking specialist, an escort cum therapist— they do pretty well, so why not me ... and there's that gift horse thing.*

"I don't know what to say ...." He took a long sip and savored the whiskey's quality. "So, I'll just say thank you, boss, and not to worry—it's a job I plan to keep for a while." He smiled, picked a Cohiba from the silver box. "Could make it a career if your money holds out." He laughed and lit his cigar.

Giles sat back. The scene was over, and he relaxed. Somehow and sometimes, he felt challenged by Izsak. Not overtly, not in any way a watcher might tell, and while he recognized it, he couldn't think why. He admired Izsak—his achievements, intellectual prowess, his appreciation for life and its offerings, and despite his loss of legs, his positive attitude—optimism, occasionally closing in on naivete. Was it envy? Was it his need to succeed, to dump this laissez-faire approach that he so enjoyed and get on with something serious?

His eyes roamed the paneled walls, the lead-crystal lamps, and the beveled glass windows, from floor to ceiling about 14 feet; the enormous Klipsch speakers, hardly noticeable in the expansive library of Italian-leather seating. He noted the burnished maple floor, soft wool carpets, books, and sculptures on glassed-over shelves and the tooled-tin ceiling. He contemplated for a moment his good fortune, his extraordinary luck. This was a job he'd describe if he were defining his ideal, and who knew the potential. He grinned. The scotch, the best, the cigar a satisfaction, and the company, damn hard to beat,

"And ..." he said, another sip across the buds on his tongue, a flame to the expensive cigar, "if there is anything else—take out the garbage, mow the lawn, you say the word."

Izsak smiled at his good fortune. He was fond of Giles and thought him a friend. Giles hadn't asked for a thing and extended himself willingly to what must have seemed an infirmed old man in a chair. Giles had appeared, from the day they had met that Sunday at the Hut, as a man without bias or fear—comfortable in his skin and at peace with his surroundings. Among Izsak's friends, Giles had become cherished ... and he fulfilled that promise to Anna.

Five

Beck Street

"WE'RE MOVING THIS UPCOMING Sunday, Giles," Paul announced, Giles on his way through the door for a night with Lacey. "You don't have much, but you can help the rest of us. The guys upstairs have a pot-load."

"And a good fucking thing," chimed Dalton, "as Giles has only his willingness to sponge."

"So ... I travel light," Giles said, a special smile for Dalton.

"And you contribute the same," Dalton growled. "I'm fuckin' tired of you scrounging in the fridge, never add nuthin, and ... and not helping a dime with the rent. It's way past time you step up ... take care of your share."

"Hold on, D," Paul said. "Giles is my guest and I've been putting in his share. You know that, so knock it off. Besides, he's in all the way now, so button it."

"Well, he's been floatin' in and outta here like queen for the day, and as far as I can tell, he still thinks he's walkin' on air."

"That's all gonna change," Paul said. "I've got *his* money now, so cool it."

"Sure ...." Dalton plopped into a chair and stuck his nose into a copy of *Motor Trend*.

"Goodnight, sweet Dalton," Giles cooed on his way out the door.

**

"WE'RE MOVING INTO THE HOUSE ON SUNDAY, the one I've been telling you about—Beck Street at the corner of Hamilton. It's not far, up Lan—"

"And I'll see even less of you then," Lacey said, not happy about him leaving the Paradise.

"Probably."

"Probably ... what does that mean, probably? That's your life, isn't it, Giles, probably ... probably this and probably that."

"Probably," he said and chuckled; his eyes narrowed and sparkled. "C'mon, Lacey, we don't have to do this. We had to move; you know that. It was crowded and taking a toll, especially on Dalton. We'll see each other as much. I'll bring the sports page and a beer and spend time on the patio here." He chuckled, walked around the counter, put his arm over her shoulder, and turned up her chin. They kissed, she reluctantly, and pulled away in a pout.

"You worry too much," he said. "You worry about things that likely won't happen. We're doing alright. How about we go up to Big Bear after the move? Spend Saturday night at the lodge there ... crackling fire, brandy. I'll bring some of Izsak's cigars ... whatta you say?"

"Sure ...." She grinned, her green eyes lighting up. "I'd love a cigar."

**

FIVE GUYS—including Dennis Delaney and Nick Gates from the apartment above at the Paradise—would move into four bedrooms, the short straw into a sun porch facing a large pool and patio in the rear. The entire backyard, walled in with concrete blocks and ivy, was bordered on two sides with a tropical-styled loggia. Under its reed canopy, a bar and sound equipment, complete with speakers, turntable, tuner, and amp, were left by the owner, Sampson—not so much generous of him, but his smaller place lacked the room, Horace Blunt had said.

A separate garage, corner of the lot facing Hamilton, was an oversized two-stall arrangement with a large work-space; the original, integrated garage converted into a step-down den off the dining room.

They loved it: more lavish, livable, and roomy than they could have imagined, and some of the owner's furniture had been left. The deal required a bond and $300 cleaning deposit as Sampson had doubts about his tenants' interest in mainte-nance—and there were threatening words in the lease should those worries materialize.

Well, who cared—a guy they had never met and proba-bly wouldn't. They were in now and ready to raise a minor disturbance.

Lanky and fun-loving Dennis Delaney, a local since birth, knew every skirt in the Valley, many of whom promised to be at the housewarming, should one occur. He worked at an asphalt company—selling, contracting, and managing the execution of paving contracts with a lot of time he reserved as his own—or so it seemed to those in the office.

Nick Gates, whose hands were ordinarily pitted with the grease, stood as the resident mechanic and pump jockey at a Signal station on Laurel Canyon—fully in charge when the owner was absent, which he ordinarily was. Nick, out from Detroit a couple of years back, was tall, dark-haired, and as serious as a soldier's memorial—except when he was drinking. Then the wheels came off, but not in a bad way.

**

"WE'LL NEED TO TAKE YOUR CAR," Giles reminded her.

"I know," she said, "gassed up and ready."

Lacey had called the lodge, a large room facing back with a bath and a view of the mountains. Giles drove her T-Bird top down.

"How did you get away on the weekend?" Lacey yelled, the proprietary smirk on her face.

He didn't respond. The Angeles Crest Highway was a driver's challenge—even in a T-Bird—but that wasn't it. He just liked to drive. He liked the attention required and ordinarily allowed, the power of the V8 expressed in the sound of its dual exhausts, and the T-Bird's stiff but comfortable suspension. He liked the smell of the leather, the look of polished paint, and the glitter of chrome. And he liked being at one with the car, and he didn't like banter from the passenger seat.

"It wasn't easy," he finally said.

"Well, are you losing money … being up here with me and away from Anna?" she joked?

"Tons."

"I'm sorry I am such an expensive date … and because of that, I'll pick up the tab."

"Lacey…."

"No, I'm serious, Giles. I don't want you to carry the entire load, to feel bogged down. I respect your need to be free—a thistle in the wind." She laughed.

He turned toward her. She was strikingly beautiful and apparently feeling it.

Her flaxen bob blew around her tanned face, and her green eyes sparkled. When she was truly happy, it invaded entirely and occupied every cell in her body—the sun out brighter after a thunderstorm, the first snow at Christmastime. She felt tingly and wiggled her toes. She was in charge of her life and, after so long a romantically barren time, in love with her man.

And she was something to behold for Giles, and he was glad she was with him. It was the first time he enjoyed folding a bet and smiled to himself … as, in this case, losing was winning. But he also felt a tiny bit of nag, a distant but encroaching whiff of obligation. But obligation was a foreign concept with no resting place in his thinking, and the road was demanding, the T-Bird responsive, and the thought passed immediately into his subconscious.

"I'll give you a hundred bucks for your car."

"Be patient, Giles; you may get it for nothing."

**

NICK GOT THE SHORT STRAW and sun porch on Beck Street. He didn't much care. There was a door to the patio and pool, one to the inside hall, and with windows shut, was adequately closed off. He was usually unconscious before he hit the bed, and his need for a large closet was nil—jeans and a tee, a Signal shirt when working. Nick seemed the happiest of the five—well assembled, content with the present and the least worried about the future. Despite the bomb shelter sales, the frightening newspaper headlines, and the rattling TV pundits, he had never given the nuclear threat a thought.

The day after they moved in, Dalton—handy with tools—built a sturdy bar in the den. It was a simple design of 2x6's and epoxy resin bolted to the floor. He then installed a draft beer system he brought in from work, and by the end of the third day cold Michelob was available on tap. Dalton earned the praise and admiration of all—at least for the moment.

**

"WHO ARE YOU?" Giles asked as their housewarming party reached a crescendo it maintained through the night.

"Names aren't important," she said, "but you can call me Mary F and you can find me in the phone book under Fun." She smiled, but her dark blue eyes blinked caution.

He stood back for another look at the woman he—along with every other bubbling pot of testosterone—had been admiring all night. At some point, it became clear that she came with Dalton, although she may not have remembered, once inside.

This was the night. The Beck Street house was awash with humanity. Everyone they knew, and friends of the known,were there, and most were watching Mary F dance. She was spectacular—every muscle working, every joint moving—reaching, retreating, her feet in synchrony with the beat. It was eye-popping breathless to watch. She could have been on stage or in a club or hanging on a pole, and when the music stopped, she held a pose while everyone applauded. Then she bowed and said, "Thanks y'all, I live to dance."

She wore a white cotton sweater dress, loose knit, that fell in length a foot shy of her dimpled knees, and as far as anyone could tell, that was it. She was beautiful, voluptuous, dazzling, sensual—easily exhausting that line of description. Her coal-black hair hung just past her shoulders, and she had a comely smile that would bring a bull in the ring to its knees.

"Well, you know how to dance. What else do you do?" Giles said, moving closer.

She tossed her head back a bit and grinned. "I'm fairly versatile, friend ... and if I'm Mary F, who are you?"

"I'm Giles... one of the few here who pays rent. You like a beer?"

"Giles ... with a *hard* G, like Gold or God and not like Gee, should we stroll around the pool? It's such a lovely night and I'm not interested in beer. I've also had enough dancing for a while. You might be a conversation. Someone I asked said you were from Kansas. Do people from the breadbasket talk or do they just plow the fields?"

Her voice was low and sultry. She should be at a piano bar singing something smokey. This was a package hard to avoid, not that he'd want to, and immediately his arousal began to churn.

"So ..." she said, "I've heard about you from the man in the blue collar that claims the tap, and it's not all good."

"You shouldn't trust gossip," he said. "My mother repeated, as mothers do, that gossip's shrouded in the bias of the teller, and the one before and the one before that." He grinned and his eyes brightened and narrowed.

"Is your mother here?"

"Too often inconveniently," he touched his head with a finger.

"Tell me, Giles with the hard 'G', what do you do?"

She sat down in a chaise by the glittering pool, reflected lights flickering over her face. She crossed her legs, her brown thighs smooth and full in the semi dark. She looked up at him where he stood and gently patted the cushion, and the only thought Giles could come up with was cherries jubilee.

**

"So, YOU HAD A PARTY," Anna said. "Did your Lacey attend?"

"She's not my Lacey, hotshot. She's Lacey's Lacey." And he laughed at the notion of possession. "Slavery's long abolished, you know. There was this guy named Lincoln, remember him?"

"Turn in here Giles, this looks like the house." She pointed to a large frame and stucco split-level three-story with integrated garage. He turned into the drive and up to a portico.

"Good evening, Anna," said a man, too formally dressed for any valley occasion, who opened the door wider and quickly examined Giles. "And this is ...?"

"Giles Anderson, a friend," Anna spoke up.

"Mr. Eastman is waiting in his study. Of course, you know he expects you. Here, let me show you the way."

As they entered the study, a large man stood up from behind a desk stacked with loosely bound scripts, dropped his pipe in an ashtray, and came around to them.

"Anna ... Anna, it's good of you to come." He spoke in a raspy voice, took her hand, and kissed her once on the cheek. "And this must be Giles. Izsak speaks of you ... in glowing terms, I can add." He extended a large hand warmly and took control with his other hand on Giles' shoulder.

"Good to meet you, I'm Ethan Eastman." He gave one downward pump with a solid grip and returned to his desk.

Ethan, a tall man if a bit stooped, Giles judged him to be in his late sixties. He had a horsey face and loose jowls, a large smile showing long teeth that were moving toward need. Giles had seen some of his pictures—drama that demanded attention, dark but mesmerizingly believable.

"Sit please, both of you," Ethan said. "You know, Giles, I've known Izsak for decades ... Anna too, of course. We're old friends—partnered on several pictures in the past—a far too distant past." His eyes lost their focus and his face fell a bit as his memory took charge. "We did that thing with Fairbanks, the junior, and then ...."

"Well shit, no need for that." He rifled through the scripts on his desk. "Anna, I think you could do this part. It's not big but it's revealing—demands a strong presence and an artful characterization." He coughed into his handkerchief. "Be a good starter for you if we can get the damn thing done ... out there where people can watch. We have the backers." Ethan seemed to have difficulty breathing.

"I am thrilled with the opportunity, Ethan. I've been working and waiting—attending workshops, some repertory, and studying ... for a long time, now, and I'm ready to give it all to ... you won't be disappointed."

"Yes, I'm sure. You look great, by the way." He grinned. His cheeks folded into his smile lines. "If this works, we might have to age you a bit. That a problem? You know with some women their vanity gets in their way." He stifled a cough.

"Not with me," she said. "I'm delighted with the chance." She crossed her legs and tugged at her skirt. "I have a strong and willing appetite."

"Good! The script ...." He handed her a bundle of papers about an inch thick and a book. "Read these. You're the Aggie Cawfield character. Now, Baker ... Guy Baker, our casting director ... uh, he'll call and arrange for a reading and the damn screen test. You know all that ... a week, maybe. And Anna ... he'll push, and I'll push too. Let's be sure you're ready." He coughed again, violently. "Eh, George will see you out." He nodded at Giles.

**

"COME IN STRANGER," Lacey said at the door to her apartment. "It seems like decades, maybe longer."

"It was last week," Giles whispered, as he took her in his arms. They kissed. She separated.

"You want a drink?" she said, "A single malt? I have a fresh 12-year-old—straight from a kilted barrel. The best on the shelf, Louie said, though it may not be equal to *your* developing taste."

"It'll be fine."

"Giles ... I've been thinking," she said, a serious look on her beautiful face, eyes that began to moisten. "I need more of you." She moved back into his arms and kissed him tentatively, then warmly. "Sometimes I wonder ...."

"Wonder what?"

She stepped away, poured two drinks, put a casserole in the oven, adjusted the heat and turned. "I'm in a sort of quandary. I'm giving you all that I have, yet you're holding back. I know who you are, and I don't want to change that, but I don't feel commitment ... like I'm the one." She sipped at her drink. "I guess that's it."

"What commitment? Tell me what you're expecting." He took his scotch into the living room and plopped in his favorite chair. "What was that you shoved in the oven? I'm as hungry as a Biafran."

She stared at him from the counter, her hands on her waist.

"Okay," he said, got up and moved to the kitchen. He took her hand. "Look, I want you to feel comfortable with us. There's zero to worry about. I feel the same as I always have."

"That's the problem."

"Let's sit down and you tell me what you're looking for that's missing."

"Oh, forget it, Giles. It'll wait. Enchiladas, that's what's in the oven. They'll be a while. You want another drink?"

Six

The Rabbit Emerges

G ILES KNOCKED LIGHTLY at the open library door. "Where's Anna?" he sang. "We're off to the Bowl to-night, Kenton's there and brother Giles is ready."

"She didn't call you?" Izsak asked.

"Call?"

"She got the part, Giles. Here, sit. Take a load off and pour yourself a drink ... and while you're at it ...." He pointed to an empty glass on his side table. "Anna's in her studio, be-coming Aggie Cawfield."

"Hadn't heard, but that's terrific. You want a splash?"

"Let's have a double, Giles. It's a double day, by God. I sent my final draft off this morning ... couriered to my agent, and damn if we don't need to celebrate." He slapped his knee. "The Padgetts are on the move. Let's call Anna ... she might join us. Ask Rose to call her down and fix a gin for her."

Giles found Rose, conveyed the message, mixed the drinks, and sat. He had the fucking tickets and he liked Stan Kenton, yet here he sat, a drink in hand and anchored. If he'd got a call ....

"And here she is ... Aggie Cawfield," Izsak sang out as Anna came in, did her pirouette, gave Giles a cheek-kiss, and plopped in an adjacent chair.

"A toast then, and let me do it," Giles said when they had their drinks in hand. He took a deep breath. "To the Padgetts ...." He smiled and took them in for a minute before his eyes found the ceiling and his wheels began to turn. "To Anna and Izsak, my good friends ... my benefactors. To their life, to their success and to Anna ..." His eyes roamed briefly over her. "...sexy, smart, enormously fun, and soon the glitter on Grauman's marquee."

Izsak laughed.

Anna stood, gave Giles a hug, arms wrapped tightly around him, tears on his face that weren't his. "I'm sorry we missed Kenton," she said.

"We better do a refill," Izsak said—pleased that these two were part of his life.

**

"I WANT ANOTHER trip to Big Bear," Lacey squeaked off in a rare childish mood as she passed her hand across his chin on her way into the kitchen. She, Giles, and Johnny Mathis had just completed a trio in the bedroom, and a rare wave of confidence in their relationship had knocked on the door. "How about this weekend, daddy Giles?"

"Can't this weekend; it's make-a-living time. Maybe the following?" Giles said, cutting through his Mexican Delight—two soft fish tacos on the smaller side, a pork enchilada, chili relleno, and the ever-present beans and rice. "This looks pretty good; nice choice, Lacey."

"It's Ernesto. He'll do what's on the menu and then a little extra. It's always good." She sat, chin in hand, pensive look. "You need a different revenue stream, darling boy, serious now .... Are you listening, Giles? A different line of work."

They sat in the waning day, she catching the rays from a setting sun as it washed through the window over her face and lit up the freckles on the bridge of her nose. Lacey was happy—almost completely happy. He had assured her he was present; her dreams seemed closer. She believed him when he told her she was at the top of the list; the list was short as no one else was there. And though he hadn't spoken the word, "committed," she felt he meant it. The word, that goddamn word, was simply a vocabulary glitch. She was satisfied, at least for now, to rationalize. Except ... except there was that tiny doubt. He was so easy, so unshackled by life's ordinary hopes and promises, so free in spirit and nonchalance; how could she believe he was hers? But then she told herself, that's what she liked about him, it was his charm. For God's sake, she didn't want to own him.

"So, what do you say, Lacey, weekend following this?"

"Sure, I'll make the arrangements."

**

PAUL HAD ASSUMED ADMINISTRATION and set the schedule. Rent was due and payable on the 21st, the house fund, including kegs and kitchen staples, came on the 30th. House cleaning duty would occur on Monday evenings, each team consisting of two, and he would do the posting on the kitchen door.

"You need to see an ophthalmologist," Dalton said, as he and Giles drank a beer during a duty break—Giles on the pool, patio, and loggia, Dalton the inside except the bedrooms. "See if he can't cure your wandering eye. You know, dickhead, that Mary's with me. I'm the one she knows, so keep your fucking fly zipped up."

"You think I'm making a move on Mary?"

"I see you ... saw you at the party, talkin' it up, tryin' to make time."

"Being civil... like any host, my friend. And if she looks my way, it's not my doing" He leaned against a patio table, took a sip of beer and smiled. "Let me say this, ol' buddy, you need some coaching. This may surprise you, but I'll be happy to share my secrets, and you know why ... because otherwise, Dalton, you'll never reach the top echelon of romantic success ... have only the discards left to attract your interest. That will make you angrier than usual, and harder yet for me to live with."

Dalton frowned, his brow furrowing deeply, anger swelling up behind his eyes. He didn't like Giles ... his fucking superiority.

"You know I'm kidding, buddy boy. But yeah, that Mary ... whew." He shook his head. "She is a peach, I'll give you that, and I might be interested but my plate is full, and she's yours, all yours, as far as I'm concerned." He chuckled and put his hand on Dalton's shoulder. "I don't need another problem."

"I guess I'm glad to hear that," Dalton said, approaching warm. "But there is nothing about you that I need, especially your fucking lessons. I ain't like you, dickhead, and wouldn't fuckin' wanna be."

**

WITH ANNA BUSY WITH AGGIE, Giles found demand at the Padgett's waning, and he spent more time at the Beck Street house, the Hut, and substantially more with Lacey. As the Padgett money continued, he wondered too about inequity, so he visited Izsak now more often.

"Yes, I want you stopping by, Giles. I enjoy our conversations and find your orientation to life a marked contrast to what I've come to accept as normal ... you know that's not a criticism. In fact, it helps with my writing. In parts and pieces, you end up in my characters."

They played chess in his library, smoked cigars and sipped the ever-present single malt scotch.

"Your move, Giles."

"Yeah, Izsak, I'm thinking."

"Don't spend the night with it."

"Ha ... you're down a couple of pieces, and I'm smelling a win, Mr. P ... if I'm careful. So, don't hurry me, sir, it doesn't happen that often. You ready for a topper?"

"And a splash."

"You know, Izzy, I'm not very complicated, and I'm thinking this arrangement we have can't last. Frankly I feel now, with Anna busy, I'm getting the much better part of our deal." He chuckled "I'm not asking you to stop it, but I want you to be aware that I know I am getting the longer end of the stick."

"Of course ... and I give you credit for that. You're on a retainer, Giles, like my goddamn lawyer. You work when there's something to do, and I rely on your talent and interest in doing it well ... and, when there isn't a play, you go to the beach." He laughed. "You see how that works?"

"Sure, but I don't want to take advantage of your generosity." He castled king side.

Izsak advanced a pawn, threatening a knight that was unprotected.

"And," Giles continued, "I don't want to screw up our friendship ... holding you to an agreement that's no longer fair."

"Giles, I moved."

"So, you did," Giles said, and moved his queen to QB3. "Check."

Izsak sat back and relit his cigar; fixed his eyes on Giles for a silent pause.

"Giles ... I know you, or I imagine I do. You are my friend, almost a son. Now don't get edgy ... that's my connotation and needn't be yours. You do me a service, one I've come to appreciate deeply. I'm stuck in this goddamn chair, and your visits are an exceptional relief. I don't want to get into details, but let me assume you enjoy my company as well." He toppled his king. "I think that's a mate. So ... let's not worry the things as they are. My money to you is a retainer for services provided to Anna when needed. She'll let us know. Your skills, savoir faire, your particular way with the world with her on your arm is unique and needed and what I am paying for, and your presence at those times of call is all you need to provide. Does that settle the question?"

Giles reset the pieces. "What is that, about two wins out of ten?"

"Be assured," Izsak continued, "I am delighted with things as they are. Yes, Anna is occupied for now, her good fortune, and she owes much of it to you—out among them, contacts, and all. The point here is that without you whirling her about, she mightn't have come by this role. She knows that, would be the first to say it. But, frankly, Giles ... well, her part in this picture is going to conclude, her involvement come to an end. She may get other parts, but she's late to the game."

Giles nodded, his attention now on the chess board, and he advanced a queen's pawn the optional two spaces and had a sip of his drink.

"It's a small budget production, Giles, and likely will see a limited distribution, and unless there are sensational reviews, it'll be on the shelf in a couple of months. And my boy, you will be back on the job full time. Exec summary ... don't worry about the retainer."

"I got it. I like your money. My concern was only a nag, and now it's gone. You don't have to go on."

Giles felt relief. The load that had been growing simply disappeared. Of course, he was happy for Anna, but the onerous prospect of finding a job and joining the lunchbox crew had been eating at him since the visit with Eastman. He'd felt it hovering, that cloud, the eventual bending into a harness. He had laughed out loud at the prospect of asking Dalton to intercede for him at the A/C and refrigeration company. What was the name? Campos something. *Christ, I might've joined a union?*

Seven

Know Yourself

"GILES," LACEY ANNOUNCED one evening at her apartment, "we have reservations ... same room as before. The one with the view of the lake, and there may be snow. I'm so looking forward to this trip. We haven't had much time together recently." She took his hands, pulled him close, a light kiss on his lips.

She smelled of lilac. His old, wizened grandmother used lilac. The smell brought memories of sagging skin, falling hair, needed hugs, and death.

"I mean extended time. You always seem to have something to do ... something right now that pulls you up and out the door."

"I have obligations needing tending," he said with a grin.

"Giles, you are the most obligation-free person I know. I want a hug."

He put his arms around her, and they embraced for a minute. He felt her body on his—her shapely body and its inviting warmth, and he kissed her. She was right—they hadn't been close for a while, and he missed it too ... now that the notion came into his mind. He tentatively explored her mouth—curious and tasty, and he wanted to go on. Their tongues met gently, the touch familiar, and the exploration continued. His arms slid to her waist, then to her buttocks and his mind's eye flashed her nakedness. He pulled her in closer and she responded. They pressed into each other, and he too was responding.

"Oh Giles ...." She breathed in his ear and nibbled. "I want you," she whispered. "I want you now."

"You haven't eaten, have you, and I'm hungry," she said as they lay on top of the bed, now breathing normally, heads back on the pillows, Giles smoking a cigarette. "Let's mosey over to Dupar's for a burger ... Okay?"

"It's right with me," he said.

Neither moved, both quiet, time passed.

"Giles ...." She rose up on an elbow. "Do we have any plans? What's out in front for us, on the horizon? You know what I mean. I want to look forward, need something to dream about. I worry about this and I'm serious, Giles, where do we go from here?"

"Dupar's?" he said.

**

"LACEY ... THE MORNING NEWS ISN'T GOOD." He glanced at his watch, which informed him it was 7:35 on their Saturday morning trip to Big Bear, he arriving from Beck Street with a small duffle.

"Shall we take a thermos of coffee?" she said. "Shall we eat here, or would you rather get going, stop on the way? Get my bag, will you Giles? It's in the bedroom."

84

"Lacey ... someone sideswiped your car. You left it out on the street. How come? Anyway, we're not going anywhere, at least not in your T-Bird."

"You're joking."

"No, I am not; the front driver's side is caved in, and the wheel is bent under. Not fatal, but not drivable either."

"I want to see." She threw on a sweatshirt, ran down the stairs, and out to the street—Giles, walking behind.

"Goddammit," she sputtered. "I love this car. Why ... some son-of-bitch. Dammit, dammit, dammit."

"The Paradise is on the outside of a curve here. Somebody sailed through too fast and lost it."

"Call the police" she said. "I'm gonna call the police."

"Might've been drunk, high on something."

"The police will find him—the asshole!"

"Well, good luck with that. My Jaguar was stolen in Long Beach a couple summers ago and when I reported it, they said, aww gee, that's a shame but it happens. Fill out these—"

"I don't care about two years ago in Long Beach. My T-Bird is now. What are we going to do?"

"You call the cops. I'll call Izsak, see if we can borrow the roadster."

The patio behind the lodge was deserted—too late in the season for vacationers and too early for skiing. They lolled. The warm overhead sun cut with a cool breeze coming in over the mountains—just right for a light sweater. The peaks held a dusting of snow, a few cumuli drifted lazily, and the area around the lodge was as green and lush as a botanical garden.

A few flowers still blossomed. Worries and frets could not survive in this ambiance.

Giles let his mind wander. This was a grand decision, coming out to the coast. He hadn't labored the notion when upon him but now that he was here, he couldn't imagine being anywhere else. His college days were good, but over. His life at home had been free of restriction as his professor father buried himself in his academic interests while his mother spent most of her life in a vain attempt at digging him out. As a growing boy, Giles didn't get or miss the coziness of a Leave-it-to-Beaver life, the motherly doting, and fatherly demands; rather, he exploited and enjoyed the independence afforded. Since there was no one pushing and no one to blame but Giles, he learned early the notion of self-discipline, motivation, blame and reward.

From Giles' point of view this unusual freedom had served him well and he held only positive reflections. He had done and gone what and wherever he wanted, and absolutely enjoyed his discoveries—happy surprise or sorrowful disappointment. He liked a panoramic view of the world and curried not excessively targeted or limited interests. Easy with following his muse, he was generally good with the outcome.

Giles checked out the mountains and breathed deep the clean air. He smiled at the notion that he was most always content. When something needed a change, he changed it. If things were alright, he left them alone.

"Giles, what are you thinking?"

"I'm thinking this was a great idea. Lacey. You seem always to be loaded with the best. What's next on your list, pretty lady?"

"Dinner sounds good. Let's dress and wander down to the bar."

THE TIME ITSELF was delicious, every minute. Lacey didn't press and Giles was attentive. It seemed to be working. Nothing more serious than the entrée selection challenged their analytical skills—until Sunday. In the morning sun, they sipped coffee and split a currant croissant on the restaurant deck near the patio while considering their choice of breakfasts. The place was essentially theirs, a brisk chill warning of winter, white-capped peaks, rustling trees, the fresh smell of evergreen—all theirs.

Lacey was fidgeting—turning in her chair, crossing and uncrossing legs, drumming fingers on the table top and roaming her eyes. "Giles ...."

"Huh?

"Giles, do you imagine we will be doing this ... these kinds of things when we're sixty? You know, these little weekend jaunts, together, just quietly enjoying our company?"

He looked up from a matchbook that he'd found beneath the table—*Know Your Private Self! Mail $1.25 to Self-Worth and Esteem, Box 1700, Ogden, Utah.*

"Heck, I'm not sure what I'll be doing tomorrow." He grinned. His eyes lit up.

"Damn, you're impossible. I didn't want to get into this, but you just won't give an inch, will you?

"Whatta you mean? You asked a question, I answered."

"It was rhetorical, Giles. But let me be literal. Do you like being up here with me? Do you want our relationship to continue? ... Do you love me, Giles?"

87

He retreated into the matchbook. *Know Your Private Self*. He didn't need advice from Ogden, Utah. He knew as much as he needed to know and was—more or less—dealing satisfactorily with his life.

"Giles?"

"Yes ... yes, I do like being here with you and I do like our relationship, and I do want it to continue."

"Do you love me? That's the real question, Giles, the pivotal question."

He thought about the question. He thought about his life and the matchbook, and he thought about Lacey.

"Look,... I don't know what it means—love. I especially don't know what it means to me, and sure-as-hell don't know what it means to you ... though I have suspicions. Do I love you? I don't know. I'm mesmerized by your looks, your manner, your ideas; enchanted by your presence and amazed with the way we join in coitus ... I'm not wild about your continual pressing for some formal declaration from me."

She dropped her croissant on her plate, pushed back a bit in her chair.

"You can't own me," he said, his voice, quiet and modulated. "People are not ordinarily for sale. Is that why Charlie bolted? He understood the bottom line, that he'd be signing over the deed to his self?"

"Damn you, Giles. You're ruining everything."

"Lacey ... my deliciously sweet Lacey ... we already have a life together. We're here. It's time for breakfast, and we don't have to wait till we're sixty." He grinned and reached over for her hand, took it gently in his and looked straight in her eyes. "But it will end, Lacey, if it's not good enough right now—as it is."

Her first reaction was to retreat, to get up and leave, get on a train to Los Angles. But then she thought, she'd already done that ... and there weren't any trains. This was different and she wanted to stay, to make this work. She leaned into him, to what he had said, tears running down her face. She put her other hand on top of their two and for a minute said nothing. Then she smiled a little, wiped at her eyes with a napkin.

Why did she push like this when she knew it annoyed him, and might end their relationship? Why did she need his commitment? It meant nothing, could be changed with a couple of words? It baffled her, and when it came out, it was reflexive and not the result of her reasoning. It made no sense.

"I'm sorry," she said. "You're right. I don't want to own you ... and I really don't want you to change. I suppose I'm locked into old thoughts ... earlier feelings." She let go and leaned back, took a hankie from her purse and blew her nose. "But I do want a future Giles ... and I want it with you."

Squirrels scampered through the wind-rustled trees, birds chirped their highwire melody, the sun was higher in the sky and warming—all going completely unnoticed.

"'Tell you what, Giles. I'll take an oath. I'll never again push on you ... press, as you say, for a promise. I may think what I want, of course. But I understand. I do, and really, I agree ... theoretically. It's my private self I'm having that problem with." She grinned and picked up the menu.

He might've said something about oaths, but he didn't.

**

THEY STOPPED BY THE PADGETT'S to move to the Bentley and pick up Arthur. Giles liked the sound of well-treaded tires rolling slowly over the gravel drive as they pulled around the house. The gentle but powerful crunch as two tons or more of iron crept slowly—indeed, he thought, a muscular rhino stalking, ready to crush. As they reached the back, Arthur emerged.

"They would like you to come in for a drink. Do you have time?"

Giles glanced at Lacey as she glanced at him and in unison they nodded. This voluntary mutual accord from them struck him as one for the books.

"Good of you to come in," Izsak said. "You are Lacey, and as elevated long ago to the height of cliché, I have heard about you often and it's my pleasure to finally meet you. Sit here next to me. I'd roll to you, but you see, this table is part my psyche and without it I crumble." He turned to Arthur. "Please give Anna a yell and come back to fix the drinks if you will. You don't mind, Giles, if Arthur takes over your pouring responsibilities ... today you are truly our guests."

Giles pulled up the chairs.

"I hear," Izsak said, "you're a producer, Lacey, and we must trade stories. Was the trip a success, Giles ... no trouble with the car?"

"As smooth as your eloquence, Izsak. Not a stutter."

"Ah, Anna, meet Lacey Haift. Lacey, Anna Galloway Padgett."

When Lacey stalled over her drink decision, Izsak suggested a gin fizz. "I bet you will love it," he said.

She liked the gin fizz, and she liked Izsak—warm, cordial without getting personal, and she wondered where and from whom the genteel manner.

"Have you done any film work, Lacey?" Anna asked. "You know Izsak spent a career making movies."

"No," she laughed, "but not because I'm disinterested. I'd move into movies in a second with the right opportunity. Isn't that what we all do or hope to do, the industry so ubiquitous."

"Yes, so it appears," Anna said, "but it is quite a challenge, and so many coming here to tinseltown, their heart on a part, a foot in the door, but end up waiting tables or selling real estate."

"And bomb shelters," Giles interjected with a wink at Lacey.

"I know it's tough," Lacey said. "I suppose you'd need a sponsor and a lot of luck, talent too, of course." She sipped her drink. "I'd have a go at it, though, if opportunity knocked."

"If you're serious," Izsak said, "we might to do something about that. I could ... eh, might use some help, occasionally ... show you the ropes, which ones to tug. We'll have to talk it over sometime."

Lacey smiled. "I'm sorry I led you into that. I didn't mean to."

"Not at all, and you may take me at my word."

With Arthur at the wheel of the Bentley and Giles nearly asleep, Lacey let her mind review the meeting. The gathering was warm, the conversation without a pause. The Padgetts were people with an interest in others—an undercurrent of care and support in their stream of conviviality. She enjoyed their company and the glimpse, if needing more definition, into a more tangible value for her should her involvement with them continue and grow. She'd see to that but there was no hurry.

"I like them, Giles," Lacey said, "contrary to my expectations. I especially like Izsak. Now what am I going to do about the T-Bird?"

"You're going to call the Auto Club and have it towed to a body shop. I'll ask Nick where to take it."

Eight
A Beck Street Disruption

ETURNING FROM THE PADGETT'S, Giles opened the
front door of his new home to find a couple of rag-
tag kids playing hide-and-seek and Mary F, in her
underwear, lounging on Dalton's couch with a movie magazine.

"Hi, Giles. How was the weekend?"

"Hi yourself, and what a surprise." He dumped the kids
from his view in favor of sultry. "Did Santa come early, leave
a gift he forgot to wrap?"

"I'm your new roommate," she said, "but just for a couple days. Paul invited me to stay until I landed this job I'm
after. It's in Avalon ... *across the bay on the isle of Catalina,*"
she sang.

"Roommate?"

Paul came in from the lanai. "Yeah, I didn't think anyone would mind ... not for a few days. She needs a place to
stay."

"I'm sure there's a story."

"There is: Nick and I were driving up to the Carnation
for an ice cream last evening, stopped at the light there where

you turn in, and who do you think we saw? Just sitting there on the curb with some cardboard boxes—Mary and her kids and looking desperate. So, she told us—"

"We were booted out," she interrupted. "The old lady said it was the rent ... always late, she said, but I know it was the kids. She hated my kids. We were waiting for the bus out to my dad's place and along comes the rescue team. Anyway, I've got a new job now, I think. My final interview is on Thursday and by the following week, I'll be gone. And you think I give a shit? I'll be glad to get my li'l ass outta this valley." She flashed her big blue eyes.

"Little?"

**

THE DESIGNATED WEEK PASSED and then another. Mary F was essentially broke. While she fed her kids canned soup, hot dogs, and potato chips, compliments of Dalton, her sink-washed undies and assorted others found their way to the phone line to dry—in plain view of the overly-interested neighbors. But the main problem was her cosmetics and the kids' rubber ducks taking up most of the space in the bathroom.

The situation was awkward, but they told themselves she'd soon be gone, and in the meantime, they were helping a traveler. The kids tossed their sleeping bags on the living room floor at night or out on the patio. Where Mary F found nocturnal quarters was not openly known or discussed.

"Giles," she said one morning while sharing coffee, "do you always play? The rest of your roomies are laboring at jobs, and you don't seem to have one."

He grinned. "I get by."

"And you seem to do it handsomely; are you rich? You dress rather nicely and except for that car, I'd think you were independently wealthy." She wore her usual attire, almost nothing, and when she crossed her legs, a flimsy kimono she had loosely draped opened just enough to bring a flush of embarrassment to Giles' more conservative nature ... and some arousal to his less.

"You do have an interesting style, Mary F ... and I stay at home, so I needn't be wasted on doing for others. More coffee?"

"You may stay, Giles, but here you don't do either." She smiled and recrossed her legs. "You know I like you, and we could engage in some pleasurable events should you decide to do while you're here ... and by the way, whatever Dalton says, or doesn't say, I don't belong to him, or anyone but me. Giles ... dear Giles, are you interested?"

He got up from his chair and came around to her, put a hand on her cheek, sliding it around the back of her neck—a light airy touch.

"Gotta go, sport, and you should know, you make a breakfast more interesting than reading a cereal box."

**

"I KNOW WHAT YOU'RE UP TO." Dalton scowled, his forehead furrowed, his eyes hardened and dark. "The two of you here all fucking day long ... and I'm warning you, prick, leave her alone. I know you, Anderson, and I don't trust your slippery ass one bit. I like her ... and I'm serious about her. So, stay the hell away from her. You got that?"

"Sure, I get it, buddy boy. You work all day long with that messy freon, turning a wrench, and none of it takes an ounce of thought so you fantasize, and your mind shows you movies of Mary F having fun being sexy. But you needn't worry. She's only a flirt and it doesn't mean much, at least not to me ... at least not now. Anyway, buddy boy, when you've got something concrete, a substantiated issue, you come back and make your scene, and if it's big enough, we'll duke it out if you like. Until then, I don't like the uninvited up close in my space. Have *you* got that?"

"Humph ... Well, you heard me."

"Whoa ... what's this about?" Paul, entering the room, felt the valences rising.

"Dickhead, he's doing it again," Dalton said.

"Doing what?"

"What he's always doing, sticking his dick where it doesn't belong."

"C'mon D ... We all know where you're coming from, but I doubt that our Lothario is interested in Mary. He's got his romantic intentions fully served by others more qualified. Anyway, isn't that up to Mary ... the preferential dick?"

"You're always taking his goddam side."

"No, I'm taking Mary's side. Shall I call her in? We'll see who's dick she prefers." Paul chuckled at the scene he might easily create.

Dalton laughed. He'd been in this corner before. "No ... you don't need to do that. Okay, maybe I'm a little out of line, but I'm not fuckin' blind. I know how she is, but just the same

.... Well, dammit, I really like her, ya know ... pretty much, I guess, and I'd like you all, especially him, to give me some operating room."

"Hmm, I got it," Giles said. "I will not advance, but as I see it, there aren't any rules for her, and when they get written, it'll be Mary F with the pen." He extended his open hand. "That's the way I look at it and I want that to be clear."

"Yeah, okay." But Dalton ignored the outstretched peace offering.

**

GILES DIALED HER NUMBER. "Lacey, we've been invited. How's your Saturday night shaping up?"

"Who, Giles? Invited where?"

"Izsak and Anna want us to join them this Saturday for drinks and dinner at their house. Can you make it?"

"Of course, I can make it. Yes! Absolutely, yes. I've been thinking about them. Got the car back today and Nicky was right; they did a great job. Never know it was hit."

"Anything from the cops?"

"They don't know. They say they haven't the manpower to chase it down, even if there was something to chase. You were right, Giles. Why are you always right?"

"Listen, I gotta run. I'm out with Anna tonight. I'll pick you up about four on Saturday. Okay?"

"Why are you always running, Giles?"

"Bye."

"Okay, bye."

**

"YOU SAID ANOTHER TIME, GILES ... did you mean another life?" Mary F brushed by slowly, leaving a touch of her fullness on his arm as she reached for cornflakes on the top shelf. "You've been as scarce as my job offers."

"Sleep well?" he said, a spoonful of cereal poised, awaiting its trip to his mouth. "It's a comfy couch, I've spent some time there myself."

"Where have you been lately? I miss you friend, you're the only one in this house who seems to know how to treat a lady. I am a lady, you know," she teased, her blue eyes flashing.

"You're something, alright, and we won't go into that. You know what else you are? You're the object of Dalton's affection."

"He's a child."

"Maybe ... but he loves you."

"So do my kids."

"You want coffee?"

"Giles, I want you." She sidled up to him, leaning in, again brushing him lightly with her breasts. "When can I have you? How obvious do I have to be? We'd be terrific together, short or long term. I'm not the clingy type, Giles." Back and forth she moved behind his chair, her hands softly over his shoulders. "We can have it and let it go ... or we might want to keep it." She reached to his face, cupped his chin and stroked his cheek with her thumb. "Humm?"

She smelled of woman, and it wasn't his grandmother.

"Well, Giles, are you a man or a eunuch?"

"Aww, screw it," he said, stood and faced her. With his hands on her inviting bums, he pulled her in, pelvis to pelvis.

"So, we'll give it a try ... see what's behind all that teasing." He guided them off to his bedroom.

**

BRUBECK SPILLED FROM THE LIBRARY and flowed through the house as they gathered in the library.

"He must have liked Bach," Izsak said, "so many of his themes are present in a lot of what our jazz friend does. Lacey, I am especially happy to see you. I have some thoughts that may be of interest."

"Izsak, for God's sake," Anna broke in, "they just walked through the door; can't that wait for a few?"

He laughed. "Of course, but it's your influence that drives me there, that get-to-the-point now, niceties later. But, I'll begin again: how have we all been, so glad you are here. Giles, I suppose by now that a few weeks have passed, you are settled .... So, how are you dealing with those many room-mates?"

"That's another thing that can wait," Giles offered, checking the furrows forming above Lacey's eyes—the harbinger of a green-sky storm.

"Isn't life simply grand," Anna said, "so deliciously complicated and challenging. Whatever would we do without its niggling surprises? It could be so very boring."

"Drinks?" Arthur offered. "Did I remember correctly, Miss Lacey, a gin fizz?"

"Perfect. Thank you, kind sir." Turning to Izsak, "I don't hear much about Giles' new roommates; you'll have to fill me in sometime ... and better when we're alone. This man," she looked at Giles, "he's not especially forthcoming."

"He is a bit of an enigma," chimed Anna, "but that's what makes him so delightfully exciting—mystery wrapped in charm." She laughed. "I can almost taste him."

"That's one way of seeing him," Lacey said. "Now, at the risk of disappointing mister personality here, I want you to know," she looked over at Izsak, "I so enjoyed our last meeting, and am delighted you invited us again, and we must find time to tug on those ropes we left hanging." She searched his eyes for a sign of recognition.

"We'll find the time, Lacey, but not tonight. Tonight, we talk of the things we cannot control, then fill our bellies with Rosa's delicious repast, and enjoy our association. Let us drink to our health and prosperity." He held up his glass.

Admittedly a snap observation, Izsak saw Lacey as rather complex—honest and naïve on the one hand, resolved and determined on the other. He thought her unusually beautiful—far more than a pretty face, which it certainly was, but competent and quietly ambitious. If he got close, she'd be a handful.

He wanted back into producing—a familiar milieu where success was essentially assured. He would regain the stature in full that had waned in recent years—the goddamn chair anchoring him to his library. Lacey could assist with that interest. She seemed hungry enough, would bend to his needs as she learned the business and be exactly what he required— his legs.

Yes, he enjoyed writing—the stretch of imagination in creating a story, and screenplays his most likely medium, but it took so painfully long to gain each step ... so many critical heads to please, each with their own agenda, often unrelated, and approval was always hard sought, never guaranteed. And, even if a script was sold, it needed production and all that it entailed. It took years, sometimes a decade, for a script to find a film. He hadn't the patience.

As a writer, he saw himself stuck in an eddy, slowly swirling around going nowhere, and he needed to get back in the mainstream. He longed for the recognition that came with producing—the credits, the "good fellow" applause from compatriots, the gratitude from all those employed, including and especially the actors. He was certain now, the notion within him, fattening on his optimism for days, that with Lacey assisting, he could resume his old role—be who he was before that goddamn horse took his legs. Of course, she too would benefit.

"So, YOU GUYS are meeting again," Giles said, as they entered her apartment that night. "You seem to have found a little of what I did, once upon a time at the Hut."

"We have things in common," she said.

"He more than hinted at that."

"Yes, and I feel I can help him. He can certainly help me."

She moved closer, took the lapels of his jacket in her hands and kissed him lightly—a brush of lips. "Giles ... I want to be alone tonight, do you mind? I have some thinking to do."

Nine
Stories Told

"HEY, MARY," Nick said one afternoon, coming out on the patio, takeout boxes in hand. "I brought some enchiladas if ya like, and some for the kids. C'mon, sit down. Where are those little rascals?"

"You're a nice guy, Nicky," Mary said. "The nicest."

"It's nothin'. It's easy to see you don't have a helluva lot. Here, over here kids, in the shade. They're good behavin' for rascals. I kinda like 'em ... at a safe distance, ya know. So, how'd you get into this fix, anyway, so, eh ... well, destitute and that?"

"It's an old story, Nick. You sure you want to hear it?"

"Sure ... we're all kinda close here, sort of a family, and yeah," he opened the boxes, "I'm interested if not buttin' in. Here, have a fork and you'll need a knife."

"Well, okay." She sighed, took a deep breath. "My husband ... we were married young, just out of school, knew nothing about commitment or kids. Anyway, we're into this marriage four years and two kids, and I came home one day early from work and there he is with a friend of mine ... stretched out in his TV chair with a beer in his hand and she's on her knees giving him ... well, a penis massage. And you know what he did when he saw me? He motioned me off like it would be rude to interrupt." Her eyes turned to the enchilada in front of her. "These are great, Nicky. Where did you get them?"

"Rosita's, down on Laurel Canyon, next to the station." He chuckled. "Ya know ... not to be flippant, I can see his point. That massage, as you call it, is damn consuming, not much room for anything else. I mean earthquakes, tornados, explosions ... not much distraction from any."

"Rosita's," she said. "Umm, I'll have to ... anyway, the bastard left that night. Threw his shit in a couple boxes and I haven't seen him since. It's been damn near a year and nuthin' ... not even for his kids."

"I get the picture."

"I'm glad you asked. I want all of you to know why I'm here, that a dickhead father—."

"What about the kids? They know about it ... you know, the whole thing?"

"I try to be honest with them. Anyway, it's no secret. My dad ... he hated my husband, called him 'the fink' from the start—could see better and father than me, and he helped with the divorce. I was getting by. Then I lost my job, next the apartment, and well ... here I am. I know I'm putting you out. You guys have been great, and Paul, he's an angel ... but I'm looking around, resumés out, and I'll be back on my feet in no time at all. I'm a nurse, you know, LVN ... and I do okay when I'm working."

"Damn, that's tough, and you seem ... well, you *are* a nice lady."

"Like I said, it's an old story." She smiled and put her hand on Nick's arm. "I suppose it's just life. Things always get better, right?"

"What happened to the job in Avalon?"

"It's a small clinic, couple of doctors, an admin and one registered nurse. They were looking for someone to empty the bed pans, watch the meds and see to the comfort of patients. It sounded great, ya know, but they didn't call after the interview ... and when I called them, they'd filled the position."

"A familiar story," he said, shaking his head. "Working for somebody else. I'll be my own boss someday, my own garage—just gotta do it."

"I can appreciate that, but I like a team, like family. My placement folks are looking, but there's not much around—a little tight these days."

"Yeah, we feel some of that at the station."

"My dad, he's sympathetic but he lives alone in a one-bedroom apartment ... has no space. My parents divorced twelve years ago, and my mom is remarried. Her husband wants nothing to do with the kids. Oh, picnics now and then, but that's his limit."

"You're kinda stuck." He looked out across the pool. And so were they, he fully realized. Without a meeting, without a vote, Mary F, her kids, and their sustenance were part of the Beck Street family.

**

LACEY RUSHED IN HER APARTMENT DOOR and picked up the phone.

"Hello ...."

"Lacey?"

"Yes."

"Lacey, it's Izsak Padgett. I'm not disturbing you?"

"Of course not. I've been thinking about calling you."

"Have you eaten? Can you come over for a bite? I would like to talk."

LACEY WAS HUNGRY, not so much for something to eat but for the words she hoped that Izsak might utter, and she wasted no time getting into his presence.

"Rose will bring us something soon," Izsak said. "Will you have a drink? You'll have to pour, Arthur's out back with the cars."

"Sure. Scotch, isn't it, with a splash? If you don't mind, I'll just have the splash for now."

He watched as she strode to the bar—a moderate movement, poised and confident. He had that good feeling about her, been nurturing it for a while and he trusted his intuition, but he would need to delve further, needed to be sure.

"I like your library, Izsak, masculine but comfortable and definitely you ... and the paintings, a breath of warmth ... eh, humanity. I have a—I'm sure you know I've been waiting for this meeting." She mixed and poured from the bar.

"As have I. Come, sit down. Put the drinks here on the table. I'm going to pry a little if that's okay."

"Fire away." She sat and faced him.

"I'm impressed with what I know, but I need more. I have an idea, and if it works, we will both be served, but first, tell me a little about your professional self—a nutshell."

"Okay." She ran a hand over her skirt, tugged at the hem. "There isn't much. I came here ten years ago—maybe Giles has told you—from a personal incident that left me a wreck. My brother has a restaurant in Santa Monica, knew a radio producer at a local public station and got me an interview. I went to work. I mean work with a capital 'devote-your-life'. I did whatever was needed, made my way up through the ranks—radio for a while and more recently, TV. I've been producing for about six years. I lead a small team. I'm happy with it, challenged by it, and now have my feet on the ground. I may not know it all—every experience—and I know it's less complex than film, but I've had some success, been on the receiving end of a few accolades, and believe I'm ready to move on. I do like a challenge."

"Humm ... well, that is a nutshell," he said. "Are you interested in making movies?"

"Yes. That seems like my next step—if a big one."

"Now, tell me about yourself," he said "Who are you, the meat in the shell, so to speak. What were your dreams before you descended on LA?"

"Of course, life has a way of changing that; it's been a while."

"I know, I know that oh so well ... Oh, Rose, come in. We'll eat in here if that's good with you, and we can continue." He glanced at Lacey, who nodded. "Trays will be fine, thank you, Rose. Please go on, Lacey."

"It's not exciting. I have a BA from a small college in Kenosha, Wisconsin—Carthage College. Not many know it. I wanted a family; my parents looked for grandkids, and we planned that I marry a high school sweetheart. Both of us were out of college when he proposed, he with a degree from Yale and a license to practice in Wisconsin. But he had other ideas ... ideas not shared and sprung at the last minute with his absence ... as my father and I waited for our walk down the aisle. It was a surprise ... big fucking surprise."

Izsak eyebrows raised but he smiled, accepting her candor.

"Excuse the language," she said, "but the memory's deserving. At first, I thought my job at the station cathartic. I bathed in it, dressed in it, took it with me to bed .... It seemed to be working but I wanted nothing to do with men." She was distant, her eyes empty as she revealed her previous years.

"Time slipped by while I immersed in the business, shunning personal engagements, and then Giles ... an awkward meeting. I had been afraid of a relationship, a comfortable place for me, and I did my best to ignore him—even to reject. But he persisted—there was a bet, of all things—and we became acquainted.

"You know how charming he is, and he pulled it out of me ... like opening an old trunk in the attic—stiff latch, frightening stuff inside. It was painful as memories unfolded and, to a degree, were relived ... but as it turned out, it was good. Giles had brought a genuine catharsis and apparently, I was ready. Anyway, now it's over and I don't feel that confining inhibition any longer and am free to enjoy a full life." She paused, giving thought to what she had said. "There is a scar." She looked aside.

Izsak sat—mesmerized through a number of ticks of the clock. The silence approached embarrassment. Not knowing whether to sympathize or celebrate, he found nothing to say.

"I'm finished; the story's over." She laughed, took a drink from her seltzer. "I like what I'm doing, Izsak. I like my work and I'm no longer the little girl in my mother's dream. I hope that wasn't too much, but I appreciate your listening. I feel refreshed these days, a new platform, and ready to begin again in a more balanced way."

"Yes, yes. That was perfect. Thank you, Lacey. I see Rose with the cart at the doorway, shall we eat?"

**

AS THE SCREEN DOOR SHUT behind him with its annoying metal bounce, and before he could level his eyes on Lacey in the kitchenette, she rushed over, threw her arms around him, and gave him a hug. She kissed his cheeks, his neck, his chin before she backed away and took his hands.

"Oh, Giles, my dearest darling, I have such wonderful news. I'm going to work with Izsak. He's going to produce—maybe his new script—and I'm going to help him. Think of that, we'll both be employed by Mr. Padgett. Come, let's have a drink and celebrate. I have to say, I'm on a cloud ... it's cotton candy, a merry-go-round and Ferris wheels." She danced through the room. "This is my lucky break, Giles. I'm going to produce a movie. Well, I'm going to help, and if it works out, I'll be listed in the credits. Think of it, Giles, my name in the credits ... Lacey Haift, co-producer, or something like that. It's just what I want, and you, my grinning something-or-other ... you opened the door. I can't wait to dig in."

"That's terrific; when do you start?"

"Soon. He said soon."

**

"ETHAN ... THAT YOU? Izsak here. How are you this wonderful day?"

"About sixty-five percent, friend, but improvement is promised ... they gave me a new inhaler." He put the phone on speaker. "Hold on while I light my pipe." He coughed. "What's on your mind?"

"Oh, checking in, I suppose. How's the film doing?"

"Gangbusters, Izsak ... simply gangbusters. Her character ... Aggie Caufield, is on the lips ... every distributor in the gawd-damn country is talking about her—makes me feel damn good ... gawd-damn good." He cleared his throat. "And it should you as well, Izsak. Anna is wonderful ... who would'a thought—so much power, emotional power ... and projection in that light-hearted woman. And natural, Izsak, like she was born Aggie Caufield." He coughed—a triple header and then a pause. "Goddamn lungs .... You'd never know you were watching a movie."

"And I hear that from others, friends ... and the early reviews. Congratulations, and good about Anna ... I want to talk to you about that. You got a minute?"

"Shoot."

"You remember the script I gave you to read, and when I asked you what your thought, you hesitated too long before your lukewarm praise— 'marketable,' I think you said?"

"It needed work."

"Trash it. I've got another now ... much better, draft near finished—not quite a sequel to *No Harm Done* but it makes use of the character, Aggie Cawfield ... a much better use."

"Hmm ..."

"Now, I've talked with Distant Star ... know a few there ... and if you're willing to direct, I think we have picture. They liked *Harm* and they adore Anna in the role of Aggie. This story of mine makes Aggie the principal character ... a noir mystery, of course. What do you say, my friend, you want another, maybe better, Aggie Cawfield?"

"You know I'm on the back side of the curve ... getting ready to retire, but I'll have a look. And don't wait to polish it up, send it over now. Who'll produce?"

"I've got ideas there, a few we'll toss around, once you're interested."

"Good to hear from you, Izsak. Been awhile, my friend." He coughed, coughed again. His chest rattled through the phone.

"God, Ethan, are you okay?"

"Fine, just a little tickle. Send over the script."

"So long, Ethan, I'll send it tomorrow."

A Fuse Shortens

66YOU FUCKING DICK-HEAD!" Dalton yelled. "You said you'd keep your hands off, but your word don't mean shit. You just don't give a damn ... not about any fuckin' thing." Dalton swung ... a powerful right cross that connected with Giles' jaw, wrenched his neck with an audible crack and left him on the floor. "Well, fucker, how'da ya feel about that?" He bent over the damaged offender, rubbing the weaponized fist, glaring at Giles, neck bulging. "Get up, you cockroach. I got more."

"Christ, Dalton!" Giles dazed, planets orbited, jaw hurt. In a flash, he could taste his blood and his tongue was thickening.

"Get up, you sick shit," Dalton yelled, dancing around, crouched like a boxer. "You sick motherfucker ... get another helping of Dalton's medicine. I'm so fuckin' tired of you ... but I'm feelin' generous. He kicked at Giles, his adrenaline peaked, blood coursing.

He'd been waiting for a while, and his while had come. He reached down to grab Giles and pull him up, right fist cocked like a pile-driver.

Giles clambered back, half under the dining room table. Nick came in through the front door.

"Hey, what's goin' on?" He went over for a better look and saw Giles sprawled under the table, bloodied mouth. "What the hell!?"

"Buzz off, Nick, this ain't none of your business."

"Ho, Dalton boy, it is my business. This guy with the blood leakin' outta his face ... he's a friend, and he pays some of the rent here. You need to cool off now, ya hear? Cool off right now or you can have us both. You got that much ta dish out?"

"Well ... okay ..." Dalton's head down, arms hanging, "okay for now. But I'm tellin' you this, Anderson ... any more of your fuckin' around with her and you're toast. I mean burned fuckin' black. You got that?" He slammed the door on the way out.

"Help me up, Nick. I may have lost a tooth."

"What was that about?"

"Nothing much," Giles said, rubbing his jaw "He's a hot-head—lights up pretty easily."

"Yeah, I know."

**

LACEY PUT A RECORD ON, opened a chilled bottle of her favorite Pinot Grigio, poured a glass and plopped on the couch. Her day was over. She was exhausted. The phone rang.

"Hello!"

"Lacey?"

"Yes ..."

"This is Dalton Dobbs. You know ... Giles' housemate, one of 'em."

"Is something wrong? Is Giles alright? Tell me!"

"Yeah ... he's fine, maybe a busted jaw, and that's what I want to tell you about. I could come over."

"What, Dalton? Just tell me now."

"Well ... it's kinda long and a little hard to understand."

"Go on."

"There's this girl, ya see ... and she's mine. I mean we're going together ... and she's living with us at the house because she's homeless. Paul and Nick, they brought her in, and Giles ... you know how he is .... Well, he ain't working and he's here all day long with her, and dammit ... well, they're like foolin' around ... sex stuff. He won't let her alone and some worse than that .... And I wantcha to get after him. Just tell him to keep his hands off her. He might listen to—"

"Goodbye, Dalton Dobbs."

**

"I THINK WE'RE AGREED in principle, Lacey—you will work with me if I produce. It's not certain right now, but as close as a Gillette shave." Izsak chuckled. "Uh ... there is interested money available. The script is done, and Ethan has agreed to sit in the director's chair, which pleases the studio and backers. Hand me that lighter, will you."

"Exactly how do you see me working in?" Lacey said.

"You'll begin as my assistant, be a lot of running around. We will talk, of course. I'll try to explain, and you will ask questions. Keep your senses tuned in, learn the process and

115

meet the people. It's all about people, you know. The producer's role is to see that resources are available when needed—not too early and not too late—the money, people, location, equipment, and so on.

"As you begin to establish yourself, and that will take time, I'll step aside a bit. I'll coach, and I'll watch you blossom. How much do you make at the station?"

"Two-fifty a week."

"Humm. I don't want you at risk, so you won't give notice until I tie the bow. There's little doubt ... but you never know in this business until the papers are signed and even then, there are lawyers."

"When will I get paid and what can I expect?" She spoke up with the bravado he was releasing in her. "Don't get me wrong, Izsak," she laughed, "I know a gift-horse, but there is that food on the table, and I'm not comfortable quitting without knowing I can keep it there." She felt strong and assertive, a new feeling, and it surprised her.

"Yes, the table." He smiled warmly. "We will be in this together, a team ... and mind you, there are risks, but here's my offer. Once we begin—all involved have shaken hands and you have taken leave—I'll pay you your current salary until we're under contract." He paused. "I'll call you, of course. We'll negotiate as a team. What comes from that is open, but I assure you, if it goes at all it will go beyond your present earnings ... far beyond."

Her mind was reeling. Hundreds of thoughts bouncing about and colliding—Roman candles released in a small, mirrored room. This was real and she was dealing.

116

"My God, Izsak. You can't imagine what you're doing to me ... for me. I can't thank you ... I could kiss you." She laughed. "Maybe I'll just fix us a drink?"

**

"GILES, I WANT TO CELEBRATE. Dress up. I'll come by your place at seven. Be ready; I don't want to meet any room-mates, especially Mr. Dobbs."

"Wha ...?"

"We'll go to dinner, Giles, and it's on me .... God I'm floating. Wear your Anna clothes."

"So, THERE YOU HAVE IT, GILES," she said, "and it's all be-cause of you and that silly bet ... truly serendipitous. You couldn't dream it up—so many pieces falling together and at the perfect time. Let's have another drink before we order."

They weren't slumming. A valet parked her car. It wasn't exclusive, but if you were there without a few hundred bucks in your pocket, it was because you were on the shift assign-ments list. And even then, it took her brother to open the door on short notice. The Beverly Hills Gourmet might have been the best there was in tinseltown and miles around. Old, well established, elegant and expensive.

"I love you, Giles. I'll always love you." Her eyes twin-kled.

"What will we have Lacey ... a little help please." He browsed the awesome menu.

She sipped her drink but didn't need it. She felt deliri-ous. She couldn't stop her joy from flooding in—a monsoon of happiness. "I don't care; we'll ask the waiter. I want to make a toast, Giles, pick up your glass and join me." She whisked her glass up from the table and spilled a little.

He obliged. He didn't quite know how to deal with this euphoria. *She is exquisite—a glistening stone, a rose in morning dew. Sunrise ... a puppy dog. She needs a poet.* He held his glass up next to hers. They tinkled. He loved her in this mood, a touch of carelessness.

"Here's to Izsak," she began, "and here's to you, Giles. Here's to all the lovely, beautiful people who made this happen ... to Charles McShithead for bailing out and pushing me West, and to Ross for the reservation, to Paul and his bet, to Anna even, and to Dalton, naïve, blue-collar, underdeveloped, Dalton. Here's to all of 'em." She laughed and chugged her martini—her third.

"Underdeveloped?" he said and laughed.

"I'm gonna have another." She smiled demurely. "Waiter ... garçon! Wherefore art thou garçon de café?"

She waved her empty glass in the air.

"You know, he called me," she said. "Your Dalton ... with some interesting news."

"What are you getting at?"

"Dalton. Your friend at the Beck Street brothel. He called, the son-of-a-bitch." She laughed. "How is your jaw, Giles? He told me it may be giving you trouble. Is it broken? Of course, it isn't broken, not *your* jaw, Giles. It's made of rubber ... flexible, like the rest of you, Giles, bends with the 'blow' as the fishermen say?" She threw her head back with a snort of a laugh.

"Jesus, Lacey, what's got—"

118

"C'mon, Giles. It's me," she said loudly. "Your casual, non-serious, noncommittal other. Let's not be naïve ... not like Dalton. Let's get it out. If you want to fuck around ... well, that's as it is. Right? Let's celebrate. Let's celebrate our cosmopolitan, bohemian, open-bed life." She glared at him, sat back and was quiet. Other patrons looked on and the maître d'hôtel whispered to their waiter as he pointed them out, the waiter nodding.

Giles wanted to be far away but knew he was there—*fucking Dalton.*

"Listen ..." he said quietly, leaning in over the table. "I don't know what he told you. My jaw is just fine and I'm willing to let this go till another time. This is your night; don't screw it up with Dalton's underdeveloped nonsense." He sat back. "She made a pass, and I caught it ... a fumble as it turned out. That's all. It doesn't mean shit. Don't make it more. Dalton is a child. His credibility stinks."

"Yeah, a child ... from the mouths of children, Giles." She had quieted down.

He put his arms on the table and again leaned forward, more intensely now. Firmly but quietly, he began.

"Lacey, *you* are important. Listen to me. You are the only one that has cut me deep." He paused. "You are a crucial part of my life now. Do I love you? Hell, I don't know ... but we'll never find out if Dalton's story takes center stage. I'm no mystery. I've always been forthright with how I feel and who I am. You are a marvelous person. I know that, and I feel lucky to be with you, but we've made no commitments. Why all this now? If you want to stem our growth, okay, just say so and I'll disappear ... and without all the noise."

She sat back, seemed a bit stunned, wheels turning but taking her nowhere.

"Look," he continued, "we may be on the cusp of something great ... true love, whatever that is, and I don't want to miss it. You punch my ticket now, we'll never find out. Let this pass. Let us grow. Don't snip our bud before it blossoms."

They were quiet. He looked at her and his gaze never faltered. She was tipsy and seemed uneasy.

"Okay, you make a point," she slurred just a little. "I don't necessarily like it. Not at all necessarily like it. You hurt me, Giles—with your screwing around. Maybe you didn't intend it, but you did."

"You hurt yourself," he said. "I did nothing. I promised nothing. We're not going to find a fulfillment that takes years in a couple of months ... if at all. Life isn't a storybook, Lacey.

"Let's celebrate your success, your life changing success, and let the 'we' of it find its own way. We're here, so let's order."

"Alright ... smooth talker, but you tell Dalton to do his reporting elsewhere." She ordered coffee.

**

THE NEXT DAY, at about one, Lacey took her place on a chaise by the pool at the Paradise—a complex she had lived in for years and had well served her needs. She opened her recent copy of *Vogue,* but her mind was on her situation. The apartment was comfortable and not especially expensive, convenient to a job she enjoyed, and for those past years, her life had been pleasant. Oh, she had cried herself to sleep now and then, hated the male ogling and the amateur attempts at passes, but by and large her life had been tranquil with little to complain about.

The sun was warm and bright, her wine cooler felt good on its way down, and the hangover she anticipated from the previous night had hardly appeared. She thought about the night—the intense give and take, and Giles. What did she want, why the frustration, and was Giles really her Prince Charming? If he isn't, why doesn't she drop him? If he is, why doesn't she accept him?

She had run before and for what—ten years a recluse. Not much of a life and no more of that. Giles is a man, a solid person, from her perspective. Not many of those around—kind, thoughtful, nice looking, enjoyable, and honest. He may hold back; he might fool around. Does she want a saint?

Where was she now? Well, things had changed, and it seemed to her they were bound to keep changing, and rapidly. A new and exciting career and she had stepped up. She had dumped the painful memory of Charles M. in the trash, what a relief. That door was shut and hopefully locked.

She had met Izsak, a movie producer, and felt professionally comfortable. He had offered the job she might only have dreamed of, that would allow a move into private digs with a no-ogling patio, and Giles—brash, unpredictable, cart-upsetting Giles, and it was all his doing.

He had yanked her out of her comfort zone to show her a life that she may never have otherwise known: a challenging, demanding, and promising life of excitement and huge possibilities. And all that he asked was to be left in a shape he enjoyed ... his shape—to be Giles. What's wrong with that?

What's wrong with loving the man who had awakened her simply because of who he was, and why should she want to change that? Well, she didn't.

She loved Giles because he was Giles, Giles Anderson. She thought about it and decided she liked that name. It had a nice ring—"solid and established," she said out loud, and then turned the page of her *Vogue*.

Eleven
A Rolling Ball

ANNA SPOKE UP FROM THE FOYER, "Ethan is here with the head of the studio."

"Good," Izsak said, "bring them in."

"Well, you're still in that chair," Ethan chuckled softly, stifling a cough, "But you look good, Izsak. You know Robert Meyer."

"It's been a while, Izzy." Robert Meyer, a big guy with an equally big presence, extended his hand.

"Yes, far too long, Bob. I've been wheeling around the library here, catching up on my reading and entertaining my muse. You look fit, been spending time at the gym?"

"Some."

"Fix us a drink, Anna. Scotch okay with you two? We need to reacquaint. Pull up those chairs over there."

"Over ice," Bob Meyer said, "and a double for Ethan. Anna, you stick around. This concerns you as well. Now, I'll get right to the point. Ethan has read your script, as have I ... when did you start writing?" He waited through a glance at Izsak, then went on. "It needs some ... well, minor stuff ... and

123

we have some suggestions regarding the abrupt ... that final scene needs more of something so as to confirm ... bring in the audience." He nodded at Ethan. "And we like the late bloomer here for the Cawfield part ... damned near perfect."

"Thanks, Mr. Meyer," Anna squeezed in.

"I know you have been scouting for money, Izzy. You have those friends; I'm not surprised, and I hear you've had some success."

"Some," Izsak said, smiling.

"Yes ... Well, don't worry about the rest. I've talked to my board; Ethan presented—slow, but inspiring and damned persuasive." He smiled at his old friend. "The sum of it is, we're thrilled, and the studio will back the film—take it all if we can. We like the story, we like Ethan directing, and we like Anna as Aggie. There is only one problem—production."

Izsak picked up his drink, took a sip.

"Ethan likes you for the job, but ... well, naturally we're concerned, umm, the board is concerned. That wheelchair has its limitations and I'm wondering ... we're all wondering if you'll agree to a studio producer, one already on contract. Now before you pop outta that chair, fist in the air, we have some pretty decent people on the lot. The guys who did *Harm* ... I'd make them avail—"

"Hold on, Bob," Izsak interrupted. "I know you have decent producers available, but as I told Ethan, I have that covered. I will produce, that's the deal ... and of course I'll want the script credit as well." Izsak lit the cigar he'd been rolling around in his mouth. "That's part of it and I think Ethan is with me here." He looked over at his friend.

Robert Meyer sat quietly, rotating his head slowly and rubbing his hands. Everyone in the room knew he needed this picture. But both his board and the finance guys thought Izsak Padgett was a has-been—out of the business for over ten years. If he agreed to this arrangement, and the picture failed at the box office, he'd be playing checkers in a park somewhere with the geezers.

On the other hand, no one in the room except him was under contract and there were other studios. Izsak had some backing and could probably get the rest. Izsak had been outstanding with production in the past—maybe again—but a risk he'd prefer not to take. Meyer smiled. He wanted this picture, but maybe another scotch first.

"Anna," he said, "if my tab is paid up, can I buy another round?" He watched as she strode to the bar. *One helluva woman.*

"Okay." Meyer turned to Izsak. "We'll buy your script, pay handsomely, and retain you as a consultant; might even work out a share of the net, credit you as associate producer." Meyer picked up his fresh drink, took a sip, looked again at Izsak. "I can see your mind is set. You've been thinking about it ... alone here in your comfort, but there are others involved going forward as certainly you know, and they too have an opinion. You name your price."

He could see the clench in Izsak's Hungarian jaw, the determined look in his expressive eyes. "Goddammit, Izzy, we have the best in direction with Ethan here; Anna is a go, and it's your story. For Christ sake, don't fuck it up with fuzzy thinking. We're firm on this. You know what producing is and it can't be done from a wheelchair."

Izsak puffed on his cigar. Whiffs of smoke curled slowly toward the ceiling while seconds ticked by. They could hear Ethan breathing, Rose shuffling pans in the kitchen. No one moved but to sip at their drinks. Finally, Izsak spoke.

"We've worked together before. You know who I am and what I can do. You've counted the money I've brought in ... lived well on a part of it. Yes, you have a point about the chair, but—now this is important—I've recruited a young woman who'll assist me. She too will have credit, by the way—an associate spot when they roll. And she'll be named in the contract. Her name is Lacey Haift. She's a natural—has the appropriate experience.

"Now, Bob, I'm not selling the script; that's not on the table. If I need to, I'll shop it around ... both Ethan and Anna are free agents and while we've not discussed it—not thinking we had to—I believe they'll agree with me and go with the story." Izsak was solid with his matter-of-fact delivery.

"This woman I've mentioned has excellent credentials with KNEW producing original drama. We will work bacon and eggs, and where I am handicapped, she will fill in ... more as time passes. You'll get what you expect, only more and better, and for close to the same cost. And Bob, the best part of this is, she's ambitious ... did I say young and beautiful? A quick study, energetic with excellent insight ... and if she stays on for you, she'll put another feather in your executive hat."

Meyer was forward, his elbows on his knees, his eyes on the floor through Izsak's speech. His head turning slowly in a defeated motion. "It's the board, Izsak. They—"

"I'm with Izsak on this trip," Ethan spoke up. "If you want the story, Bob, and you want me directing, you'll need to buy the kit and caboodle." He paused for a breath. "I'm afraid that's how it is."

"I don't really have much standing here," Anna added, "but I need to say this. I know Lacey Haift, and I also think she's a comer. She's sharp, attractive, and eager. She and Izsak as a team ... well, they'll set examples—teach those studio guys you like just how to run a show." She laughed. "And here's the real thing, Robert Meyer—we like each other, and we like the script, and after all, isn't the role of a studio boss to find a collaborative team?" She got up and sauntered to the bar. Meyer watched—fluid movement, all woman, with legs that should be insured.

He remembered her in *No Harm Done* and the positive commentary from her performance—Hollywood, New York, Timbuktu. She was a handful, confident and tantalizingly new for the audience—*tough, comely, another Patricia Neal ... maybe better*. He also remembered the money her film was bringing in, Ethan's skill with a crew, and the low-cost budget. He wasn't going to pass up another high-profit hit. He shook his head and held out his glass.

"Shit, we'll do it your way, Izsak." He smiled. "The papers will be ready next week ... someone'll call. Here's to Aggie Cawfield, and I'll have one of those cigars."

LACEY'S PHONE RANG. She picked up.

"Hello Lacey, this is Izsak. Give your notice tomorrow and drop over in the evening to sign papers. It's time we got to work."

"Izsak, oh, Izsak ... thank you. Oh my God, it's happening. Yes, I'll see you tomorrow night." Tears rolled down her face. She hung up the phone and danced into the living room, back into the kitchen, twirling about, arms outstretched, and then she dialed.

"Giles, can we celebrate again? This time it's—"

"This is Dennis. Giles isn't here."

**

"WAKE UP, GILES," Nick said. "We're playing poker here and the bet's to you ... drop, call, or raise—pick one. Dalton's high with sevens showing."

"Uh, yeah ... call." He threw a buck in the pot.

Nick dealt. The last card down. Paul bet a dollar.

"Raise a buck," said Dalton, sitting back and grinning.

"In," said Dennis.

"Call," said Giles.

"Five more to see 'em," said Nick.

Paul dropped.

"Fuck you," said Dalton. "You're bluffin'."

"Only cost you five to find out."

Dalton edged forward, looked again at Nick's up cards, the stack of bills in front of him, then back at his own hand.

"Shit, you're tryin' to buy it again," Dalton said. "I'm raisin' another five."

"I'm outta this." Dennis folded his cards.

"It'll cost you, Dobbs." Nick grinned and raised ten more.

"Damn," Dalton said, "that's three, the last raise, or I'd break you." He pushed the last of his chips into the pot

"Jacks full," Nick said, as he turned up his hole cards.

Dalton turned over a straight to the ten, pushed back from the table, and rose. "Son-of-a-bitch," he growled, dirty son-of-a-bitch .... How can ya lose on a straight?"

"I'm finished," Paul said.

"Me too," Dennis added.

"I guess that's it," Giles said as he put his remaining money into his pocket. "Congratulations, Nick, lotta luck tonight."

Nick raked in the pot, stacked the new bills—ones and fives here, tens next, three twenties—and began rolling the change into wrappers, while Dalton smoldered and paced, mumbling to himself, clenching his fists.

"Thanks guys," Nick said. "Y'all just sent Mary and me out on the town. Live music tonight at the Broncin' Saddle if anyone care to join us."

"You gonna do what!?" Dalton swiveled toward Nick. "What's that you say?"

"Calm done, Dalton. It's only a game," Nick said. "There be more. You'll have a night."

"You said you and Mary ... that's what I heard."

"Yeah, I'm takin' her dancing because she likes to dance ... thinks you have club feet." He laughed. "You wanna watch? You can watch if you come with us."

Dalton snarled as he pulled Nick from the chair by his shirt front and hit him hard with jab to his chin. "You take my money ... you take my girl?" He loomed over Nick, now sprawled on the floor rubbing his jaw.

"Back off, D," Paul yelled. "No need for this."

"Fuck you. This asshole's been doin' shit with Mary behind my back ... first your penis-head Anderson, now him. Get up; I've got another knuckle sandwich for ya."

"D ...." Paul stepped back.

Nick rose slowly. Taller than Dalton but lighter by about twenty pounds, he was muscular and, Detroit raised, knew how to fight in the streets. Without a word, he picked up a roll of nickels from his stash on the table as if to put them in his pocket but curled his hand around it and in a flash, Dalton lay dazed on the floor.

Giles moved to step in. Paul pulled him back. "Let 'em go, it's time."

The only noise from Beck Street was the soft, mushy, thud of fists and flesh colliding, the heavy gasps for air, and the grunts that followed collisions. When it was over, and it didn't last long, Nick was standing, essentially unbruised, and Dalton was sitting on the floor, back against the wall, knees pulled up, hands over his bleeding face.

"Nuff, dammit," he said. "I'm through."

Nick dropped the roll of nickels into his pocket, picked up his money and left the room. Dennis shook his head without a word. Giles wet a dish towel and patted the blood on Dalton's face while Paul prepared an ice pack.

Later that night, Giles approached Dalton, who sitting on his couch, holding the ice pack to his jaw and rocking back and forth.

"You're lookin' pretty bad there, Dalton," Giles said. "You wanna see a doctor?"

"No." Dalton grunted and didn't look up.

"You up for some conversation?" Giles asked.

"Say it. You're gonna say it."

"Look, if you'd rather not, it's okay by me. You want an aspirin?"

"I said, say it. You're gonna fucking say it anyway, so say it."

"Okay, you like Mary, right?" Giles said.

"So ...?"

"You're showing it the wrong way."

"Yeah?"

"I've no idea how she feels about you but acting like a bully is not going to improve it .... Do you want some aspirin?"

"Took some. Jesus, my head hurts."

"Show her some interest; she's the one, ya know? If you want her, she's the important one, not you. Take her out, make nice ... and do some of it with her kids."

"Whatta you know?"

"I know one thing. Your current technique isn't working. Beating up on the competition or trying to ...." He chuckled. "That isn't gonna cut it. She isn't Guinevere ... and you sure as hell aren't Lancelot."

"Who are they?"

"My point is, go to her directly. You know, court her. Take her to a movie, Carnation for a sundae. Take 'em all on a picnic and be nice. Show her that you care."

"Yeah, like you did?"

"Jesus, you're a hard nut ... but you can do it if you want to. It's about affection, Dalton. Take her hand ... smile ... ask her about her life, show her you're interested, and for Christ's sake, don't punch her out."

"That's funny ... but I can't laugh, and ... well, you're prob'ly right. I s'pose I could try."

**

"GOOD MORNING," Izsak said, Lacey at the door to his library on a Saturday morning. "Come in, take a seat. Rose will bring us some coffee. Had breakfast yet?"

"And good morning to you, boss, or is it Mr. Producer? I've had breakfast, but coffee sounds grand." She took a seat, opened a thin case, and pulled out a pad.

"You won't need that now," he said. "Here's how we will work." Izsak handed her a binder, empty except for a goodly number of blank pages. "I'm not telling you how to organize the notes you will take, the information you'll collect, and I will not say that by the time our film is in the theaters, this binder will be full as will its siblings, but I hate to repeat myself and there'll be a lot of words between us, and in the past I've found this system to work the best." He sat back and lit a cigar. She put her pad back into its case.

"First off," he said, "you will listen. Movies work a little different than TV ... more complicated and far-reaching, more God than gospel. You might think of it as an estate dinner. We, you and I, will put the guest list together, send out the invitations, and purchase and prepare the food that matches the menu. We'll clean up the kitchen after it's over, and absolutely everything in between. If it needs doing, we will do it. The only thing we won't do is the table conversation; that'll be the actors coached a little or a lot by the director."

"I'm listening."

"We'll work as a team, both pulling the load, but we'll start with you assisting. I'll give you assignments, you'll carry them out, I'll give you more and along the way you'll learn the ropes. By the time we're finished, I'm hoping you'll know what I know. You will also do some rather complex things, things that will test your intelligence ... like pushing me around and occasionally helping me into and out of a van." He laughed. "You up for that, Lacey?"

"Of course. I'm your protégé, your intern, your server."

"Oh, and by the way, we are a team. I am Izsak and you Lacey—no 'sir,' no 'boss,' no genuflecting. And here's Rose with the service. Thank you, Rose. You've met Lacey, right?"

"Yessir. Good morning, Miss Haift."

"Good morning, Rose, and thank you."

"Will there be anything else, Mr. Izzy?"

"Not now, Rose."

"In a nutshell," he turned to Lacey, "we will present the filmmakers with all that they need to make it. We will see to sets, travel, meals, schedules, equipment, journeymen, and helpers ... we will budget the spending, see that the cash is available, and that the right people are spending it on the right things. We will see to schedules and timelines, and emergencies when they come up. We will wipe asses if needed ... and of course we'll get help. The producer is a project manager, Lacey, a whip cracker, therapist, and occasionally a mother. The picture belongs to the producer ... ours, in this case, and we need to think that way. It will succeed or fail as an investment, depending on how well we manage. The people, the entire crew ... their selection and performance is our responsibility."

"Wait," she said, "we have a director, don't we, and star, and ...?"

"Yes, and the director works with the casting director, and they with the musical director and costume designer and those doing the scenes settings will see to the artistic side of the film, although we can exert influence, help resolve problems ... if and when necessary. Operations, finance, and art all together make up the team and good to remember this—they are experts and know what's expected.

"The studio depends on our making the film a financial success. Every day on the lot, more on location, these people are paid and it's money going out. We need to see it properly spent—the plan is executed, that schedules are met, and progress is made. There are accountants, of course, and we'll meet with them regularly."

"Got it," she said. "I've done this, though at a smaller scale. Umm, good coffee."

"You have the fundamentals. That's why you're here, and the people we will bring in have all worked before, know what to do. Our job is one of ensuring cohesion, collaboration, cooperation ... the glue that holds them together ... and, that resources are there. The crew must act as a single force. And all that I've said, Lacey, is the tip of the iceberg."

"Good ... I'm not intimidated, Izsak. I expect it to be a challenge and I'm ready."

"Yes," he said, "I believe you are, and I want you to ask questions whenever you're not sure. There'll be problems you've not encountered before."

"Honestly, I've never felt better about a new job ... ah, new profession. I've given notice at the station, last day is

Friday, and then my slate is clean … well, except for Giles. But I'll devote all the time that is needed, no other demands as important. And …" she reached over and put her hand over his, looked into his graying eyes, "thank you again, Izsak. This is a wonderful opportunity for me, and I promise you, I'll give it all that I have."

Ordinary Times

136

Twelve
A New Direction

GILES ... LET'S STAY IN TONIGHT," Lacey said on the phone. "I'm exhausted. Spent the whole day with Izsak. It was intense and I'm tired. This is a broad sweep of a business, this moviemaking, and I just want to be with you ... quiet, Giles, in your loving arms.

"Uh hunh," he mumbled, holding the phone away from his ear; he looked at the receiver as if he could see her. Talk between them wasn't working so well—still and always, a bias toward "serious" and questions of "future," while he wanted a lighter, airier interface. Sometimes, he thought, he'd rather go to a movie.

"Okay, I'll be over about seven. Should I pick something up?"

"Would you?"

He stopped at Chin's Chinese Cuisine and ordered a 27. "And a 13. Umm," he scanned the menu, "and an 8 for two."

"Steamed lice? Come with two."

"Yeah, steamed lice and add egg rolls. That'd be number 4."

"Three minutes, you wait."

Numbers ... the universal language, his dad always said, "Everyone knows how to count, and everyone uses the same mathematical concepts." He thought about his dad, a math professor at Lawrence—integrals, differentials, regressions, derivatives. They were the old man's escape, wandering around with Greek theoreticians. Well, he had part of it in common with his dad, the wandering, though he was using a different map. He had visited and revisited his lust for wandering, and considered his dad's situation, his refuge from the emotional entanglements of marriage buried in numbers—and the subtle encouragement for his only son to consider the same. And he recalled his mother's continuing admonishment about settling down, leading a normal life—an advanced degree, Harris tweed with elbow patches, join the faculty, and marriage with kids and a dog, of course.

Well, he had escaped all of that and was happy. He'd been responsible enough through earlier times, fulfilling expectations and bringing pride to his parents and mentors. Now he had the reins, if held loosely. He liked a life without obligation, and he liked it without bounds.

He picked up a bottle of cold chablis at Louie's and turned his old but dependable Plymouth toward the New Paradise where he felt a tether waiting.

"YOUR FIRST meeting went well?"

"Beautifully," she said, "big picture and admonishments."

138

"Good. I was thinking he might be a little stiff, eh, instructional." He focused on getting food into his mouth—chopsticks a challenge, his appetite losing out. "I need a fork."

"You know where they are, although that's cheating, you know."

"I'm not a citizen, just like their food."

They sat at small table, across from one another, a sea of white containers between them, flaps open like sails hanging, masts of serving spoons, breeze steady and the forecast clear until from the calm, a threatening wind blew in.

"Giles, I want us to get married ... not tomorrow, but when the picture is finished." She looked up with curious eyes.

"Not now, Lacey. Let's have a night free of life's planning. What's on TV?"

"I haven't looked. I'm not planning, just telling you how I feel, Giles. I love you and want to be your wife. God, you certainly know that."

"Yeah, I know that."

"Things are going so well," she said. "I have a great job, now ... good money and more to come, so that can't be the problem ... even if you were laid ..." she chuckled, "laid off, that is. Darling Giles, I'm not pushing ...." She reached out for his hand, which instinctively he moved back. "I'm just telling you my feelings. It could work out, you know. Do think about it, darling."

Darling ...?

"Will you think about it? Just think about it?"

"Okay, I'll think about it." *What I'm thinking about is this 'darling' shit, and the load of commitment it brings.*

"You could show some enthusiasm."

"Great idea, Lacey, I will give it my serious considera-
tion ... now, may I have the rice?" He grinned, his eyes sparkling. "Please, the rice."

"Okay ...." She pushed it toward him, and as he reached,
he knocked over the open soy sauce.

"Giles! Watch what you're doing." She got up, went for
a towel.

"Sorry," he mumbled. *Just when you think the sailing is
smooth, the sky turns a threatening green, the wind kicks up
and tries to capsize your boat—fucking Chinese.*

"It's not going to happen tomorrow," she said, wiping
the table with a wet towel.

**

"I THINK IT'S WORKING," Dalton said. "I hate to say it,
dickhead, but I think your advice is helping me out. We're going out this Sunday, Mary and the kids ... a family picnic, no
less."

"Your wounds are healing." Giles grinned.

"Yeah, s'pose you could say that, so thanks for the tip."

"Say, Dalton, how about you return the favor, lend me
your Triumph for a ride. I need a little fresh air, a little relief.
Can you handle that?"

"Huh?" He looked away. "Well, sheeze ... I dunno." He
ran his fingers through his hair and looked down at his feet.
He didn't want to mess up this new amenable interface, but
he also didn't see any fucking reason why he needed todo anything for Giles.

140

"You know how to ride? I don't like lending my bike, too easy to screw it up. Dump it. Most riders can't handle a Thunderbird."

"Yes, dummy, I can ride," Giles said, "and I'm not going to screw it up ... and if I do, I'll make it right. I'm living here, remember, and not going anywhere."

"Well, shit ... I don't wanna but ... okay. Okay for this one time, and be careful in the damn traffic. Where ya headin' anyway?"

"Not sure ... up by the dam, maybe, or out toward Lancaster. Just need a break ... get away, clear my head."

"Damn good for that, but ya gotta be careful, keep your focus on the fucking road. Keys ..." he held them out. "It's in the garage, and check the gas; you'll prob'ly needs some soon."

"Thanks ... and good luck on Sunday."

THE TRIUMPH THUNDERBIRD, red-trimmed and powerful, was a meditation on wheels. He cranked her up, could hear the parts moving, the clicks and clacks that would morph into a scream as he throttled her up on the highway. This was a machine for the road, one of the best.

Giles pulled out of the garage and headed west toward Henderson Dam. He ran the big bike through the gears, stretching out revs before shifting. But before he could get into fourth, it was time to slow for the upcoming intersection. Shit, he needed a highway. He liked the wind into his face, through his hair, though he'd forgot his sunglasses and stopped at a Thrifty to pick up a pair.

141

"Nice ride, mister." The clerk said. "I like the color. Custom?"

"Dunno."

"I'd give my sister for one of those. Nothin' like it ... open space on a bike, out there on the highway, jus' you and the planet."

Giles picked up the freeway ... west seemed right, out to Oxnard, a cut towards Chatsworth and maybe from there to Lancaster. *There's plenty of time ...and anyway, who gives a fuck about time?* He laughed at the abundance of time.

The motorcycle performed. It whined easily right up to 100, screamed on to 110, crept to 112 and then to 120. Freedom! Wild-assed, unassailable, freedom. He was enthralled with it and felt at one with the machine. When he thought he'd reached the bike's top speed and his apogee of singleness and self-direction, he throttled back and settled for cruising—70 was comfortable and allowed his mind to wander.

Did he like his life today? It was okay. Was he in love with Lacey? Well, he didn't know about love. She was great in bed, though she could dump Mathis and that marriage need. She was good-looking, ambitious, and no one could fault her intelligence. Once through the ice, she had a great personality and outside of that deal with McNaughton, seemed well put together. Her huevos rancheros were great in the morning and she knew how to brew coffee. But what about him, was he ready? There was that "darling" thing—sticky sweet, and smacks of ownership while he was the only one with the deed.

And what about his job? Was it really a job? How long would it last, and what about future? Fuck future—you can't think intelligently about what you don't know. Anyway, he knew it would come and be whatever it would be.

He adored Anna. She was outstanding. If he were twenty years older or better yet, she younger .... Well, he liked Izsak too, a great fondness ... and the guys on Beck Street and even Mary F. They all seemed to fit, so what the hell was his problem? Did he have one? He should stop for gas.

"That'll be a buck-sixty-five," the guy said. "How far do ya get on a tankful?"

"Don't know," Giles said. "Never measured."

"I s'pose it ain't very important, 'les you're goin' somewhere. It's sure a nice-lookin' bike, though, bet she gets up an' scats." He was slender, brown with the sun, and wore a small beard sprinkled a little with lunch. Seemed a friendly sort to Giles, asking nothing, just out there serving gas.

"That's the truth, friend," Giles said with a grin. "She gets up and scats. And thanks ... maybe catch ya on the way back."

"So long pal ... you take her easy." And he waved as Giles left.

Back up to speed, through the desert now and Lancaster almost in view, it occurred to him that it wasn't his surroundings that bothered him; it might just be him. Had he built his nest where it didn't belong? He glanced to the sky where the hawks were circling low. *Now what about that?*

"HERE'S THE KEYS, DALTON, and it's all in one piece ... as am I. Nice ride. Might ask you again."

"I wouldn't," Dalton said. "I'd hafta turn you down and you wouldn't like that. Why doncha buy one a your own? I know a guy—"

"Never mind. It was perfect as it was, and thanks again, sport ... good of you."

**

A WEEK OR SO LATER at Izsak's chess table: fresh drinks, cigars waiting, Rose's assemblage of honey-ham and cream cheese topped with a slice of olive layered over a wheat cracker, and Giles, reaching out from his favorite chair to pick up a canapé.

"Nice, these," he said with a sigh. "You must be pretty damn busy these days, Izzy. Don't see much of either of you. Haven't had a call from Anna in over a week."

"Very busy," Izsak said, pondering his move.

"I guess," Giles said, "this is our third try at a game ... don't see much of Lacey either."

Izsak moved a knight. "There, that ought to bring on some Anderson cogitating. Well, we've been at it. Lacey's doing great, much better than hoped, in fact. She's a bright woman, Giles, and knows about work."

"Yeah, damned near perfect; I don't know what I'd change." He grinned. He was thinking, motorcycle.

"And things will get tighter as we move closer to filming. Will happen soon, you know, a few weeks."

"Humm," Giles said, studying his situation.

"Well there, Kansas boy, presents a dilemma, huh ... one way you lose this, another you lose that. A knight fork is a lot

144

like life, Giles. Great game, chess—India, sixth century, I think."

"Yeah, like life," Giles said. *Like life with Lacey—if he said no he would lose and if he said yes he would lose a little slower.* "So, what's Anna up to these days?"

"She's into her character, working with Ethan on selected scenes and we're making a few early changes. A film is consuming—got a huge appetite—and a lot to do in a short period of time. Every hour spent chews up a load of money.

"This time with you and the chess board is a gift to me, Giles, and one I dearly appreciate. Thank you for your part of it. I've said this before, but it bears repeating. You're a good friend and I don't count many in that group."

"I feel much the same way." He moved one pawn and sacrificed the other. "So, is Lacey gonna be a producer? I mean, does she have a future in films? Your opinion, of course."

"No doubt about it, Giles. She wants it, she's capable, and she's willing to put in the time. So far, she's well-liked in the community. She'll be around for a while. I'd bet on it."

"That's good to hear—uh, that she's focused and challenged, and gaining ground." *Keep her mind off the marriage kick.*

"Hiya, honey-pops," Anna sang from the library door. "I thought I heard your lovely masculine voice. You busy tonight? I've got some time and a pent-up need for sweet ... and you, delicious boy, are my favorite confection." She danced into the room, did her pirouette, and kissed Giles on the forehead, then in continuous movement, twirled into a hug for Izsak.

"Anna, Giles is facing a problem here and needs to concentrate. There are downstream ramifications to his choice. This way he loses his—"

"Izsak dear," Anna said. "I have the solution to all Giles' problems—a night on the town. What do you say, Giles? We'll dress smart, take the Jag, and go bar hoppin'—you and me. Pick me up about eight, honey-pops. It's an offer you don't wanna refuse." She drew her hand across his cheek and skipped out of the room.

Thirteen
Decision Time

"SAY DALTON," Giles said, "tell me about the guy with the motorcycles. You know him well?"

"Yeah, pretty well... he mostly sells Triumphs. Got a shop down on Ventura just west of Laurel; it's where I got mine. I'll call him if you like."

"He a friend, a good friend?"

"He ain't givin' 'em away, but you'll get a fair deal."

"I'm only thinking," Giles said, cupping his chin between index and thumb. And he'd been thinking about it since the ride on Dalton's bike nearly a week ago.

"Well, yeah, call him. Tell him I'll be over this afternoon."

"His name's Hank ... that's for Henry. His shop is called 'Cycle Specialties'. We went to high school together; well, he was a grade ahead ... then later his old man got sick and Hank took the business and—"

**

A BELL RANG as Giles wandered into Cycle Specialties—moving slowly, checking the inventory, running his hands along the seats, cupping the gauges. The aroma was intoxicating—tanned leather, fresh-baked paint, a little petrol blended in and *whoa ... does she come with a purchase?*

"Hi stranger, can I help you?" she said.

"You don't look like a Hank."

"No, and I don't smell like him either. So, what can I sell you?"

"Dunno. I'm sorta in the market. Did a guy named Dalton call ... talk to Hank?

She smiled. "You must be Giles Anderson. I'm Suzy. Hank had to step out and I'm s'posed to help you."

A real straw blonde ... and tan. A beach-bunny here in the Valley. She sparkled. She wore a big grin under her pale blue eyes. *Where'd those eyes come from—angel painted, so alive and welcoming.* And he saw a sprinkling of freckles on the bridge of her nose—a hint of a turned-up nose.

"So, Suzy," he said, "you work here, own the place, or just here to attract the customers?"

She smiled big. "I work here. I like bikes and someday I'll own one but now I just take your money and wave as you ride out the door."

"Well, I don't have a lot of money. Maybe Dalton mentioned, I'm poor, but I'd sure like to ride out the door."

"Like I said, I'm s'posed to help you with that ... but first, let's decide what you'd like to ride, Mister An-der-son ...." She let herself drag out his name, just a little.

"It's Giles to you, and I'm pretty much set on a Thunderbird. Are they cheap?"

"Well, being the cream of the showroom, they're not real expensive, and most we handle now are new, but for you, my dollar deprived, I have a nice used one ... hardly used at all, actually."

"I've heard about those."

"Seriously ... a guy came in here about a month ago, signed a contract and plunked down a few hundred bucks. Two days later we had the bike back. Seems he'd forgot to check with his wife. It's now on consignment. We'll make him right if someone picks it up for less than asking; would that be you? Let me show you." She walked around from behind the counter, "Over here."

Umm... He watched her move. *Wonder if they need any help here.*

She pointed out a green tank—British racing green. "Here, throw a leg over and have a seat." she said. "Grab the grips and settle in."

He followed instructions, folded his hands around the grips and smiled.

"Now, how does that feel between your legs?" She grinned.

"Humm, gets a close second place; mind if I take it out?"

"Sorry ... can't let you do that. We can wheel it out to the back lot, and you can do a few brodies if you're serious, but our insurance won't—"

"Yeah, I guess I know about that."

"Tell you what I can do," she said "Since it is a used bike, and you a friend of Dalton's, you can give me some money and sign a contract. If in a week or so, you're not as happy as you think you should be, bring it back and we'll put you on something else. No loss to you."

"That's fair. How much do you need from me?"

"Come into my office and try out the couch. Well, it's really Hank's office. We'll talk a little about your attributes and work up a deal ... then I'll let you know." She nodded at a cubicle in the corner of the showroom and started over.

Giles tooted the horn a couple times, got off the bike and followed.

After the interview—her explaining the forms and tossing numbers, he watching her and signing when told. She looked up from the papers and flashed him a smile.

"Now comes the easy part," she said. "You give me two-fifty and I'll give you these keys." She held them up in front of him, twirling them in the afternoon light. You bring in the balance within 30 days and the bike will be yours. If, like I said, you're dissatisfied, I'll credit your cash to another."

"Tell you what," he said, "I'll do all that if you'll add to our contract a beer with me at the bar across the street."

"I'd love to, Giles, but ..." She looked around at the floor full of bikes, "I'm the only—" A bell over the door rang and Hank walked in.

THE ROUND UP PRESENTED a casual ambiance with wooden booths, dim lights, and sawdust over the floor. There were two plus the barkeep in the place.

"Hi ya, Suzy, what'll ya have?"

"Giles?" she said, nodding at him.

"Couple beers sound good, let's see ... whatta you have on tap?"

"I got Pabst ... and over here I got Pabst and if you'd rather have it packaged, I've got chilled Pabst in a bottle," the keep said with a chuckle

"So many choices," Giles said. "We'll settle for Pabst from the tap." He glanced at Suzy, his eyebrows arched.

"Me to, Slugger," she said. "Give us a pitcher."

Slugger drew the beer and pulled chilled mugs from the cooler, while Suzy dropped a quarter in the jukebox. Stan Kenton's "Just a Sittin' and a Rockin'" filled the room first.

"So, Giles," Suzy said, "have you ridden much? What are your plans for that Thunderbird?"

"Honestly, I don't really know right now, but something'll come up. I don't do a lot of planning."

"Hey, I like that," she said. "A sort of take things as they come kinda guy."

"At least for the moment." He shook his head.

He watched her lips kiss the rim of the mug as she pulled a cool sip—*nice lips*. When she laughed, it was a quiet laugh full of mirth.

"You know," she said, "if I had one of those freedom chasers, I'd cut my hair in a bob, grab an extra pair of jeans, and be on the road in a minute—headed south, a little east. I'm not loaded down with strings and obligations right now— oh, the usual trivial stuff, you know—but the idea of the wind and the road just do it for me ... someday."

He listened. A lotta people had those kind of "somedays."

"Just think about it," she said. "Going where your eyes take you, changing when you feel like it, staying there or not, getting acquainted with yourself ... pure freedom. That's what a motorcycle is to me. It's exhilarating ... thinking about it sends a shiver up my spine. And maybe it really isn't all that, but freedom is what it represents to me, and I simply don't know where else to find it. Oops, sorry Giles, didn't mean to make a speech." She reached over the table and cupped her hand over his.

"I think you've touched it," he said quietly. "You're very close to my Triumph."

**

GILES DROVE HIS OLD PLYMOUTH back to the house, found Paul in the den with a beer. He'd pick up the bike on Thursday. They wanted a couple days at Specialties to check out the vitals and say goodbye.

"Say, Paul," Giles said, drawing a beer. "I'm thinking about a trip ... I don't know, a couple of months, maybe less, maybe more. I'll keep up my rent, give you a couple months before leaving and mail you more if I'm not back. That work?"

"Humm ... It's that time, is it?" Getting up from his chair, needing to stand. "I've been wondering when ... knew it would come." He put his hand on Giles' shoulder. "I don't want to see you leave, like that you're here, but okay, it's good. Where're you going?"

"Haven't the slightest, though I know what I'm leaving."

"I get it, ya know," Paul said, thinking that was one part of Giles' life he admired, might like a little to rub off. "You've been tied up ... and for you, tied up pretty tight. I'll miss you." He laughed. "And Dalton will too, but I know you gotta do what you gotta do. I'm on my way out about now, but if you want to talk, I'll be back late, if you're up."

152

"It's not a big thing," Giles said. "Just need some time."

"Yeah, I get it, and don't worry; we won't rent your bed."

"HI LACEY," Giles said into the phone in the den while eyeing an empty mug on the bar and thinking he'd rather be somewhere else. "Have you got some time tonight? I want to talk."

"Gosh, darlin', I'm kinda busy, orders to run through; can we do it tomorrow? Uh, how much time?"

"Maybe an hour."

"Sounds ominous, Giles, what is it? Can't you tell me now?"

"You don't want to hear this over the phone. Can we say seven?"

"Make it eight, that'll work."

Giles settled into his usual chair and thought about how to proceed.

"So, you see ... I'm at odds, been feeling pinned down—a butterfly under glass."

"More of a wasp, I'd say."

"You're busy, Lacey ... seems night and day, Anna and Izsak as well, and that leaves me with those at the house for sociability ... and they're working."

"Well, that's heavy, Giles, but ... well, what about Mary? Seems she's been entertaining in the past."

"You're not listening."

"Oh, I am, Giles—crocodile tears. Have you thought about a job?"

"Hmm ... any of that scotch left?"

"You know where it is."

He got up and into the kitchen, poured a double shot neat. It wasn't his ordinary, but the clouds were moving in.

"I don't want or need a job, and I've not been involved at the house ... not much into the scene there, and really don't wanna be, and Mary F has taken up with Dalton. Anyway, it's not a puzzle, and it has little to do with any of that ... or with us. I'm taking some time and I'm doing it because I want to."

"Well!" she said. "You bought a bike, want to take a ride, don't know where or how long gone ... what else is new? If you're gonna do what you want to do, why are you here?"

"That's a puzzling thing to say."

"Look." She backed away emotionally, thought of the broader picture. "I have work to do, backed up and highly important to me. We can talk through this later if you want. So, good night, Giles, darling. I'll call you when I have the time."

**

"IZSAK, CAN WE TALK? I need your advice ... maybe your affirmation—an hour or so."

"Certainly, Giles, come on over. Tomorrow will be fine. I'm always here and will take the time."

**

"GILES, IT'S ME ... LACEY, calling you at the brothel you call a home. I hate it, you know—calling you there. How many extensions do you have?

"Oh well, listen, I havtta to say this ... didn't get the chance earlier, when you were over. Didn't take it in—what

154

you were saying—is probably more the truth, but now its hit me .... And I'm saying it now, and ... Giles, are you listening?"

"Yeah."

"Okay, and please don't reply with something clever, unintended that'll fester, cause irreparable damage. But I've been thinking about what you said about taking a break, and—"

"Can you get to the point?"

"Well, I understand. I know I've been pushing you ... the commitment thing, and pushing too hard, I guess. And, well ... I love you, Giles, and I don't want the 'us' in you to end. I want you, Giles, and it would break my heart if you left me."

"Want or need, Lacey?"

"Damn you, Giles ... damn ... Okay, I honestly don't know, I'll give you that. But whatever it is I'm not willing to lose it. And I really don't need to get married. I called to tell you that. I'll be happy just rollin' along like you want. You don't have to do anything drastic. Please say you'll spend some time and talk this out before you do whatever it is you are going to do."

"You're making too much of this—too fucking much."

"Giles!"

"I'm not going to the moon. This doesn't change how I feel about you. You're important ... got that place in my heart. I simply need some time alone, and I'm taking it—living *my* life ... while seeing you do the same."

"But Giles ...."

**

"SIT DOWN, GILES," Izsak said. "No, wait. I get the idea that this meeting calls for a drink. Are you willing to pour?"

"Well now," Izsak said after hearing the plan that wasn't a plan. "You're just going to crank her up and go ... south and east, did you say?

"Isn't that enough? I've got enough money, a change of socks, and a sleeping roll."

Izsak chuckled. "Giles, I've always thought of myself as self-made. It was a while back, you see, but I too needed a look around... check out the landscape, see where I was, and where I might want to go. Not the same motivation, it seems, but the same result. You seem to need the freedom from obligation and expectation, while I was searching for a place to commit, to dig in and assume responsibility—work and reap its rewards. Cigar?"

Giles found the lighter and lit them up. Not for the first time noted the Padgett comfort—not so much the wealth represented but the whole of it that was Izsak—the classics of literature on the shelves, his broad interest in music and the marvelous speakers that poured it out. Picasso, Gauguin and Cézanne copies, not prints, hung on the walls and more modern originals throughout the house, the rich wood paneling, beveled lead glass and eclectic furnishing. It all spoke to Izsak Padgett and to the life that he'd hewn from his scant education. Giles admired the idea of the comfort that surrounded them, and the immense effort required to bring it, while in the specifics, it wasn't him right now—though maybe someday.

"I can't tell you what to do," Izsak said, "but I can tell you what I've learned. The first thing anyone needs is confidence, and for that we need to know ourselves, who we are.

For me that came slowly and organically, much of it forming along the way with how I saw things there on the path and how I responded. Fortunately, I paid attention. Then we must know where we want to be and some of how to get there, and for that we need to know where we are.

"A little soul searching, adventure, and discovery for you may well be in order. A man must know who he is, where he is, and what he wants—build the house before installing the furnishing. And, my friend," he patted Giles's knee, "that seems exactly where you are today—somewhere along that path. And, when you know all that—the who, where, and what—and you find your target, you must be prepared to take the associated risks, and that gets us back to confidence. In all of it, Giles, awareness and belief in oneself is the key."

"Uumm ... you put it clearly, no surprise there. And I think you're right, nail on the head. I'll be leaving tomorrow." He flicked his ashes in a tray and sipped at his drink.

"Leaving?" Anna said from the door. "Did I hear leaving? Where are you going, honey-pops and how long will I miss you?" She waltzed in dressed in shorts and a tee, her effervescence spilling throughout the room.

"Just a jaunt around my life," Giles said and laughed. He would miss her as well, maybe more than any of the rest.

"Sounds exciting," she said. "I'll go; take me with you?"

"Like to, darlin' ... but only room for me."

Ordinary Times

158

Fourteen
Repercussions

"HELLO," PAUL SAID, aroused by the phone late on Friday night.

"Is Giles there?"

"Eh ... no, this is Paul, who's this?"

"It's Lacey, Paul. I'm sorry to call this late but I haven't seen or heard from Giles in a couple days and then this morning I got a cryptic note in the mail ... it says to the effect he'll check in when he gets back. Do you know what that means, where he is going and when he'll be back?"

"Well, not exactly ... but I can guess."

"Okay, guess."

"Why don't we have a coffee, Lacey, and I'll tell you what I know—the Grotto on Vineland, shall we say ten in the morning?"

PAUL SIPPED on his Columbian dark roast espresso—a slow sip that was taking unusually long. Finally, he put the cup down and looked into her eyes ... dazzling eyes, he thought, intense, yet pensive and inquiring. He had known Lacey for several years now as the "porcelain cat." He imagined her to be intelligent, culturally aware and accomplished, but unapproachable and he wondered just how the hell the Giles he knew had become such an integral part of her life and why, now, she was talking to him.

"Tell me," she said, "what do you know?" Lacey held a latte with both her hands.

Paul—a benchmark of appropriate behavior, who provided direction, solved problems, and attempted to advance the welfare of any group a part of—took Lacey's inquiry to heart, and intended to provide her his best possible answers.

"Giles is a very good friend," he said, "from long before college."

"He has told me as much."

"I'm gonna be truthful, Lacey, but I'm not going to judge him."

"Yes, go on, for Christ's sake, I'm eager to hear your thoughts."

"Okay ... first of all, he's a straight shooter and would never do anything intentionally hurtful or underhanded."

"I know that, Paul, and I respect his honesty and straightforwardness. I just want to know what you think this note means." She unfolded a small piece of paper she had been massaging between her fingers like a shiny new quarter. "Look, look at this!"

He took the note. It was from a memo pad that was embossed across the top with "Cycle Specialties," and below, "Lacey, I'll check in when I get back. Giles"

"Yeah, that's his scrawl," he said. "Lacey, I'll level with you, and it's all I know. He bought a motorcycle a few days back, packed a change of clothes and some rain gear into a sleeping roll and just took off. I don't know where he's heading or when he'll be back, or, frankly, if he will, but he left me a couple month's rent, if that's any indication."

"Oh God ..." she mumbled, "I guess he mentioned the bike; I've been so busy." Her eyes watered up. She was going to cry.

"He's like that, you know," Paul said. He might as well hit her with it all. "He's always been wandering, though earlier, mostly in his head. But he's never been devious, always up front. He must've given you a hint."

She shook her head slowly, "It's me, isn't it? He wanted to get away from me." She began to sob and then a heavy, convulsing, releasing cry.

She wasn't as attractive when she cried, he noted, as he scooted around to her side of the table and extended his arms as she fell into the crook of his shoulder. He rubbed and patted her back while she sobbed and shook.

"You'll be okay. It wasn't about you. He'll be back, probably soon. No need to cry." He felt embarrassed, but also touched. He wanted to comfort on the one hand and to leave on the other but felt inadequate to both—she essentially a stranger of her own accord. He watched his espresso grow cold.

Suddenly she pulled away. "You know Giles ...." She wiped her eyes and blew her nose on a hankie from her purse. "You know him better than anyone out here. Tell me about him from a friend's point of view. I love him; why would he leave without saying a word? All he said was he needed some space." She managed a smile through her final trickling tears.

Paul relaxed, took a sip of his cold espresso—"Ack." He pushed the cup to the side.

"As a friend, huh? Well, let's see—at his core, I'd say he's— Here's the thing. Each of us looks at another through eyes that differ ... as we all differ one from another, and what I see in Giles may never enter the view you may have, and if it did, would be essentially useless, maybe misgiving. So, I don't think my thoughts about Giles would help you or him in the least. I've already said more than I should as he's a good friend of mine and I don't want to misrepresent him."

"Umm ... so why do you suppose he didn't say anything?"

"Maybe he did, and you weren't listening. You know, sometimes we're distracted by our own perceptions of what's going on, sort of what we'd like to be happening, and we miss the real message."

"He could've said goodbye."

"He left the note. One thing I will say ... he's never made a promise he didn't keep."

"He doesn't make many," she said, her voice breaking.

"And I suppose that makes it easier, but the statement holds."

"Oh Paul, what will I do? He's become so much to me." Again, she began to sob, and he put his arm around her shoulder. What could he do; he'd said all he wanted to say.

In a few minutes she pushed her chair back and stood. "Thanks for seeing me. Can I call if ... will you tell me if you hear from him?"

"Count on it, Lacey, and call anytime."

162

She wobbled off, He noted her uncertainty, then ordered a fresh espresso.

**

"Izsak, did you know …?" Lacey, reporting for work the next Monday, put her things on the table and sat down. "Did you know that Giles has left … uh, parts unknown?"

"Good morning, Lacey, and no, not exactly. I know he was feeling a bit antsy, needing a little personal space. You don't' know where he went?"

"No, or when, or if he'll be back."

"Are you okay?"

"Yes. I'm a little bent that he didn't say goodbye, but I'm fine." She turned her head away. She was angry and might nurse it a while. Was it Giles who deserved her anger? She tossed it aside, too early for such a question.

"Are you sure? Maybe you'd like to talk about it."

"You know, Izsak …" She dabbed at her eyes with a hankie, then turned to him. "I love Giles … and more, I'm growing fond of the idea of Giles, though he's different than me, very different. But I admire that difference now and had hoped to bring it my way, some of it, at least. I'm already missing him. He's been good for me, Izsak." She did a final rub at her eyes and put her hankie away.

"Good, we have work to do. I want you to visit the Guild's offices today. Introduce yourself and our project. There will be forms to fill out and you'll want copies. And take note of the names you encounter."

SHE GRABBED THE PAPERS they'd gone over, stuffed them into her briefcase and headed out to her car parked toward the back of the house. She sat for a minute behind the wheel, looking out at the trees, the rolling lawn, the pond, and the statuary in the garden that fronted the carriage house. It was all so verdant and inviting, and she imagined a horse or two. Someday she would like the same. As her eyes roamed the landscape, her mind was struck by what seemed a revelation—a man that she loved had escaped again. The recognition came suddenly and without introduction; a soul-splintering bolt tossed her back to her earlier loneliness and emotional paralysis. She had been deserted again ... by Giles.

He had abandoned her on the threshold of their beginning. All they had and more they might yet get was gone. The place was too familiar. The McNaughton pain had been excruciating then and she shuddered with a repeat of it now.

She tried to straighten it, to apply an objective view and make better sense of what seemed so apparently obvious to her, but her mind's eye was a kaleidoscope with images of Giles Anderson and Charles McNaughton in sharp, irregular pieces swirling around. She drew her lids closed and wept. When her tears ran out, she slumped toward the vacant but familiar place she had known before. She didn't want to be there, earlier thought it behind her, but now in the Padgett's back acreage, on the cusp of a new career, it seemed inevitable.

"MISS LACEY ... MISS LACEY, are you okay?" Arthur tapped on the T-Bird's window. "I hate to ... eh, I don't want to interrupt, but you've been here for over an hour now, and the evening's drawing on. Mr. Izsak said I should leave you alone, but it's getting late, and Rose thought I should check ... eh, see if you're all right."

Her smeared cheeks were roughened red with rubbing and smudged with liner, her eyes red from crying as she turned toward the voice. It was familiar but she couldn't and didn't want to focus.

"Arthur? That you?"

"Yes, ma'am."

"Can you bring me a drink?"

"A gin fizz, ma'am?"

"A double scotch, neat, would be better—thank you." She began slowly to deal with reality. She didn't like it; she'd need time, and when Arthur returned with her drink she said, "Thank you, kind man, and please tell Izsak I'm going to take a few days, that I'll ... I'll call him ... probably later this week." She got it out, though the statement a struggle. She needed to crawl in a hole somewhere and be left alone, and as soon as she recovered enough to drive, that's where she'd go.

Book II–
High Jinks and Shenanigans

Fifteen
An Ambiance Adjustment

"YEAH, I'LL MISS HIM," Dalton said, "like a fuckin' hole in the head. He never had no idea where he was going and took advantage of those he called friends. Never gave a fucking thought to anyone. Him and his free-wheelin' attitude ... where's he goin' anyway, did he say?"

"So, what's the difference," Dennis said. "He's gone, bon voyage."

"Well," Nick piped up, quiet to this point. "I'm interested in the rent. I s'pose it'll be going up. But I'm with Dennis on this, wishin' him luck. We shoulda had a dinner." He chuckled.

"I've no idea where he's heading," Paul said, "and D, you're being a little careless with the truth, don't you think ...

and with his absence, I thought you put most of that loathing behind you."

"Naw ... hell no. Ya can't hide the facts. He's a dickhead and a mooch, and frankly, man, I'm glad to see him gone. He won't be fuckin' around with Mary, or takin' my bike, and like Nick said, he's left us with his share of the rent. Who'll take his place, anyway? I'm not gonna pony up any more, already payin' too much."

"He's taken care of it," Paul said. "Left us two months in advance. Does that shut you down? Anyway, I thought you *gave* him the keys to your bike."

"Well, I'm fuckin' surprised at the rent thing. Okay ... maybe I'm being too harsh, but he always rubbed me the wrong way. I dunno why, he just did. Anyway, if you say, I s'pose I could wish him well. Say, Mary and I are goin' out tonight; you gonna be here, maybe keep an eye on the kids?"

"Yeah, I'll be here, D ... but let me say, and I want you to listen to this, take it all the way into that hardwood head. Giles is a longtime friend of mine, which means I think highly of him ... and you know that. When you slander him, you're ridiculing my judgment and I'm personally offended. Is that your intent—to offend me? You have your thoughts about Giles, and that's fine, just don't share 'em with me. I'd prefer you didn't share them at all. Are we square with that?"

Dalton looked to the floor. He checked the others—saw eyes in the room that seemed glaring at him, shoved his hands down deep in his pockets. "Well, I didn't mean anything by it. I know he's your friend ... and I'm sorry, I guess."

"HEY PAUL," Nick said later. "You wanna take in a movie tonight? *Psycho*'s down at the Lankersham. Think it's the last night."

"Can't ,Nick, told Dalton I'd watch the kids."

"What's he up to anyway?" Nick said, plopping his lanky body **down on the couch. "He's gonna get burned, you know,** screwin' with her ... thinks he's in love while she's just toying with him. Though I dunno ... she's attractive all right, and smart ... over his head by a mile. And ya know, once in a while I think I might try a little a that myself. Then I realize ... she's the kind of gal that'll take your heart as you will freely give it, then toss it in the trash without a thought. And with two kids, who needs it? Nice kids, though. It's all such a handful. Whatta you think about that whole thing?"

"I think you oughtta stick around tonight. We'll have a few beers and talk about life. Cole may be over."

"Umm, Cole?" Nick raised his brow. "He's a hoot. Yeah, okay." He chuckled. "I don't wanna sit through *Psycho* without your emotional support and protection."

"So ... Giles is gone ... that's gonna change some things, and what about Lacey? I mean, she seemed pretty well into him ... a mystery to me. I wasn't that close to the whole thing, but it *was* pretty weird. I remember the bet you guys made, and who'd a thought it'd be Giles pickin' up the money." He got up, then down a couple steps into the den, drew a beer from the tap that Dalton had installed. "You want one?"

"Sure," Paul said, "one of the small glasses."

"I remember sayin' to Dennis, it's gonna be downright hilarious watchin' that Kansas hick tryin' ta crack the veneer on the cat. Shit, we'd been there at the Paradise two years before you came around and never once did she say hello, much less respond to a pass." He clinked glasses with Paul. "Mud in your eye … maybe I will stick around tonight."

"Ya know," Paul said, "he left that bet on the table. Said he didn't want it, that it'd be like making him a John … and then me being a pimp."

**

"HEY COLE, PAUL SAID, "Good to see you. What's new at the dump? Have a beer and let us in on life's major challenge—processing the valley's trash."

"It's *refuse*, good friend," Cole Stringer said, "refuse in a landfill. Time you got your vocabulary right, and it's a serious job, my good fellows—every day caring for our citizen's hygienic needs. You think about it, citizens of Beck Street, everything goes into a house has to come out, one way or another, and without we sanitary techs, refuse be piling up in the streets till you can't find your car, stink that'd scare off a skunk… and the rats, my friends, they would populate your lovely community, run for office, maybe fire off the bomb. Oh yes, it's a serious job."

Paul sipped his beer. He'd heard most of this before.

"You think about it," Cole continued. "The mayor can leave for a week, and no one misses him. A cop, a doctor, can go skiing in Switzerland and no one misses him. We take a day and it's like your pool out there, overflowing with sludge, algae and scum to your ankles and the water line as low. Yes, my friend, we have a challenge most would prefer not to face, a role to play, an important role, and you're damn lucky we're playin' it, though we don't get the respect we deserve—no regard, no reward. Is there beer? Is it cold? Is it Pabst?"

Paul laughed. "Credit where it's due. We citizens do thank you and when I become mayor, I'll declare Refuse Day to be celebrated with parades, balloons, and dancing bears."

"You'll see that a statue's erected?"

"Damn right, and it will be of you—Cole, the head collector ... and there is beer, and it is cold, and it's Michelob ... but you don't have to drink it." Paul was trying to keep up if ever amused with Cole Stringer's banter. A high school chum of Dalton's, he came with the draft system—a beak-nosed, narrow face, laughing eyed, get-along sort of guy, who dropped in unannounced on occasion.

"The pool filter's broke, by the way. I called the agent couple weeks back but nothing yet. If we don't get some action soon, the Health Department is next. And help yourself to the beer."

"Check out this mug," Cole said, "came in this morning with the second load from the elites south of the Boulevard. They would've preferred to build on the Hollywood side of the hills but there's only so much space over there and they ran out of room.

"Look at it, here. I'd say it's lead crystal from maybe Latvia as it's got etching I fail to understand on the bottom. Get a load of the size; ain't she a beauty?" He plopped the big mug on the bar, the handle a nude form of a well-endowed woman arched from the rim to the bottom, the most interesting stuff facing out. "Now puttin' your hands around that'll make any beer taste good. It must've come from a Muslim house cause no red-blooded bible-thumper would ever part with this doll.

You know ... one man's brightening Quran is another man's life-long prize."

"Hey Cole, howzit goin'?" Nick entered the room. "Jee-zus, turn on some light. Ever since Giles painted the living and dining room black, all the light is sucked into those walls. It's like a damn magnet, and him, the only one that wanted it, and he's gone."

"Hit the lamp," Paul said. "And it's charcoal."

"Maybe we get the paint bucket out."

"Yeah," Cole said, "I heard Giles was gone, Dalton said something ... a cheerful note for a change. Why'd he leave? I liked Giles ... a lota Midwestern integrity there, and a good sense of humor ... might say a hip kinda guy ... nothing like you, Paul. You sure you came from the same state?"

"And black his color," Nick said.

"Charcoal," Paul said.

"Black, charcoal, it's the same," Nick said. "I like to see who I'm doin' it with before the next morning."

Paul chuckled. "Not a lot of concern there. You're not doin' it that often and by the time you get agreement, you're blotto for the night."

"Sez the pot to the kettle," Cole said. "Say, wise one, what caused your good friend to leave so suddenly? I'm interested in detail.

Paul rubbed his chin. He knew why. It wasn't a short story but he began.

"... AND SO, IN THE END," Paul said, "it was Giles, not Lacey, and not us. He's had a roaming way since I've known him, and not much tolerance for strings—doesn't like obligation in either direction. I admire and envy his freedom."

"He fucked over Lacey?" Dalton said, popping in, waiting for Mary. "She got the shitty end of the stick, if you ask me—though every stick Giles held out had some shit on the end."

"Is that right?" Paul said. "Well, as Giles took care of himself, he thought others would do the same. I had a talk with Lacey, and she tried like hell to admit he'd never made promises.

"Okay, we've about wrung that dry, Cole said, "You know what you should do with the cesspool out back you charitably call a swimming pool? Drain the rest of that mosquito hotel, clean it up some, and have a poker game down there in the deep end—Friday noon to Monday morning. We could spread the word and guys could move in and out, leaving their money with me."

"Hmmm, I like that idea," Nick said, "and I got the money magnet."

"Yeah, I'd go for that," Dalton said, "a big poker party."

"And you might win a few hands, now that Giles is gone."

**

"HORACE BLUNT, RENTALS," Blunt drawled into his phone around a dead cigar.

"Mr. Blunt! Victor Sampson, here. You called about the pool, and I'll get right to the point. I don't like those turds living there, didn't from the start, and if I hadn't been flat on my ass at the time, they would never have crossed the threshold.

And you can count on this, Mr. Blunt. I'm moving back the very day that lease is up—been counting the hours." He took a breath. "In the meantime, I'm doing nothing ... nothing, Mr. Blunt. Fuck the pool ... let 'em swim in the muck."

"But Mr. Sampson," Horace said, oil from his cheek smearing the receiver, a fly buzzing his head, "If the pool isn't maintained and full of water, the gunite will crack; the grout will mold, and the system generally degrade. You don't want any of that."

"Screw 'em," Sampson said.

"In the end, Mr. Sampson, you'll need to replace the filter anyway and why add the rest ... besides, your lease agreement calls for pool repair if things go wrong."

"Who the fuck set that up? What's their part of it?" Sampson said. "What the hell do they hafta do?"

"I'm reading the lease," Horace said, cigar ashes falling on his desk. "'Sweep and add chemicals' is what it says. You know they could sue you."

"I should never have signed that gawddamn thing ... and you, Blunt, you had a hand it it. But, okay. I'll get over there Monday, have a look around. Shit, how'd I get into this mess, anyway? Can you get me out?"

"No can do, Mr. Sampson, the lease is a bona fide contract and they're holdin' up their end." He swatted at the fly with a rolled-up newspaper.

Sixteen
Sparks, but No Fire

A S HE CRUISED DOWN HIGHWAY ONE, ocean air through his lungs and a clear head, Giles was thinking he had never felt better. Sleep came easily, stomach knots gone—no calls to make and none to take. There were 360 degrees on his compass and all of them beckoning; life couldn't be much better. But he did have a decision to make. A fork in the road was coming up.

Bearing to the right would be Mexico with its whiter, finer, and sparsely populated beaches, cheap living, gay señoritas, fresh seafood ... and scary banditos. He'd heard tales related to risk, and not just from drinking the water.

To the left was dry hot air, religious morality and small-town suspicions, cacti, jackrabbits, and the more desolate parts of Arizona and New Mexico—friendlier faces perhaps, a familiar language and known, if not reliable, law. He pulled up at Chico's Bar and Grill alongside the highway.

"I'll have a Budweiser," he said to the guy behind the bar.

"You bet ... great day, uh? You come in on that Triumph?

"Yep."

"Nice. Always wanted one a those."

"Whatda you know about 94 into El Centro?"

"Good ride," the barkeep said. "Two lane black-top. Not much along the way, few prairie dogs, arroyos, a jackrabbit now and then. Be good to have a couple extra gallons of gas, maybe double the water you carry."

"What about straight down ... into Mexico, TJ, Ensenada, then south?"

"You just bummin'?"

"You could say that."

"Well ... ya hear stories," his expression more serious, "yep, stories ... people goin' and not comin' back ... eh, here's your beer," and he put an icy Bud and a chilled glass on the bar. "Guy on a Honda stopped by a year ago or so. Said he was goin' down for the beaches and people. They found the bike—frame and fenders—about fifty mile south of Ensenada but nuthin of him. Made the papers in San Diego. But me, I ain't never been down there. People say it's great, that Mexican folks are gracious ... you know, friendly and such. The price is sure right, 'bout twenty-to-one, but ...."

"But?"

"Well ... I s'pose I'm a coward, but if I was jus bumming' ... I guess I'd grab an extra gallon or two and head off toward El Centro ... it'd be safer. There's trouble everywhere, a'course ... especially when you're bummin'. Folks in parts to the east don't take too well to bums, ah know that for a fact. Careful is good to have ridin' with you, either way you head, and that's another fact ... though, like I said, I'd go east. Hows the beer?

176

Had some trouble with the cooler last night, had to ice it up in a tub."

Giles bought a gas can and a couple extra gallons just after he turned left at the fork. There wouldn't be a whole lot of civilization from then on.

**

"CALL THAT BLUFF, and that calls for a beer," Dennis said as he reached into the ice chest. "Hey Mary, we'll need a new load down here pretty soon," he yelled up from the bottom of the pool. "Bring some of the Pabst, and by the way, I thought this was a topless bar." He laughed. He had company.

Six players sat around the dining room table, now in the lower end of the pool—empty beer cans closing in on a foot deep, well into the third day of the game that started on Friday at noon. At least twenty friends, friends of friends, and some without friends had sat in at one time or another and the word was still spreading with affirmative nods. Ten bucks got you onto the premises and chits for six beers, twenty more got you into the game. Of those hosting, Paul was ahead but currently sitting out for a few. Nick seemed next up; Dalton sat off to the side sulking and occasionally kibitzing. Dennis seemed either down to his last buck or packing it into his pockets—a mystery but assumed far ahead. They would play until those interested dropped out, as long as one host was present, or until the hosts pulled the chain. Blue Monday, what's that?

"Hey Paul, some man here to see you," one of the out-players yelled from the house.

"Tell him to hang in, we'll soon have a chair open."

"Says he's the landlord; his name is Sampson."

"Oh shit ... I'm coming in."

VICTOR SAMPSON, a bald but muscular man, "in my fifties," he said to those having the courage to inquire, had a life membership at Vic Tanny's Gym where he worked out religiously every day in front of mirrored walls. It was one of the few pleasures left he could afford, as his membership there was paid, while his discretionary funds were "no more than vapor," he was often to say. He hadn't had an assignment in over a year—a special-effects technician at what was left of Republic. "Those fat fuckin' assholes were right next to bankruptcy, probably filing," according to Vic, who had only a few kind words in his vocabulary. His resumé was out, though, and things could be brighter soon as he'd had a few "fucking nibbles" from competing studios.

Most of Vic's romantic encounters were with males—though not all of them. His reasoning was that he didn't have to deal with the "tedious foreplay or subsequent commitments." Vic sustained a few good friends, as he could occasionally be amiable, and when absolutely needed, midland at "charming"—the acting he'd picked up from his ordinary but currently dormant employment environment.

Victor's serious problem was his nuclear temper. When going off, though not often, he was completely unpredictable, enormously threatening, and when unleashed, especially damaging. He suspected this trait, which he admired at times when in front of the mirrors at the gym, could be responsible in some odd way for his financial predicament.

"Mr. Sampson, good to meet you. I'm Paul Smythe, the guy who sends you the rent checks." Paul stuck out his hand in a business-like manner.

"What the fuck is with all this black?" Victor responded. "Who the hell gave permission to paint my walls? Paintin' ain't in the lease." He looked steadily into Paul's eyes, burning the retinas and demanding the answer he couldn't act on anyway. "Black, I cannot fucking believe it." He stiffened, his arm muscles bulging and stretching the sleeves of his t-shirt.

"Well, you see, sir ... It's really charcoal, and I was as surprised as you when I first saw it, but don't worry, Mr. Sampson, we'll restore the original color before we leave ... now if you—"

"You'll *restore*? 'Mr. Sampson, we'll restore.' Shit, I doubt you know which end of the brush I should shove up your ass. So, let's get on with it; what's the fuckin' problem with the pool? I haven't much time for screwing around with you imbeciles." He moved into the den. "Shit .... What have you done here? Where did this bar come from? I'll be a son-of-a ... it's bolted to the floor ... God dammit, Smythe. Now who the hell ... You're gonna pay big here, pea-brain ... real big." He pounded his substantial fist on the bar that Dalton had built and installed and noticed it didn't move. The glasses there didn't jump, even waver.

Sampson turned a bright red. His heart, hammer on anvil, was pumping blood through his stretching vessels more forcefully than oil in a gusher. Those bulging in his neck were throbbing, and might rupture momentarily, and Paul began to consider the need for an ambulance—wondered where he might find the number.

179

"Look, Mr. Sampson, please chill out here. You'll have a stroke. We'll make it right. You have a sizeable deposit from us, as well as a surety bond that will see that we do. Please calm down now ... and prepare yourself for the pool."

"You're gonna pay, asshole. I may just have some of you now." He shook his fist. "This is my house ... mine. Before you came, I lived here for twenty years, did the work myself ... love this place ... it's my home." He looked through the glass paneled door to the outside. "I added the pool, the cabaña and bar—put in the stereo, the garage." He shook his head in disbelief. "Jesus Christ," he mumbled. "What's going on out there in the pool?"

They moved out into the brighter light of the sunny afternoon, the clamor of inebriated voices and Mr. Sampson's pool—empty of all but the game and its players, near calf-deep in beer cans.

"I'll have you evicted tomorrow. I'll throw you sons of bitches out myself if I hafta. It's no wonder the pool isn't working. Where's the goddamn water and what's goin' on down there?"

"Let's go out to the pump room and you can see what the problem is," Paul said, making a big effort to remain unafraid and calm—like reciting a love sonnet to an approaching dragon.

The bunch from the bottom of the pool looked up. "Who's the old geezer with the dome?" Dalton yelled up. "Ain't seen him before."

"Yeah," said Dennis. "You think he wants in? Hey buddy, we gotta seat openin' soon ... soon as ol' sour-puss here loses this hand." He nodded across the table at Schrader from down the street who was trying to squeeze a straight from a blend of primary numbers. "We can use some fresh money."

Paul, needing reinforcements, called out, "Hey Dalton, c'mon up here a minute. I may need your assistance. We're going out to check on the pump and maybe could use your expertise."

"Huh...?"

"It'll take only a few minutes ... c'mon up." Dalton and Nick had the only big arms among them and at this moment Dalton, bare-chested, tanned, and looking pretty trim, was, for once, a godsend.

"Mr. Sampson, meet Dalton Dobbs, one of your renters. Dalton, this is our landlord. He's here to check out the pump and filter ... validate our complaint."

"Hi ya, Sampson, the pleasure is mine." Dalton patted Sampson on the shoulder.

Victor Sampson staunched and moved away. "Lets get on with it. I don't like a thing I'm seein' ... hurts my eyes to look around, remembering what it used to be. I'll have you all in jail. You're destroying my property and my lawyer will be servin' you tomorrow."

"Now, Sampson, no need to get shitty with us, we've done no damage," Dalton said, with the help of the Pabst he'd been drinking, stretching his nominal height to near six feet. "We just want the pool fixed. It's in the fucking lease. We can't use a pool that don't fucking function."

They opened the door to the pump room and brushed the cobwebs aside. Sampson threw a few switches, then examined the faulty filter box and rusted-out tank. "I'll call a service," he mumbled. "You get that shit outta the pool."

Sampson slumped. He was worn down now and moving fast toward the latter half of the "fifties" he claimed. He felt tired, was ready to get his sagging ass outta there. He'd had too much, the whole damn visit a nightmare. On his way out to the street, through a side door to the walled patio, he gave a last glance at the party still in full swing and felt weary with disappointment. He didn't want to be a landlord, didn't want to understand why he was one, and when the lease was up, he'd move back in, if he could muster the will—maybe sell the damn place.

**

"NOPE! NO CAN DO, MR. SAMPSON." Horace Blunt said. "Emphatically no. You cannot break the lease because you neglected the pool." He poked at his ear with the striking end of a match. "Your best bet is to fix the pool and sit tight—figure out how to minimize their grievances. If anyone has a claim here, it's them. Here, have a cigar."

"What the hell am I paying you for? I didn't like this deal in the first place. They're ruinin' my house, painted the fuckin' walls black, and—"

"Here, let me give you a light. You need to remember … it was you who came begging. Couldn't make your mortgage, you said, needed a quick lease and wanted me to scramble. I can't do anything now." He rubbed his nose. "Those boys are good till the clock strikes mid of November one, as long as they're on time with the rent. After that, of course, it's yours."

Sampson crushed the cigar on Blunt's desk. "Fuck you," he seethed. "Keep your stinkin' cigar," and he slammed out of the office.

**

"HEY MARY," Nick said one night, "I'm going down to the Hut for a beer. You wanna come along—get outta this place for a couple of hours?"

"You buying?"

"I'm good for a few. I'm kinda celebrating my good luck."

"Oh, how's that?"

"My brother's coming up for a few days ... gonna leave his new car with me. He's in the Navy—San Diego. He's a little younger and smarter than me, in the Navy and all."

"You're pretty smart, Nick."

The back of his neck flushed a bit. He liked being told he was smart. It didn't come often. He had no recollection of parents. He was no more than a number in that place in Detroit—that home for delinquents.

"He'll be shippin' out in a week or so on a cruise ... and just after he bought this new Ford. Can ya beat that? Paid cash ... a brand-new Victoria, hardly got the seats warm and he's gone for a month. He's got no place to leave it, except with me ... or pay for storage. I like cars, understand 'em too, and he knows that. One day—if the Ruskies don't blow us all up—he'll be out with nowhere to go ... and I'm thinkin' he figures it best to be on my good side then."

"You're a practical man Nick, I like that in you."

"Well, until he arrives, we'll take the old Morris. It's a likable car, picked it up for a song. Guy came into the station one day and said fix it. When I told him how much, he said sell it. I offered him a hundred bucks, he signed on the pink, and said good riddance—all in less than an hour."

"Yep, you are a practical man, Nicky."

"So," NICK SAID. "You gonna have a draft? They got Pabst on tap here ... and they got bottles—most any domestic. You ever been to the Hut before?"

"No, and I'll have a draft." She looked around, didn't see much—a shuffleboard machine, three-quarter size pool table, jukebox. The mahogany bar was about twenty feet long. There might've been half dozen tables, booths along one wall.

"Hey Bogie, couple a drafts."

"Comin' up, two glasses of the best," Bogie sang out.

"Harry Bogasen was a route guy for Pabst. Says he got tired of throwin' cases and kegs and bought this place from Slick Eddy and Mitzi, who themselves bought it from a pair of guys who wanted to retire in Tahiti. In all that, the place hasn't changed a wit. I guess I've been coming here for a while ... they bring in jazz on Sundays, open up the walls there and set the front lot up with tables and chairs and a lot of folks come. Bogie's an all-right guy—says I'm a loyal customer, and once in a while I get a beer on the house."

Nick thought about Mitzi, a tiny woman with big breasts and hair the color of pearls. She was there every night and flirted something fierce while Eddy looked on.

He felt bad about it, but what could he do if when they danced, she did the askin'—crawled in near under his skin.

184

She was firecracker hot, but Eddy had that sawed-off behind the bar, and even when his auto-rhythms had taken over, he was dissuaded with the blast he knew would be coming. Mitzi was cute as a bug, but she was married to Slick Eddy and Eddy's big gun.

"What's grabbed your attention?" Mary asked. "You seem a hundred miles away." She looked into his eyes. "Nicky ... If I was asked, I'd agree with Bogie ... I'd say you were a loyal person through and through." She touched his arm. "A straight shooter and a real nice guy and I'm just plain old happy to know you."

He smiled at her warmly, if some embarrassed. "I already said I'd buy the beer."

They sat at the bar drinking Pabst drafts and talking for about two hours—two friends passing the time—when Nick said, "Tell me about you and Dalton."

"What? There's nothing to tell."

"Well, he doesn't think that."

"Why, what does he say?"

"He says you're his girl."

"He should ask me before he makes such a claim."

"Well, I guess I'm askin'."

"Why, Nick? Why are you asking?" She grinned at him.

Nick was not only a loyal-straight-shooter, he was also a shy loyal-straight-shooter and he knew it and dealt with it the best he could. He swallowed hard.

"Umm, I think maybe I been cornered."

"Look," she said, taking his hand. "I don't belong to anyone. I did once but not anymore—maybe my kids—but certainly not Dalton. I'm open season, Nick ... until I say otherwise. Me, Nick ... I'm the one to say otherwise. And I like it that way, beholding to no dumb-as-a-post, year-in-and-out erection. Though, that's not you, Nicky. You seem understanding and gentle ... not to mention loyal." She laughed while running her fingers through her raven, wavy black hair, her fluttering lashes drooping a bit now over her deep blue eyes.

He thought she was beautiful—the most beautiful woman in the world, the whole damned world—but he didn't know what to do about it, or even if he should.

"Now I'm really cornered," he said.

**

THAT NIGHT AS NICK, comfortable in his head, waited for sleep, thoughts of Mitzi stealthily entered before the last sheep jumped over the fence. She was unavoidable. Mitzi had early-on confided her story and he had been empathetic—a young woman caught in a bind: an undesirable suitor on one hand, an immediate bleak future on the other. Slick Eddy had offered security while her father was threatening eviction. With little love between them, her father wanted her out—to support herself and provide him relief. She was seventeen.

And for Nick, her story was near déjà vu, as in an earlier life in Detroit, he had met another with a story like Mitzi's; he may have been twenty-three. He was unsure of the details now as he had intentionally put them aside.

In Detroit from Seattle, and except for a girlfriend traveler, this girl was alone. Both girls, then in their late teens, had escaped from the bonds of a "home" run by a fundamentalist church--both orphaned as toddlers or so they were told, left on the doorstep. Seattle Maxine had no skills and was shy of an education as she had left her "prison" at the top of her junior year. Dorothy was in the identical boat. "Why Detroit?" he had asked her once. Her reply, a shrug of thin shoulders and, "It's where the bus brought us."

When he met Maxine, she was desperate. Dorothy had left with a boyfriend and the income they depended on—both waiting tables at Wally's Wholistic—was now insufficient to handle the load. She sat on a park bench one Sunday morning when Nick wandered through on his regular trek with Sporting—a Jack Russell terrier that belonged to a neighbor who was old and unable to walk. The young woman on the bench seemed to be crying and he stopped and looked down.

"Hey, what's a matter?"

"Nothing, it's jus ... nothin'." She looked up, pale blue eyes wet and reddened.

"It can't be nothing or you wouldn't be crying like that. What can I do?"

Sporting raised his leg to the bench and splashed a mist on the one crying.

"You ..." a smile came to her face through the tears. "You might teach your dog better manners."

Nick sat down, not so close as to be offensive, but what he thought neighborly.

"Well, he's not really my dog, but I'm serious. I've lived here all my life and like being helpful. There's a lot of us needs it here in the city."

"I appreciate your interest, but it's too big," she said, wiping her eyes with the back of her hand.

He'd taken an interest and now began to notice her—petite was the word, though waif might fit ... cute face, with hair a platinum blonde and a bunch of it full over her thin shoulders. She was pale, had obviously not spent much time in the sun, and from the looks of her, not having much fun in it now.

"Can't be that big," he said. "Let me buy you a coffee, and you can tell me about it. There's a place nearby, just across the street from the park."

"No ... that's nice, but I don't know you. Anyway, what I need goes far beyond coffee."

"You don't know me, that's right; I may own a lamp with a genie."

This was unusual for him, being so forward ... "brazen and shameless," the mistress that earlier headed his dorm would say, but this little gal seemed so vulnerable and help-less, small and certainly not threatening.

She finally did agree, and he listened as they nibbled at croissants and sipped coffee at a sidewalk table, his favorite bakery—Sporting tied to a lamppost off to the side. She told him her story. She really was cute ... and disarming, he thought. He also noticed, in time, she was not overly shy of the feminine attributes he ordinarily noticed first.

"I don't know what to do," she said. "My job is okay and I like it, but it doesn't pay enough to keep the apartment alone." She looked down at her lap or her legs or a place under the table. "I don't know a soul besides Walter and the kid who washes the dishes. I'm being evicted on Saturday, and I ha-ven't packed a thing ... and what would I do with it anyway? Dot has run off with a furniture salesman; they're gonna get

188

married, and I don't blame her, but I don't know where to go, and—" She was crying again.

"Wait, wait," he said. "First, let's get acquainted. My name is Nick, Nicholas Gates, and ... that mannerless mutt is Sporting." He gave Sporting, now sitting up and growling low, a piece of his croissant.

She laughed. "I like Sporting, despite his free-wheeling inclinations. I'm Maxine Smith. There's little else to say."

"Is that a real Smith, or just the name you put on your lease?"

"Why would I do that?" She laughed. "Well, if you must know, it's McCluskey and it is the name on my lease. I guess I'm a little defensive. I don't feel I have both feet on the ground."

He smiled. "Never mind." He leaned toward her across the table. "Listen, Maxine, please don't think of me as some crazy with strange motives, but I've got this small place just around the corner on the second floor, a one-bedroom apartment, and ..."

She was desperate, she said, and had no alternatives, and he seemed an okay guy. He must've been an Eagle Scout, so kind and concerned in this encounter. She liked his smile, she said, and thought him handsome, found no fault with his behavior, and told him it would be silly not to move in, to say no to a safety net.

He slept on the couch. He wanted to, said it was part of the arrangement. They shared the rent, the food, and their ideas. He fell, for the first time, hard and utterly in love ... as did she, but not with him.

When she moved out to be married to Walter, he cried for the first time he could remember, hard and without limits. Then he packed up his belongings and hitched to LA and the Valley. He met Dennis at the Signal station, and ....

NICK FELL INTO SLEEP. He relived his story often; it warmed him. Maxine was a friend and meant him no harm. Knowing that left a smile on his face.

**

"SO ASSHOLE, WHATTA YOU DOIN' OUT WITH MARY?" Dalton yelled from the door.

"Beat it, Dalton," Nick mumbled. "I'm still sleepin'."

"Out late drinkin' with Mary—my Mary, ya hear! Well tough shit that you're sleeping; you explain yourself, you asshole. You got no business out with Mary. We been through this a hundred times."

Nick rubbed his eyes—*fucking Dalton.*

"Look," he said, "there's no cause for all this—your rampagin' around like a bull elephant with a lonely erection. We just went down to the Hut for a beer. I don't need to explain that to you. You got a problem with your girl, you talk to her." He sat up on the edge of the bed, shook his head, chasing the Pabst foam out. "I'm getting a little tired of your 'my-Mary' shenanigans anyway. I doubt she shares your view about who she belongs to, but I sure as hell don't want to fight over it now. You talk to her, and get outta my room, I hafta be at the station by noon."

THE WHOLE THING about MARY F was like a cyst coming to a head that needed lancing, and Mary was the one with the scalpel, the most motivated and stood most to gain. And she knew it. She liked these guys, all of them, and that would suffer if she caused a riff. And, while she found them each individually attractive, she wasn't especially enamored with any of them, leastways not now. She had to step on the brakes. Not having much official standing, she asked Paul to call them together.

They sprawled in the living room, Dennis sucking a beer. These meetings were never any fun—a large telephone bill or someone late with the rent, a neighbor complaint about any number of behavior anomalies related to this locality misfit. Mostly it was too much noise, the police coming by late with their bright lights and squawkers.

"So. what's this about?" Nick said.

"It's Mary's meeting," Paul said. So go ahead, Mary, what's it about?"

"Okay." Mary stood tall, looked around, catching each with her fascinating eyes. She felt beautiful and strong, standing in front of them ... her full, unvarnished presence—jeans and a tee. They retreated a little, giving her room. "I have an announcement and I want it listened to 'cause I'm not gonna repeat it and I'll try to make it simple and brief."

Dennis put down his beer.

"There's a rumor goin' round that I need to squelch ... that I belong to somebody, that I'm somebody's girl. I'm not gonna say who; I am gonna say this." She scanned. She had their attention, four pairs of eyes looking her way. "I don't! I don't belong to anyone! Got it? I am nobody's girl." She turned as she talked, catching each individually. "I'm a free agent, a very free agent and furthermore, *I choose!* Meaning, if you don't get my drift, that I ..." She planted an index finger square in the middle of her magnificent breasts, "I choose who I associate with, go out with, lie down with, etcetera, etcetera—and not anyone else, ever!" She turned again to see, did it sink in. "Anyone got any questions?"

Stunned, Dalton started to raise his hand but sputtered and coughed, his clutch slipping some, but with a deep breath, he mounted the insurmountable: sat up, squared his big shoulders, and open his mouth while a half-minute passed before any words came out.

"But ... but I thought we were a ... you know, goin' together, at least kinda." Beads of sweat emerged and collected on his prominent brow.

"Dalton," she said, "I don't want to upset you and don't intend your disappointment." She looked into his wide brown eyes. "I am not your girl ... not now and never have been." She softened her strident approach and moved in next to him. "Look ... your affection is sweet, but it's misdirected, and you need to understand this—you may have thought I was your girl, dreamed it and believed it ... but it simply wasn't true, it didn't and doesn't exist." She put a hand on his cheek. "I'm sorry, Dalton, but I can't be responsible for your thoughts." She smiled, then briskly turned to the rest. "Any other questions?"

Seventeen
Grotto, Arroyo, Miscellanea.

"YOU'D LIKE IT THERE, Paul," Dennis said, "Romano's Coffee Grotto. Great music, folk stuff and New Orleans jazz. I take my guitar sometimes. Good people there, friendly thinkers, I'd say. The kind that can explore ideas without getting emotionally entangled."

"Uh huh," Paul said. "So, you've found a nonalcoholic outlet for your money."

"Well now, that's real funny. I'm tryin' to be serious here and you're lettin' it fly right on by."

"I'm sorry, Dennis, your serious happens so seldom, it's hard to recognize. Please go on; you have my attention."

"Okay, ya see, Romano's brought in chess boards. You can check out the pieces, no charge—heavy pieces that stay put and easy to recognize ... and the coffee varies—Java and Sumatra, Kenya, Ethiopia, Vietnam, all sorts of places. You oughta come down. It's not too expensive, and good place to meet chicks. Those coffee shops, they're comin' on strong, got a future, ya know."

"You just drinking the coffee, or do you own the place?"

"Ha, wish I did. I'd do a little more with it, like add some weed—the kind that grows in Mexico and in the hills around Mendocino. Big margins there."

"That's the business that will get you room and board paid in advance." Paul smiled at Dennis—bright and affable, maybe short on experience.

"I'd like a little business of my own," Dennis said, "and a coffee café would do it just fine. Someday..."

"Yeah, if we all don't go up in a nuclear cloud."

**

DUSK WAS MAKING ITSELF KNOWN, the heating rays depleting. His bike needed gas, and he needed nourishment and a look at his map. He had left the main highway looking for the appropriate replenishment. In a while, a small roadside with a gas pump out front found his view—"Diner and General Provisions" above a weathered old Coca-Cola sign featuring a blonde woman in a nurse's cap, a tray in her hand ... and below: "Habla Español."

He killed the engine and dusted himself off. Hot was the dominant condition. He pulled the air cleaner from the engine and banged it hard against the frame. A bit of New Mexico let go and was picked up by a breeze. "Dry" fit in there somewhere. A person would need some time to get used to this climate.

He wheeled the Thunderbird to a pump, uncapped the tank and loosened the lid on his spare can. There were a couple old cars to the side, but not a soul around. He hand-pumped the glass cylinder to the top mark, then drained five gallons and two tenths into his tank and the spare can. Replacing the hose, he wheeled the bike up to the side of the entry door—still no one in view.

The screen door squeaked and a bell on a string rang as he entered a dim room, food to the left, provisions to the right. He took a seat at the counter. A small man with a large mustache and a cigarette dangling beneath appeared from back of the store.

"Si señor, como esta?"

"Hi ya, you understand any English?"

"Si, un poco." He smiled.

"I want to pay for some gas, five and two tenths, and get something to eat. You got a menu?"

"Si, eet's on the chalkboard, señor." He pointed to a scrawl above an empty pie shelf on the back wall. "All fresh, you will like it," the cigarette still in his mouth ... a long ash forming as a wisp of smoke found its way up the side of his lined and darkened face.

Giles looked around, his eyes adjusting to the relative dark. In a back booth four men in boots and workers' garb drank beer and talked quietly. Each at his own, glancing over to notice the gringo who just walked in.

Giles ordered two burritos and a beer and added "dingy" to the hot and dusty of the place—broken linoleum floor, some of it missing, some worn through. The red leatherette stools were cut and bruised, and their chrome trim rusted. A ceiling fan turning above kept the flies away from a catcher hanging just beneath. He pondered that as he waited—a fly-catcher under a ceiling fan.

The burritos arrived, mostly beans but otherwise spiced and respectable. The ash on the man's cigarette threatened but didn't drop. Giles was starting his second bean wrap when he noticed two more men had pulled up chairs to join the booth in the back. Their laughter was louder now and sounded like beer.

As he ate, Giles reminisced about Lacey. Staring blankly over the back counter into a smudgy mirror, he saw her face— green eyes, flaxen hair, a comely smile. He wondered how she was and hoped her well. He wasn't much for dealing with the past, a poor use of time. He had never learned to season his life with remembrances, preferring to spend his perception on things of today—the vivid acuteness of this instant. Things either worked or they didn't and the "didn'ts" he easily discarded. He felt a presence, and the stench of bad breath filled his nostrils.

"Hey señor, where do you go on the nice bike out there?"

He hadn't noticed them gathering around—smudge on the mirror and the one in his mind.

"I like the beer," one said ... picked up and drained the remainder in Giles' glass. "Maybe you buy me another?" He laughed. "You are a wealthy man?"

"Si amigo—maybe for all of us," another said. "We like the beer." They laughed and crowded in.

The man behind the counter picked up a telephone and dialed—hard chatter in Spanish. With a scowl, he put it back down. There was more talk and laughter among the men who hadn't noticed the call.

Giles laid a five-dollar bill on the counter and started to get up. "This should cover the burritos," he said.

The man behind the counter smiled with worried eyes. He glanced toward the door.

"Hey amigo ... you don't go now ... you buy us a beer? We would be happy." The one speaking put his hand on Giles' shoulder, heavy enough to push him back down.

Giles nodded at the counter man and pulled another five from his wallet. The men surrounding watched closely.

The café man brought six dripping bottles from the cooler, put them on the counter and opened them. The men laughed louder, passed them around. Their chatter was in Spanish. As they drifted away from the counter, one turned back to Giles, "Hey señor, did I tell you? I like your bike ... maybe you give it to me?"

Giles looked at the café man behind the counter. The man shrugged, his eyes wide, rolling, and directing Giles toward the door. His lips trembled. The cigarette was gone. He reached in his cash drawer, added the two fives and brought a dollar in change to the counter. He motioned for Giles to pick it up. "Leave, pronto," he whispered.

Leaving the dollar, Giles moved slowly and deliberately. The screen door squeaked, and the little bell rang. He straddled the Thunderbird and kicked on the starter.

"Hey amigo, where you go in the hurry? Come back. We have some beers. We get acquainted."

"Si hombre," another said, "you come back ... we want to be friends. We take care of your bike."

Giles kicked again on the starter. The engine sputtered and caught. He revved it up a couple times and, as two grabbed onto the rear rack, he let go of the clutch, leaving them stumbling. One fell in the dirt, the others were left in the dust, mouths agape. "Hey amigo," he heard as he turned onto the road, "Hasta la vista."

Looking back, he saw one of the old cars pull out and turn after him, a man on either side running board. Clouds of loose gravel and dirt churned behind them.

On a smooth surface, he could easily outrun them, but the road was gavel and mostly dirt, rutted from last season's monsoons and he hadn't had his look at the map. He doused the headlamp. The moon was up and casting sufficient light to see the road and the surrounding flats. Ahead looked straight, until it wasn't as he remembered that county roads followed property lines and when they turned, they turned at right angles. He'd need to be attentive.

A bridge was coming up. He could see the abutments and slowed. It was an arroyo and probably dry. *Well, what the hell.* He steered the bike down into the bed and under the bridge and cut the engine, hunkered quiet. Soon he heard them pass over, yelling out their charge. He watched their taillights disappear into the night and waited.

In about ten minutes they returned, moving much slower. The men on the running boards seemed to be searching the flats. There was chatter among them as without hesitation they continued over the bridge. When they were out of sight, Giles cranked up the Thunderbird and headed in the opposite direction. The burritos weren't half bad.

**

LACEY KNEW SHE WAS RAW NAKED, fully exposed, and vulnerable—a familiar place she had been before. Whether he

198

knew it or not, she had given herself completely, fully invested with every joule of her soul ... and she gave him credit for not knowing. How could he; she didn't know much of it herself. It wasn't a knowing kind of thing.

She loved him. Or as he had offered, did she need him? She might love the idea of him, so different in many ways from what she might've expected ... but that she admired. She knew he wouldn't be good for her but felt that he would. When she tired of crying, she began to wrestle with the mystery of him—her mystery. She wondered if it was need ... well, what's wrong with that? And when she stopped thinking about herself, she wondered what he was doing ... and then, if he thought of her at all.

Occasionally she'd get a glimpse or a thought of him so close he seemed to be present. It felt good and she anticipated those moments with eagerness as she remembered Christmas again as a little girl—the ornament brightness, music, and the presents.

Jesus Christ, she must grow up, get a hold. She must call Izsak and soon, or all with him would be lost, all of it over. It had been days, maybe a week, maybe more. She didn't want to remember.

*

"SO, DENNIS, you gonna have a date for this shindig, or are you going to spend the fucking night cadging attention from ours?" Dalton said with a confidence not often seen.

"You gonna have one?" Dennis chuckled, recalling Mary's legendary speech. "I don't remember your coughing up a name. And it likely won't start with an M."

"You don't know, do ya?" Dalton ran his hand through his hair. "Well, smart ass, as it happens, I have a date with her sister. So whatta ya think about that?"

"I think Mary should see a psychiatrist."

"And she's cute, and she's single ... and she ain't got any kids."

"I didn't know she had a sister. How old is this sister?"

"Old enough ... and she's built jus like Mary. Wait'll ya see her."

"I'm pissin' in my pants."

"Be me that's escorting Mary." Paul entered the room, "So, what about you, Dennis, what's the answer? Are your breaking the unspoken rule?"

"Well, I may surprise you. I met this young woman down at Romano's, name of Maxine. Looks a little like Slick Eddy's Mitzi, though not as busty. She's from Seattle. Seattle, she says, is quaint, open, and friendly, and she sure fits—"

"Wonder what happened to Mitzi," Paul said.

"She split," offered Dalton. "Bet she took him for a bundle. I saw him at the Hut a couple nights back ... looked like he belonged at the refuse center."

"I suppose we deserve what we get." Paul said. "I didn't mind Eddy but didn't like the deal she got or the way he treated her ... and her father was a dick."

"How come you know so much?" Dalton said.

IT WASN'T OFTEN they prepared for a party; usually, they just happened. A few guys drinking a few beers, a few phone calls, and that's all it took. But this one was different. It would be planned. They would all have dates, a rule advanced by

Paul as he thought it might keep it less rowdy, thus the police at bay. There would be eats; they would invite agreed-upon people; someone would actually tend bar, though they didn't know who. Dalton had a friend.

Paul took command, his usual post. "D, you see that a fresh keg is available and maybe some of those hanging paper lamps for the cabaña. Dennis, you take care of the food. I'll do the utensils, paper, and music—know a little group that plays over at the Broncin' Saddle on Wednesdays—they'll come over, and if not, we'll use my system. We'll need some booze and wine ...." He glanced at Nick

"Yeah, I'll do that," Nick said. "Where's the money for all this?"

"I'll do a quick estimate and we'll chip in—equal amounts. Any objections? We'll put a jar on the bar and request donations. Say we start with twenty bucks each ... might as well haggle this out now." he said as he surveyed the frowns.

"What if we go over? Booze ain't cheap, ya know." Dalton spurted.

Cole, more of a regular now and being nudged by some to move in—take Giles' place—raised a hand halfway and said, "So fucking what ... you'll have your share, you usually do."

"Screw you, Cole. You're not on the roster so clamp it."

Dennis said, "Hold on, always time later for that. Paul has the right idea; we'll chip in whatever it costs, and Cole's money is welcome. The booze won't go to waste. It's not perishable, you know."

"Okay," Paul said, "anything else? Hey D, I hear you got a date with a pleated plaid skirt. Will you be carrying her books?"

"Fuck you."

LATER, WHILE ALONE WITH DALTON and having a beer, Paul asked, "So okay, tell me ... how old she is."

"I'm not so old myself, ya know."

"I know your age; I am asking about hers."

"She didn't say."

"Who didn't say/"

"Mary didn't say. I didn't ask and she didn't say. Is that good enough for you ... and what the hell does it matter? It ain't you she's gonna be with."

"Look, I'm not concerned about any difference in age, only that's she's over the threshold. There's drinking, partying, and sex, and then there's underage drinking and statutory rape. You don't want any of either."

"Yeah, yeah ... I know. I didn't just come in from Brazil."

"Brazil?"

"Yeah, Brazil ... you know, the place where they're havin' a family as soon as they bleed. Well, it's somethin' like that I read in a book."

"Jesus D, just find out—make certain she's at least eighteen."

"Yeah, okay."

EASTMAN CALLED.

"Izzy, I'm coming over. Tonight, okay? Tell me what time."

"I suppose it *is* time to talk."

"Meyer certainly thinks so."

"Maybe about eight."

"See you then."

This wasn't gonna be easy for Eastman. Izsak Padgett was an old and dear friend—he'd directed several of Izsak's productions. They went way back. And Anna ... Christ, what about Anna? Well, maybe they could salvage this thing. He'd see.

"GOOD TO SEE YOU ETHAN ... not fond of the occasion but enjoy your company. Let Arthur fix you a drink. C'mon over here and sit down."

"We have to do something, Izsak. We're losing money and credibility. Oh yes, and same with you, my friend." He pulled over a chair. "Scotch over, Arthur, please. This fucking movie, or lack of it, is getting to me. Sorry if—"

"Yes, and you know what it is ... so let's get to it. Anna's coming down, wants to sit in if it's okay with you."

"Sure, and ... and, here she is." Eastman got up and stepped over to meet her, took her hands in his and gave her a kiss. "Lovely tonight as always, Anna."

"Hello, Mr. Director, Anna said. "My, you are sweet after working hours—grizzly to teddy when the sun disappears." She smiled demurely. "The usual, Arthur."

They sat. They sipped. They took a moment together. Ethan felt the warmth from Izsak and the wealth of the room, and it soothed him. He felt at home, more at home, he thought, than in his own place. Izzy was, from every angle and on every account, an excellent thinker and good close friend and it would be extremely difficult to feel anything else.

Izsak broke the hovering silence. "You think I'm not worried? I'm worried ... and I know you're shitting bricks, you and especially Bob Meyer. Yes, we have to do something. We are behind ... nearly a month on some lines, and it's not all Lacey, although—" He took a big sip of his single-malt scotch—"her absence is certainly contributing, and yes, I'm worried, fucking worried."

"Please," Anna said, "she needs time. She's a competent producer. She's taken a hit ... a monstrous whack to her heart. You guys need to be patient—give her a break."

"We've got people," Ethan said, "drawing money doing nothing. The studio doesn't like it, and some have other op-portunities. I talked to Meyer today. He's got his hand on the plug—sez if we don't come up with an answer soon, he'll pull it. And I know you're getting calls from the guys with the money and know they are whispering as they bleed. I've got some in it too. We've got to act now, Izsak. What do you sug-gest?"

"I understand. We've all got a stake in this picture. It's not that I haven't thought about this possibility. I've hired a van and a driver, one of those things with a lift. Hate the god-damned things but ... well, it's time for severe measures. The driver will push this chair around and on top of that, I've lined up some experienced help—knows his way through the pro-duction maze. You know Anthony Giotto, did a couple of 'Bs' at Republic. He'll sidle up until we get this thing back on its track."

"How long you suppose that'll take?" Ethan asked.

"Assuming clear sailing," Izsak said, "less than a month. You can begin shooting the simple stuff on a soundstage in a week. I'll have the assets lined up."

"You sure of that?"

"Ethan, my love," Anna broke in. "You must settle down. He said what he would do; what else can he say? Nothing is certain, you know ... except for those beastly taxes and that unspeakable thing." She leaned in and gently took his hand. "You know, we're in this together ... and we'll win. We'll win if we don't toss the towel."

"Of course." Ethan smiled. He didn't often smile but he liked to, and he was somewhat relieved with their confidence. There were always risks, he admonished himself, and he'd been here before. They'd all been here before. Sometimes it seemed just part of the game.

"Has Arthur retired?" Ethan said. "I'm ready for another scotch."

"I'll get it," Anna said. "Over those sparkly cold little things, that right?"

"You know," Izsak said. "I heard from her last week— Lacey. She called. She may have been a bit ... a sedative, I suppose, but she said she was recovering. She's sought help. It's working, and she plans to return soon. I was encouraged." Izsak smiled and looked off. "I do have hopes," he murmured.

Anna rose. "I'm going to leave you two weathered giants to enjoy your camaraderie and don't put the bottle away half full. I do agree with Izzy and share his hopes. I too like Lacey and she has my best. Good night, honey-pops, and you, Mr. Eastman. See you both in dreamland." She sauntered out, very much the total woman, and they were both uplifted by their proximity to her feminine aura.

Ethan smiled and took a sip. "How did you get so fucking lucky?"

Eighteen
The Party

ECORATIONS HUNG, booze and mix behind the bar and a new keg of Michelob chilled artic cold. Dalton had found an old high school chum, Oliver, to tend bar; several trays of deli were over ice on the dining room table, and the band would arrive at nine. This indeed was a party, and they were appropriately dressed, jackets and ties except for Cole.

Cole came in a tux with Beth, dressed in a revealing gown, hanging onto his arm. Beth worked weekends at Ernie's liquors on Victory Boulevard, and while often seen by this group, never in anything but jeans and a sweatshirt. Cole looked good in a tux—narrow, chiseled, face, nose like a parrot's beak, and eyes so intense they often frightened the one on the receiving end of a glance. He sported unruly black hair that pushed back resembled a bramble bush. Cole was slender without being skinny. And while he shined in a tux, he garnered not a glance from the voluptuous red-headed, freckled-faced Beth, and they wondered what strings he had pulled. The night was young, of course, and her early broad-based attention may simply be good manners.

Mary F. also wore a gown that could've been a Hartley design as it was splendidly regal—a light gauzy thing, ivory white with pearlescent sequins.

"Do you like it?" she asked Paul. "Will I fit in? I do want to fit in, you know ... now that I'm *your* date." She grinned and her eyes sparkled—a comely look, displaying a hint of her skills and the ability to melt most men into a tepid pool.

"Shee ... you are beautiful—a rose among thorns, a single lily on the pond, and I am duly impressed."

"And you are so eloquent, Paul. Is that why I adore you—so many well-chosen words from your flowery mouth?" She put her hand on the back of his neck, drew him into a kiss. "There, that's for being a man—the only one now at this address."

Dennis arrived with his newest discovery, Maxine, and her looks were as demanding as earlier related. A bobbed platinum blonde, mature in comportment, who presented herself as an experienced sophisticate. It was easy to see why Dennis was smitten. After introductions, Dennis took her hand. "C'mon, let me show you around."

Nick arrived next with a fresh-looking all-American peach he had met on the tennis courts. "Shelley," he said, nodding toward her. "I want you all to meet Shelley." She did about an eighth of a curtsey and showed them her very white teeth. She was blonde with freckles in a pleated pink skirt, high collared blouse, cute as a button and just as Nick had proclaimed.

"No bobby sox?" Cole laughed. "Or did you leave them with your baton?"

208

"And if I'd remembered, it would be mostly up your ass about now," she whispered back.

Dalton, proud as a new father, strode in with Heather on his arm and nodded around with a grin on his face the envy of Jimmy Durante. "I ... I want you all to meet Heather Martinez, my date for tonight, and maybe through the year." He chuckled and winked at her. She smiled. While not quite up to Mary's exotic standards, Heather showed promise.

The crowd thickened.

The neighbors stopped in after the combo cranked up about 10—Ilene and Larry. Ilene, a sassy 45 with a pixie look, a slender but shapely body, and already primed for the night. Larry, a special effects guy buried deep in his active imagination, was generally not inclined to get sloshed—and a good thing, as someone would need to guide Ilene home before very long.

"C'MON, LET'S GO OUTSIDE," Nick said to Shelley. "I'll show you the layout. Nice pool, now that it's in working order, a bar, piped sound, lanai around, and cabaña. We'll take a break from the noise,"

"Oh, I love that idea," she said. "My ears ... they're so sensitive, you know, and they're hurting with all that sound." They left the house to wander out and around.

"It's beautiful out tonight," she said. "I jus love the Valley, so balmy and comfy in the evenings, and the lanterns you all hung ... they're so romantic and Japanese. I love the Japanese. Nicky, don't you love 'em too? And, well, isn't it all just wonderful? Life is so inspiring."

"Hey, I think that's Dennis there in back under the lanai. Let's say hello ... Dennis, that you?"

Dennis stood. "Yeah. Come on over and meet Maxine."

Maxine—and immediately Detroit crossed his mind, and the girl that occupied his dreams, and as he got closer: "fucking Christ," he murmured to himself. "Maxine? I don't believe it. What the hell ..." He hurried now, put his arms around her in a hug. "I don't believe it."

"Seems you already know her," Dennis said.

"Oh, Nicky ..." She wiped her eyes. "I'd heard you had left Detroit but didn't know you were here. You look wonderful ... I don't know what to say."

"My God, how have you been?" He stood back. "You look fabulous. How long have you been here... in the Valley? What happened to Wally? Is he here too? You are a sight ... I'm so glad to see you." Tears rolled down his face.

"HEY, YOU GUYS, you know any slow ones ... maybe *Cry Me a River*? You know that one?"

"Sure, a slow one for Dalton," the drummer said."

"C'mon, Heather, I love this tune ... Now you say you're lonely, You cry—"

"Please, just dance, Dalton."

"You do like me, don't-cha? I like you." He pulled her in closer and she came without resistance. "You're so beautiful and ya smell so good—your soft hair .... Now you say you're sorry ... dum-dum-de-dum."

"Shhh ... I like you too, but you can't sing. This place is so cool, all you guys just doing what you want to ... and this party." She slid her hand from his shoulder up onto his neck, softly stroking. "Well, it's ... it's professional, sort of, and you're part of it. Is Paul the chief? I mean, does he like, head things up? You know, the group. He's nice. Mary likes him ... but I like you, Dalton. You're Paul's oldest friend, right? Are you number two?"

"Yeh baby, that's me—numero dos." He nuzzled her and took a deep breath—intoxicating. She felt so good next to his body—fit exactly.

"LOOKS LIKE THEY'RE HITTING IT OFF," Mary said to Paul. "Heather's a smart gal, though—might be too much for Dalton."

"He *can* get forceful. You know about that, I suppose."

"We Martinez gals can take care of ourselves. Heather? I've seen her in action."

"Runs in the family?"

"Maybe." She winked. "You gonna find out?"

"Might check it out later, though I'm not into violence. Listen, I've been wanting to talk to you ... got something you should know. Let's go out on the patio."

"Sounds mysterious, what's up?"

"It's the kids. You know we all like you; you've become part of the group. And we like Kenny and Margie ... though I hafta say, we're not accustomed to kids"

"So, this is my eviction notice?"

He laughed. "No, of course not. Here, let's sit here." He had led her to a bench across from the cabana. "It's just that ... well, we're concerned about the kids, their welfare, so to speak, and the pool imposes its risk, and well ... now that you

211

have a job, they aren't getting the attention or care they did before, and they need. So, we—"

"So, tell me," she said with a bit of an edge, "is this about right: I needed the job so I could pay my share and now that I have one, my kids are in the way? Don't you think I'm aware of my circumstances? Don't you think I know they affect you ... that I'm in everyone's fucking way? Jesus, Paul, you more than anyone know that I'm trying, and none of you know how much *I* want outta here ... my own place."

"Look, it's not that at all." He reached, took her shoulders to bring her closer. She didn't come.

"No one asks how I feel ... what I need. Believe me, it's no fun being an unwanted guest." Her sobs were beginning to come. "God knows I'm looking ... I need a better position so I can afford some care for them ... you know that. You know things are working and that it takes time. You want me out of here ... okay, I'll leave. Just park me where you found me. I'll find something."

"Hold on." He backed away. "You're jumping to the wrong conclusion. Let me, eh, look: first of all, we like you here; you're one of us now. It's the kids. Well, they're okay but we're concerned for them, worried—they could have an accident ... the pool, for example, no one here to pull one out.

"We know you're taking steps—your grandmother and your mom, maybe others. There's a plan. We think it's the right thing to do and it's a temporary fix ... until you get on your feet. These things take time, we all know that."

"I love my—"

"Quiet. You'll know when I'm finished; there'll be punctuation."

212

She smiled and moved closer.

"Now, what I've been trying to say is that Dennis has called someone at a Catholic children's services, or something like that, and he thinks they will help. They have the facility to take the kids for a short or long period of time. You would have access whenever you want, for as long as you want, overnight and permanently when you are ready. It sounds ideal."

"I'm not Catholic."

"Doesn't matter. They're going to send out a representative to interview you. I suppose there'll be papers to sign, and it's only one alternative and strictly up to you. Dennis is trying to help. We like your kids. We want them to have a safe life ... and healthy meals."

"You mean Tootsie Rolls don't make the list?"

They both laughed. It wasn't personal. The situation wasn't good for the kids, and everyone knew that something had to be done.

OLIVER, STOUT, PALE, BLUE-EYED OLIVER, held court at the bar with stories about prison life—from gutters in to gutters out. Round cherubic face, small mouth, blond hair parted in the middle, his arms were a gallery of hearts and moms, naked woman, anchors, omni-directed love and roses, with plenty of room for more as his arms were the size of hams.

"Yeh, I spent some glorious time at one o' the larger dormitories, compliments of the state—the one up at Chino. They treat ya okay, I guess. Love green ... second is gray—them are the colors, one-er the other wherever ya look. Screws on your ass all day—like warts they was." He bellowed. His laugh was more of a roar. "The screws, they's worse than the cons. They brought in the dope, and we did the usin' but don't never mis-behave, turn on a screw and get caught. Now ain't that a laugh, usin' big while servin' time for usin' a little. Jus business, of course." He took a big drink of the bourbon he brought.

"What were you using, Mr. Oliver, if I may ask?" Ilene said, her breasts attempting escape from a low-cut crepe.

He pounded a hand on the bar, threw his head back and bellowed—a freight train barreling down the track, metal grinding, ugly smoke roiling into a quiet blue sky.

"'H', a-course little lady—capital 'H' .... There ain't noth-ing else. It's the Chino vitamin—keeps the wheels a turnin' anyone can see, even ol' one-eye me." And with that he nod-ded his head toward the bar and dropped his left eye into the glass of scotch and water Ilene had been drinking. "With a lit-tle 'H', li'l lady, ah can stick my thumb in the ground and turn the whole wide world upside down." He roared again, his thumb in the air, while everyone gasped—everyone but Tom.

Tom, a quiet man, sat comfortably in the upholstered wingback in the corner away from the bar, sipping quietly from his preferred bottle of claret. He abhorred this sort of situation, any man's conspicuous state of over-wrought exist-ence, a bit of a sneer his only response. He had been in the chair since he arrived, undisturbed and not disturbing but simply sitting and sipping—a muscular man with a short-cropped head, flat lips and narrow eyes, slouched in a loose black blazer over a black linen shirt and faded jeans ... his at-tention grudgingly drawn to Oliver's exhibition. He wasn't unhappy enough to move.

"WHY ARE YOU OUT HERE in the back by yourself when the party's going on inside?"

"Wha ... Who are you?"

"I'm Betsy. I live across the street and down a house or two. Who are you?"

"I'm Dennis, and I want to be left alone, so fug off." He took a drink from his bottle. "Beat it now or can't-cha hear?"

"I like the music so came in through the back gate. You are my first acquaintance." She squatted down in front of the chaise and the hem of her skirt slid down her thighs, exposing some parts that most assumed were ordinarily covered but weren't tonight.

A sharpened attention flooded his psyche. He took a drink and reconsidered the moment.

The light was dim there next to the filter room ... she might be a redhead and still in the Girl Scouts.

"Betsy, huh? Well, Betsy from across the street ... I been jilted. My party date has found another, and I'm just sittin' here tryin' to enjoy what's left in this bottle ... and frankly, Miss 'cross-the-street, would like to do it in peace." He lifted a bottle of rum from between his legs—still half full—and took a long pull.

She moved onto the chaise sitting next to him.

"You're cute." She put a hand on his shoulder. "I like these kinda parties." She reached over and kissed him full on the lips. "Do you want me to hang with you?" She found the bottle and took a few gulps, and without a reaction put it down to the side. She pulled him closer and guided his hand up to her breast. It needed no further coaching.

Dennis forgot about Maxine and his rum and turned his attention fully to that at hand. "Betsy, huh?" And he kissed her back. Wow, did she have a tongue.

She found his manhood, or maybe it found her as it was moving in her direction. Wanting to be helpful, she rubbed and assisted. Unzipping his fly, she released the captive, springing forth like a jack-in-a-box. She fondled it gently, and before he knew what the hell was happening, she was kissing and inviting it into her mouth. Of course, it responded in a positive manner—a lost prodigal now eagerly returning.

"Ohhh ... ahhh ... oh my god, you are talented," was about all he could manage, and then he exploded. A wonderful celebration of nature, a glorious reason to survive Maxine. Fireworks, the philharmonic, then dew on a rose ... and for a moment, he was in love with whoever the fuck was sitting beside him. She straightened, swallowed, and chased with a gulp of his rum.

"Ah Betsy, you are an artist beyond comparison—Puccini, Rossini, and Donizetti all rolled into one. How old are you anyway?"

"Sixteen. Not bad for sixteen, huh? My dad works at Pep Boys and can get you discounts. Can we go in now?"

"HI PAUL, I'M JOHN TEAGARDEN ... live down the street a couple doors. Got that new turquoise Chrysler Saratoga you probably see out front. Where's Giles? Thought sure he'd be here. And oh, by the way, this is my friend, Wayne Gundersen. Wayne's just out of the Air Force. We both work over at Lockheed." John extended his hand. "Our dates, Ellen—a misty eyed brunette and Wayne's tall, strawberry blond, Vicki, are around somewhere—hard to keep track ... if one wanted to. Great party, by the way—the talk of the neighborhood, you guys and your parties."

"Welcome to both of you," Paul said, shaking their hands. "Good to see you here and hope you're enjoying your-selves. I've already met your ladies. They're around ... yep, complicated keeping track of anyone." Paul laughed. "Oh yeah, Giles? He's off on a Thunderbird ride ... who knows where and who isn't talking, ha-ha."

"Yeah.... Well, if you hear from him and say something back, tell him hello for me, and that I've got the pre-amp he was looking for and he owes me $200."

"Okaaay, and luck with that." Paul grinned, beginning to feel a little light-headed. "Nice to meet-cha Du-wayne."

"It's Wayne." He chuckled. "We'll be around."

C'MON BABY," Dalton said. "Let's mosey off and I'll show you the house." Heather had her arm around his waist, her thumb tucked under his belt, as they slid into the back hall toward the sunroom. They sat in the dark on a daybed and looked out toward the lanai, now more visually available with the colorful Japanese lanterns hanging the length of the struc-ture, and the pool lights giving off a flickering glow. The combo was back from a break and their music was now soft and dreamy as it came down the hall. He turned to her, kissed her lightly on the lips.

"You know I really dig you, Heather."

"Yes, I know."

"We could be big together."

"Maybe."

He tightened his hold around her a bit and said, "Maybe?"

She kissed him on his neck and pulled them down. She breathed into his ear, "I do like you, Dalton, but don't take me for granted. You won't do that will you … take me for granted." She purred as she snuggled down into him.

God, she is something.

He was consumed by her, everything about her—her fragrance seeped into his head, his gut ached. She was so fresh and lovely—a fantastic woman who was young and soft and firm and cuddly. He loved every part of her and wanted to crawl inside her—they could be one. His mind was exclusively focused, and it seemed she was his.

They rolled and squirmed on the daybed, trying to get closer. He touched her and she him; they intertwined their legs, and he ran his hands from her thighs to her breasts— back and forth, up and down. They kissed and their mouths were one, their tongues swathed in identical raiment. The windows steamed up, and the room took on a musky scent. The rest of the world was somewhere but it wasn't with them. He was beside himself, respecting but wanting, respecting *and* wanting, and then wanting won out and he unzipped his pants and wanting popped out.

"Dalton Dobbs! What the hell are you doing?" She bolted straight up. "Oh no you don't mister, not with this girl. Who do you think I am? You think I'm stupid?" She bounced out of the daybed and turned to him. "Zip it up, friend. There won't be another opportunity for that, I can assure you."

218

"DENNIS! DENNIS," Shelley gushed, "where have you been? I've been looking all over. You wanna dance? It seems my date is otherwise occupied."

"Sure ... why not. I think my date is with yours."

As they swayed to the late evening sounds, she whispered, "I don't care anyway. I been watching and sorta like you. Nick's a shit, isn't he?"

"I guess they had something back in Detroit. I didn' know she was from Detroit. You're not from Detroit? I dun wanna fug around with any more women from Detroit. It's gettin' late, you know. If you're from Detroit, you better go." He stumbled and it was only a two-step. "I don't even like Detroit. Where you f-from?"

"Silly ... I live right here in the Valley. I love the Valley. I went to school at Van Nuys High. I Jus' love the Valley, don't ever wanna leave. Maybe we should sit down; you're scuffing up my shoes. Where's Detroit? I never heard of Detroit."

"Shit, I dunno ... it's some place, I guess—where ya wanna go?"

She nibbled on his ear. "We'll see, Mr. Dennis Delaney ... we're gonna find out."

"C'MON, OLLIE OIL," Ilene slurred. "I wanna see that trink ... trick again, you know, the one where you lookin' at me from inside my drink ... I'll need another one first." She leaned on the bar, her knees wobbled—her perky breasts had lost some perk and her eyelids drooped a bit.

"Sure doll," Oliver said. "A drink for the lady comin' right up. Though maybe ya might wanna taste of the 'H'? I got some, ya know."

"Nooo, sh-scotch will be fine … I like sh-cotch and maybe some sparkly, but not too much." A heel turned under and she almost fell. "Ollie, ol' boy, ju hear me … I dun wanna get drunk" She laughed.

"Here ya go, doll, the ole half and half. Half whiskey 'n' soda, and half Oliver." He reached over the bar and pulled her toward him. She pushed back, spilling her fresh drink down her blouse. "S'okay, doll, here lemme lick it off." He came around the bar, grabbed her arms and began licking her neck.

"Hey, you shtupid, get off me!"

Tom rose from his comfort, carefully placed his claret on the bar and grabbed Oliver's shirt, one hand on each side, and doubled Oliver backwards over the bar until his spine began to crack.

"Now, we've had more than enough from you. Get back where you belong before you lose that good eye and go totally blind."

"Okay … okay!" he squeaked. "I'm goin' … goin'. Leggo, you're breakin' my back."

With a final vertebrae crack, Tom picked up the claret and returned to his wingback, slowly crossed his legs, took a sip from his bottle and enjoyed the quiet.

"DALTON, WHERE'S MY SISTER?" Mary F said.

"I dunno … went home, I guess. I called her a taxi … was my fault, shouldn't a taken her for … well, I made some fucking assumptions." He looked rough, wrinkled shirt, hair astray, cheeks chafed.

"You aren't the first puzzled player." She laughed. "Last out, sides retired just as you're rounding third. Gotta admire her ... she liked you, though."

"Say, Paul, we're shoving' off," John said. "Thanks for the party and ..."

"...leaving sho soon? Jus' getting' started."

"We need to get Vicki back; she works tomorrow."

The doorbell rang and there was a loud knock—baton on wood. "Who's in charge here?" A gruff voice came in through the open doorway. The band stopped. The chatter waned, then quickly went silent. Paul came up as the rest moved away.

"I guess that would be ... be me." Paul straightened. "Come in, officers. Yeah, c'mon in."

"What's going on here?" The first officer in said. "It's after twelve. You got some ID? Anyone underage here—under eighteen?"

Paul pulled out his wallet, opened it to his license behind the clear plastic window and extended it to the one asking.

"Take it out."

Dennis, standing behind Paul, muffled a chuckle.

"You think this is amusing, funny man?" The second cop spoke up.

"No sir."

"Who's out back?"

"No one," Paul said. "Uh, well, maybe a few. Most are right here. He looked around. "It's just a party, officer."

"Who owns the Chrysler parked on the front lawn?" He handed back Paul's license.

"I really don't—"

"I do." John spoke up. "I'll move it right now.".

"You look familiar. You Teagarden's son?"

"Yessir."

"Umm, okay … you all look legal. No drugs here, right? Get that car off the lawn and shut down the noise … if we have to come back," he looked at Paul, "some of you will spend the rest of your party in a cell—got it?"

"Let's go, Ed," the second officer said. "Ain't nuthin here. We're wastin' our time. We may all be ashes tomorrow anyway."

"You're right. Okay, keep it down here," he said to Paul.

"What's goin' on?" Dalton asked, entering the living room, buckling his belt, Betsy behind him.

"Who's the girl?" The second officer asked as he moved quickly through the living room toward the den. But Betsy had gone.

"Tom! Didn't see ya there in the corner," the second officer said.

"Hi Roger, night shift?"

"Yeah, Grodin's out sick."

"Okay we're leaving now," the first officer said. "Keep it down, all of you. We don't wanna come back … and move the goddamn car."

"DAMMIT, DOBBS, who was that kid?" Paul pulled Dalton aside. "What was she doing here … just a kid. You're startin' to piss me off, D … I mean really piss me off. We coulda been in big trouble."

"Screw you!" Dalton said. "You're not my mother ... so go take a flyin' fuck ..." He stepped back and fell into a chair. "I ain't never seen her before. Anyway, who put you in charge?"

"Say Paul," Larry said, taping him on the shoulder. "I'm sorry to interrupt the tête-à-tête, but you s'pose you could help me get Ilene home—her legs have turned to rubber."

"Sure... sure Larry. Where is she?"

"On the floor in the den."

THE GUYS IN THE BAND cased their instruments, collected their money, and departed. Soon after. the keg sputtered its last, and the crowd thinned out. Unconscious bodies reclined in convenient locations leaving heavy breathing the only party noise. The cops had corked the bottle.

**

AT TEN THAT NEXT MORNING, Dennis opened his eyes, looked around from the couch and shut them again. At noon, Cole pulled his head from a cushion in the fireplace and stood. Quickly, he grabbed a chair and sat down.

Dennis stirred and Nick came in from the patio, rubbed his eyes, "Uuuh, what a mess; a bicarb would be good."

Wayne, behind Nick, said, "I need a pitcher. You guys own a pitcher?"

"You came back?

"I didn't leave. John drove Vickie home."

"A pitcher?" Dennis sat up on his elbow. "There's one in the cupboard. Ohh, my head may need a doctor."

"And a strainer?" Wayne asked

"In a drawer—second over from the fridge."

"Got it."

Mary F came in about five minutes later, looking showered and fresh. "You know what Wayne is doing out on the patio?"

"Don't keep us in suspense a moment longer." Cole sniggered into a laugh.

"He's straining drink remnants into a pitcher, then whackin' the strainer on the side of his shoe to get the bugs out."

"Hair of the dog without the fleas," Cole said, shaking his head. "Technology at work."

Nineteen
Settling In

GILES PULLED INTO LAS CRUCES at 10:30 in the morning. He stopped at a "Y" in the road and cut the engine. Right would lead to El Paso and across the river, Juarez ... both within a few hours. Left, and to the north was Albuquerque, a full day and more of riding. His butt was talking; he needed a break. Bolstering that, a curiosity about Mexico had been swirling around in his head since the conversation over a beer near San Diego. He'd never been and that alone seemed reason enough. He turned the front wheel south. Half a mile down the road, a lunch stand caught his eye and he stopped for a Coke and burrito. A thermometer in the window said, "Drink a Pepsi – 101 degrees." No one eyed his bike.

In El Paso, he headed straight for the crossing and into Juarez. The city was a mess, though not unexpected—titty bars, street peddlers, and little-boy pimps, dancing music from open doors, some asleep on the walks with their sombreros holding the night. The tourist thing was geared to shaking pockets clean. Well, he didn't want any, and rode farther south into the outskirts and some beyond.

At a little cantina on a side road just off the blacktop and far out of the Juarez limits he stopped. There would be beer and food—a late lunch and perhaps nearby, a siesta. He turned the bike in toward the building and parked next to the door. Dust rose, then settled. Two old pickups looked worn and neighborly. When he walked in, a little bell jingled and three at the bar lazily looked up and smiled. One waved his hand, a signal Giles read he was welcome.

This is the right place, he thought, and stepped up to the bar. "Un cerveza, por favor."

Her white teeth enhanced a smile and her brown eyes twinkled. She might have been twenty-five … twenty-seven.

"I am Maria," she said. "Maria Castillo, and this mi cantina. Americano?"

"Sure, Americano," he said.

"Un cerveza." she said as she plopped an ice-cold bottle onto the bar, wet from the tub. "Glass?"

"Si un vaso, por favor," he said, trying his high school Spanish.

She smiled again and someone dropped a coin in the jukebox.

"You want to eat?"

"Si... menú?"

She laughed. "*Usted es gracioso, no tengo un menu … tengo enchiladas, burrito, frijoles, huevos y beans, chiles rellenos—*"

"Stop. Two enchiladas will work. Gracias."

"Work? They will work?" She laughed. It was a wonderful laugh, full of merriment and joy, and her eyes lit up.

He laughed, then she laughed more, and he tried to imagine what he thought she could see—a couple of enchiladas wearing sombreros, each with a sack, picking beans in the field. Would they be drinking a Coke? He laughed again. It had been a long day.

The food, "delicioso" by any standard. Maria was a treat for his motorcycle bones, and the place, out here on a rural road seemed safe and friendly, and maybe what to expect of the ordinary folks.

"Anywhere nearby I can stay for a while?" he asked. "I don't need much, a room maybe ... or just a bed?"

"¿Cuánto se paga?" she asked.

"What?"

"How much will you pay?" Her smile was alluring.

"I don't know. What should I pay?

"You can stay weeth Juan and Maria for ... umm, maybe five, six pesos a day."

"Juan?"

"Si. Él es mi hijo, es pequeño."

"Small?"

"Sí, él es de siete. He is seven. We are in a small house in the back. I have a bed you can use. You can eat here. Is it good?" She opened another beer and placed it in front of him. "You like these enchiladas? Cómo te llamas?"

"Giles... estoy Giles." He reached in his wallet and pulled out a ten spot. "How long will this keep me?"

"Oh goodness." Her eyes ambled from the bill to his grin ... "a very long time."

**

THE TEMPERATURE was up in the Valley, often over 100, and Friday noon was the start of the weekend at the Beck Street house. Beer came out with the music and if the keg was dry, quarts were generally cold in the fridge. A swamp cooler struggled on the utility porch, lowering the inside temp by several degrees. A little maintenance would've helped, but no one had the will or skill, and everyone cringed at the thought of a visit from Sampson.

Dennis and Mary F were dancing a jitterbug step in the living room, he for comfort in his Jockey briefs, his gangly frame limbering up as the beer went down. Teagarden had left his latest Stan Getz.

"Wait a minute," Mary said. "What's good for the goose, is good for the gander." And she shed her blouse and her skirt, leaving her marvelous body in bra and panties to luxuriate in the semi-damp air. "Now that's much better; brother it is hot."

They were good together, natural in the moves—as if they taught at an Arthur Murray studio.

Dalton sprawled on the wingback in the den while Paul, at the bar, was saying, "Yeah, he'll come through, D. He has in the past and, anyway, he's good till the end of the month. If he's late, I'll front him if need be."

"You're fuckin' kidding yourself. The guy's a deadbeat ... always has been. You don't even know where he's at. Likely ran that bike into a gang of banditos that didn't speak English so didn't cave to his bullshit. I say let's put what little he had in the garage and rent his bed—bring in some fresh cash. Wayne might be interested."

"What ... you're talking this up with Wayne?"

"Don't get your tits in a ringer ... all I said, it might be open."

"Well, it isn't, and best you stay outta this, D. That's my bailiwick—establishing the need, reviewing and making recommendations ... and then, only then we all decide." He pulled a long draw on his beer. "We don't know him, barely know the guy's name," his voice taking on an edge.

"You know," Dalton said, "I'm damned tired of you calling the shots. Just who the hell voted you king?" Dalton on his feet now, stretching his frame and moving towards Paul, his jaw tightening up. "You're always at this ... makin' the fucking rules, tellin' what do to ... and I'm up to here. You need to come down a peg, and I might be the guy to do it." He shoved Paul against the bar. "You're fucking due."

The doorbell rang, though the front door was open.

"Sure, c'mon in," Dennis yelled over the music and they kept up the pace. They were into it now and moving fast, sweat running down their hot bodies, the music loud.

It rang again.

"Get the damn door," Paul yelled from the den.

Dennis stopped, shrugged, and went to the door where a little old lady stood. She was dressed in black with a small hat and a gray veil, her faded blue eyes as wide as the horizon.

"Oh my, do I have the right house? She checked a card she held. "Does a Mr. Delaney live here? I must have the wrong address." She looked through some papers she had in her hand, "Mr. Dennis Delaney?"

"Shit ..." he mumbled. "John," he yelled over at Teagarden, "cut the music ... uh yes, I'm Dennis, eh, how can I help you? Maybe you'd like to come in." He couldn't imagine what she was thinking but he had an inkling that he knew who she was.

"I'm ... she glanced around. Her eyes stopped with Mary. "I don't want to interrupt ... eh, maybe I should go. I could come back—"

"No, it's alright, please, we were just trying to cool off, Friday you know, and it so hot ...." He glanced around—*what did I do with my pants?*

"Well ... I just don't know ...," She glanced over at Mary, then quickly away. "Eh, my name is Miss Elizabeth Bryne. I'm from the Catholic Children's Services. I'm here to—"

"Who the fuck is it?" Dalton yelled from the bar. "Is it for me?"

"Eh ... please come in Mrs ..."

"Bryne, Miss Bryne."

"Yes, Miss Bryne. Come in. Uh, give us a minute, here ... to, eh, you know it's so hot here in the Valley ... eh, to put on some ...." He turned to Mary and under his breath: "Get dressed, for Chrissake. Please have a seat, Miss Bryne. Would you like something to drink?"

"Well, I don't know if I should stay. I should talk to Father ... he's in the car ...." She looked around at the black walls. "Are you Mr. Delaney? Does Mrs. Martinez-Torres live here?"

"Yeah sure ... yes, that's me. You have the right place ... and she'll be right back." He had found his pants and was holding them where he thought she might want him to hold them.

"Who is it?" Paul asked as he came into the room with a quart of Pabst in his hand.

230

"Whoever, sure saved your ass." Dalton's anger following along from the den.

"It's Miss Bryne," Dennis got out as he stumbled into his pants. "She's come about the kids I guess."

Mary F reentered the room in a kimono. "Hi, I'm Mary Frances Martinez-Torres," she said. "It's my kids are the problem." She extended her hand, tentatively taken with a scornful look from Miss Elizabeth Bryne.

"I'm very sorry," Miss Bryne said. "There's been a mistake, I fear," and she trembled a bit as she put her papers on the table. "I'll leave you this application, but we look for qualified Christian families with domestic problems. Those who are seriously interested in placing their children under our care. I ... I'm afraid I don't see that here."

"Look, lady, we're serious. And we're Christians ... I ain't a Catholic but I believe in God." Dalton blurted out. "And we gotta get those kids outta here."

"Button it!" Paul said. "Look, Miss Bryne, you've caught us at a very bad time. If you could come back—"

But she had turned was out the door on her way to a black sedan with its door opened by a smiling man in a collar and black suit.

"Well, if that ain't the shits," Dalton said on his way back to the den, "fucking uppity Catholics."

"You know something," Mary said, "You guys ... I'm sorta glad that didn't work out." Her eyes teared up. "You didn't have the courtesy or the balls to ask *me* ... if I wanted my kids slurping their narrow-minded gruel, up and going down with a bell."

"Yeah ... well what about your kids?" Dalton said. "What about that?"

**

NICK WALTZED IN WITH A SAILOR'S CAP ON, a set of keys he jingled in front of him, and stood behind an empty seat at the poker table.

"Boy, that San Diego is some kind a town—more swab-bies than tourists and together they outnumber the residents. That is to say, it's a party, twenty-four, and we gotta visit sometime. Can I get in the game; there's only five?"

"Sure, take the seat. How's your brother?" Paul asked.

"He's doing great. It's not a bad life if the Ruskies don't blow us up, and even then, being out on the water might be the safest yet. He gets three nutrition-packed meals a day, a bunk, clothes, medical care ... shit, everything but wipe his ass, and then it's shore leave." He sat. "On top of all that, they pay you real money. Shit, I might join up."

"You gonna play cards or make a fucking speech?" Dalton grumbled.

"Didja get his car?" Cole said.

"And whata set of wheels," Nick said. "Spankin' new Ford Victoria. I put on more miles driving back here than were on it when I started."

"Okay ... you got a thrill. Can we play the damned game?" Dalton growled.

"You must be winning." Nick grinned, not a bit affected by Dalton's perpetual gloom.

"And he can't stand it," Dennis said. "Ahead so seldom, he doesn't know how to behave."

232

"Yeah. Well, behavior's a problem for Dalton anyway," allowed Teagarden, "and not just at cards." He turned to Dalton. "But you pay attention, young man, maybe take notes, and you may get the gist of it someday."

"Fuck you, John. Just deal the cards."

"Where's Wayne tonight?" Paul said, picking up two pair on the deal.

"He's out with Vicki at some dance; think it's her high school reunion."

"You'll never see me at one of those, everyone outdoing everyone else—or trying to. Aces full," Dalton announced.

"Sheeze," Paul sighed, turning over his house full of sevens.

"Not again," Cole muttered, "and I had a straight. Good hands tonight, we oughtta be in Vegas."

"Yeah, trips can't win a hand here," Dennis said, "but would clean the table in Vegas."

The game continued. The deck seemed loaded with royalty—flushes, straights and then in one hand, a straight flush beat out one of lessor denomination and Dalton hauled in another major pot. With the big hands, big beer flowed, as Dalton had brought in a fresh keg of Michelob early that afternoon.

"Maybe we do it, maybe we go to Vegas," Cole offered, "with the cards that are coming, we might buy the place. We leave now, we'll be there by one ... one-thirty."

"Not quite eight," Paul checked his watch. "I'm game—and we take miss lady luck along with us."

"Let's go," Nick said, and pushed his chair back. "I've got no restrictions—James said, use it as you would your own. You guys buy the gas—it likes that dinosaur juice."

They pocketed their money, grabbed quarts from the fridge and in less than it takes to talk about it were on their way.

"Keep the lights on, Vegas ... here we come," Cole said.

"How far is it?" Nick said.

"About 270 miles," Dennis said, "and in this chariot, maybe four hours. What happened to Teagarden?"

"He's decided not to come," Paul said. "Got tickets to the Bowl tomorrow night—an evening with Tchaikovsky."

"Chi what?" Dalton said. "That guy and his foreign music. Why don't he ever listen to American stuff?"

They drove fast, San Bernardino, Victorville, Barstow, only blurs as they sped through, and the nearer they got, the faster they went, often burying the speedo needle.

"Pit stop!" Dennis yelled out, the wind noise overwhelming conversation. "Gotta pee and best that we stop now."

"Me too."

"Yeah, floatin' here."

From 110, Nick brought the car down to a less lofty speed, pulled off on the shoulder and they all got out and unzipped. As they filled the storm gully with the residuals of barley and hops, a car pulled up with those funny blinking lights and a state trooper got out with a flashlight.

"Hey, what's going on here?" He caught a few of the cascading steams in the beam.

"What the hell's it look like?" Dalton said.

234

"It looks like you want to go to jail, wise-ass. You been drinking?"

"We just stopped to relieve ourselves," Paul said. "Not many restrooms here in the desert; where else would we go?" He stumbled a bit, off balance.

"Well, you got a point," the trooper chuckled. "Who's driving this rocket? You guys went by me back there about ten miles and I've had it to the floor trying to catch you ... and these CHP cruisers aren't slow."

"I guess that'd be me," Nick said, zipping up his pants.

"Come over here." The light beam went into Nick's face. The officer drew a long line in the sand with his baton. "I want you to walk that, heel to toe ... hands in your pockets."

Nick positioned himself at one end but then it happened. The earth tipped, and Nick received a hug from mama nature. "Wobbly planet," he slurred, "s'posed to be steady on its axis." He rolled over on his back and laughed. "Do I get another try?"

"Anyone else?" The trooper asked, a grin on his face they imagined, though it was too dark to see.

"I'll try," Cole said stepping up. He got down the line three steps and lost it. "It's my vertigo actin' up, does that out in the desert."

While they all wondered what might become of them if no one was able to pass, "What about you, big mouth," the trooper pointed his baton at Dalton. "You want a shot at the kewpie doll?"

"Yeah, okay. I'll do it." He took a big breath and brought all of what there was of his concentration to bear and started off.

"A hand for Dalton, he's our man," Cole encouraged. But just before the end, Dalton too lost his balance.

"Shoulder's uneven," Dalton grumbled.

"Well," the trooper said, "You're the best of the lot, and frankly, I don't want to haul the five of you twenty-five miles back to the station. Nevada's about three miles up the road. Let them take care of you. You got a license, smart-ass?"

They piled into the Vic, Dalton now driving, and sped off, leaving a token of dust on the cruiser.

"Something's wrong here," Dalton said when they'd reach about 50. "The steering wheel's wobbling and ya hear that thump in the front end."

"Pull over," Nick said.

They stopped, got out, and walked around the car. Everything they could see looked alright. "It's a goddamn Ford." Dalton said. They pushed at the car, ran their hands along its side, kicked at the tires—shook their heads and put their hands in their pockets. No one but Nick knew a wrench from a shop towel.

"Shit, whata we gonna do now?" Dennis said.

As they stood in a group in the beam of the headlights, a smokin' eighteen-wheeler honked and pulled up on the other side of the road—Jake brakes barking and its frame howling out in protest.

"Hey, you got car troubles?" The driver yelled down from the cab.

A young man in a sleeveless tee-shirt, jeans, and an old Yankees cap with the bill turned up slid down and came over.

"What's the problem?" he asked through a chuckle.

236

"There's a thumping in front." Dalton related his experience as the guy kneeling down ran his hands around the driver's side front wheel.

"Shit, your tread's gone, ripped clean from the casing ... you can't see it standing there. Get down here and feel it." He moved his hands up over the back and around under the fender. "All gone except for this one place here, pro'bly the thumping." He stood. "I get some a that myself when it's hot and I'm drivin' too fast. You guys must've really been burning up the road ... and you're leaving that shit for the rest of us to drive over. These new tires? A damn good thing she didn't blow when you were crusin' .... You're sure lucky fucks, alright. You gotta spare? "

"I s'pose so," Nick said.

"Open 'er up, I'll help ya get it on ... and let's get her farther off the road—don't wanna get kilt by some wide-eyed, long-haul driver, frozen up tight on bennies."

THEY ROLLED INTO LAS VEGAS at two; by four they were broke, Dalton with enough left from his earlier winnngs for a tank of gas and coffee all around. The ride back was slower and dreary. Dennis got a phone number from the cute dealer that took his all his money, so not all was a loss, though as he sobered, he knew the number was bogus.

"What time is it, anyway? The sun's comin' up," somebody said.

"Shut the fuck up," someone answered.

Nick wondered how long his headache would last, how much a new tire would cost, and promised himself nothing so careless with his brother's car in the future.

**

"HEY MR. SMYTHE, I got my first raise today, thirty cents an hour," Mary Frances announced with pride, her right thumb cocked under her shoulder, a big grin on her face. "I want to celebrate. Care to take me dancing, Mr. Smythe?"

He smiled from the sofa and put down his book. "Tell me about it."

"You remember I said the office manager had eyes for me?"

"Yeah."

"Well, I've been working him a little, cashing in on his interest—a look, a touch, a comely smile, and it's paying dividends." She laughed. "He's a hungry dork, looking for affection. God, I could do so much more with someone I liked." She tossed her head back to move her lustrous black hair over her shoulder, eyes sparkling with her success.

"It's a long story and likely agonizing to listen to so I'll summarize. I'm new to this rep business—but not unlike nursing—I'm patting popos and fixing egos, while the salesmen I'm supporting are selling to the user, because the manufacturer has yet to set up his inhouse sales force. I just support the salesmen with gofer runs and diaper changes ... they're the ones haulin' in the big commissions—bucket loads. They report to my boss so I'm keeping my senses on and tuned so that someday soon I too will be hauling with a bucket.

"Well, this afternoon he calls me in, and says something like: 'Mary, I like the way you're working out, much better than expected ... bright woman,' and such he goes on, and then finally gets to the point where he announces my raise.

"His boss, the owner, said fifteen cents, he tells me, cozying up some, but he ... he said, had the authority to add another dime, making it a fifteen percent raise.

"Fifteen, I think. Well, not bad but not terrific, so I drop the smile and move to get up and then he says, 'But damn, Mary, I didn't want to insult you.'

"I could smell his lunch—a Polish and kraut, and awful in the methane state. And while I'm trying to avoid the rot, he says, 'I'm going over his limit and makin' it thirty. I can do that, you know, I have that authority.' He patted my shoulder a couple of light ones, and then, thank God, he retreated some as I was about to pass out. 'You're a big help to me,' he says, 'and I see a future for you ... eh, here with me at the company, you know. We're a darn good team, doncha think?'

"I told him yes, we were a good team, and I would do as much for him as he would for me. So, I'm thinking now, thirty, not so bad, and worth a celebration so, Paul ... be a dear and take me dancing."

He laughed. "I can't. I don't think I can move ... plumb wore out from attentive listening."

"Get up. Walk around, and keep this in mind, I'll buy the first one ... if it's less than thirty cents."

"Wow ... now that's an inducement; the Saddle okay? He laughed. It was close. He didn't have plans. She was very attractive and about the sexiest woman he'd ever known ... if only she weren't such a flirt.

"What about the kids?"

"Dalton's here. He seems to like them now that Heather has him tethered. I'll ask him."

"SHIT," DALTON COMPLAINED. "Why don't Paul watch the kids and you and me go dancin'?"

"Now, Dalton Dobbs, be a good friend ... I could put in a good word, you know, where it might do you some good."

"Ya think? Heather and me, we talk on the telephone, but she won't agree to see me."

"She might ... with the right encouragement. You do me this and I'll try and return it ... okay?"

"Yeah, okay. We have fun, the kids and me, and I'm not doin' anything anyway."

**

THE "BRONCIN' SADDLE," about five blocks away on Lankersham, hosted live Western music on weekends. The guys called it the "Boinkin' Saddle" for all the single skirts that attended and later the groans and sighs in the parking lot, but it was fun and a great place to "kick up your heels"—their tag line and strongly encouraged. There was the occasional scuffle, but usually confined to those wanting to fight, and they didn't last long because the bouncers wore spurs and were good at kicking themselves.

"YOU KNOW I LIKE YOU, PAUL," Mary said. It was late, the music was slow, and the Saddle emptying and preparing to close. She reached across their table and put her hand over his.

240

"You make sense to me, the only who does, and if I were wishing … well, I'd wish we were closer. You know. romantic-like." Her eyes were wet, her brows arched in question.

Shit, it was fun until now. He pushed back in his chair.

"I guess I'm supposed to say something impractical, only I'm not sure what it would be."

"You don't have to say anything; I'm just talkin'. It's just a feeling I've got. I guess I need some stability, some future. Sure, I like to have fun …. You guys, nothing seems to bother you, any of you—just skipping along, doing your thing. I'm envious, I guess. Christ … when you're so close to living under a bridge with two kids you adore, and you're tryin' as hard as you can to do what's right, and at every turn you seem to be failin' … Well, it's hard to refrain from cutting your wrists, and even then, where would the kids be?" Her wet eyes began to spill over. "I've got nowhere to go."

"C'mon." he pushed his chair back. "It's the last set; let's dance."

"I'm sorry. Paul, didn't mean to put you in a corner like that."

"Shh." He pulled her in closer. She felt good next to him. He didn't have a steady girl, or really one at all, and he liked the fragrance coming from her hair. As they danced, he kissed her lightly on the forehead. She murmured softly.

"What?" he whispered.

Twenty
Getting It Together

L ACEY LOUNGED BY THE POOL with a copy of *Cosmo*. It had been over two weeks since Izsak had first inquired and she promised her presence, but as the days had passed, she had increasingly become hesitant about a return. "Frightened," a better fit. Rejection once and then reawakened to be rejected again was powerful emotional stuff.

Izsak had called in the interval expressing an urgency, and quite unprepared, she had nervously given hope to them both, but it was a lie and she hated herself for it. *Such a coward.* She was hiding from a future of success in an area of competency—a once-in-a-lifetime opportunity—and was letting it pass her by while those she respected were suffering loss in her hesitancy. There was no credibility, no honor, in her lack of action and that made her angry.

How many times had she gone to the phone to say she'd be over, when would be good? And how many times after dialing had she heard his phone ring and hung up. Damn, she couldn't go on like this. She simply must square this away. Tomorrow was Sunday, jazz at the Hut. They used to attend. *Jesus Christ, what will he say?*

She stood on the sidewalk in front of the Hut after spending half an hour in her car wrestling with fear. The front shutters were open, a Sunday usual, exposing the inside to the street. A combo was playing, and Izsak was at a table alone on the patio, thumbing the rhythm with his hand. Anna stood at the bar, flirting with a young guy in a Vic-Tanny tank top.

She rustled up what was left of her diminishing courage, approached from behind, and whispered in his ear, "Can I get you a drink Mr. Padgett—scotch over?"

"Lacey!" He looked up. "My God, good to see you. How are you feeling, my girl?" He turned his chair toward her. "You look marvelous. Sit down here. There's a break coming soon, and I want to hear all about you." With a stretch, he dragged a chair over beside him.

"I'll be right back," she said. "Give me a minute at the bar. Can I get anything for you?"

"The ususal." He smiled and took her hand. "Hurry back. Anna is around here somewhere."

Wow, what a relief, and at the bar, "Tequila sunrise please."

The group was not the usual brass but two flutes, a violin, a bass, and drums—the music, rhythmical and blue. Seems to fit the occasion, she thought. Giles liked Bud Shank, she recalled.

Lacey put her drink on the table and sat.

"So, Lacey," Izsak said, "how are you doing and don't spare the details. Both Anna and I are concerned, and ... and here she is now."

"Lacey, Lacey, how very nice to see you," Anna sang. "You look quite fit, and you've been out in the sun. Your tan is coming along beautifully." She bent over for a touch of their cheeks. "Did you find a drink for me? No? Wait now, not a word until I return." She sauntered back to the bar to find her gin and tonic waiting.

"Why, thank you, Mr. Bogesen, you've read my mind. I hope that drink was the only thought I prompted."

"Your secrets and ours are mine," Bogie said.

"Okay, children," Anna said, coming back to the table. "I'm here and I'm ready to listen. Do tell us all, Lacey."

"It's been difficult ..." Lacey began. She owed them this although she objected to paying. She wasn't too sure about the how and why of it or herself or what it might mean, whatever it was, and she wasn't certain she wanted to share. "... too difficult, God knows. I'm afraid I've been locked onto Giles' disappearance, occasionally afraid; I still am, a little. But I'm shaking it and need to get back to work. I'm functional, Izsak, I am. If I could begin with ... well, maybe edge my way into the fray a little at a time. I believe I can be productive, and the work would be therapeutic—get my mind off me and onto something else." She looked off through the tall windows, the greenery of Encino, the reality of the day. "I'm being totally honest here in revealing what I feel."

"Yes, of course," Izsak said with a smile. "I can arrange that—a position of less demand—and you needn't go on. We have a new primary assistant, you must have assumed, but I do want you back—work you in somehow."

"Do you hear anything from Giles?" Anna asked.

"No ... not a word, not a goddamned word, and as far as I know, neither have his friends. There was a postcard from Juarez at some point, Paul mentioned."

"So," Anna said, "how are your emotions? Are you up or are you down, are you bouncing around like a tennis ball at Wimbledon?"

"Anna!"

"Well, between us girls then," Anna said. "Izsak is all business, you know."

"That's not entirely true," Izsak said. "I am concerned but see no need to push it right now."

"Oh, it's okay," Lacey said. "I have a hard time sleeping some nights, better recently. I drank too much for a time, but it helped. There are books dealing with this sort of thing, depression—not the clinical kind, but more like the blues. I want to get over it, put Giles out of my mind ... yet I can't stop thinking we had something special." She began to sob, pulled a handkerchief from her purse and blew her nose. "I'm sorry. I hate this ... damn him."

"It's okay," Anna said. "You don't need to say another word."

"I know," Lacey said, "but it helps to talk." She wiped her eyes. "I suppose I was only a good time for him—a romp in the sack, he might say, and I guess he provided me the honesty he could, though I haven't quite internalized that. I'm afraid I fell for him all the way, while he didn't stumble. And now I'm climbing back; I want my feet on solid ground. Can you understand, Anna?"

"Some ... you may need to think that way, putting it all on Giles, but sweetie-pie, I think you might be selling him

246

short. I knew Giles too, remember, and never knew him to be anything other than straight arrow. And my dear, that honesty crap goes both ways. I mean, were you honest with him ... and even more important, honest with yourself in what you were getting back? And another thing ... you might be loading Giles up with some of your former disappointment—that left at the alter bit."

Izsak put his hand over on Anna's and smiled.

"We both understand," Izsak said, "and we are both here to help if needed ... and pleased to have you back."

"Oh, of course," Anna said. She took Lacey's hand and broke a big smile. "Truly pleased, Lacey."

"Getting back to work will be good for you." Izsak leaned in. "Of course, and turning your attention to other demands will draw your mind from its meandering. You must decide where you are now, Lacey, and then move ahead."

"You bet, sweetie-pie. Izzy does that, doncha dear; every day gathers himself together and moves on."

"Oh, quiet Anna. When will you come back, Lacey?"

"Tomorrow if that's okay."

"Ring the bell about ten. Now, let's have a celebratory drink."

**

"HEY WAYNE," Dennis said, "how about we latch onto a couple of skirts and head up to Waterman this afternoon ... take the Lincoln, put the top down."

"Yeah ... what'll we do there?"

"Giles told me once there's a hip lodge he and Lacey ran across on their way to Big Bear. Says a lotta young folks hangin' out and if we get lucky, there's rooms to rent."

"Humm." Wayne pondered, rubbed his chin. "Sounds bitchin', maybe I'll ask Mary ... have had a hankering to ask her out. Yeah, I'll ask Mary."

"I'll give Shelley a call ... leave about two?"

"WITH YOU?" Mary said, her expression puzzled, a haughty tone in her voice.

"Yeah, with me. Something wrong with that?"

"Sorry, Wayne. You're not my type. Besides, Paul and I are going out tonight."

"Paul ... so, maybe I get in line?"

"I'll let you know when it's worth your time."

"SHIT," DENNIS SAID, "can't find Shelley either. What the hell, you wanna beer?"

"Yeah ... long way to go on an empty stomach."

Dennis filled two mugs from the system and they sat.

"Beer's good," Wayne said. "How you and Shelley gettin' along? She's kinda cute but kinda young."

"She's not so young; just looks that way. She's twenty-six."

"You'd never know it ...uh, from appearances and talk."

"Yeah, I get tired of that sometimes, her Valley-hip and dress. But there's those other things, you know. She can get serious ... I'm not too fond of that either, but there's the other things." He looked up and grinned. "I tell her it's hard to plan ahead these days. You don't wanna invest too much on the come, better ta spend it now. She wants to get married and I'm sayin' why? I mean, who fucking knows what comes tomorrow. I mean, it's awesome, the news. Who knows what lurks in the head of Khrushchev?"

"You ready for another?" Wayne said.

"Sure. Good idea, this system—only good thing ol' Dobbs has done."

"He's a bit of a rowdy ... hot tempered, that guy."

"Impressionable, I'd say—and a hard time leavin' adolescence. I'm okay with Dalton, just hope he makes it to adulthood before he kills himself ... or somebody else. So, what's goin' on with Vicky? Every time I see her, a different coif."

"Yeah, fascinating. She works with a stylist, a coiffeur, they call 'em. There's contests and prizes for original, best done, and ... they got categories and stuff. She's goin' to Vegas next week. I'm havin' another ... you?"

"Yeah, nuthin' like an ice-cold Mic."

There was a pause as both seem to ponder what might come next. Wayne's foot slipped off the rung of the stool and he spilled some of the beer he was holding.

"Shit, sorry about that."

"No need."

They drank in silence.

"I'm likin' that job with Lockheed," Wayne said. "They need techs and pay well ... Teagarden's kinda set me up, knows the right people, but I hate the idea of workin' for a big corporation—just a number—and all that you make is known by the goddamn government ... had a lot of that in the Air Force."

"I getcha ... one of the reasons I like the job I've got, most of the time on my own."

"What's that? Don't think I've heard."

"Paving ... asphalt sales and paving ... lot of field work, lot of driving—gettin' around to the sites, see that things are progressing according to plan. I do the research and write the contracts. It's like my own business, and a lot of free time ... well, time I can sort of manipulate." He got up to draw another. "You ready?"

"Sure, fill me up. I gotta pee." He put his empty mug on the bar, missed a step up into the dining room but caught himself before falling. "Sheeze, not too familiar with this house."

They drank and talked for a couple of hours before Dennis caught a glance at his watch.

"Hey, man, we gotta get goin' if we're goin'. It's closin' in on ... eh, six o'clock and it's a least a couple to get there. I'll grab a couple quarts from the fridge."

THE ANGELES CREST HIGHWAY, a two-lane mountain road, was well paved and infrequently used. It took those traversing it from Pasadena up over Mount Waterman, a small ski resort, into an expanse of altitude and peaks, Arrowhead, and Big Bear beyond. A beautiful drive began with a curvy mountain route, then switchbacks through scrub brush and Manzanita, then higher and steeper, tall pines and fir—a challenge under any circumstances.

As he drove, Dennis felt conflicted as his eyes were drawn from the needs of the road to the beauty of the topography—the saw-tooth peaks dropping precipitously into colored canyon walls, the blue of their igneous age bearing streaks of rust glistening in the seepage. Here and there, a seed of scrub found footing in the vertical walls and surprisingly flourished while the fir and spruce danced to northerly breezes coming down between the peaks unhurried, but otherwise the mountains as quiet as a chapel. If God was anywhere, He must be here, and as Dennis was taken with the grandeur, the Lincoln slowed to a crawl.

"Step on it," Wayne yelled. "We don't wanna be late; all the good babes will be taken or gone." Dennis came out of it and pressed on the pedal. The tires on the powerful and heavy Lincoln squealed as they shot through the turns.

"I'm pushin' this chariot now," Dennis yelled back, "about as fast as I care ta go." And the tires spoke louder as they wove back and across the center line, straightening the snaky road where Dennis could see through the turns. As they moved higher, in and out of the mountain's shadow, Wayne got an occasional glimpse of the chasms on his side of the car.

"Holy shit, there ain't nothing down there but space."

"Grab me another brew," Dennis yelled through the wind.

"We're out," Wayne responded after reaching back into the cooler.

"Shit," Dennis said. "It be pure thirst that's drivin' this wagon now—yahoo Waterman." The tires screamed as he corrected through a curve he wasn't watching. "Whoops, don't wanna end up in a ravine."

As they sped along, top down, radio blaring, they relished what a day it was and the night more promising. Through a long curve coming up, Dennis pushed hard on the accelerator, his mind on their destination and its probable offerings.

"Holy fucking shit!" Dennis yelled. In front of them came a car in their lane careening and closing at about their speed.

Avoiding a certain head-on, Dennis steered quickly into the oncoming lane, edging the Lincoln in close to the mountain.

Metal hit metal and they heard a scrunch. Wayne dove toward the driver's side as the Lincoln was jarred, pushing its driver's-side wheels into a drainage ditch at the bottom of a sheer rock wall. And then, from the rear they heard a long screech of tires and in seconds, another series of colliding forces, lower pitched. Then nothing.

Dennis slowed the Lincoln to a crawl, pulled back into their lane and stopped, his hands and arms trembling.

"The bastard sideswiped us," Wayne blurted out, "on my fucking side. And he just drove on ... that was close."

"Ya th-think we should we go back?" Dennis croaked, after a minute of paralysis. "See what happened back there ... if anyone needs help?

"What the fuck for? He's gone, and he's not gonna stop ... all over the fuckin' road. Dammit, I need a drink. We coulda been head-on with that asshole and down in the gorge ... eh, good thinkin' on your part—movin' into the oncoming lane against the mountain."

"Wh-what about him?" Dennis said. "Maybe he went off. Maybe that last crunch was him hittin' the bottom. M-m-maybe he needs help."

"F-Fuck him," Wayne said, his voice now quavering, his body shaking. "What could we do? He was on our side. Damn, that was close ... anyway, the road's too narrow to turn around. Let's get moving before someone comes up on our back. Shit, Dennis ... we're just sittin' here."

They moved along slowly now, and around the next big bend, a sign appeared— "Waterman Lift." "Dennis steered the Lincoln into a lot and turned off the engine.

"Where's the lodge?" Wayne said. "Don't see a lodge."

Dennis was surveying the damage—entire passenger side from front fender to tail light lens scraped and dented. Wayne got out, the door obstructed but with an extra shove and a clunk, opened up.

"Coulda been worse," he said.

"Not your car; looks bad enough to me." Dennis said, recovering some from the shakes.

"So, where's the lodge?" Wayne said again. "I see a ski lift and a shack, no lonely women, no bar, no big fireplace, no band. You sure we're on the right road"

"It's what I heard."

"Someone has made a big damn mistake ... and it might be funny if two of 'em weren't us. And shit, we're out of beer."

"I keep thinking about that other car. They might need help ... they might need—"

"There's nothing we can do about what's already done. Whoever it was is on his way down the mountain, and if he didn't drive off it, he be long gone." Wayne put his hand on Dennis's shoulder. "C'mon, man, calm down; let's go back. That guy's either dead or he's having a drink in Pasadena. Either way, we can't affect it."

Dennis thought about the "guy"—could of been a woman, a family—he saw him or them at the bottom of the ravine—bloody and screaming for help. He thought about his Lincoln and its busted-up side, front fender to back. He noted their reward—a ski lift and shack. There were some things even a beer won't help.

**

"SEñOR GILES, you go fishing with me?

Giles lolled in the morning sun in a hammock, one hand on a light rope tied to a small tree so that occasionally he could give it a tug and keep himself swinging, the other hand resting behind his head. He doodled in his mind's sketchpad, sometimes recallable notes.

"And a buenos dias to you, Juan. You speak pretty good English."

"Si, mi Madre, she teach me. She say some day we live in Texas and need to speak the English of Estados Unidos."

"Yeah." He chuckled. "Like someday hablo Español y vivo en México."

"You want to live in Mexico?"

"Maybe. I like it here ... quién sabe, Juan."

"I don't know that is your thinking. You stay, and we go to Texas. So, Señor Giles ... you want to go fishing now?"

"Yes sir, Mister Juan." He chuckled. "Be glad to go fishing with you. Where do we go?"

"There is a small river, not far, that flows down from the hills. You see, I have you a pole and the ... the ..."

"Tackle?"

"Si, tackle, Señor Giles." Juan held out two long bamboo poles wrapped with string. "We tie on the hooks later." He held out a bag. "Bobbers too. We will dig worms by the river." He held up a garden trowel.

IN THE DAPPLING SUN through breezy leaves, they sat on a large, exposed root of an old sycamore, their bare feet planted in the mud of the shore. They watched their bobbers bobble in the eddy that Juan chose for their most likely success. The light breeze cooled the sun on their backs as squirrels scampered in the branches above. A frog leaped after a water spider. A dragon fly buzzed over the eddy. Crows, high in the tree, cawed out their gossip to one another.

"What will you do when you grow up?" Giles asked.

"Quién sabe?" Juan said, "I don't know ... and you, Señor Giles ... what will you do when you leave?"

Giles thought about that. "Am I leaving, Juan?"

"Me Madre says. She says someday you will. She cries when she says it."

Was he leaving? Why would he do that? He'd not taken the time to ask the question; in fact, it had never occurred to him, and it wasn't that he had someplace to go, someplace waiting. How long had he been here? He didn't know. Weeks he guessed, but likely more. It seemed he had been nowhere else.

"You tell her I am not leaving ... not soon ... hear?" He reached over and ruffled Juan's hair. "I am happy here, amigo."

For the first time, Giles thought about it. He glanced at Juan playing his line—a bright, curious boy who made no assumptions. And Maria ... vivacious, sexy and brimming with good humor. In fact, there wasn't a negative thought at the cantina. He hadn't heard an argument, not even a disagreement—everyone content with their lot. Moreover, there seemed an aura of happiness and he too felt the easiness and joy. It was becoming a part of him. Why would he leave?

He took in the trees—the pines up the slope and the occasional oak, felt the quiet of the stream, the hills beyond. The sun warmed his back as the breeze cooled his face, and he listened to the water burble as it flowed around the eddy and across the stones downstream. There was nothing looming here—no threat from across the ocean, no political rankling or concern for the outcome, no need for commitment or hopeful thoughts, and no recollections of a jumbled yesterday. Everything was right, and right was now, and now was fine with him. He looked down at his feet in the mud of the bank and smiled.

"Juan, you tell her not soon, I'm not leaving soon ... and look, your bobber going under." Yes, he would stay for a while, but would need to do something. He would write—a low-risk investment. A pad, he thought, and a pencil ... and he already had the ideas.

He recalled from his lit classes, the 20s expatriates who left for places in Europe to write and paint, and had concluded back then their departures weren't about going but more about leaving—abandoning societal obligations insinuated into lives over time, the shedding of tradition and expectations that began when getting on the boat, like stripping off your dirty and worn work clothes before a hot shower.

It was all about freeing their minds, he thought, to better encounter their muse. Paris? Why not Juarez—God knows, he didn't have much to shed. He smiled as Juan lifted a struggling bass from the eddy.

"Nice work, Juan," he said. "Now I'll have to land one," and he raised his line from the surface to see a bare hook.

As the sun approached overhead, they packed up and went back, three nice-sized bass in Juan's sack, heading straight for Maria's pan.

"You do better, Señor Giles, when you pay more attention. I will teach if you want to learn."

Giles smiled. Next time he would bring a notebook.

**

"Morning Paul," Mary spoke softly, standing in the kitchen entry yawning, her arms outstretched. "How're you this morning?"

Paul glanced up in time to see her fill out her night shirt, smiled and lifted his coffee in a toast, "Fine, I'm just fine. Coffee?"

She sat next to him, early and no one else around. He poured.

"I had a wonderful time at the Saddle the other night." She put her hand on his arm.

"Me too."

"So, I'm wondering, would you like to catch some breakfast with me this morning ... maybe to Bob's? They do a great Benedict."

"Me too"

"I can be ready at ten," she said.

"Me too, and we'll take the kids."

Wayne rushed in the front door, yelling, "Dennis, where's Dennis, is he here?"

"He's still sleeping," Paul said, "out on the sun porch."

"Gotta wake—" he took note of the two of them looking chummy, then turned quickly toward the porch, patting a rolled newspaper against his thigh.

"Dennis, wake up. I got news ... good news"

Bleary-eyed, Dennis turned his buried head from the pillow. "What time— What the hell you doing here this ... goin' back to sleep; shut the door on your way out."

"Wake up, buddy, you gotta read this." He opened Tuesday's *Pasadena Gazette* to the third page. "Here, right here ... read this!"

Dennis raised on his elbow and rubbed his eyes. "Whatta you want?"

"Read! It's an article about us." He pushed the newspaper at Dennis and pointed out the headline and Dennis read.

Another Accident on Angeles Crest. A fifty-six-year-old man from Pasadena was pulled from a wreckage in a ravine just south of Waterman Ski Saturday about 8 o'clock pm.

He was found by tourists, Frank Bealey and his wife, Betty, from Toledo, Ohio, who made the call from Edy's Quick Shop in Pasadena. "We couldn't tell if there was anyone in the car," Mr. Bealey reported, "It was way too steep to go down, but we could see the car alright, hung up on a tree about thirty yards down the embankment. It looked pretty beat up and we knew it was recent because steam was still coming off from the radiator. Lucky thing that tree was there, must've been over a thousand feet to the bottom. Good thing we came along too, Betts and me."

The victim (name not disclosed) was pulled from the wreckage by Officer Joe Baderman of the Pasadena Fire and Emergency Crew. He was taken to Los Angeles General where he's reported to be in stable condition with a broken collarbone, multiple leg fractures and numerous abrasions and contusions. His blood alcohol level is unknown, but Officer Baderman said he suspects alcohol was involved. Fragments of red glass on the road led police to suspect there might have been another vehicle involved. "But," said Sergeant Wills of the Pasadena Police, "It just as likely he passed out and drove off by himself. It's a dangerous road and he appeared to be coming around a curve pretty fast. We need guard rails up there on those curves."

The car, a 1946 Ford Coupe ... no further investigation... man recovering may be cited ....

As DENNIS' EYES began to close down, Wayne shook him and blurted out "Don't you see what this means? We're off the hook. The guy's okay and no further investigation ... well, we need to get that taillight fixed pronto and the fender rolled out."

"Yeah, yeah, it's great," Dennis mumbled as he laid back down. "I'll take it to a garage when I get up. Now get outta here and let me sleep."

"No! No, you won't take it to a garage. We'll fix it ourselves, wrap this thing up. Now get your ass up, and lets buy a tail-light lens."

Dennis, again on his elbow, eyes open, "You know, now that I'm thinking ... it wasn't our fault at all ... if the guy was drunk." He swung his legs out over the bed and sat up. "Probably not at all."

"Yeah," Wayne said, "probably not at all. I was feeling a little edgy too, once I sobered up ... the screeching and crash and all ... couldn't get to sleep that night for thinking about it, seeing ... well, imagining that car goin' over, but now ... now I'm feeling a lot better, a hell-uv-a lot better ... maybe we get a bottle."

**

"I QUIT MY JOB," Dennis said. "Well ... maybe I was fired."

"You've been bitchin' about that place for months," Dalton said. "I could write a fuckin' book."

"You'd have to make it up because I'm not gonna tell you about it. But I will say this: I got royally screwed ... and you know what, I liked that job and the people I encountered—construction types and businesspeople. It's kind of funny, you know ... the way it happened." He plopped down in the wingback in the corner of the den.

"I'm havin' a beer; you want one?" Dalton said. "I'm feeling kinda of social. It don't happen often, so why don't you spill your sad fucking story. I'll be like a shrink." He laughed. "Think about it. They say it's good, confessin' ... liftin' the weight, gettin' it off your chest. The Catholics do it regular and it's free to them ... like here, it could be free to you." He laughed. "I thought about being a Catholic once, saw the advantages, but then I thought who the fuck needs it? I ain't goin' up there anyway."

"You do go on when you're feeling social."

"Sure, but like I said, you spill the beans, I'll shut my trap."

"Um, okay ... might be good for me to review a little ... some of the high points, and yeah, I'll have a glass if you ever get 'round to pouring.

"Well, here's the thing. I never met the guy that owns the place—Mr. Sparks. He's an old guy I'd only heard about ... never came in. It's a small company—only about ... maybe twenty employees and only three of us actively doing the design and contracting work ... sometimes four, but mostly three. A bunch in the yard makin' the stuff—asphalt concrete—and more doing the grading and paving.

"Anyway, when I went in this morning, Besler, my boss, says, 'the old man wants to see you.' So, I knock and go in. Now, this guy is old. He's thin, brittle, and I'm reminded of a communion wafer, you know."

"How the fuck would you know about communion wafers? And, don't make this into literature, Dennis, the fucking lease is over in a few months Here's your beer."

"I'll summarize. First thing, he wanted to know is why I was late. He's sittin' there smug, chewin' on a stogie and sippin' a coffee. So, I explained that often I stopped at the sites I have going when on my way in ... saves time and mileage. He doesn't respond right away, relights his cigar. Then he says that Besler had told him that on some Mondays he doesn't see me at all, and that yesterday was one of them."

"Ha! Didn't you explain your deal with them called for three-day weekends?"

"I told him that I had earned more for the company than any of the others in my end of the business, yet not a dime of bonus at Christmas. And I said that was disheartening, that I worked just as hard, pulled in more profit than Jimmy who picked up a bonus and a turkey."

"So ..." Dalton said, showing interest.

"He said I'm a decent performer, but I have to be with them a while, that they're paying me for five days a week, not four, that I needed to demonstrate an interest in the company—the little family there, and then he gave me the evil eye and sipped from his coffee.

"'Decent,' he said ... my work was decent. I had this one job, Burk's Haul-away—a big storage lot with a drainage challenge— that brought the old fuck thirty-five thou ... cream, right off the top. I told him that, the wizen old fucker, and then I'm getting pissed. I stood up. 'Should I quit?' I said. 'I gotta a good mind ....' I turned to leave his office, thinking he'd cave— give me the bonus. 'Wait ... wait just a minute there. You have some equipment of mine. Quit if you like but leave that transit and whatever of ours you have in your possession.'"

"And then, hot shit, what happened then?"

"Well, I just sortta huffed out of his office, went out to the car, got the transit and rod outta the back, and leaned it up against the building. Ol' Besler came running out all upset

... never seen him run before—big pear-shaped guy, sits on his ass all day. He said to forget the ruckus, whatever the old man said, that he needed me at my desk. There were jobs I needed to address. I s'pose I could've turned, kinda wish I had, but I'd made such a scene seems I had to go through with it, so I just said, 'No thanks,' and got in the car and left. Kept seeing that pompous old fart, never came in except that one morning, sittin' in his office, sippin' coffee and suckin' a cigar."

"He does own the place."

"Yeah, I s'pose you got a point. I'll find something. Shelley's talkin' serious now—be pretty disappointed with this, my losing my job. Got plans, she says, big plans that I'll like." He finished the beer he'd been holding. "I gotta find something."

"There's a help-wanted sign at that new coffee shop. You got an apron?"

**

"Señor Giles ... Señor Giles, a letter for you," shouted Juan, running full speed back to the hammock, waving an envelope. "It has come this minute. Read it Señor Giles, read it!"

Giles opened and read out loud.

> *Dear Mr. Anderson,*
>
> *We are happy to enclose a check for $100 in payment for the exclusive publishing rights to your short fiction, "Living in a Juarez Cantina." Our editors here enjoyed your story and are delighted with the tone and the style of your writing. Your piece will appear in our June issue. Please feel invited to send*

*us more of your witty and clever composi-
tion.*

*Note: in redeeming this check, you
agree with the Publication Provisions and
Conditions attached.*

Respectfully,

H. H.

Owner and Managing Editor

"BUENO! THIS IS GOOD ... muy buena... right, Señor
Giles?"

"Si, Juan, it is good. It is money ... dinero, and I can pay
for my beans and bed."

"Now you stay longer, and we do more fishing, and you
catch the big one ... and mi Madre, she will like." Juan took
Giles' hand. "Let's go to the cantina ... *esta es una buena no-
ticia para todos.*" And he pulled Giles from the hammock and
feeling proud, maybe somewhat older, led Giles up the path
to the back door.

"*Eso es maravilloso,*" Maria exclaimed. "We must have
a toast." And with a flourish, she brought cold beers from the
ice tub for everyone and told them the the news—that Giles
was a writer now, and that his story about the cantina would
be published, and that maybe they all would be famous someday—and then she held up her beer and exclaimed, "*Toma-
mos a nuestro amigo, él puede estar con nosotros durante
mucho tiempo y todos estar orgullosos de su trabajo.*"

They all drank and applauded.

"What does that mean?" Giles said.

"It mean we are glad for you, that you are a friend, and that you may stay a long time," and there were nods around with approving looks, as she pulled him across the bar and brushed his lips with her kiss. "And you may stay with us very long time if you wish ... si lo desea," and her eyes filled with pleasure.

**

COLE POKED HIS HEAD IN from the lanai where he was drying off after a swim while taking a break from a poker game in the den. Some Saturdays were laid back and lazy, with nothing much planned. A few beers, some leftovers, the pool operational—no immediate demands. "Hey Dennis, there're some Mexicans out here on the street, want to know if you want your car fixed."

"Send 'em in; I can't leave this hand. I'm ahead, and it's a rare and exciting feeling I don't want to break."

A little man with a brown, wrinkled face and deep, twinkling eyes stepped in. He wore a tattered plaid shirt and held a cigarette in a hand that was blackened with old grease.

"Señor, is that your car, the big Lincoln out on the street? She is almost beautiful—such a fine leather inside and good paint. But señor, she has a dent I can fix. Big dent, you want me to fix? My sister, she is outside with her husband, a very good man with the dents."

"Aces full," Dennis said, and pulled in a pot that added to his needed and substantial winnings. "Sure, mi amigo, you 'fix'—how much?"

"Umm, only a little."

"Don't go for that shit," Dalton said.

"How much?" Dennis said.

"Maybe only one-hundred dollars." The man's smile took up most of his weathered face.

"That's fucking outrageous," Dalton said. "I'll do it for that."

"Twenty-five," Dennis said.

The little man laughed and shook his head. "Oh, señor, we cannot do it for so little ... maybe we do it for fifty. We have children to feed."

"Thirty-five."

"You drive a hard bargain, señor." and behind him came up a small smiling woman missing teeth, an infant in her arms. Behind her were two other niños and a large man with a bag of tools.

"If you can spare forty, we will do a good job. You will not know the big dent was there."

"Yeah?" Dennis shuffled the cards. "... a very good job, eh? Well shit, okay."

"You give the money now, and we won't bother you again." The little man assumed a slight bow and held out his hand.

"Deal the cards," Paul said, "or go fix your car, one or the other. We're havin' a poker game here."

"Okay, forty." Dennis picked a couple of twenties from of his substantial pile of cash and slapped them into the weathered hand. "Now, I'll be out to check ... that includes paint, right ... paint's included?"

"Si señor. We do the paint. You will like it." And the body repair entourage left the den with a chorus of "gracias."

"You're fuckin' crazy," Dalton said. "Those people can't even mix Bondo. They're Mexicans, ya know ... they pick lettuce."

The hammering began with chattering heard between blows.

"They can't make it any worse than it is," Paul said, "and it seemed they could use the money."

"Yeah, Dalton," Dennis said, eyeing the cash in front of him. "So maybe it's charity ... we all gotta eat."

Wayne stepped in from the front door, drew a beer and sat down. "See ya got a hand-picked team of skilled body men out there working on your car." He laughed, his hand on Dennis' shoulder. "Nothing like putting experts to work on a problem. Mind if I sit in?"

**

"SO WHY ARE WE HERE? I hate these fucking meetings. Where the hell is Paul?" Dalton growled, clenching his hands into fists and working his biceps—one arm pitted against the other, veins popping. "He called the damn meeting."

"Yeah, and where's Mary?" Dennis offered. "Bet the two are playing footsy somewhere and forgot the time. I gotta leave soon, got the evening shift at Romano's and he don't like us being late."

"Yeah, how's that going?" Nick said, pulling his nose out of *Motor Trend* and taking a sip of a Coke. "I hear you're doing okay there, making the big bucks." He grinned.

"Tips help out," Dennis said, "and yeah, I like it there okay—brewing coffee and learning the exotics. The folks that come in are intellectuals; they talk instead of fight."

"Uh huh," Nick said. "And that's why you'll never see Dalton darkening the door."

"Sorry we're late." Paul with Mary coming in the front door, hand in hand. "Detained a bit."

"So why are we here?" Dalton, breathing heavily, admiring his bulging arms.

"It's the rent," Paul said. "We're going to be short this month. It's due in a couple of weeks and yesterday a card from Giles postmarked Juarez/El Paso saying he wasn't coming back, and we'd need to find another source for his share."

An a cappella of groans filled the air.

"Here's what he says," and he passed the card around.

> *Dear Paul,*
> *Quest for answers finds only questions and I'll not be returning soon. Please box up what I left and rent to another. Hope everyone is well.*
> *Your friend,*
> *Giles*

"His quest!" Dalton said. "His fucking 'quest' … in Mexico? There ain't nuthin' down there to find, Billaba already looked."

"Balboa," Dennis said.

"That fuckin' guy's been a pain since he landed here and even now that he's gone it don't stop."

"Don't hold back, Dalton," Nick said. "Tell us how you feel … not that we don't already know in spades."

"So anyway." Paul nodded toward Dalton. "If you're finished, D, we have three possibilities. One, we can pack quickly and bail, forfeit our deposit and leave no forwarding addresses. Two, we can each pitch in the difference, about fifty dollars apiece including the utilities, staples, and beer ... and three, we can find another renter to take Giles' place." He waited.

They glanced at one another, but no one offered their choice of the three, or a plan four.

"I told you before, goddammit," Dalton cutting through the silence with an axe. "I ain't payin' no more. I've had enough of his shit. He's on the fucking lease ... tell Blunt to go after him, send out the posse or those head-huntin' types. It ain't our fuckin' problem."

"Bounty hunters," Dennis said.

"Whatever you call 'em," Dalton scowled.

"That's not the answer," Nick said. "I'll put in another fifty, if that's what's called for ... mostly because I don't like the other alternatives. Don't want a stranger hangin' around and don't like the idea of skipping out on a promise ... never mind the legal shit; we signed for a year."

"I can't do that," said Dennis. "I just don't have the means right now. Why don't we ask Cole if he want's in, or maybe Wayne?"

"Yeah," added Dalton. "They both live here most a the time anyway—shit, maybe half from each of 'em, maybe more."

**

"I APPRECIATE THE OFFER," Cole said, "but Paul, I gotta nice studio over the pizza joint, ya know—cost me fifty dollars a month with utilities. Aside from an old dentist and two lawyers with offices down the hall, I'm the only one there. I have my own special parking spot, a wafting Italian fragrance that comes in on pop tunes from a jukebox, a 20-percent discount and near instant delivery of the best in the Valley. And that's not to mention Sophia, who does the deliveries. She's a cutie and is not at all averse to dallying a while on my Murphy. Now, my friend, why would I trade that opulent style for a two-hundred-dollar bunk here with Dalton?"

"Humm ..." Paul chuckled. "Would you like a room-mate? Okay, I'm taking you off the list."

"Have you talked with Wayne? You know his address is Pasadena ... and with his folks. Seems to me that's a big dis-advantage for him. He works here in the Valley, spends most of his other life here as well ... and he sure as hell can't bed any sweeties in a room that shares a wall with his mother. Seems to me he's your best bet."

"Yeah. I was planning to talk with him, soon as you re-fused."

"Not a refusal, just the best of my current options—weighin' the puts against the takes."

"WAYNE, BUDDY," Paul began. "I've got an offer you can-not refuse, save you traveling time and open new horizons. I can give you a freedom you have never experienced and along with that, cheap beer. You'll be help—"

"Yeah, I'm in." Wayne put up his hand. "Dennis has been telling me, and I got the whole story—Giles and his searchin'. I been thinking of approaching you anyway. Here, I gotta check in my wallet ... two hundred, that right?"

"Wow, that's right. Two hundred takes care of rent and utilities, pantry, and beer. Dalton handles the beer. I do the kitchen, the basics—milk and cereal, some canned chili and spaghetti for the rough times. If you buy something special that you want exclusive, put your name on it."

"I've got some shit in my car; where do I park it?"

"You'll take the other pad in the sunroom ... there with Dennis, and welcome aboard."

"Thanks. It's prob'ly time I was weaned. Be in with the rest on Saturday."

Twenty-One
Serious Losses

"COME IN LACEY and sit. Coffee? Fresh service, Rosa just brought it around."

"And those tasty croissants."

"Help yourself there and top me off if you will."

"Here you go boss ... so, you want a status?"

"No, Tony keeps me up to date. We meet every morning ... early, and it seems we are moving along at this point—something we all are delighted to hear, by the way. I have a few problems but that's normal. What I wanted to know is how you are doing. Tony says well, but he's talking performance; I thought it nice if you and I could chat on a personal level—don't seem to see much of you now ... with Mr. Giotto there. Is that working out okay with you?"

"I'm learning a lot and he's very forthcoming ... well, a bit of a perfectionist," she sipped at her coffee, "but a lot of experience there and I love picking it up."

"He's been around the industry most of his life, started off as a grip a long time ago." He smiled contentedly as he reflected on old times. "It was Tony's father that brought me into the business, taught me the ropes and politics."

"He's said as much that you were close to his father."

"So how are you doing personally—I ask as a friend."

"I'm fine Izzy—back to normal."

"We are friends, aren't we Lacey. I think of us as being rather close ... family, you know. Do you mind my saying that?

"Of course not. Why the concern?"

"I have something I'd like to ask you. It's of a personal nature."

"Sure ... what is it?"

"It's Anna."

"Anna?"

"Yes. Anna is very occupied with the filming and ... well, she spends a lot of time at the studio. And there's location and she's gone for days. The short of it is I see little of her ... and frankly hear even less. It's very much like she doesn't live here now."

"She is the star. Isn't that expected?"

"Yes ... to some degree. Look, I'll be frank. I've talked with Ethan. We go back ... like brothers, and he tells me she's not always where she tells me she is. It's not all that obvious, but I can read between his lines ... I mean, she'll call and say she's held over to confer with Ethan and he'll be sitting where you are. Well, Christ ... I hate this, but I'm worried I'm losing her. There, dammit, it's out."

"Izsak ...."

"You're a woman ... and a friend, and I'm wondering if you have any insight here. Can you tell me to shut it down, that everything is okay, that I should stop with my schoolboy

274

suspicions?" He choked out a chuckle. "She's been a flirt all her life ... part of her charm, you know, and I accept that. But look at me. I'm getting old ... and stuck in the damned chair, and no use to ...." He began to sob. He tried to muffle it, but no use. Tears ran down his face.

"Izsak ..." She got up and came to him, put her arm around his shoulders and kissed him on the forehead.

"You are a dear man," she said. "You are thoughtful and kind ... and patient above all, and you are family. I don't see Anna, except on the set occasionally, but she loves you. And I'll say this ... if anything, she's honest and speaks her mind. If she was having an affair, she would tell you, lay it out in plain view ... and even if that, it would not affect her feelings for you."

He wiped his face with a handkerchief. "Yes, I suppose you're right. She's had them before, little flings, and yes, she's always been honest ... or obvious. I think that's what worries me this time. It seems secretive and ... and well, this time seems different."

"I lead a private life, Izsak, not by choice so much as circumstance. You know that. It's a lonely life ... one I would easily trade for a little excitement—dancing and dining and frankly, sex. It would be fun ... sporting, but it wouldn't change an iota of how I feel about life, my friends, my family— those I deeply love. Women too need a laugh now and then, need to be tickled. They need to chuckle at an off-color joke, swear at the gardener. We aren't all apron strings and welcome home. So, think about Anna, her steadfast resolve to love and cherish, to be your wife, and think about giving her a break ... if that's what this is about.

"You don't really know that 'this time is different'. You only suspect ... and you sit in this library all day and your imagination, bountiful as it is, runs down dark alleys, finds only the worst ... and it's likely all bullshit ... just bullshit.

"Izzy, my friend ... my collaborator, mentor, and head of my table, please compose yourself ... wait for the reality if it comes. Things are as they are, you know, not as you imagine them to be." She took a sip of her cold coffee.

"But," he mumbled, "but I don't know what I would do without her—this career of hers. I want her to succeed on the one hand and on the other ... well, that would be the end of me." His eyes turned gray and began to leak. He shuddered.

"Oh, for Christ's sake, Izsak Padgett, get a grip." She turned to him. "Listen to the sermons you've offered me. Your life is robust. You are a talented man with endless challenge and skills to match. You want for nothing." She looked around. "You have it all." She scooted around in front of him and caught his eyes. "Now how about a drink of that prime single malt that most of us cannot afford."

He looked up with the beginning of a smile and wiped his eyes. "Let's do have a scotch."

**

"What if I don't want Wayne livin' here?" Dalton's discontent with what he perceived to be a growing weakness in influence was fueled by an afternoon alone with the keg.

"Nobody said anything," Paul said, home early from his shift and anticipating some relief from his week at the plant. "You seen the afternoon paper?"

"I'm saying it now," Dalton scowled, beginning to pace back and forth. "Maybe I don't want him livin' here."

"Too late, D. I asked and he's movin' in the rest of his stuff this weekend. You were the one most vocal about not paying the extra money."

"What if I don't want him here?"

"You got something against Wayne?"

"It ain't about Wayne, it's the fuckin' decision ... and whata ya always calling me 'D' for? My name's Dalton."

"You might have said something earlier. Where's the paper? You seen it?"

"Why do I hafta say something earlier? You know my names Dalton ... known it for years." He went down into the den and drew himself another beer, drank it while he stood at the bar and refilled. Returning to the living room, he stumbled on the last step and sloshed beer on the carpet.

"You should clean that up before it soaks in and leaves a smell."

"Fuck it. Not my carpet." He leaned against the door jamb and in a few minutes of silence, glared at Paul and sipped at his beer.

"Okay ... out with it. What's behind this attitude of yours? You been here all afternoon ... what, just drinking and stewing?"

"I'll tell you what's behind it—you! You and your bossy fucking ways. We shoulda voted on Wayne. We shoulda voted on a lot of things you decide for us. You think yer fuckin' king ... king prick, I'd say, running the goddamn show. We shoulda voted." Dalton was back in the living room, pacing.

"You could've said—"

"I coulda said, I coulda said ... you got any other wisdom for me? You gonna teach me more ... how to behave? You and your fuckin' uni universh college da-gree." Dalton's face reddened and the veins in his neck began to bulge, his empty hand doubling and redoubling into a fist. "You jus' piss me off, Smythe—you and your 'D' and your superior ways." He came closer to where Paul was sitting, beads of sweat on his brow, his glare intensifying.

"Hold on now." Paul got up from his chair. "There's no need for this, D. You gotta beef, okay, we'll have it out in a meeting ... have a vote."

"Don't call me 'D'!" Dalton's voice rose in amplitude. "You're really pissing me off with that 'D' shit. You been telling me what to do for too long, an' I been takin' it ... eatin' your shit since we met, and now I'm fucking tired of it." He gave Paul a push. "You hear ... I'm tired of it."

"Okay! Okay. Calm down, for Christ's sake. Get ahold of yourself."

"You and your mooch of a friend ... your faternilly brother, what a batch of shit," he spat out. "He's the one should be paying the toll, not me and not the others. Nobody made you boss." He reached up to push again and Paul backed out of the way.

"C'mon, knock it off and calm down. Giles isn't here. He can't pay. It wouldn't make sense. Even you must see, it just doesn't work that way."

"You mean it doesn't work your way ... an' you're the only one with any sense." He finished off his beer and put the mug down. "I been doin' it your way ever since we met, and I'm up to my eyeballs with you ... you fucking shit. An' then you took my girl, whisperin' your uppity smartness in her ear. Damn you." He took a swing ... landed a solid punch on Paul's ear and neck. It knocked him back into the chair.

"Jesus, Dalton." Paul raised his arm in defense. "What the hell are you doing?"

"Get up, goddamn you, an' fight ... you lily-livered shit," and he punched Paul, one-two in the face. "Git up ... see where your brains can take you now." He pulled Paul up from the chair and hit him square in the nose—blood splattered. "I been waitin' for this ...." His breathing heavy, adrenaline flowing, his muscles bulging. Dalton snorted and growled. He had lost control.

Paul swung once and connected. Dalton recovered, moved in, and hit him again and again as Paul lifted his arms and tried to defend. "Dalton, stop. For Christ's sake ...."

"Yer not even from my state ... fuckin' foreigner—you and your freak-fuckin' friend and now we're gonna see ... gonna see a lot of shit." Dalton swinging wild and carelessly, Paul trying to get out of his way but more than enough hit the mark, and when Paul fell to the floor, Dalton pounced on top of him, beating him with his fists, slobbering, crying. "...good as you ... make as much ... took my girl ... damn you, damn you."

Paul turned his head back and forth, trying to avoid Dalton's fists—blood flowing from his nose, then his mouth, sweat burning his eyes—in a blind maneuver kicked Dalton in the groin and pushed him off.

Dalton, his face screwed up in pain, grabbed a fireplace poker, and as Paul tried to get up, brought it down on his head—a glancing blow that ripped through Paul's ear and stopped short at his shoulder.

Paul lay quiet on the living room floor.

Dalton stopped, slumped, arms hanging loose and heavy. He saw the poker in his hand and dropped it.

"Paul! Goddammit, Paul, get up, you fucker."

Nothing.

Dalton stood over him, looking down, sobbing, "You son-of-a-bitch, get up ... Paul, dammit get up ...."

He reached down to pull him, but Paul didn't move, blood oozing from his face and the wound in his head.

**

NICK ARRIVED HOME FROM THE SIGNAL STATION, Dennis immediately behind him. They'd heard the sirens as they approached. There were police and a fire truck down at the corner behind the house. An ambulance was leaving, red lights flashing as it sped off. A man who seemed somehow familiar was with Paul, sponging his head with a wet towel and pressuring the wound.

"You guys got bandages? We need something to stop the bleeding. Son-of-a-bitch. Get some bandages and call a doctor. You know a doctor?"

"No, we don't know a doctor. Should we call an ambulance?" Nick said. "What the hell's happened here? Who are you?"

"I'm Mackey, George Mackey ... live in the house behind you. What a mess. Your housemate here is not in the best shape, needs a doctor now. And the other guy … he might be dead."

"Dead? What!? What the hell's going on?" Nick could hardly believe his eyes. "Paul, what happened?"

"It's Dalton … we got—" Paul, sitting up on the floor, groaned, an awful sound, then shut his eyes and drooped into unconsciousness.

"Good God," Dennis said, "we don't know a doctor. What'll we—"

"I do," Mackey said, "a friend … office close by. You got a phone? I'll call my wife and she'll get ahold of him." Nick took over the pressuring and Dennis paced while Mackey called.

"We need some ice. Dennis, wrap some ice in a towel." Nick's voice in a pitch higher than usual.

Paul groaned again, put a hand to his head.

"And George," Nick continued, "give me a hand and let's get him up on the couch." Mackey and Nick lifted Paul. They waited for the phone to ring.

Paul drifted.

With pressure and ice, the bleeding subsided.

Paul muttered between groans, but nothing coherent.

"We have to keep him awake," Mackey said. "Keep him upright and talk to him."

"Dalton …."

As they propped him up, kept the ice pack in place with occasional dabbing and relief from the cold, they wondered in silence—stunned with the scene they were in and trying to imagine what had preceded it … and what was Paul mumbling? The phone rang and Mackey picked up.

"The doc should be here soon." Mackey said.

"What do you know about this?" Nick asked. "How did you happen to be here?"

"Yeah," said Dennis, "what the hell happened?"

"The other guy?" Nick said. "A burglar?

A knock on the door and a man with a black bag walked in. "George, what do we have here?"

"We have head injuries, a dangling ear, and a guy in pain ... maybe shock. He's been drifting in and out for about half an hour."

"Okay, You guys take a break, give me some room and I'll have a look ... see what's to be seen."

While the doctor examined and treated Paul, the three, Nick, Dennis, and Mackey, stepped into the den.

"Okay," Nick said, "thanks for being here. What do you know about this ... digging in?"

Mackey sat quiet for a minute, hands in his lap, fingers against fingers like a spider on a mirror—and then he began. "I was out on my rear deck working a script when I heard this argument from your house. It got pretty loud and then quiet. The next thing I heard was the roar of that motorcycle starting up and revving up again and again. I walked to the side yard there adjoining the street and out of the side gate comes one of your roommates on that Triumph of his ... screaming up the street full throttle. Must've been doing about 60 into the intersection there to the front of my house. Heard him shift into second and jump on it again just as a car was passing through. I guess he didn't see it because he didn't brake or turn to avoid it ... and without a helmet. Well, shit ... he smashed into the car broadside—a terrible sound of metal and glass as he was thrown into the car just about at the windows, and over the top and onto the street about thirty or so feet to the other side. Saw the whole damn thing. I know the guy in the passenger seat let out a yelp that could be heard around the neighborhood. Never in my life ....

"Well, I yelled at Josephine to make the calls and ran over to see if I could help. Your buddy was a mangled mess, legs twisted and broken ... head battered, clothes torn—he must've rolled and slid seventy feet after coming down. There wasn't much I could do ... used my shirt as a tourniquet on the worst lookin' leg, both of them bleeding. The young guys in car ... standing around, didn't seem hurt.

"They all came quickly—the cops, the fire department, an ambulance ... and then I came over here, see what the hell might've started the whole thing.

"You know the rest. I suppose they took your buddy to Valley Memorial—closest around. The car was damaged, door caved in, but nobody in the car was hurt—shaken up a bit, I imagine. The motorcycle's junk. Funny thing ... the car that he hit was four police cadets on their way to the academy. I know a couple of them."

The doctor came in.

"He'll be okay. Smacked around a bit, lost a part of his ear, and a possible concussion. He's bandaged for now, and I want him in my office tomorrow morning when I'll x-ray his shoulder—big bruise—might've fractured the clavicle. Keep him immobile and resting but awake for a few hours ... water, no food. If he dozes off in the meantime and you can't wake him, run him down to the ER and don't waste any time. Same if he becomes nauseous, but he'll likely be okay. That was a glancing blow to his head, mostly contusion and bruising ... and the ear, lost some of that. Good you called, though. Watch for bleeding. We'll know more when he comes in. I'll be in my office tonight until nine and in the morning till noon—best in the morning. Any questions?" He looked around, in turn catching the eyes of each. "Stay sober tonight and alert to his condition."

"Thanks, Ben, glad you were available," George said.

"You're certainly welcome ... and it's damned hard to turn down a plea from Josie. I overheard some of your talk in the den, by the way, and yes, Valley Memorial is where they'd have taken him. He'll either be in the O.R. or the morgue downstairs. Take care, you guys, and I'm guessing you might turn it down a notch in the future."

"I'm leaving too," Mackey said. "Hope our next encounter will be under better circumstances. If you need a witness, you know where I am."

"Thanks, George, you've been a good friend. Don't know what we—"

"Forget it." He waved his hand in a gesture of kinship, left through the den and out the side gate. They heard the gate latch click, then silence as they sat—Nick next to Paul, attentive to his condition, Dennis in the big chair, his eyes on Paul, his mind in a state of wonder.

"I'd like a little water," Paul said.

MARY DANCED IN THROUGH THE FRONT DOOR, thrilled with the end of her work week and the start of her time to relax, let down, maybe a party—her kids spending a few weeks with her grandmother.

"Hi all, TGIF? When do we—" She stopped short, dropped her purse and a sack of chips on the floor and rushed over to Paul, his head wrapped in gauze. "My God, what's happened? Paul, what happened to you? My God, Nick ..." She sat down next to Paul, put her arms around his shoulders, a light touch. "It was Dalton, right? He finally exploded. I knew it was coming ... well, I thought it might."

"We don't know, so don't jump. We really don't." Nick tried to bring her down. "We don't know and Paul's not sayin' ... not saying much at all. So ... Dalton's in the hospital and we need to go over and it's good that you're here."

Nick told her what Mackey had told them.

As she listened, tears flowed, dropped off her chin, her hands clutched and wringing.

"Dalton may be dead, certainly seriously injured, so if you keep an eye on Paul, Dennis and me, we'll go over to the hospital." He repeated the instructions the doctor had given them.

"For God's sake, Nick, I'm a trained nurse. I know what to look for. This is terrible. Oh Paul, I'm so sorry."

**

"YES, MR. DOBBS IS HERE ... came in a couple of hours ago."

"Can we see him?" Nick asked a cute redhead behind the desk at the ER of Valley Memorial—a pale green place with a pre-war look and the smell of bleach. "I'm Nick Gates and this is Dennis Delaney."

"Are you family? It doesn't sound like you're close."

285

"Close?"

"Yes 'close'." She smiled up at him. "His parents are back in the waiting room, a private room set aside for family."

"Is he alive?" Dennis asked.

"I'm sorry. Unless you're family, I can't tell you a thing." She allowed a perfunctory smile.

"We're his housemates," Nick said, a bit of whine in his voice. "We share a house and ... and lots of other things, some I can't mention. We're close, piston and cylinder, and all we want to know is his condition." He gave her a puppy-dog look. "We just gotta find out ... you do understand. We're almost family, about as near as you can get without sharing the blood line. You must sympathize—you seem like you're a part of humanity and can appreciate our concern."

"Please back away," she said. "I'll call security."

"You're beautiful," he said.

"There are rules. You can sit out here if you like, but if you continue to insist on taking my time, I'll call the head nurse. And you don't want to deal with her, believe me." She glanced up. "She'll have you out in the street on your ear and then it'll you in the ER."

They sat on old Danish-style American with only enough padding to cover the wood and spent their time reflecting and wondering. An hour ticked by and another while Dennis, relieved by the wait, began fantasizing with Shelley. Nick found a pay phone and talked to Mary: "Is Paul okay?" The answer, reassuring.

Not much activity where they sat—too early for highway collisions, knife fights, overdoses, and gunshot wounds. The occasional buzz at the desk was the only interruption to the hospital silence.

A hulk of a woman, who presented like a warden, would roll in occasionally and speak to the cute little redhead who in turn would nod toward them. The look from the hulk then coursed over them like a cold blistering wind—penetrating and disarming. Like it was because of them, the intruding visitors, they were there and not at a party. Dennis tried to sink deeper into his chair but there was nowhere to go.

About ten, an official-looking hawk of man—young, tall and gangly, in a green smock with a stethoscope hanging loose from his pocket, came in from the back of the hospital. "You the 'almost family' of Dalton Dobbs?" He leaned in.

"Yeah," Nick said while Dennis nodded. They shuffled and stood.

"I'm Doctor Eisenberg, and I have some bad news ... eh, we should sit."

They sat and the Doc pulled up a facing chair and leaned forward. "I can't tell you much, but I can tell you this—he's in a very serious condition ... but will probably live. Despite the worst mangling I've ever seen in this volcanic hole of a valley, he will likely survive. He's lost a leg however, poor guy, crushed and broken beyond repair—a disjointed line-up like elbow macaroni—and we had to amputate above the knee.

"And he'll have some scars, physical and mental. He'll be a sick young man for a very long time and will be here for a while, in and out, as we patch him up—bone and skin grafts, joint replacements, reconstruction, ligament repair ... the list is long. Your friend is really banged up and it's God's miracle he's alive at all. And I'll tell you something else ..." He took a

287

breath. "In a week or so when you come in to visit, avoid his parents. We don't want to be patching *you* up as well." He stood, looked over at the admittance desk, then back at them.

"So, you talk to the that cute little red-headed triage nurse when you visit, she'll tell you if they're here or when expected." He turned to Nick, "It's been observed you have an eye for her, but let me say be careful. She's a fiery one with a razor-sharp tongue and a temper—been known to terrify men, send them running." He smiled. "She's loveable otherwise."

"You wanna stop for a beer?" Dennis spoke in the parking lot.

"Yeah, let's stop. I'll want something amber, and it's not gonna be beer."

At the Hut they ordered from the bar and sat at a table. Dennis opened his mouth to speak, "Uh ... umm, nothin'."

"What?"

"Jus nothin' ... hell of a day, don't know what to say."

"Yeah ...."

"Like a bad dream."

"Only it isn't."

"Yeah ... I mean no, it sure as hell isn't."

"I can't believe it ...."

"Whadda you suppose will happen now?"

The question lingered as they sat in silence, each to their own, time slipping by. They had another.

"I don't wanna get drunk," Dennis said.

"Me neither."

Twenty-Two
Pogo Hops

PAUL KNEW HE NEEDED to visit Dalton and he knew he would, but what to say to the man you caused such a calamity, a personal setback that would last his entire life? He didn't know, and until he did he simply could not face him. He hadn't the courage. He fibrillated emotionally—will without courage.

As days passed, and then a week, and all the time this question of what to say ... *Fuck it, I just gotta go ... can wait no longer.*

He visited Dalton in Valley Memorial, private room in a hospital bed, his right leg in traction, the other one gone, his left arm and shoulder in a cast from fingertips to chin, the right forearm, tips to his elbow, and some sort of immobilizer around his right pelvis. His head was completely bandaged with one eye to the world and a slit at his mouth.

"Jesus, Dalton, you nearly bought it. I'm so sorry, and I know I'm responsible—all that scepter waving for years. I know now ... I'm responsible and I'd trade places ... uh, it should be me in that bed. I don't even want your forgiveness. It's me needs to be punished, I guess."

289

Dalton motioned him closer with his single functioning appendage and whispered, "Call me 'D'."

Paul thought he saw a smile coming in from under the bandages and felt more at ease. "I don't know what to ... I'm so sorry we had that fight. I see your side now—those years of my acting superior though I hafta say, I didn't mean it ... it wasn't intentional, and okay ... eh, yeah, I had it coming, the beating you gave me ... denying the vote, correcting behavior ... though you ... you started it ... and damned near finished it. But yeah, I'm sorry, real fucking sorry ... and in thinking about it, I'm gonna change if that means anything at all and I wouldn't be surprised if it didn't ... you lying there as you are. Dammit to hell, Dalton, I hope you understand that I'm really fucking sorry." Paul shuddered a little, put his hands in his lap.

Dalton lifted his right arm a little to wave off the effort, then motioned him in and whispered. "Call me 'D', you fuck."

A nurse came in to warn Paul that the senior Dobbs were on their way and Paul should leave by the back door.

Paul stood, took Dalton's fingers and leaned in, "I'll be back ... eh, 'D'. You try and take care of yourself. Your motor-cycle is junk, you know." He paused, searching for positive and added, "But not like you, my friend, who will be back and stronger in—"

"You must leave, Mr. Smythe. You must leave right now."

Dalton waved goodbye with his finger.

IN THE LIVING ROOM AGAIN, all together with a question gaining familiarity. "Whatta we gonna do now?" Dennis asked.

"I dunno, whata you want to do now?" Paul said.

"We still have the rent problem," Nick said. "Can't expect Dalton to pay for his hospital digs and also pay here."

"His name's on the lease," Paul said, as a token of fondness for 'D' who had said and would have said just that."

"I can pay more," Wayne said, "pick up a share of his share, and if everyone could share, those shares would not be so punitive."

"What?" Dennis said.

"They don't pay me when I'm on leave," Paul said, "and if they did, I would share in Dalton's share. As it is, I can continue to pay only my own." It hurt him to talk.

"I can share," Nick said.

"How many months do we have yet to share?" Dennis asked.

"Till November one," Paul mumbled.

"How about this?" Wayne said. "Um ... Paul pays the share that he already does, and so does Dennis. Nick and I will pick up Dalton's share along with our own. Of that, I'll take the largest share as I prob'ly owe for the time I was living here when I wasn't and had no share to pay ... and I saved. In fact, I saved big and I'm buyin' a new car this weekend. Not spankin', but new to me. How is Dalton? Anyone seen him today?"

"Today he waved his finger," Paul said, "and he's been swearing at me."

"Sounds like he isn't dead," Nick said, "and I suppose that's a good thing."

"Who's gonna pick up the beer, now that Dalton's not here?" Dennis said.

"Whoever draws the last glass?" Nick offered. "How much of a share of Dalton's share will I pay?"

"I guess we will know when it's time to pay," said Paul, not wanting anymore to be king. He put his head in his hands and shook it, "What the hell has happened to us," he said to the floor, "... and whatever it is, I don't even care."

**

GILES SAUNTERED INTO THE CANTINA through the back door, another check in his hand. He had won first place in a contest—a literary review in Louisiana, and the notion of writing to pay for his supper was beginning to take on dimension. Slightly less than what he'd received for the sales of first two, but fattening his confidence and filling his wallet nonetheless.

"Maria, let's all have a cold one, por favor, and include yourself. I had another sale and I'm buying." The four regulars nodded at one another with a smile, held up and waved a hand. Giles was already their hero and would put the cantina on the map.

"Oh Giles ... You do so well. We are proud. *Te felicito!*" She reached into the ice tub and pulled out six beers and rang up 'no sale'. "Thees one is on me, mi amor." The boys smiled again, tipped their bottles toward the bar and Miguel said, "*Caramba, Señor Giles es un hombre muy bueno.*"

She reached across the bar and took Giles' hands. "But I am afraid," she spoke softly. "You will leave and we will not see you again and that would be sad ... a sad day for us here. Oh yes, it will happen," she said, as he shook his head in denial. "I dream ... I worry and dream it will happen."

"Of course, it will happen," he mimicked. "We will all leave someday. Even you, Maria, someday ... but now we are here and now we will celebrate." He dropped a coin in the jukebox. "C'mon, dance with me."

"*Que son incorregibles,*" she exclaimed as she came around the bar and into his arms. "I hope it is not so soon."

As they danced into the evening and talked warmly to one another, a separate part of him wondered, why *would* he leave? Why would he part from this wonderful company and this land. He was enchanted with all that it offered, had never been so content. He had grown quite fond of Maria and Juan and had easily made friends with her patrons—and while all poor, they were happy. Farmers some, others worked odds and ends. Some had small businesses; Manolito a repair-everything garage. Some worked in town, and they all had goats, but no one he'd met in this village that was little more than a crossroads on the outskirts of Juarez complained about anything. And he was learning that one bath a week was more than needed to maintain an acceptable hygiene. No, he thought, there was no reason to leave now and none on the horizon.

Occasionally he'd take a ride south and into the hills where the roads were rough and the population thin and then nonexistent. He felt the wind and took in the smells of the terrain. The land around was the same as it had been for

293

centuries, and distance was the same as forever. He could not catch the horizon no matter how fast or far he rode. It was hypnotic—the freedom. Seldom had he felt so in charge of his life with so little effort.

But somewhere back in a cranny of his mind, something was missing. There were no obstacles to overcome, no argument to defend, no puzzles to solve or avoidances, and sometimes as he rode, he thought that he missed it—a challenge.

And sometimes he'd think about Anna, Izsak, and Lacey, and what had become of the guys on Beck Street. And one day, upon his return from a ride, he wrote a letter and dropped it into the box.

"GILES, MY SWEET, it is the anniversary of my birth, and I am taking a holiday today. *Como un día de fiesta*, and I want to go fishing with you and my Juan. I pack a basket, okay?" She danced around him as he lay in a chaise in the yard behind the cantina and sipped at the dark coffee she had made. She bent down and kissed him lightly on his forehead as her rhythmical movements were tracked with his smiling eyes.

"Can you fish?"

"I don't catch the fish ... I only cook them. I don't like to see them die ... to be on the hook, to struggle ... and such a wild, frightened look in the eye. Oh no, you catch. I will just be there. I will be in the water and in the sky and I will hear the birds sing ... but I will not catch the fish."

He laughed. "Me neither. I too don't catch the fish," he mimicked. "Though not for lack of trying. Sure, you come ... pack a basket and I'll throw on some shoes. *Dónde está Juan?*"

"I think he is with Manolito at the garage."

CHALLENGED WITH the complications of bicycle repair, Juan had no interest in fishing and declined to join in.

Giles grabbed his fishing gear, only because lately it seemed, as he lolled for hours on the bank along the river, he needed a reason to be there.

"Will you be at the cantina for the rest of your life?" Giles looked for conversation. It had been quiet throughout their walk, Maria pensive and he no reason to talk. But. now settled, hook baited in the water and bare feet in the mud, he thought it time to recognize he was not there alone.

"No. With Juan, we will go north."

"North? Into Texas ...?"

"Si, into Texas."

"What will you do there in Texas?"

"I will open a diner, serve American foods. Juan will go to school and learn to be a good doctor."

"Humm .... You'll need lots of money, mucho dinero. And you'll need a work visa. Have you thought about that?"

"The cantina is mine. Was my father's and his father's before ... and now it is mine. I will sell ... and I have saved. We will make it okay. It is in our future."

"The visa?"

"I don't know about visas. You want to eat now? Give your questions a rest?" She threw her head back, let her luxurious black hair float over her shoulders, and she was beautiful.

"I love you, Giles, you are a good man ... and someday a famous writer, but now we will eat." She poured wine into glasses and held one up to him. "Here ... this will help you to relax your curiosity. Drink and give me a kiss."

He smiled, sipped, and leaned into her for a touch of their lips.

Songbirds sang, crows jabbered at one another. Squirrels—were they always the same—scampered as a breeze tossed the sycamore leaves and they replied with their gentle rustling. All rivers flow, and this one seemed lazy to Giles as it meandered contentedly in here and out there on its way downstream to somewhere. A fish jumped and the water rippled, insects hummed, and when he retrieved his hook, the bait again was gone, and it occurred to him he was there only to feed the fish.

North to Texas? Suddenly, in all of this, a disruptive thought. Would she be leaving before he was ready?

"Great sandwiches, Maria. You *are* a culinary artist."

"Que es 'culinary,' Giles?"

THE LETTER he had hoped for had arrived.

> *Hello good friend,*
>
> *Anna will leave me for another I fear ... and I suffer. But I am also delighted you are having success with your life in the South. I miss our talks, the drinks and cigars and winning at chess. Take care of yourself, Giles, and don't forget us here in the Valley.*
>
> *Izzy*

"Umm."

THAT NIGHT, Giles lay on his bed in the dark, tired from the day, but his mind would not shut down. What would become of Izsak? He teetered on the edge of vulnerable as it was, and Anna's leaving might tip him into despair, maybe drink, maybe worse. This concern for his dear friend swirled about in his head, and he considered a return to the Valley. Izsak had done so much for him, and he felt indebted—a very personal obligation of care. His eyes closed. He didn't want to leave. Here he felt in balance, settled, and until now, not a worry or pressure. He was fond of Juan and very much taken with Juan's mother; he felt free to write, to create, to discover himself. Life here was indeed a bowl of— *What's that? The bed moved.* One side seemed to have sunk a bit and he noted a familiar fragrance.

"I have come to lie down with you," Maria said, ever so softly. "Is that to your liking?"

Twenty-Three
Some Progress Some Loss

"NOW AIN'T SHE A GODDAMN BEAUTY!" Wayne exclaimed as he ran his hand over the fenders of his new-to-him 1955 white T-Bird, parked on the front lawn and filling the eyes of the admiring beholders. "Only nine thousand on her, hardly broke in, and let me tell you, this baby knows how to scat."

"Be hard to disagree," Dennis said, as with a scowl, all envy, he joined the approbation. "Things are lookin' up for old Wayne I guess, but not for the rest of us. Shit, Paul's probably out of a job, I'm at the grotto servin' coffee for tips. Dalton's broken up in the hospital and probably won't be back. You and Nick got the only income these days, and he's talkin' about buyin' a garage. Jesus, things have changed."

"Nice car, Wayne," Paul said. "Good that some of us are doing better."

"Little V8, right?" Nick said. "And light as a feather. No wonder it scats. How's the suspension?"

"Stiff, but comfortable. You wanna see under the hood?"

"Sure, let's have a look."

"Wow! They really stuffed it in there," Paul said. "Not like a Corvette where at least you can *see* the spark plugs."

"Don't matter," said Wayne. "There's a special tool, makes it easy."

"You got it? Let's see the tool," Dennis said. "I wanna see the tool that can wiggle in there and pull a plug."

"Dealers have 'em," Wayne said, all grin. "When they need changing, I just drive her in."

Mary sashayed out, looking fresh and sexy but not unusual and drew no attention.

"It's gorgeous, Wayne," she said, "and, if anyone needs a fancy chariot, it's you, Cyrano."

"You wana take a spin, beautiful?" Wayne asked, a playful grin on his face.

"With you?"

"Of course, with me; you don't see a chauffeur, now do you?"

"It's always been no, Wayne. A jerk is a jerk, even dressed up in a new car." She took his arm in her hand gently. "You know I'm kidding, doncha ... well, a little kid and a lot of perspective."

"I getcha." He laughed. "But it don't bother me none. You're not the only chick in the yard."

Paul smiled. He felt like laughing, but it hurt.

"Be nice to the man," he said, "he's paying his rent and most of Dalton's to boot, and we still have months to go."

"Yeah, I got a vote and a half now." He glanced at Mary. "And it might see you out on the street." He laughed. "Anybody else? Only room for one and the driver, which, of course, is gonna be me."

"Okay, I'll go," Dennis said, "but I got no margin now, so take it easy ... can't afford a hospital bill or a funeral."

"It's got belts."

**

"GEE, PAUL, when will you go back to the plant? It's been well over a week since ...." Mary shrugged. "I'm not naggin' or anything, but won't they miss you?"

"No ... not anymore—I'm walkin'. I talked to my boss yesterday. He's filled in my spot with a woman he wanted to promote. Did it the second day I was gone. Needed to, he said." Paul slumped in his chair, talking to his shoes. "I knew, well, sort of suspected ... they do that, you know—assembly line from the shiny front door to the crapper."

"That's not fair ... what an asshole." She crumpled her face.

"It's okay. It's the way it is out there. You're either in on time every day or you're fired. I knew that when I signed on. White collars aren't in the union." He was mumbling low now and she had to lean in to hear him. "I can take an entry job, he says ... if I come back, he says ... if one's available, he says. If I were on the line tightening bolts, I'd have Dave Beck in my corner, but salaried folks ... well, our noses are too high in the air when it comes to unions."

"What'll you do then?"

"I don't know ... when they have openings, he'll give me first crack, he says." He looked up and caught her eyes. "I've got a few bucks saved up and maybe I'll take some time ... um, look around. Find something less regimented. No need to hurry."

"I could help. I'm doing better now. Imagine, an LVN peddling parts as a sales rep for electronics companies."

He let out a painful chuckle. "You could sell anything ... hell, I'd buy a bucket of transistors just to have you come to my office. What happened anyway, you get a promotion?"

"Well, he said—you remember I told you this—if I'd do for him, he'd do for me, the sleaze. And sure enough, he's coming through." She winked, got up and sashayed around. "Gotta raise too, and I get a commission on everything I sell over the counter."

"Humm, so whata you doing for him?"

"I'm cooperatin'." She grinned.

"What does that mean?"

**

"WOW, THAT'S SOME CAR, that T-Bird of Wayne's," Dennis said to Shelley while parked in his Bondo-rumpled, Lincoln convertible out in front of the house. "Had her up to one-twenty down on the freeway, and boy is it quick. I mean, a jackrabbit off the start, and clean. I mean, clean lines ... and better'n that Corvette of Cole's in my opinion."

"Wayne ... he's such a slug."

"Why do you say that ... he's a friend, ya know."

"Maybe ... but he's not gonna be in our wedding."

"Wedding! What weddin' you talkin' about?"

"*Our* wedding, silly. We're getting married ... soon as you propose." She laughed, moved closer and gave him a kiss on his cheek, put her hand in his lap.

"You know I love you, Denny ... and Daddy says when we get married, he'll give you a job in his company ... sellin' insurance, or something else if you want. I'm his little bunny and we'll never have to worry about lettuce." Her fingers began to move, a light, selective, but effective maneuver. "You could have your own T-Bird then."

"I know nothing about insurance, and don't care about learning. I don't even have any. And I don't know about marriage either, and I—"

"Hush, silly. We don't need to talk about it now."

"When we gonna talk about it?"

"Later," she whispered as she unzipped his fly.

"Wait, Shh-elll ... 'least lemme put up the top."

**

ON A BALMY DAY, somewhat cooler than usual, Wayne and Dennis took the bird out for a cruise. Wayne had said, "Hansen Dam, there'll be some lookers out, soakin' up rays."

As they putzed along, no hurry, the usual chatty Dennis spoke not a word, seemed distant, like in another world.

"What's up with you? Got nothin' to say?"

"I'm thinkin' about my financial situation and runnin' low on jack ... wallet's as flat as those pancakes at Bob's. I like the Grotto, you know, but it isn't enough money to see me through."

"You could get a real job," Wayne said.

"Yeah ... I've been lookin'. Paul said the Chevy plant, so I went out, took a number and filled out their application ... a hundred fuckin' guys waiting for an interview. I hung around.

Every fifteen minutes or so a name'd be called. I left." He laughed. "I'd be there today, still waitin'."

"I could get you on at the pool company—Patio Pools. It's nights. They're runnin' some new filters through, need unskilled help and you might qualify." He laughed, punched Dennis on the thigh.

"Yeah ... well, if you're employed there, it obviously don't take much."

"I just go in when I wanna. Pop set it up, knows the foreman. So, when I got nothing going on, or need the cash, I go from Lockheed to Patio and pull another shift ... pretty informal. We'll go over this evening if you're game. I'll introduce you to Homer. Grab me one of those beers from the cooler, will ya?"

**

"So, DELANEY, you wanna glue up our filters, do ya ... stinkin' damn job, you'll wear a respirator and the pay ain't much. I guess he told ya all that ... Gundersen. Did he?"

Dennis looked around—part machine shop, part warehouse, part assembly area, mostly disorder.

"Well ... you wanna sign up? Print your full name on this here timecard, and when you're ready to work, slip it in the clock for the time punch, same when you leave—target, one a.m. We pay on Fridays, hold back a week. I'll start you at two dollars an hour, raise ya as high as three if your production warrants, and you need to fill out this thing for Uncle Sam. You gotta pen?"

"Eh, no sir."

"Use mine, then, and leave it and the form here on the desk when you're done. I be going now ... quittin' time for me, so punch in. Wayne'll be here soon ... damn near always late. He'll show you the ropes."

"Yes sir, eh, thank you, sir."

"Name's Homer."

Patio Pools was big in the Valley.

> *"Build and service swimming pools from the first shovel of dirt to the last kid in,*
> *and our Star Filter is the very latest in crystal clear water.*
> *If you swim in the Valley, you're in a Patio Pool."*

.

"HERE, LEMME SHOW YA," Wayne said, taking the gun from Dennis's hand. "This is a hot glue gun—pulls glue through this insulated hose from the pot on that burner. The hose and pot's under pressure ... that gauge, ya see that gauge on the bucket—"

"You're late."

"I know it, but now that you're the very punctual glueman-two, you can clock me in when you get here."

"I can't do that."

"Sure you can. I gotcha the job, didn't I?"

"What if I punch you in and you don't show up?"

"Well, sir, that's a bridge too far ... and we'll only cross it if we get there. Now, you see these mandrels ..."

THE NEXT NIGHT Wayne arrived with a box of parts and went directly to the machine shop.

"What the fuck," Dennis said. "What's all that?"

"Engine parts. The old man is building a plywood boat. He's using an old Chevy engine, but he needs these pistons and connecting rods balanced so the boat won't shake apart ... drowning him and his passengers."

"They pay you to do that?"

"Aww shit, Dennis, won't clock in till I'm finished ... whata you, a company spy?

Dennis went back to the gluing—awful stuff, respirator helped but damned uncomfortable. There was a radio. It had one station—a gospel one that sang to Jesus. Dennis made up his own lyrics: The wafer goes into the sleeve/ sleeve assembly into the mandrel/ glue on one side then the other/ an eight sleeved mandrel becomes one star. Then the chorus, six stars every hour/ hour after hour/ change the respirator filter when you can't breathe anymore.

In an hour, Wayne joined in and with two guns working, the air unbearable. There was no breeze.

At ten, Wayne threw down his mask and put his gun on the rack

"I'm goin'. Had enough of this shit tonight. Clock me out when you leave. There's a saloon on the corner. I'll be there till it closes."

"I can't clock you out."

"You don't get it, do ya ... life is short and it's gettin' shorter. There may not be tomorrow. You gotta grab what ya can while you're able—keep your engine revved, your tank full of hi-test, and don't waste a fuckin' minute—so clock me out when you leave."

"Okay...."

Twenty-Four
Joey

WAYNE WALKED INTO HUGO'S SALOON, let the screen door slam behind him. He shambled up to the bar and took a stool near the front door, and let his eyes adjust. He didn't know this place and thought it best to be near an exit. The saloon, essentially empty and stone quiet, reminded him of a church on Saturday night. Did no one know the weekend was starting or it was just this spot—worn thin with loving care, no doubt.

The barkeep shoved a basket of peanuts his way—more shells than nuts. He followed it down, running a rag along the bar.

"What'll you have, pal?"

"Whiskey sour if the bourbon's any good."

"Old Crow unless you call it."

"It'll do."

Wayne looked around. Most of the light came from a juke box in the back and the neon beer signs against a mirrored wall behind the bar. The floor was worn bare along the traffic paths—varnish gone and some of the wood. Three guys sat at a table midway back; one glanced up. Bare empty booths along the far wall spelled discomfort. A woman sat on a stool at the far end of the bar. He couldn't make her out, but her hair looked a rusty red. The ashtray in front of him needed emptying.

"Here ya go, pal. One whiskey sour with the Old Crow ... a double shot, first of the night."

They guy was male pattern bald, but he didn't look old ... an ordinary fifty with bottle-brush, pepper-gray above each ear.

"Name's Jed if you need another. I'll be down to the end with Joey." He nodded toward the woman in the dim at the end of the bar.

Wayne sipped at the sour. He was feeling down ... a little bitter. Vicki had left him flat—said goodbye and gone. After near two months, there was little talk. She said it wasn't him; she wasn't meant for a man. He wanted to fix it, but she had already met another. Her name was Sharon, and there was nothing he could do. He liked Vicki—straight arrow, no bull-shit about her. Their only problem was her goddamn or-gasms—they were absent, and never, not once, came around. He shook his head. Well shit ... easy come, easy go. *That fuck-ing glue ... it's making me sick. I'm losing my damned per-spective.*

"Hey Jed," he yelled down. "I'll have another when you can break away."

"Comin' up, pal."

On his way, Jed opened and shut a few doors behind the bar.

"The crow done flew the coop." He laughed. "How about Early Times?" He presented a fresh bottle.

"Yeah, I don't care. What's with the girl?" His nod went down the bar. "She belong to you?"

"Joey? Nuhuh, not mine, though dreamin' sometimes." He smiled. "Mine's ta home toastin' the bed ... at least she s'posed to be."

"What's she drinking ... the girl?"

"Champagne cocktails."

"I'm buyin' her one. You think that's okay?"

"It's just cash in the register to me, pal. You wanna run a tab?"

"Yeah, okay. Tell me about her ... Joey, you say."

"Don't know much ... you want a double again? It'll cost ya this time."

"Just the regular. She come here often ... alone?"

"Fridays. Sweet ..." His eyes rolled once. "But I don't keep track, and I'm not your fancy-man, either. You interested? You go talk."

Wayne sat back, sipped on his drink—not as mellowing as the double Old Crow. He thought about approaching. Timid socially, even shaky at first, never been good with small talk, hated the awkwardness, he chugged the drink and walked to the back, put a quarter in the jukebox and punched in a couple of tunes.

She turned toward him. "Thanks for the drink, mister. You got a name?"

"W-Wayne." He took the few steps toward her. "He told me you're Joey."

"Jed? I know Jed. I've been here before, but I haven't seen you."

"It's not on my regular beat, ya see." His eyes dropped to the side, saw the planks in the floor. "But I hafta say, eh, I'm glad I found it."

"You don't live around here?" She crossed her legs, brushed down her skirt.

"I do a shift some nights over at Patio Pools ... little antsy tonight ... unfocused. So, I thought a drink might fix it."

"Antsy, huh, and why is that?"

"Lost my girl."

"Do you need a hug?" She laughed.

"You're getting close." He put his hand on her shoulder and moved in a bit.

"Uh oh, you move too fast, buddy boy, or you've made a colossal mistake." She turned back to her drink, her back toward him.

"Look ... I'm sorry, just a smart-alecky crack. Didn't mean nothin' by it."

She didn't respond, but he could see in the mirror a grin on her face. He found her appealing—cute turned up nose, big blue eyes, wavy auburn hair cut short. He imagined freckles though it was too dark to tell.

"If I ask you to dance, can we erase the arrogant statement? It wasn't really me."

"Go back to your place at the bar and maybe I'll think about it."

He did, and he ordered another sour and a champagne cocktail for her. *Fucking women.* They always win. Whatever the game, they end up on top. Vicki came back to his presence.

310

She was different. He could see her plainly in his mind's eye—tall, a substantial build but no fat and a little light on the breast size, but damn good-looking—glamorous a better description, and she loved him ... so she said. Those missing orgasms. They could fuck till the cows came home ... but they didn't ... ran the other way and not for Ferdinand. God's plan, he thought, and his bad luck.

"Would you like to dance with me now?" The voice was in his ear.

"Sure," he said without turning. He remembered her voice—soft and low and smoky. "I have the coin; you pick the tune." They went to the box, currently quiet, and she picked three slow ones—"Wheel of Fortune," Kay Starr; "Cry Me a River," Julie London; and "More Than You Know," Perry Como.

He had been warned, and he made no advances, holding her loosely—Arthur Murray would be proud.

"You seem a little stiff," she said, moving a hand to the back of his neck. "I don't want you to feel uncomfortable."

"I don't plan to offend."

"You won't."

He pulled her in closer and by the end of Como, they were dancing as one. He produced another quarter and they continued to dance—saying little.

"I think I might like you, Wayne, but I don't know you."

"Uh huh, same here," he managed.

"Why don't we take a booth—talk a little and get to know one another?"

"I'm game."

They talked. She lived nearby, worked as a med tech for a doctor, never married and no particular male interest—liked a casual relationship. She came to Hugo's on Fridays, and she gave him her phone number.

At 1:30, Jed, the bartender came over, put a round down.

"This is it, kiddos. You're the only ones here and I'm closing. This one's on the house, and Pally, your tab is $23.50." He looked at her. "You want I should call you a cab, Joey?"

Wayne waited with her while she awaited the cab. She declined his T-Bird ride, but he might call her.

"I don't want to push this," she said. "We may have something here, let's savor and protect it."

Oh course, he agreed. She gave him a light kiss before entering the cab.

As the cab drove away, he thought, what dumb fucking luck—*Goodbye Vicki and God's blessings.*

**

"Rob's Auto Repair" could almost be read from a dingy sign near the street. A low building set back on the lot, where out front a few older wrecks were parked—one on jack stands and missing its wheels.

"This is the place," Nick said with a grin. "Not much to look at but I hear well equipped."

"It'd give you a start," Maxine said. "Let's go in."

Through the main bay, they navigated a clutter of car parts strewn about—worn tires, empty wheels, an engine missing its head, an axle and differential housing, an assortment of gears, and a scattering of other automobile parts that had apparently been there for years. They entered the office and a bell, back in the shop, rang too loudly. An old man, dressed in coveralls that could stand by themselves, came in.

"Howdy, what can I fix fer ya?"

"I'm lookin' for Rob," Nick said.

"That's me. Ya got some repairin' fer me ta do?" He gurgled out of a mouth that was leaking brown, turned back to the door he'd come in, and spat.

"No. I'm Nick Gates. We talked on the telephone ... eh, and this is Maxine."

"Oh yeah, you called. Yer the one want's ta buy this place. Well sir, it's fer sale. I'm gittin' too stiff ta be crawling around all this iron, ya see, and maybe we can strike us a deal."

Rob was dark with age and dirt, had blue eyes that twinkled through a white-bearded face showing years of accumulated wear. His hand, black with garage residue, extended and Nick took hold for a quick business-like shake.

"Sit yerselves down there. You a mechanic? Lemme git another chair for the lady." And he disappeared into the shop to soon reappear with an old wooden folding chair which he opened for Maxine. "Can I git you a sodie?"

"I'll want to see how you're equipped and to look at your books," Nick said. "And if you have a customer list, any debt, and—"

"Ain't got any books, no lists and no debt," Rob said. "An' the place is equipped, got all that ya need—got a pit and and a lift, honing machines and every hand tool in the book.

313

Bought a new Sunnen shaft grinder last year. Got vises and presses, arc an' 'cetylene weldin', and lots-a air. Got it all, ya know ... been here since nineteen and twenty-seven. Belonged to my dad, old Rob senior. Died in '42. Never got outta here none but that ain't gonna be me ... some life yet ta live, ya know, and, by George, it's time I start livin' it. How much can ya pay? Need about fifteen thousand cash, ya know—the whole kit-n-caboodle includin' the land. Now, that's a fair deal, doncha think? Durn near a giveaway."

"Whoa. You're getting ahead of me, Rob. We just walked in the door."

"Yep, I s'pose ya did. But I tell ya, young feller, I ain't got no time ta be wastin'. Either ya wants this place er ya don't. Got work at do, ya know ... an' there be some other interested parties. Now whata ya say, mister Nicholas Gates ... you be one of 'em?"

"Might be," Nick said.

"We'll go back. I'll show ya around." He got up, slapped Nick on the shoulder, and turned to the door to the back. "C'mon now. Sittin' there on yer keester won't git it done." And as he walked through the door, he replenished himself with a fresh chew.

"HE DOESN'T SEEM THE KIND who's much into bargaining," Nick said as they sat in his brother's Ford, still parked in the front lot.

"He's a character."

A silence settled in.

"Well," she finally said, turning to him, her hand on his arm, "what do you think?"

314

"I don't know. It's a big step." He pulled away and put the key into the ignition switch.

"It's what you want. You've been talking about it since the party."

"Yeah, but I may not be ready. I may need to think about it." He cranked up the engine.

"What's there to think about?"

"It'd be a lot of work, you know ... and there's the money." He revved the engine.

"You're not afraid of work."

"It's more the money." He turned off the engine.

"You haven't tried? At the bank, I mean."

"I opened the discussion." He looked ahead and a longer silence ensued.

"I have a little money," Maxine broke through. "You want a partner?"

"You? You got a toolbox tucked away somewhere?" He laughed and turned toward her. "And the place would need few bucks to straighten it out—new signs, paint, and the rest. And there's the cost of transactions and getting rid of the junk. Look around. I'll bet some of this stuff was here before the old senior Rob was running it."

"It does have a history," she said, "but isn't that good? People will know it."

"Suppose so ... and his reputation is good; I hear that at the station."

"Well then, let's get a move on. Like the man said, 'times a wastin'.'"

He turned to her. "You're serious?"

"Damn square," she said. "Always wanted to set the rules."

They looked at each other and laughed. They had Detroit, and while it lasted it was good and now it was back and better. He took her hand in his second business-like shake of the day. "Partners?"

"Partners," she said, and she kissed him.

"HEY ROB," NICK CALLED OUT, reentering the shop.

"I knows it ... plum had the feelin'."

"How much do you want for good faith ... and, what the hell's your last name?"

"Dobuninski's the name ... an yer word's good enough, ma boy. But no chislin' or welchin' or wastin' my time ... ya hear me?"

"Dobuninski ... Okay, Rob Dobuninski, we'll be back within the week with the cash."

Twenty-Five
A Weepy Loss

WHEN DENNIS POPPED INTO THE DEN, he found Wayne slumped over the bar, a glass in his hand, a quart of rum at its side. He didn't look up.

"How they hangin'?" Dennis inquired, his early shift over and free for the rest of the day—Saturday, and off until Monday at seven.

"Kinda low, to and fro ...." Wayne said to his glass. "You remember Oliver, the guy who tended bar at your first big party? The guy with the glass eye who was all over that biddy from next door?"

"Yeah."

"He's dead."

"Dead?"

"He got ahold of some bad stuff, I heard, and OD'd. His ol' lady found him lying on the bathroom floor, face in his foamy puke. Jesus, what a scene ... if you can't trust your dealer, who you gonna leave ...? He wasn't too smart. Never did no harm." Wayne looked up now, his eyes glazed with tears. "Didn't know him real well but just the same, big loss when any of us .... You wanna drink? I'm holdin' a wake here ... a private memorial."

"Um ... I'll have a beer, but don't wanna interrupt your private mournin'."

"You remember him, doncha? Little noisy sometimes, but a nice guy ... do anyone a turn if they needed it."

"Yeah, I remember him, noisy's right. On parole, wasn't he? A bum."

"Well, he's dead."

"Sort of asked for it ... using the hard stuff."

"Dead is dead ... no one asks for that."

"'S'pose your right. Okay ... pour me a fucking rum."

"It's not *fuckin'* rum, it's the best I could find ... in memoriam, ya know."

"Didn't mean to be disrespectful." Dennis plunked a glass on the bar and pulled up a stool. "Fill it up then; I'll try ta get in the mood."

"Got a quart here," Wayne said, "and another in the car, jus' in case."

John Teagarden walked in. "Hey ... ja hear about Oliver?"

"Yeah, we heard," Dennis said. "We're holdin' a wake. C'mon, you might as well join in ... he was your friend."

"He was an idiot, and he wasn't my friend, but I'll have a beer."

"That's kinda harsh. Wayne here thinks anyone who dies needs a sendoff."

"Yeah ... a proper send off."

"Maybe." Teagarden drew a beer. "He wasn't going to last. Knew it and didn't care. I've known of him since high school. Always reckless ... not courageous, just reckless. Doing stupid things all through. I remember one night he climbed up the water tower with twelve beers—drunk when he started. Stood up there at the railing and yelled out some shit about the meaning of life. Went on for hours while he drank all those beers and threw the cans out, one by one, at the 'nonbelievers.' Fire Department had to haul him down. Yeah, destined for greatness, he was."

"You know him well?" Wayne asked.

"Not well. He was closer to Dalton. Steered clear when I could. He was brigh, though—good grades, excellent papers printed here and there with formal recognition. Whole thing a waste, stupid drugs."

"Don't like it when good people get sidetracked," Wayne said. "Somebody throws a switch and there they go, down the wrong fuckin' siding ... a dead-ender." Wayne poured himself another rum and topped off Dennis' glass. "I feel sorry for the guy ... a bad turn somewhere. Lost his eye, and—"

"Don't go maudlin," Teagarden said. "The guy had plenty of opportunity to change ... didn't take one. But then, who can tell, maybe a screw needed tightening. Not much can be done about that." He turned toward the door. "Maybe I will have a rum. Pour me a drink, Wayne. I have some music in my car. I'll get it ... a fugue by Bach ... just what we need."

"What the fuck's a fugue?" Dennis said.

"It's for the old man with the scythe, it's what plays when he's taking you away—Johann Sebastian Bach most notable. Hold on, be right back."

"Maybe we should be wearing black," Dennis said. "At least an arm band."

THEY LISTENED TO BACH, OVER AND OVER, and talked of life, and death to the extent they allowed they knew it—and they mourned. And they thought and talked about destiny and Ollie, and it all was most unusual.

"I'll never forget his dunking his eye in that broad's drink ... and she just as drunk," Dennis mumbled after an hour had passed.

"Yeah ... fuckin' drunk," Wayne said. "What was 'er name ... can't remember that broad's name,"

"Broad! Tha's her name. Jus' Broad," Dennis added to their collected wisdom.

"*Miss* Broad?" Teagarden said in his most serious tone. "You're s'posed to be polite at a wake."

"No, dummy, tha's her first name," Wayne explained, "the name sh'as given. You know, the one she got when she 'as christened—Broad somethin'. Anyway ... she's married now, when she was here with ol' Ollie, so she's a Missus, Missus Broad somthin'. And my god, wash she drunk."

"Yeah ... and sexy," Teagarden responded. "Tha's why ol' Ollie ... ic, went for her ... thought she was invitin' him in ... a first for ol' Ollie. Where ya s'pose ol' Ollie is now? Think he knows we're talkin' about 'im now ... though never before, talkin' over his dyin'? Ol' Ollie—thas gettin' hard to say."

"Well, what about that Missus Broad Some ... Smoothening? Tha's kinda hard too." Wayne chuckled "Though *she* ... kinda sexy an' might've been easy. Sure as hell acted like it."

Teagarden got up from his stool, reached into his pocket and pulled out a small vial. "Less do somefin else. This wake is over. Take a drive. I'm getting' tired a ol' Ollie and ol' Ollie's passin' ... and tired of Bach too. I got good sounds out in the Chrysler. C'mon, les take a drive. We'll go somewhere." He popped a couple pills and washed them down with his drink. "Here, have a bennie or two ... wake you up."

"Agreed," said Wayne, stumbling backwards. "I'll fix ... fix us some coffee."

They had finished two cups and a couple of bennies each when the front door slammed and in strode big blonde Vicki with orange hair. "I need to borrow a car ... Wayne?"

"You gonna say hello, for Chrissake? We're mournin' here," Wayne said as solemnly as he could muster. "You're breakin' the damn mood."

"I need a car, and I want to borrow yours."

He laughed. "Can't do that babe ... of limits. Sorry, new rules for new ... doesn't yet know it belongs to me." He laughed again. "You know I don't let anyone drive it, 'sides, you need your own. Told you that before."

"C'mon, just this once? It's important to me. I hafta go to a birthday party in Long Beach. It's a family thing and I promised I'd be there. Please, Wayne, be a doll ... it's really important, and I don't have time for your lectures." While running her hand through Wayne's hair she glanced over at Teagarden. "I see your Chrysler out front, John—don't suppose ..."

"Not a chance, Vicki girl. Brand new, same rule ... besides, we're on our way out."

"Take the Lincoln," Dennis said. "Needs gas, jus be careful .... Ya will, won'tcha, Vicki ... be careful?"

"You're my fav, Dennis." She grabbed the keys from his hand and passed a pretend kiss. "Wayne ... take a lesson," she threw back on her way out the door, "and remember this next time you think you're horny—no one drives my taxi but me."

JOHN'S CUSTOM STEREO, with big ovals on the back shelf, was packaged into a spanking new Chrysler Saratoga—an emerald-green car with large tailfins and chromium flash. John loved his car, even more the sounds its customized radio emitted. He had all the pushbuttons fixed on music stations, three of the five on the PBS classical. Passengers would not ride in the rear seat without the muting headphones John provided for their comfort.

"Where're we going? Not far, I hope, don't like it back here," Dennis mumbled as they headed north down Lankersham. "Ya bring the rum? I'm wearing thin toward sober ... though I'm fuckin' wide awake," he spoke louder.

Wayne passed what was left in the second bottle. "Don't drink it all."

"We'll head up the grapevine to Santa Clarita," John said. "Grab us a burger there."

"I know a gal lives in Bakersfield," Wayne said. "Used to have a thing when I was stationed at Vandenberg. Nice body, very nice ... and she didn't mind sharing it. Those were the days ... ya belonged to the government, so what ever happened, ya know, you were already as good as dead."

"We're as good as dead anyway," Dennis said, "now that that Nikita guy's got the bomb."

"Forget about that," John said, "can't do anything about it anyway. So, Wayne, what's she look like, this Bakersfield chick you know?"

"Brunette, kinda tall, big smile, good teeth—what all you wanna know? She was hot and built like a brick shithouse, liked strawberry daiquiris ... and the more she drank, the warmer she got." His mind wandered back, and he remembered the bomb shelter burried in the rear yard that they used for a boudoir—quiet and private and something about fucking in a bomb shelter quelled all inhibitions and the whole damn thing was outrageously erotic.

"Bakersfield, huh?"

The radio was alive and too loud for conversation, so they zoned—still numbed by the rum if wide-eyed awake with Benzedrine. Coming down the other side of the 'vine, John slowed to the right.

"What's up?" Dennis leaned forward. "Why you stoppin'?"

"I'm pickin' up Pedro—looks like a man needs a ride."

"Why ya doin' that?" Wayne, reluctantly leaving the bomb shelter.

"Don't get your balls twisted up. It's just a ride." John pulled the car onto the shoulder.

The man ran up, short-sleeve khaki shirt and denim bibs. "You give a ride? Gracias, gracias." He held a grocery bag full of clothes in one hand, flashed a worker's card in the other.

"Sure thing, hombre, get in the back there with Dennis. Move it, Wayne, let the good man in."

"Muchas gracias, señor. Me llamo José. Muchas gracias."

"I'm John. Where're you headed?"

"Headed, señor?"

"Going ... where are you going?"

"I go to Bakersfield to work." He produced his card again for their inspection. "I was there, but had to leave with an illness in my family ... and now I am back. I come every year to work in the fields. It is on the program; it is on my card. Thank you."

"You got family in Mexico?"

"Si. I have wife, two sons, and hijas tres. Son bellas. The youngest very sick but now she is well ... gracias a Dios."

"We'll take you to Bakersfield, my friend. You're lucky we stopped."

"Bakersfield?" Dennis said, confused by it all and tired of the Tchaikovsky cannons pounding on his head.

"Sure, Bakersfield. Wayne can look up his old girlfriend ... the one that likes sharing."

Wayne, eyes wide, straight ahead, was remembering the delicious experience but could not, for his life, remember her name. It would come, he thought. *No point in confessing it now. anyway.*

Teagarden tuned down the music and they talked. They talked to José about the program, his wife and his kids and his little bean garden. And they talked among themselves about the girl in Bakersfield. And they talked their way into Santa Clarita where John bought hamburgers, ravenously consumed, and they talked between bites. They boosted their high with a couple more pills, then talked their way on to

Bakersfield where, at the now-darkened bracero office, they left José to sleep until morning. Nowhere in town were three pairs of eyes so wide and tongues so active.

The time was near ten and the town was dead, except for a Chrysler Saratoga idling at a curb and Wayne in a phone booth, studying the directory. *It was something like Lannie … was that her first name or her last?*

"We never met at her house, ya know," he told them. "It was always somewhere else. We'd have a Coke at the drug-store or maybe see a movie and then when it was dark, slip into the bomb shelter back of her house. Her old man was a bull and didn't want no daughter of his out with a guy the likes of me." He flipped pages. It was useless. Even if there was a needle in this haystack, he wouldn't recognize it. "I'm fucking sorry, just can't remember … it's one those blocks."

"Forget it," John said. "Let's pick up a six-pack and go over to the park. Maybe lie down, sip a few, then get some shuteye. Can't drive back tonight."

"Jesus Christ, Wayne, what were you thinking … talkin' up a broad like she was a combo of mink and Gina Lollobrig-ida, and you can't remember enough of her name to find in a phonebook."

"She coulda moved," Wayne offered, wanting to hide somewhere. "Anyway, it wasn't me decided on Bakersfield, it was fucking Pedro."

"José," John said.

They drank one beer each, gave the rest to a vagrant, and lying on their backs in a park in the middle of Bakersfield, closed their eyes on a starlit night and beckoned sleep—needed, desired, longed-for sleep. Their bodies were exhausted, every muscle humming a lullaby, but their Benze-drine brains were dancing around the maypole and about four in the morning John stood up and adjusted his pants. "Let's go. I'm not sleeping. and my money says neither are you. We might as well go—maybe some coffee."

"A big cold water for me," Dennis said.

They were exhausted, hungover, and wide awake as John guided his Chrysler back to the Valley. No one said anything. Up the grapevine about halfway home, "Bannerman," Wayne shouted, "Lucile Bannerman."

**

"HEY, DENNIS, why you here in the morgue on Saturday night... and *readin'* a car magazine?" Wayne bounded in through the front door. "It's party time, man. You the only one here?"

"Yep, just me ... got nothin' goin'. Shelley's out with her friends. Where's Joey? Thought you'd be out with her."

"Saw her last night ... God, I love that woman. Never met anyone like her before, makes my gut ache just thinking about her ... but she has obligations tonight ... obligations."

"So, that leaves me free. You wanna go to a party? I got a lead on a happening over the hill in West Hollywood—cou-pla teasers with a flat and one of 'em's havin' a birthday. No idea who's gonna be there; don't even know them, but two of those attending could be us."

"Tonight? You mean now?"

"No ... my engraved invitation delivered by unformed courier says next Valentine's Day—potluck, bring hearts and

326

bunny eggs for the fucking stew. Of course tonight, asshole. You game?"

"Sure, I guess. Gotta be better than hangin' around here."

"Yeah, pretty dismal here these days. Whata you gonna do when the lease is up?"

"I haven't a notion." The question had once tripped fleetingly through his mind: *what will I do?* and he had no answer, so he put it aside. There was time.

"I'm headin' back home," Wayne said. "The old man wants me to help him fix up his boat."

"Yeah ... so when do we go, to the party, I mean?"

"Starts at nine, so anytime now."

THEY PULLED UP AT AN ADDRESS ON MELROSE, a large residential of brick with a chiseled white keystone over the entry and in embossed gold letters on the heavy glass door, "3945 Melrose/ No Solicitors Allowed/ Deliveries in the rear"

"You sure this is it?"

"It's the number I got, fifth floor, 503."

"Looks pretty quiet."

"It's the snobbish neighborhood. Gotta park here, I guess ... no fuckin' garage. Shit, I hate leavin' the Bird on the street."

In the elevator, Wayne pushed number five and as soon as it started moving, they could hear music, and it sounded like party.

"Think they'll let us in?" Dennis said.

They walked down the hall to 503 and knocked; no one answered. They knocked again louder, then opened the door and went in.

No one noticed them as they mingled in the noisy crowd, shoulder-to-shoulder, some dancing, others talking loudly and laughing. Seemed, in a while, that few of them knew any of the rest. The music came from a small combo—sax, muted horn, drums and a bass fiddle.

"Wow, this is great. Wonder who's place this is?" Dennis said.

A girl overheard and replied, "It's Belle's, and it's her birthday." She pointed to a young woman dancing. "I live here with her. And who might you be?"

"God, she's beautiful," Dennis said. "How old is she?"

"She's not saying, and neither am I." The girl yelled in his ear. "But I'm Jeanie; you wanna dance?"

"Sure, I'm Dennis, and this here is ... where the hell did he go?"

"Doesn't matter; c'mon, put your arm here and your other one there ... no, not so low, not yet."

When the band took a break, Dennis moved toward the birthday girl and waited for a lull in her conversation. She was even more beautiful up close, and sexy, though not flaunting it around.

"Hi, I'm Dennis and I hear you're Belle. Great party and I also hear congratulations are in order. So what's the number? How many years you been gracing our planet?"

"You're cute, and that's so nice to say." She batted her eyelids.

"And you're gorgeous," he replied. "I dig your red hair." And she was an armful, he thought. Cute baby blue eyes, small nose surrounded with freckles, and everywhere round and cuddly. As they swayed with the music, he moved closer to her fresh-looking body, plumping out of a thin cotton dress, and she didn't retreat, not a fraction of an inch. He looked into her warm blue eyes, and she looked back. She turned into him and kissed him with full lips, and he almost fell over. "Jesus!" He smiled at her, lost for words, and put his arm around her waist and returned the kiss—a tender pressing of lips, tongues saying howdy, and foretelling, he hoped. Her soft body fitting nicely against his.

"So, your name is Belle?"

"Annabelle, but I like Belle." She looked up at him and smiled. "I'm glad you came to my party. All of these people …. "She looked around. "Where did you come from?"

"Doesn't matter, does it? I'm here … and I think I'm in love." He laughed a little, quietly, and she laughed back. When the band started up again, they danced. And they danced the rest of the night. And when the party ran down and the band left, and they were the only ones there, they kept dancing while she hummed.

"Where the hell's Wayne?" he idly mumbled.

"Your friend? He left with Jeanie. They said they'd probably be gone all night—back to the Valley or somewhere." And she kissed him again for the umpteenth time and his hand explored her breasts—full, firm, round, and warm … hiding behind almost nothing.

"Jesus, Annabelle, I love you."

"I love you too, darlin' Dennis. You're cute and you say such divine things."

They stood, swaying in the dim light for a while, cooing and nuzzling, and then she said, "You wanna stay the night? I make a really good breakfast."

He couldn't handle it. Was this a dream? Better'n any he'd ever had. *But, what's going on here?. Shouldn't I be careful? But damn, she's so hot, so aggressive, maybe got a penis between her legs. Aw, stop it. I gotta just go for it, what the fucking hell, it's a party.* He wondered about it for about a second, then lost perspective, could only react. And he was as hard as a railroad spike when she ran her hand down the front of his trousers.

"Huh, Denny, you wanna?" she repeated. "I can call you Denny, can't I?"

"Holy cow yes!"

They undressed in the moonlight, a warm yellow coming in through the bedroom window, bathing her in its glow. She was a goddess, perfectly put together, and tonight, 'untouched' he imagined—an early morning violet, radiant in the dew, whatever the hell that was. How did he get so fucking lucky, another of his fleeting thoughts. They moved together in her large bed, his arm around her shoulders, his hand caressing her thighs, wonderful thighs that would lead him to glory, while she ran her finger around and around the spike.

"Be gentle, my love," she whispered. "Go slow, make it last; it's my birthday, and Denny, you are my gift." She spread her legs invitingly, coaxing him in. He thought he might come before he arrived, and when he began to enter, the doorway was small, seemed guarded, and he would have to squeeze through.

"Go ahead," she whispered again. "Do it. Just do it gently."

He pushed a little harder, negotiating carefully, moving it around from side to side in the wetting warmth until things began to give. He pushed a bit more and she moaned, then squealed, and then he was there, and nothing was like it. With only the slightest movement came his explosion followed immediately by hers ... and then again. And when they were finished and pulled apart, there was blood, and he looked at her quizzically.

"Oh, Denny my love, you are my first ... and now my only, my only ever love. You took me to womanhood and now you are my man." She giggled and threw her arms around him. "We will be together forever, and I knew it as soon as we met."

"Huh?"

"I can't wait for you to meet Mommy and Daddy. They have a flat downstairs. My mom will be excited, utterly thrilled and so will my dad."

IN THE MORNING, he thought, what the hell, he'd meet the damn parents ... and maybe he'd make this trip often. "Boy, this scramble is good, what do you put in it?"

"MOMMA ... DADDY, this is Dennis. We're going to be married."

"Huh?" *She's fucking crazy! Married, no way ... at least not now.* "Eh ... Hi, Mr. and Mrs. Rosenthal."

Mr. Rosenthal nodded—a tall man with a chiseled appearance and salt-and-pepper hair—and looked up from his paper. She, a well-dressed, slender, and nice-looking woman, sipped from a small cup of coffee.

"You're going to get married?" she said with a smile, and more of a recognition than a question. "Now that's a big step, Annabelle, my dear. Don't you think you're a little young for family? You might want to wait until after you graduate." She put down her cup and crossed her legs. Nice legs he noticed, but only momentarily.

"I'm a woman now, Mom, in the Old Testament way, and can make my own decisions. Dennis and I are in love, our first love ... we've found each other. Daddy, you understand, don't you? Love can make you grow up in a hurry."

Mr. Rosenthal looked up. "I see." He folded his paper deliberately, laid it carefully on a side table, then turned his eyes toward Dennis. "Dennis, my boy, tell me ... what do you do? Are you able to support a wife? Over the years, our Annabelle has developed many frivolous demands."

"Eh, well ... I work in a coffee house, sir. I'm doin' pretty good." *I shouldn't a come down here—fucking Wayne. I can see only trouble.*

"And what do you do there, son?"

"Eh, sorta wait tables, sometimes brew, sometimes clean up. I'm learning the business."

Rosenthal smiled. "And you had sex with my daughter?"

Dennis was dumbstruck, had no idea what to do or say next—totally in awe of the situation. He looked around at a room, well-appointed, rich-looking furnishings encompassed a sedate and comfortable ambiance. *Must be some money here,* his thoughts idle and listless.

"Dennis?"

"Eh, yeah, I guess so but she—"

"And you love her?"

"Yeah ... I guess ... we just met last ni—" *I gotta get out of this.* He glanced at the door. He might just run for it.

"I can see you are a serious young man if somewhat impetuous, Dennis .... You're not Jewish, are you?

"Uh, no sir. I'm not anything ... eh maybe a little nervous."

"You just relax, my boy, you can convert. Many do. Rabbi David does very well with instructions. We're family now, apparently .... Sit, my boy, no need to be shuffling about like that."

Dennis took a chair. Annabelle stood behind him, her hand on his shoulder.

Rosenthal cleared his throat. "We love our Belle, of course, so let me make a proposal. I own a big furniture store over on La Brea, perhaps you've heard of it—Cosmopolitan Luxury By Rosenthal. It's a thirty-million-dollar business with twenty employees and half again in designers and decorators .... I need a manager. When you marry our Annabelle here, the job is yours. If you do well, you'll earn real money and live a good life here on Melrose. If you fail, I'll have your adolescent ass ... three ways from Sabbath. Now, you understand that, don't you, my boy ... it's all business, you know, and back to the coffee house for you both." He smiled, picked up his paper and began to read.

"Now Aaron, don't be so gruff." Mrs. Rosenthal winked at him. "You know you will help him out. You know he'll have *some* trouble. It's a very big load to put on an inexperienced man. Coffee, Dennis? Do you take cream?" And she poured him a cup from a silver carafe on a tray full of like-styled accoutrement, exquisitely engraved.

"Momma, we're truly in love. We are meant for each other, want to grow old together. We knew it the moment we met. You understand, don't you?"

"Why of course, my dear. You've given Dennis your precious virginity and now you're a woman in love. You've always been mature for your age, dear, hasn't she, Aaron?"

"Humph ... Yes, a mature young woman, our Annabelle. Well, Dennis my boy, I've told you what I can do; what do you bring to this marriage?"

"Er, well sir, I'm not sure. I don't have much—I have a car and—"

"A car?" He got up and began pacing—a tall man of stature, debonair in his smoking jacket and velvet morning shoes, a black onyx signature ring on his right hand.

"You have a car! Who in hell do you think you're dealing with ... you here to insult me, boy. You ask for the hand of our only child, our baby Annabelle ... and you say you bring a car! Now I'm not sure about that position I offered; you don't seem sufficiently responsible. I want you to explain yourself, young man. How will you support our daughter, a mature young woman of sixteen? She yet has a grade to finish at high school." He walked over to Dennis and put his sculpted nose in Dennis' face. "Tell me, young man, how the blazes do you plan to support a family with table waiting?"

Sixteen? Holy Jesus Christ ... am I in big trouble ....

"We'll elope. We'll do alright on our own," Annabelle sang out and took Dennis's hand. "Love conquers all, you know ... others have done it. Please Daddy, give us your blessing; we're so much in love."

"Yes, Aaron, your blessing." Mrs. Rosenthal topped off her coffee, delicately placing in a lump of sugar with the silver tongs. "We welcome you into our family, Dennis. Aaron isn't really so nasty ... can be rather charming once showing your metal." She smiled and sipped from her cup. "You kids are excused now .... Why Dennis, your coffee, dear, you haven't touched it. Maybe next time when we chat about your plans for a family. Toodle-oo for now. Aaron and I will want to discuss the wedding. I'm sure we will see you soon. Belle, you stay for a moment, I want just a word."

"JESUS H CHRIST, WAYNE. Where the fuck've you been? I been out here pacing for a lifetime— shoe leather's gone ... and I really need to get outta here; woulda waved down a cab if I'd seen one. And I'll tell you this, Mr. Shit-head, I ain't never going to a party with you anymore, not ever. Now goose it. I need outta here pronto."

As they raced down Melrose that Sunday and up Gower to the freeway, wind in their hair, tires squealing through turns, Wayne yelled, "This fast enough for you?"

Book III--Graduation

Twenty-Six
Some Changes Made

"MISS LACEY IS HERE, SIR."

"Thank you, Arthur. Send her in and fix me another drink, please."

"Another, sir?"

"Yes, another, Arthur ... and you might ask Lacey if she would like one."

"As you wish."

"Good morning, Izzy."

"Lacey. Nice of you to respond so quickly. I want to give you some news I don't want you getting from others."

"Okay, it sounds important ... not a problem with performance, I hope? Tony and I are getting along very well, and things are moving on schedule, and ... well, there is this hitch with—"

"No, no, it's none of that." His eyes looked tired and watery. His hand shook a little as he picked up his drink. "Sit down, Lacey, and I'll get right to it. Anna has left ... packed up yesterday. She ...."

"Oh, I'm so sorry, Izzy." She reached over to him, a hand on his arm.

"There's more. This morning they found Ethan dead in his car in the garage, probably a heart attack, but the motor had been running, ignition still on and the car out of gas."

"Jesus ...."

"Lacey, I'm resigning. I've been up all night with thoughts about Anna and then the phone call from Ethan's daughter, and well, I'm through. I don't need this and likely cannot take it, and for my health ... my general well-being, must not continue. And, of course ... this means you are out of a job."

"My God, Izsak ... I can't believe this. It's all ... well, there's so much. What do you need? Anything I can do, of course ... anything."

"No, no, I'm worried about you. We had such aspirations ... you, your beginning, me ... a return—our very own trip to the moon. Fortune has not been our friend, my dear."

"You mustn't worry about me ... I'll get along. I've always thought you two were solid ... well, ups and downs, but everyone has those. You have to take care of yourself. What a blow. Would you like to tell me about it ... you and Anna? What happened?"

"You're quite thoughtful, Lacey—a good friend, but I don't know that I'm ready for that. I have a lot of strings to tie before I collapse on anyone's shoulder." He laughed a little and finished his scotch. "Need to talk to Meyer; haven't done that yet. Meyer will need both a new director and producer.

And you might be ready for this—while your deal was with me, as was Tony's, he might stay on with a new producer. That would be smart and lend to continuum—and Tony might want you to remain—working for him, of course."

"Oh, I don't know. I'll need to digest all this, a huge serving of change and then the unknowns."

"Will you fix us another drink, Lacey? I find I'm in need today."

"Yes, I'll do yours, but then I am going to leave. I want you to call me tomorrow. If I don't hear from you then, I'm going to come knocking. Hear me, old pal ... I'll come knocking."

"Okay." He chuckled. "It's a deal. Thank you for understanding. It appears that you do. You do, don't you Lacey?"

"Of course. We're okay." She put his drink on the table and gave his shoulders a squeeze as she kissed his forehead. "Take care now ... call me tomorrow."

"Or you'll come knocking." He laughed.

**

"SHIT, I'M NEVER TAKIN' ANY MORE OF THOSE," Dennis declared, sprawled out on the couch and after two days of sleeping, finally recovered from the Bakersfield trip.

"What are those ... the those you're not takin' anymore?" Cole said, sitting in the opposing upholstered chair and sipping slowly on a beer.

"Bennies."

"Oh yeah. Bennies with the big 'B' and it ain't short for benefactor, although they give ... like a migraine. I've always thought they were zombie food—like the tired cannot sleep as the dead cannot die. As when you are starting up that tunnel toward the blue light—like your old friend Ollie did—you could be pulled aside, 'cause while you're ready, it ain't your time. They stoke you with Benzedrine, and you get to roam while you're waitin', and for entertainment, you show up in young ladies' dreams. You wanna expire something awful, get back in the tunnel speedin' toward the blue light, but it's still not your time and you just gotta roam—not alive but not yet with the light. And if you drift too close before your time, they give you more pills. Get it?"

"Wow, Cole, so you're sayin' we had a taste of things to come."

"That it may be, Dennis. That it may be."

"Yeah .... Well, I gotta say, I'm not comfortable with that shit—don't want any more, don't even want the talk. So, how's it goin' at the dump? Any more lead crystal?"

"Ah yes, the refuse disposal site. Things are swell, my friend, and I wanted to talk to you about that. I'm thinking of a change in career. Nothing dramatic, you understand, at least not now—but a gradual withdrawal from refuse management and into the field of comedy. And I've been wondering, good friend ... could you get me a standup gig at the Grotto? Is it possible that you could praise my skills and exert your influence?" He clapped his hand on Dennis' shoulder. "I could do the same for you, should you like. A stint at the disposal, might do you a world of good. As you've been told, the pickin's are fine, and you might enjoy the steady income ... as things stand."

"I'm sorta happy at the Grotto."

"What, then, do you think about a gig? I could come over next Sunday afternoon."

"Yeah ... okay. You kinda lost me there for a minute with the zombies, but yeah. I'll talk to Ray, maybe get you in. Going over tonight ... though I've never seen any stand-up there. Mostly guitars and singing and only when the mic is open."

**

LACEY PICKED UP HER TELEPHONE. "Hello."

"Hi Lacey, it's Tony. Guess you heard the news—disrupting. Meyer called this morning. Wants me over tonight to talk over the future. Didn't mention you."

She liked Anthony Giotto—spirited, friendly, and straight to the point, not a charm on his bracelet. She was goddamn tired of men looking to get into your pants. "Hi Tony. Yes, Izsak and I talked. I'd like to continue, if that works out."

"I'm not certain even I will be his man. Meyer and I are not buddy-buddy and he's got other producers in line. The best I can hope for is an assistant's role with one of them. Me ... I think the entire project is up in the air. I'll put in a word if I have a chance, but if I were you, Lacey, I wouldn't bank on continuing. We were there because of Izsak and Izsak is gone."

"Yes, I've been officially fired, tied to his wheels, so to speak."

"Yeah, me as well, though I get my checks from the studio. I feel sorry for Izsak. I mean, he really wanted this, but with Eastman's death, the cookie has crumbled."

"Okay. Listen, Tony, don't risk your own future by attempting to drag me along. It's been fun working with you, and I've been well paid ... not to mention the fabulous experience. I wish you luck. If they don't pick you up to finish *Sugar Cane*, you'll surely get something else."

"Bye, Lacey. If something good comes up, I'll call."

"Bye-bye, Tony."

What a fucking disappointment.

SHE KNOCKED. Arthur answered the door. "Good afternoon, Miss Lacey."

"Hi Arthur. Izsak in? He should be expecting me."

"Give me a moment, please."

She waited. He hadn't called; she didn't think he would, but she also thought he needed to talk and she needed to listen. It was the least she could do ... had to do ... must certainly do, considering his doing for her.

"Come in, Miss Lacey, he's in his study, though not in the best of shape."

"Thanks Arthur. I'll take it from here." She stood tall, her full presence, shoulders back, and with a deep breath walked into the study, heels clicking on the hard oak floor.

"Lacey ... I know ... I should have called. Well, I didn't and the hell with it. You're here anyway and I knew you would come. Sit down. Rose will bring us a bite. You hungry?"

"Thanks, but no. How are you? I talked with Tony. He too is concerned."

"Yeah, we're all concerned. Poor old Izsak, stuck in his chair ... can't get around, lost his wife, his friend, and his job ... depression. My-oh-my, what will become? They're all shaking their heads. Well, fuck 'em. Let 'em stew in their suspicions, their goddamn speculations. I don't give a shit, not a drizzling shit."

"Izsak, Izsak, such an awful attitude. It's not you. You must try. Things aren't that bad."

"Drizzling ... it's the worst of it, you know—nothing more distressing than a drizzling shit when what ya need is an explosion." He chuckled briefly. "Fucking life ...."

"C'mon." She put her hand on his shoulder. It seemed she had little patience for sniveling in a man, but he was a friend, and she would give it a go.

"Stop it now. You're a man of great wealth and I'm not talking money. You have your genius, and time to use it ... to enjoy it, to offer it so that the rest may benefit. For Christ's sake, Izsak, step back away from the details, find a more distant and broader view."

"Step back? You mean roll back." He coughed. "But I need another drink. And you too will need one. And you mix. The good stuff is out and there may be some left in the bottle and when we run out, we'll call Arthur. "

She mixed: ice and single malt. "Here ... now go slow so as I can catch up."

They clinked. "Here's to you, Lacey. May your life be the 'bed of roses' as mine a forest of cacti."

She laughed. "Okay, Mr. P., I do like roses, but here's the rub: they both carry thorns for those getting too close."

She sat. There was quiet for a minute—some tinkling ice and glass—and then she said, "Okay, I want you to tell me what happened with you and Anna. And spare me no personal inflections. This is your time, and I will listen ... unless, of course, you ask for my opinion."

There was an explosion. It seemed far off. The house shook a little, noise from the kitchen, a horn honked down the street. It might have been a tremblor. It might have been construction. Time had a way of slowing things down.

He looked at his drink, twirled the glass, watched the ice run around its perimeter. Why would he go through this again; it won't change. If he ran through it countless times for as many days, Anna would still be gone, her closet empty. Ethan would still be dead.

But then, there was little else to say, and he had to say something. She had come to listen. He took a sip. The drink was good. He liked the scotch ... it never ran out on him.

"She left. She's been leaving for a while ... I think since the picture was released and came the applause. She wanted it, you know. She's always wanted it ... likely wanted it most. When we were younger, and I had legs, we thought I could give her that, but then the accident and my producing days were over ... and my influence waned. Not that she wouldn't have succeeded herself, but someone needed to open the door. It's always the case; no one in this business opens that door themselves. Of course, you know that.

"She had been looking, but until Giles came along, her sight was restricted—like a milk horse with blinders, but you don't remember them. We didn't get out. We didn't circulate—down to the Hut for the music on Sundays about the extent of it. Of course, he changed that—Giles—and she loved it. Then the part in *Harm* popped out of nowhere. A small part but she did well ... and things changed even more. She was

344

noticed for her ability, and I could see she didn't need me after all—Giles had facilitated the opening—though they knew she was married to this chair and the lump that occupied it—the 'has-been,' they likely whispered.

"I guess that's when you entered the frame, a help-mate—and I thought I might produce again and gain back my reputation and be of some value. A Godsend, I thought, and things were looking up ... through those lying rose-hued lenses it turned out. Fix us another drink, Lacey, my glib is drying out." He laughed. "I suppose I'm boring you to death. I know I'm boring myself."

"No, not at all. You are a good friend and I'm interested. Keep talking. It's good to go through it, perspective, you know, and I can hear you from the bar."

"Well, she's attractive. Men find her appealing, no surprise there. She's bright and fun ... vivacious and loves to joke around, and to dance. Likes a party and is generally its life, yet here sits her husband, anchored, rust-coated, and old.

"When she began *Sugar Cane*, and Giles was gone, new opportunities popped up and they could see he wasn't around. Well, a cast likes to party. And she liked the cast, her co-star, the despicable asshole-in-particular, I believe. Forgive my editorializing.

"Rory Randle. I don't even know him. He might be a nice asshole, but certainly he knows she is married. I hear he's a bit younger than Anna—you'd be surprised at her age, actually, and I doubt that Rory knows. Maybe doesn't care. God, I hate this ... a fucking soap opera.

"Anyway, she came in late one night, very late ... although I was up. When she was gallivanting with Giles, I didn't worry. I trusted Giles, a friend. But I got to staying up after he left, waiting for her. Oh, I had valid reasons, working on this and that—the script or some production detail—but the reason, of course, was her.

"All that aside, she came in that night all laughs and frolic and sat down here next to me and became immediately serious. She lit a cigarette. She never smoked before, you know, hated the damned things—kissing an ashtray she used to say.... Dammit, God damn this life I have to live.

"Well, she started. It was a 'new chapter' for her, she said. A challenge had come her way, 'opened up,' she said. A 'life-long dream, another page.' She went on. She would always love me. We were connected somehow, and I believe she even called us soul mates, but to cash in, to exploit this new opportunity, she needed to be single. It was excruciating. Sitting here listening and not even able to reach out, to touch her, hold her, express a manhood I have continued to feel despite it having left long ago.

"I can't tell you ... the devastation ...." His eyes turned downward and began to leak. He shuddered. His frame convulsed and he began to cry. He griped the wheels on his chair until his knuckles turned white, and in his eyes, a massive anger ... clenched jaw and trembling head. Then, in a moment, he pushed it back.

"I'm sorry. Christ, you'd think by now .... I've gone through this before, you know, too many goddamn times." He wiped his nose with a cocktail napkin and sniffled. "The next day she packed a few bags and left."

THEY SAT IN SILENCE. Her instinct was to hold him, to show him she cared, to demonstrate her affection for him—a man of the few she held in esteem. She wanted to bolster his courage, to help him stand ... stand up and face his adversity like she expected he wanted to. But she didn't. It seemed she couldn't ... maybe because she believed he wouldn't—that he liked that chair; it had become his excuse, a convenience to use when needed. So ... she simply sat, and there was little she could think of even to say.

"I guess it's time for a refill." She smiled—a meaningless movement of lips. It seemed that all had been said.

Relieved, she rose and went to the bar; poured them both a full glass of scotch over ice. She felt honored to be awarded his confidence and wished she was competent to return it with some sort of genuine, meaningful help. She wanted, beyond all else, to assist but hadn't the foggiest notion of how. Then, in reviewing her own situation, the best she could do was nothing—self-loathing is internally controlled.

"Izsak ... dear Izsak, I am your friend. If there is anything you think I can do for you ... beyond pouring scotch." She summoned a shallow chuckle. "I want you to tell me ... now or anytime. Anytime at all."

"Thank you ... thank you, Lacey. I know that. It's good that you've listened ... um, in itself a big help. No one has been available, you know ... and apparently, I needed to unload. I feel a little better."

She sat, took his hand, and caught his eyes. "Anytime, Mr. Padgett, anytime"

SHE SAT IN HER THUNDERBIRD parked in the drive in the rear of the lovely Encino house and looked out at the fountain and foliage, the carriage house where Arthur and Rose spent their private life. This was the second time here, immobilized by what had gone on inside, but this time she was angry. What the hell was she doing here—the whole damn thing, starting with Giles. Not very long ago she had a great job and a good life—not the most inclusive but it was working—bills got paid.

Giles had brought risk. She didn't like risk then or before ... and look what's come from taking it, *embracing it*, and totally contrary to her, all that she ever was. Damn that Giles, so different than what she believed she wanted, and he wheedled his way with his charm. She thought she was immune to all that bullshit after McNeveragain. And then she laughed. She laughed at herself ... her naiveté, her gullibility, the defenses she thought she had but were actually a mote of shallow water.

Giles is gone, though, and that had its upside. Though he was a lot of fun ... and he was honest ... and he was certainly good looking.

She rummaged through her purse for the ignition key. *I don't know what the hell I am going to do, but I need to get out of here before Arthur comes out with his long face and a drink.*

Twenty-Seven
Looking Up

NNOUNCEMENTS HAD been up for over a week, inside and outside the Grotto:

FIRST TIME EVER

SUNDAY AFTERNOON, AUG 22 AT 3PM

ON THE HOUSE FEATURING COLE STRINGER.

"Eh, hellooo ... and welcome to the Grotto. My name is Cole Stringer. I work at a refuse center ... so it's called by hoity-toity in the Hollywood Hills. The flat-landers call it a land fill—a commoner expression, and those like me who work there ... we call it a dump. <a few chuckles >

"I say that I work there, but the word work in this context is overused ... misunderstood. It's more like I sit at the entry gate waving the trucks in and out ... point to that part of the fill they can dump ... like a FedCo greeter, 'Have a nice day ... doorless refrigerators to the left, broken TVs straight ahead.' < more chuckles)

"When a civilian arrives—a pickup with a load of lawn clippings—I'm supposed to check eligibility. Did they pay, have a pass, but mostly I'm into making friends. 'Cause we're a family, you know. This coming Sunday we're havin' a family picnic ... we'll BBQ there next to the junk appliances and old stoves; the Edgars are bringin' last week's potato salad that's been setting out, the Joneses will provide left-over dogs and moldy buns, and the Smiths a case of flat beer. < laughter >

"We'll spend some time lookin' for valuables—the stuff that Beatrice don't want but Bernadette finds a need for. < titters > It'll be a contest. We'll hop around in gunny sacks and the one with the most valuable haul will get what the rest have found. < laughter >

"... and then during the week, there's the pickers, those people dressed to the 'twos' that wait for the trucks. The 'twos' ... that's when the holes in your shoe soles are now in your feet ... your coat is so ragged, to take it off you just stand still with your arms down. < laughter >

"It's like someone is watching and the needier you are, the better you'll fare when the back opens up and a rush of other people's trash comes cascading out. < a few chuckles >

"We don't associate. The pickers got their union. It hasn't got a name ... it's informal and there isn't any dues. We wear a uniform, a military press, and we're formal and gotta pay a bit out of each damn check ... but we got a name. There is some animosity due to competition. The pickers can't BBQ at the refuse center and gotta go to a public park where there's grass and drinkin' water, and slides for the kids. < laughter and some applause >

"Some of those trucks pick up in the neighborhoods where the trash is good ... and we call it discards < laughter >

"That's the almost-new stuff that's tossed aside when racing after the Joneses. Some from mansions on Laural and Mullholland. The seasoned pickers wait for them ... but the others, the newbies ... they havtta stand aside and wait for the poor folks' trash—empty milk cartons and toilet rolls. < chuckles >

"And the pickers, they know who's bringin' what, especially the veterans know ... and they line up behind the trucks with the good stuff, 'Here comes Ed. He's got the "A" route today. C'mon, no cuts. You ... You get yo ass to the end of the line.' < laughter >

"Seniority rules at the refuse center—old-timers first. Those trucks back up to the downside of the hill, the gate's released and the hydraulics whine, the bed goes up and the trash comes exploding out like the truck's had an enema. <roaring laughter > There's all sorts of shit, a lotta noise and it comes pretty fast. If you're there, ya better stand back....

"You gotta be close enough to be there first and far enough back so as not to be carried down the hill and buried in the biggest outhouse in the Valley. < laughter and applause >"Yeah, it happens ... but it ain't like anyone cares. If you end up under the good stuff, you might be pulled out and saved, otherwise bye-bye. <roaring laughter >

"It's a contest, ya know ... among the pickers, who can locate and tag the best ... pull it aside. Put a dog on it if it's valuable enough—a snarlin' mutt tied to a find is kinda like homesteading in the earlier days, or stakin' a mine. They work in teams, the kids and their folks ... a kid could grow up to be a principal picker ... make his parents proud. 'Look at Lonie there, got himself a radio.' < laughter >

"I'm lookin for investors. Start a conference, maybe two—the APL and the NPL. The American and National Pickers Leagues. Get enough money together, get the cities behind us, we'll build some bleachers at the Center—a pickers stadium ... and once it catches on and teams have formed, a world series. Anybody? Anybody wanna get in? < applause >

"So, whatta you think about this homosexual thing—men making it with men? Friend of mine boasts that he knows a gay guy that works at a studio here ... he's nice, ya might say sweet ... says he's not afraid of bein' raped—actually looks forward to it. < scattered chuckles >

"And they do it with each other, ya know ... in through the back door, and then there's that fellatio thing—guide it in, move it around, and swallow it down. I might like gays ... maybe even love gays ... but I don't think I could do a whole one. < groans >

"Women do it too, you know. A girl I was dating ... was pretty hot too. She told me one night after a couple hours of grinding away that she didn't want to anymore. She wasn't havin' any fun, and frankly, she said, 'I don't think you're havin' any either. You go, and you go, and you go ... but you never come.' I used to drink a little then .... < standing laughter >

"Anyway, she hooked up with a woman and I saw her once later on ... said she was happy, that things were workin' out ... that neither of them needed go very far before they turned around and came. < mild chuckles >

"This drinking thing's not so good. You're with a woman. She's a looker and you've been thinking about her for a while ... dreaming about how she'd be in bed ... or over the kitchen table. So, you get up the nerve and you call her on the phone. You stammer a little as you try to ask her out and you can't believe your ears when she says okay. < light applause >

"You spend the afternoon, ahead of time, thinking about what you'll say ... where you'll take her ... and what happens then. You have a drink to calm your nerves and then another for the road.

"She looks terrific when she comes to the door, and you take her to a club. She wants to dance. You aren't much good at dancing, so first you have double. She's nice, you think ... much better looking than you thought, and smart. So, what's she doing here with you? < laughter >

"Intimidated by the thought, you have a drink. It's only your third if you don't count those at home and the one or two at the bar. She doesn't seem to mind your drinking and it helps ... so you have another as it loosens you up. < yeah, yeah >

"You close the place, the last to stumble out and you take her home. She has her own apartment and invites you in ... a nightcap, she says. This is great. So inside and anxious, you have two, maybe start another. She's taken off her jacket but doesn't stop there and pulls you into the bedroom. It's your dream come true. It's happening. You're gonna get laid by this beautiful woman. < yeah, yeah >

"Then ... you know what happens .... You can't find it. That big, throbbing, hungry-eyed, pleasure-seeking friend you expect when you unzip ... he isn't there. She looks too and fails to arouse. He's just pulled up his hood, like a wee little baby and gone to sleep ... not even a nighty-night. < big laughter >

"Thanks folks. You've been great. I'm Cole Stringer and it's been fun. See you all again and you have a nice evening here at the Grotto." < standing applause >

"THAT WAS GREAT, Cole" Dennis said. "Where do you come up with that shit? Really good ... and the applause ... they liked it."

Ray came up. "Good stuff, Cole, they liked it. You want next Sunday? Tell you what, you publicize a little, bring in the coffee drinkers, and I'll give you a part of the revenue ... say twenty percent of the net when you're here. As it is, I've put a tip bucket up on the counter with your name on it. Yeah, great stuff ... and the presentation, that dry-martini droll ... perfect for my crowd."

"Okay, I'll be back next Sunday. Let's say at two, and maybe two sessions ... one at two and one at four. That be okay?"

"It'll be your afternoon."

**

NICK HELD MAXINE'S HAND as they walked through the front door of the North Hollywood branch of the Bank of America. He had doubts about getting the money. He had doubts about Maxine as a partner, and he had doubts about running the garage. The whole thing, all of it, left him feeling empty and anxious. What the hell was he doing, taking on this

354

obligation ... three obligations. He didn't feel comfortable with one. He stalled. She turned to him.

"You're worried about this, aren't you," she said and squeezed his hand. "We don't have to do this, you know; it *was* your idea, but you can stop any time before we sign."

"We're here; we'll talk to him."

"Nick, wait ... we'll talk to him. We'll pitch this idea. We're going to be enthusiastic and convincing and when he says yes, we're going to do what? We're gonna say no, just a test run? Let's stop now. Let's talk this though once again. We know what we know ... how to proceed. We've been over it enough times, but we've never talked about how we feel about it. You know, the emotional strings .... We may be tying some knots we prefer not to tie. Let's take that bench over there and explore that part of the deal."

"Okay, you're right. What are we getting into?" Nick said, leading them over.

"I'll start, and here's my thinking, Mr. Hesitant Gates ... and I'm gonna be candid with you. I love you, Nick. It would be dishonest to say I didn't see a future with you ... marriage and kids, the white picket fence. But while I want that, and it's about the only thing I want, I don't need it tomorrow.

"Now, I'm pretty sure you want this garage ... and the only thing holding you up is the money. It seems like a good deal to me and I'm willing to invest as a partner ... a partner, Nick, not a wife. I know I'll be putting up the bulk of the money, along with yours, to get the loan. You'll put up your part and we—the two of us—will both borrow the remainder. You will bring the know-how, hard work, and contacts, and that, with your money, will match my investment and we'll be fifty-fifty on the books. I'll work the front office and we'll each take a draw related to the work we do and its value to the business … and, if our personal relationship doesn't work out, we'll be adults. How does that sound? I mean, is it consistent with what you think?"

Nick nodded, eyes on the floor, his load lightening some.

"If we never get married, if we both, or one of us, falls out of love, or in love with another, it will not affect my attitude or involvement related to our business. Now that's where I stand. I absolutely will hold no special claim on your heart as a result of our partnership. Now, how's Nicholas Gates? Does it help?"

He looked at her, her fair skin and bright blue eyes, the hint of freckles around the bridge of her nose. She was smiling at him and still holding his hand. *Shit! What problem?*

"Yeah, let's get the money."

"AH, MISTER GATES … and this must be your partner."

"Miss McKlosky, Maxine McKlosky," Nick said. "Maxine, meet Noah Nestleman. He is going to lend us the money."

"Well," Nestleman said, "it's the bank, of course, and we'd certainly like to …. Very nice to meet you, Maxine. Please sit down. I want to hear all about your new venture and, assuming the best, I'll have some papers for you to sign. We've heard a little about Rob's Auto Repair from Nick here, earlier … and now, I want to hear the rest."

"GOSH NICK, that was a whole lot easier than I thought. Are we good or not?" Maxine squealed after they got into the car. "I can hardly believe it."

"Yep! We're partners, partner, put her there, partner." He reached over and kissed her.

"That's not what partners do." She laughed.

"We've got the money now and the next thing we need is a more detailed partnership paper, like Noah said. And he needs a copy as will Rob, maybe. I think I'm over my head here. We need to talk to a business guy, get books set up and the rest."

"Yes sir, Mr. Gates, but first we need to open the champagne."

**

JUAN WHEELED UP ON HIS NEWLY TUNED BICYCLE to the hammock where Giles dozed in the sun, corralling the parts of a story.

"Señor Giles, what will you do when we are leaving?"

"Huh ...? You're leaving?"

"Si, Señor Giles. We are leaving for Texas and the USA."

"And when would that be, little friend?"

"Soon, I think. Mi Madre, she is selling the cantina to Manolito. You know Manny, the friend at the garage."

"Humm ...."

"You will go with us?"

"Quien sabe, Juan. I'm not real good with the future."

"You must ... I want you to be with us. Say you will come ... mi Madre say you might come. She would like it, I think."

With some resistance, Giles rolled out of the hammock and headed toward the cantina. Maria was at a table with a man wearing a serious face and a three-piece suit, and Manolito in his ordinary grease-filled coveralls. They were talking in hushed tones.

Giles sat at the bar, pulling his stool up with an intentional squeak as it slid across the floor.

"Un momento." She looked up. "Oh, Giles, you get yourself a drink, okay?"

They were looking at papers and nodding. Soon the man in the suit got up. *"Todo está en orden,"* he said. *"Nos podemos encontrar en mi oficina mañana y terminan con esto, ¿de acuerdo? El director del Banco tendrá que firmar. Se hará a continuación."*

"Bueno," Manlolito said. "Muy bueno."

"Si, bueno." Maria nodded as she too pushed back her chair and got up. They shook hands and the man in the suit left with Manolito, his hand gingerly on the coverall shoulders.

"Oh Giles, my good, wonderful Giles, it is almost done. We will finish tomorrow. Manolito will buy, I will get money. It's my dream come true ... almost, you know."

"I am happy for you, Maria." He gave her a perfunctory kiss. He felt it was coming but so comfortable in its absence, hadn't given it a thought.

"Is it happening soon? When will you leave?"

She put her hand on the back of his neck and pulled him in for a Maria kiss. "You may come with us? There is room, you know ... in my heart, and Texas is big."

"I will need to think," he said. "I ... I just don't know. I just really don't know..." the last of his words tailing off.

"Tomorrow night we will celebrate. We will have a big party. I will cook tamales for all." She exclaimed, "I am so happy, and my beautiful Juan ... he will go to school in the USA."

THE PARTY WAS GETTING UNDERWAY as Giles lay in his hammock, a chilled can in his hand. He pondered his next move. He would need to make one, but what would it be? He liked Mexico ... the people, the attitudes, the sophisticated humanity among common folks. He was picking up on the language enough to get along, and the people he'd met were all to his liking. As he knew it, Texas held nothing for him.

Maybe he'd go south, up on the high plains into the hinterland. He could camp out, writing about what he'd discover, maybe more about himself and about life. He might stay right where he was, work for Manolito to earn his keep. He knew most of the patrons. Or back to the Valley to re-establish old haunts and friends. Maria and Juan ... they wanted him to join them—toasty nights with the lady and days working a diner. Those seemed his options. He took a long draw on his beer. None of it was pulling at him. Elimination, that's the trick. Which of the four was less appealing - okay, one at a time.

"Mi Madre sends these for you, Señor Giles." Juan placed three cold ones carefully on the ground. "And something to eat—quesadillas? Why do you stay out here when the party is inside?"

"*En poco tiempo, mi amigo,* I am coming in soon. I have to think about what I will do."

"Please, Señor Giles, you will come with us to Texas. We are familia now."

Giles laughed, reached out and ruffled Juan's hair. "Si, familia now. You go back in; I'll follow soon."

Familia ... that would be a change, and all the stuff that went with it, the problems with their immigration; he'd probably need a job, need to settle in, and there would be pressures in ways he couldn't imagine now. Well, that leaves three, he thought.

"COME SLEEP WITH ME TONIGHT." Maria beckoned, as in plain sight she slid her bountiful tan body into her negligee. "I think you are leaving but we must say goodbye in ways to remember. Come into my bed and we will make love. You will always have a place in my heart ... because I am fond of you, Señor Giles ... very fond." She laughed.

THE NEXT MORNING, Giles packed his Triumph with the basic survivals, gassed up at Manolito's, gave teary-eyed Juan and his Madre a big hug, and headed out to the road ... a phone number in San Angelo where she thought she might be reached, six fresh burritos and a new poncho in his backpack.

**

"DALTON'S FOLKS WERE BY," Dennis said to Paul as Paul entered the house. "Took his things ... and boy are they pissed; thought the old man was going to hit me."

"Yeah, he's due to be discharged on Friday."

"The old man ... the guy is big ... I mean line-backer big and movin' around in here like a tank into battle and cussin' all the time. Wasn't for his wife, I'd be comatose on the floor. You know they blame us ... say it's our fault. Say it's the way we live ... and I don't get this—they say we're not Christians."

"Yeah, well maybe some of that's true. We do some things I wouldn't want to bring up at a church ... and you know, Dalton didn't have a full voice here."

"Didn't have a full voice? Shit, he was louder than the rest of us combined."

"I mean we didn't listen ... I ... I guess I mean I didn't listen. There's some truth there, Dennis. I think we made him feel inferior ... ignored in a way."

"Don't getcha, man. Dalton's no kid. A guy's gotta stand up if he wants to be heard ... and instead swinging his big fuckin' fist, he's gotta explain ... persuade and convert. Shit, if anyone's to blame for his feeling inferior, it's his fucking parents ... and probably the old man."

"I suppose ...."

"And isn't it funny, they're the ones so angry .... And something else, now that we're on this. You been moping around here like a sick dog, takin' the blame for something that wasn't your fault. You gotta remember, Paul, it was you ended up on the floor looking like an overused Kotex ... face through a grinder. And it was him went flyin' down the street like a crazy man ... under his own steam on his own bike. Weren't no one else, so pull your head outta your ass ... you're not responsible."

"That it?"

"Yeah, I guess, but I'm not the only one who feels that way—I got a lotta company here. So, where's he gonna live, Dalton? Do ya know?"

"He's going home ... his parent's house. Says till he gets used to one leg and the cast comes off ... and his arm ... needs its use with the crutches."

"What then? He got any thoughts about then? Given his parents' behavior, he'll not be lastin' long there .... You wanna beer?"

**

"LET'S SEE ..." Cole said, eyeing the menu. "I guess I'll have the roast pheasant under glass, a toasted Norwegian bun ... and not too dark on the toast—maybe a Hawaiian brown after three days at the beach." He looked up quickly to see if she was smiling. "And green, we'll need something green ... I don't see watercress but feel certain you have it ... with rough-chopped Amaretto-soaked hazelnuts, and to drink, a glass of your best French sauvignon blanc."

Cole was ordering at Dupar's a late Sunday dinner after completing a successful gig at the Grotto and feeling inde-structible.

Dupar's, the Valley's late-night stop-over between the office party and go-home-to-your-wife, wasn't crowded to-night, in fact, unusually empty. Three uniformed cops with a substantial presence of Danish at a far table, a couple of three-piece gabardines at the bar, and a carhop zone lacking a car. It was time for fun with the waitress, who wasn't busy at all.

"Do I have this straight, Mr .... I didn't get your name, but you can see I am Lacey." She touched her name tag. "You don't have one of these, do you? How will you *ever* know who you are ... or does it matter?"

"Stringer. Cole Stringer. You see, I do remember because, if to not a single other concern, who I am matters to me ... and who knows; it may matter to you as well at a point in our future."

"Yes .... Well, Mr. Stinger, there are substitutions tonight. In place of pheasant, we have barnyard sparrow from before the big war, you get two. We're all out of buns, but we have croissant made with parsnip dough served on a green paper doily, but don't despair, the doily is laced. Today's order of watercress came in short somehow, but we can offer you fresh mown fescue. It's the golf-course variety garnished with Canadian goose poop and sure to satisfy your fussy culinary taste. We do have the wine if from Napa, and I recommend it first ... maybe two tall glasses with a whiskey chaser."

He smiled and nodded. "That was good ... really good, and I presume unrehearsed. Clever, Lacey, and cute."

"Cole Stinger ... rings a bell. Who do you know that I know?"

"Ever been to the dump?"

"Dump?"

"Yeah ... that's where I am thought to work, occasionally."

"No ... wait a minute ... the dump? Do you know a Giles Anderson?"

"Sure. Not around these days, but yes, I knew him reasonably well. You're not *that* Lacey?"

"Afraid so."

"Whata you doing here? I thought you were a movie producer."

"Long story, Cole. Let me get your wine and ..." she looked around "... I'll have some time, should you want company. Oops, just got a signal from the kitchen, Mr. Stringer. Sparrow is out tonight, no barns here in LA, but we have some fine roast beef au jus on a French roll with a salad side."

"That'll do, medium rare, and Roquefort."

"SO THAT'S IT, COLE. They're making the picture, *Sugarcane Blues*—new director and new producer who came with his own assistant, leaving me out of a job."

"No other like opportunities?"

"Nothing immediate and there is this: I needed a break. Wandering Giles leaving me flat, the movie that almost never was, Izsak's personal problems, the director's suicide ... all too much for the likes of me, and I could spend half a year at the beach mending my ego or get a no-stress job and my act back together. I couldn't afford the first, so here I am."

"And the act?"

"There's always hope, I'm told."

Twenty-Eight
Severances and Partnerships

H IS TRIUMPH THUMPING AT IDLE, Giles pondered the decision once more. He'd never been this unsure of direction, so stymied and halted. He glanced left toward Juarez, then right to the desert. It wasn't like him to second guess; that itself was unsettling. Even his momentous decisions were easily made and quickly pursued. And it didn't seem just a matter of which way to turn, or maybe go back ... even 'go back' still lingered as a possibility.

Once a professor friend of his father's had asked, "Giles, sit back, close your mind to the present and imagine your demise. When people walk by your coffin and look in, what sort of person do you want them to see? What will you want them to think of you, and would you like for an epitaph?"

He smiled at the recollection. It had been something foolish he'd did, something spontaneous ... a "fuck-up." But to his father and his analytical psychologist friend, it was more ... something serious—a harbinger of his future ... although as he scanned the road, seeking invitation, he couldn't remember what it was.

As he mused, the Triumph's engine died, and he let his mind go untethered with the question.

He also couldn't recall what he wanted on his stone—something smart-assed probably, and he thought about it now. If he came to his end out on the highlands, the only stones around would be those weathered by centuries of the hot blistering winds that had formed the desert in the first place, with not enough space for a line from even a ball point. The only eyes peering in would belong to a coyote or maybe a buzzard—and what would they think? Umm ... a Kansas-steak dinner.

Fuck it. He grinned. *I'm turning right. That's what I decided when I thought on it last night.* He cranked up the engine and started off into the high desert of Mexico with a handful of burritos and, with the decision made, no more on his mind.

He felt the dry air on his face, saw the endless horizon ahead, and his mind cleared of all things past. He loved, if he loved anything, the freedom of the road and its lack of entanglement. There'd be time enough for that in years to come. All of his life was out in front—a panorama of adventure and discovery—and what could be more enticing than that?

The miles passed by; the road narrowed and got rougher, and signs of life diminished. In the last half-hour he had not seen another soul or signs of one. Toward evening the air chilled and he stopped for a burrito and warm beer. While he was eating, a scorpion wandered by within a couple feet, and he shared a part of his tortilla ... and would the bug like a beer? He chuckled quietly and looked away as the scorpion tended to its business.

The sky, a blinding blue forever, seem to mirror Giles' meditative aspirations for a clean, clear slate ... and there wasn't a sound except for his breathing. He would be in Chihuahua soon, find a bed and sleep that night without the desert visitor. Giles mounted his bike and again headed south, curiously looking forward to a human exchange, and happy with his direction.

**

"I'M LEAVING," Nick said one night as he and Paul were watching the TV news, mostly a swing at détente with mutually assured annihilation there as the kicker. There was little doubt in anyone's mind; the nukes were going to fall. The only question then was when.

"What do you mean?" Paul said, glancing up.

"Maxine and I are looking for a place."

"Humm ... expected, I guess. There's the lease ...."

"Yeah, the lease. I'll keep up my part of it—only a couple months to go."

"When do you occupy, I mean, start up your business?"

"Next week ... hard to believe, my own repair shop ... Max's and mine. Like a dream."

"Yeah, totally, and I'm happy for you on both counts—the rediscovery of hidden love and the garage. You okay with money?"

"Yeah, we're good. Be tight for a while. Maxine will stay with her job, keep us in bologna and beer, and we'll have some left from the loan. It was her got this started, ya know. She pushed on me some ... and then she put up some money. I didn't think we were ready, but then she asked me some

367

questions ... got to the heart of my worry and boom! It went away and we'll be fine ... I think."

"We should celebrate. Dennis and Cole should be back soon, out looking at cars. Dennis wants new wheels, wants to trade in his Lincoln. That poor car ... cherry less than a year ago but since sure taken a beating—belongs more in a salvage yard than on a public street. Since Vicki's accident in Long Beach—the birthday party, you know—she drove that Lincoln all the way back in lo-range, something about the accident fucked up the transmission. And now, he's using a shower curtain for a top—classy."

"Comes of lending it out. Wonder what he's using for money ... of course, there's Shelley. She has a way. And I s'pose he'll be leaving soon too."

"I don't know, maybe not," Paul said. "The way I read it, Dennis is not so hot on a formal coupling. He likes Shelley but he's not real game on marriage—be the last one into a nest and I gotta few bucks for that. Care for a wager?"

"Sure, I got ten ... even odds."

"You're on. Let's say by the end of the year. Now how about a beer? He took down a glass, put his hand on the tap handle.

"Sure, make it a tall one," Nick said. "Okay to turn off the TV? It's depressing ... all that crap about falling dominos and a nuclear holocaust. People digging holes in their back yards, burying those big iron tubes filled with dried beef and canned corn. Good God, we've all gone mad."

"People are frightened. I find it a little spooky myself. I mean, we peasants ... we don't know enough of the truth to form a decent opinion, so we just go with what we are told ...

TV and newspapers. And you know their motive is profit. It's all about money, Nick, and when we're scared, we spend it, and if we're scared shitless, we really unload."

"Yeah, I guess …. The beer. You gonna pour or preach?"

"BOY, I'M BEAT" Dennis said, coming in the front door. "Saw a lotta cars out there on Van Nuys Boulevard, and salesmen … funny thing though, they all wanted money and not one was interested in the Lincoln. They'd take one look and start talking to Cole."

"So, where's Cole? Wasn't he with you?" Nick said.

"Pussy-whipped. Soon as we stopped out front, he jumped in his Corvette and took off … said he had a date with Lacey. Can ya beat that coupling … Cole and Lacey? And he says she's waitin' tables over to Dupar's. Man, what a comedown for that hoity-toit… wearin' an apron."

"Have a beer," Paul said. "We're celebrating."

"Sure, whata you celebrating; somebody die?"

"Pour your beer and shut up for a while," Nick said. "You might hear the news."

"Nick's leaving us," Paul said.

"You going back to Detroit?"

"Nope, Maxine and I are moving in together. The deal is closed, and Max and me, we own the shop now and we're thinking it would be handy … living together."

"Oh."

"Um, so we're celebrating his good fortune," Paul said. "You gonna be next?"

"Me?"

"Yeah. I heard that Shelley's dad has offered up a job with his agency, and ... and here you are out looking at cars like you just came into a big paycheck. So ... you next? It's a question that's beggin'."

Dennis emptied the glass in a single chug, eyes watering. "You gotta be fucking kidding—not me. Got no such designs. Yeah ... he offered, but I like it at the Grotto. Ray's considering expansion—another place that I might manage." He drew another beer. "Sure, I like Shell ... we get along ... great sex and all that, but I'm here for the duration. Shit, I'll be here when ol' Sampson shows up with a moving van. Ha, maybe he'd like a roommate."

"So, what's the deal with the cars?" Paul said.

Dennis chuckled. "Just checking things out. Wanted to see what the Lincoln was worth on a trade. Runs okay since the transmission replacement. Tops gone and winter's comin' next—I looked at the calendar." He chuckled. "I'm just planning ahead."

"Planning? You're planning?"

"Yeah, we all gotta look out for ourselves ... sometimes. Besides, Shelley may make me a loan. Getting tired, she says, a riding in a junk-heap, and I never discourage her feelings. Fact is, I encourage her good taste." He grinned. "You know ... that car was cherry when we moved in here—I mean, pristine clean. I got my hand on the tap here, anybody ready for a refill?"

"Umm, so there it is," Nick said, looking over at Paul. "Seems you're gonna have company, you and Wayne—Dennis, to the bitter end. And if you're all here when Sampson arrives ... wouldn't wanna miss those fireworks. Sure, pour, Dennis; this is a celebration. Too bad Dalton's not here."

"Speakin' of Dalton, what about this beer thing—his system? He gonna take it now that he's gone?"

"No," Paul said. "I talked to him about that and it's here for the duration. He'll have someone pick it up just before the end of October."

**

"STEAMIN' JESUS, LACEY ... your place is ... well, it's leaving me speechless," Cole exclaimed, looking around. "I got the idea you were a classic lady, but ... wow, can't think of another thing to say."

"And nice to see you, Cole. Can I fix you a drink?"

"Most certainly and let me play tourist while you're mixing. I like the art."

"You almost remind me of someone," she said, "all that wonderment. Do you like scotch?" ...*as well* crept into her mind.

"Yes... and a double with soda would suit me."

"I know how to mix them." She laughed at her reflection in the window over the sink. It all seemed so familiar, and its lesson learned, yet here she was again, entertaining a man in her apartment.

"Let's see ... we have an Alvar screen and a Pollock litho, and here is Newman. Wow, this is original."

"It's my brother's donation," Lacey said. "The Newman's probably on lease ... but he's never asked for it back.

He's a sports nut with money, has a restaurant over on the beach."

He let his eyes scan the room. "Place looks fantastic. Gotta say, I'm impressed."

"Cole, please ... don't fall overboard. Let's get back to the reason you're here. A dinner, you said, on the Strip."

"Yeah, the Gourmet. Been there? It's quite nice—an elegant restaurant for an elegant lady."

And another flash of Giles lit up in a corner of her mind. "Yes ... I've been there, once ... and you're right, it is elegant. Here's to comedy." Lacey held up her glass to his and they clinked.

"Sit, Cole, and tell me about yourself."

His lanky body stretched comfortably over the white Italian leather. He sipped the scotch, a rich single malt, and let his mind travel the short path that led to his new comedic role. It made him smile.

"There isn't much in the prologue, but the succeeding chapters may get interesting."

"I'm talking about your earlier times, Cole. Let's leave the new pages blank for a while."

"Oh ... well, let's see. I enjoy my life. I have a few friends. I'm reasonably healthy, above average smart, seethe with ambition, polish my shoes ... and generally, what you see is what you get. How's that?"

"Why that's quite encouraging, Cole. I appreciate honesty without flourish."

"Thank you, and you are lovely tonight."

She smiled, her sparkling emerald eyes framed in her ash blonde hair, "Now tell me about yourself."

"I have plans. They're not specific or definite, but I don't like to waste time and I have an appreciation for quality and the associated value. Let see ... early I began saving, then investing in the market. Did my own accounts and discovered from listening wherever I could, how to research, follow trends, and when to get in and out.

"My father, not just a dad but a good friend, teaches microeconomics at Valley and that served me well. I had some downers ... no one knows everything. Well, that's kinda it, Lacey; most people find this boring as hell." He smiled. The intensity in his eyes diminished as he reached for his glass.

"No ... go on. I'm really very interested." She had moved up to the edge of her seat.

"You're kidding, of course, or playing the good host."

"No no, I want you to tell me more."

Well, okay ... despite my educated forebearers, I'm not at all interested in college. I like to work and got a job—"

"I heard you work at the county refuse center."

"Yes ... well, the dump isn't particularly demanding—waving folks in and out—and I am able to dig in ... study opportunities and work my portfolio, and .... Look, I'm just a regular guy who got his priorities in line, early-on in the game. I'm not bothered by threatening doom, don't have bomb shelter, though I do own a few, and I keep an eye on the times. And, I like to have fun but it's not why I get up in the morning."

"You own bomb shelters?"

"Yeah ... picked up a small piece of Sheila's Shelters down on the Boulevard—friend of a friend thing, a trend investment. Big mark-up on the dried food and some on the tanks." He crossed his legs and slid back in the sofa. "Okay ... I'm buying into fear. People spend emotionally. I'll get out soon, got a buyer sniffin'. It won't last, you know."

"You mean the Red Menace?" She leaned in toward him with a curiosity just short of wonder.

"Yeah, the menace." He laughed. "First, not much one can do about it ... either way. Second, the Ruskies have tastier fish to fry in Asia ... and soon, they'll be havin' trouble at home. Finally, I have a lot of faith in our own ... the Philbrick guys, livin' those three lives." He chuckled. "Now enough of all this. Is there another scotch or is it time to leave?"

"Humm ... I like the way you think, Cole. So where do you hang your hat ... still living at home?"

"With my folks, you mean?"

She nodded.

"Not for years. Got a couple rooms over a pizzeria ... Tony's over on Lankersham. Nothing like this," he looked around. "But it works for me, stimulates my appetite—both the modest arrangement and the pizza wafting up from be-low."

"Humm ...." She scooted back in her chair, took a last sip.

"And what about you, Lacey?"

"What about me... I guess I'm finding my bearings—looking around. Freshen your drink?"

"Yes, to the scotch, but you're not getting off that easy. I want to know about you. I've heard a little, but let's hear it from you."

"What have you heard?" she said, getting up and taking his glass. "Same?"

"Sure, though lighter on the scotch. Only that you're a producer, radio and films."

"Well, not so much with the movies, but that's about it. And I'm not into history, Cole, especially my own. I've learned a bit over the years and prefer not to repeat the lessons." She returned with the drinks, the late sun behind her as she passed by the dining nook window.

"You are an appealing woman."

"Yeah, appealing ... now here's something I *will* say about me up front. I'm not interested in romance. But it strikes me, Cole, that we might work something out ... uh, professionally, you know."

"Really ... how's that?"

"Well ... and I've been thinking about this over our last couple meetings, and maybe I'm off base ... and you say if I am ... but you're wanting to get into stand-up, and I have a few connections. I might like to get back into producing, or something related, and maybe we could hook up. I manage while you focus on routine—push your career while I'm working a little on my own."

He settled back in the comfortable cushions and took a sip from his scotch. A smile came over his surprise as he hadn't been thinking of this, not this at all.

"You know, Cole, and I'll be honest. I'm a little awkward pushing out like this. I intended a more subtle approach. But you seem to appreciate things straight up, so what the hell ... it's not such a crazy idea, you know, and the more I think about it, the less crazy it seems."

"So, what's your deal?"

"Deal?"

"Yeah, what would you want? What sort of financial arrangement?"

"Twenty percent of the gross. I'll get the gigs, negotiate your fees, and keep the books—schedules and finances and such. You do the shows. We could begin like that and if what we see now gets different in the future, we'll be open to change. Doesn't need to be formal—a simple piece of paper. You want to sleep on it? We can talk more about it after."

He grinned, got up from his chair and went over to her. He bent down suddenly and kissed her on the cheek. Her eyes widened but she didn't retreat.

"It's a deal, Lacey ... partner. Draw up that paper and we can start as soon as you put down your pen. I like your 'straight up'."

She got up and extended her hand. "It's business, Cole."

"So, now it's your turn," he said. "Tell me about you."

She offered, a coy smile that hardly broke a facial line. This deal with Cole, its quick conclusion a surprise, was returning the budding confidence she had been feeling with Izsak. If she wasn't back on the track where she felt she belonged, she was getting damned close. In the days short of this meeting, a fantasy had been born and had grown as she repeated the scenario, from sheer speculation into something approaching reality, and now ... now it *was* real.

"I've said all that needs to be said ... for the time."

**

MARY F LIKED HER JOB more and more each day. She loved the attention her good looks brought from the in-house sales team she worked with, and occasionally they bought her lunch. She enjoyed her success in the office, reflected now with sizable and frequent increases in title and salary. And she felt she would fit in the larger network of field reps she was planning to join, and the buyers and design engineers she would meet when soon she would hit the road with her own accounts—earning big money.

She didn't like her slimy boss, who seemed obsessed with getting into her drawers, and the continuing tightrope she needed to walk to make her aspirations a reality—encouraging enough interest to hold his favor without sullying her own constitution. He was a pig, she thought, married with two kids and acting like some acne-faced, teenage grease-ball—always with his dick in his hand and ready to spew.

She also didn't like the fact that Paul couldn't seem to land a job and each day of failure brought him less interested in trying. Something had happened to Paul, she thought. He'd lost his confidence and she could understand why he wasn't succeeding in interviews. She loved Paul and thought Paul was her future and that of her kids, and he loved her, it seemed, and that sort of bonding didn't come very often in her book.

On the other hand, there was Las Vegas, and Las Vegas might be the solution. Out of this place and away from the immediacy of near memories, he would repair. There he would work, and she would spend her time with the kids. She had been quiet about her conversations with friends there, friends who would like her to move and would make accommodations. She only needed to establish his interest.

"HI PAUL, HON ... any luck with Graul and Weston?" she asked in a subdued and musical voice as he came in through the door and plopped down beside her.

"Don't know yet. The interview went okay, I guess, but ... well, it's hard to tell but I think they're just collecting applications." He stared at the wall and felt like a robot. He had no interest. "Guy there said they had new work coming in. How many times have I heard that. I guess it's tough for everyone. I don't want—" He was just talking. It wasn't for her so much as closing the door on Graul and Weston.

"You know I have friends in Las Vegas. They say things there are booming. Mac works for a casino. I think we should drive out, you know, talk to Mac and Charlene. He's said a couple of times ...." She moved closer in, put her hand on his, catching his attention. "He said ... okay, Charlene said, that you'd have no problem. They need financial people ... keep track of all that money. In a little while, who knows? Las Vegas is growing, and if nothing else, we'll have fun, and it will lift your spirits. Anyway, you'll like them. Mac's a swell guy."

He moved his eyes from the wall reluctantly and turned to her. She smelled good. She always smelled good—a single flower. Not overwhelming, just enough, and he felt comfortable. She was strong but not aggressive, and it made him feel warm and secure.

"I dunno ... if you think so. I guess I'm willing. I know I need to do something ... feeling kind of useless these days and my funds are running low."

"Okay, mister." She got up from the couch. "You just sit. I'm calling right now. If they're available, we'll go this weekend and stay as long as you need. It'll be fun, the casinos and

378

all, and you'll like Mac. Cheer up, for Christ's sake; despite what they say, the world's not ending tomorrow."

Twenty-Nine
Ups are Down and Vice Versa

"NAME?"

"Dalton Dobbs."

"Umm ... I guess I knew that. Address?"

"2698 Mari ... look, why don't you just let me fill it out? Arms working fine."

"Okay, didn't mean anything by it. Just that most of the times I can't read the scrawl you guys put down. Besides, it's kinda my job, what receptionists do .... I'm a girl Monday, Tuesday, Wednesday, Thursday, and Friday. Only thing I don't do is bench saw and grinding."

He took the application, and on his crutches, hobbled over to a chair. *Kinda cute, ask her name.*

"You wanna pen?" She was right behind him. "I know who you are ... you're a big deal around here, son of the boss's best friend. And I know how you lost that leg, too, and I'm real sorry about that. Must be kinda tough, those crutches and stuff."

He wasn't sure how to answer. He wasn't sure of anything, though he used to be sure of it all. He didn't know whether to smile or turn and stumble out, but his old man was out in the car and he was expecting him to move on—get the job. His old man .... He looked back.

"You want to talk, or do you want me to fill out the application?"

"Sorry again. I need the app."

He laid it on the table. "Meisner's Wood and Fine Furniture Shop - Specializing in Custom Cabinets" and below that, "*We Do Amazing Things with Wood.*" He didn't know a thing about building furniture or even how he'd keep up with one leg, but old Meisner had said, "Plenty to do for a man with one leg. Start 'im vacuuming and as he progresses, work him on the line. Yep, plenty to do. Got my start like that ... plenty." Melvin Meisner and Fred Dobbs were close friends in kindergarten and except for the war, neither had moved out of the other's reach or engaged in a serious argument.

Dalton finished and, on his three legs, made his way back to the reception desk and laid the application in front of her.

"That was quick," she said, "and I can almost understand it." She looked up at him with sassy blue eyes and big smile. "I'm Daisy ... and since you can read, you already know that." She pushed a small wood block with her name on a brass plaque toward him. "When you're here for a year, you might get one of these and maybe a desk to put it on ... and I hear if you're around here long enough, and don't die beforehand, you'll get a gold watch. Now that, Dalton Dobbs, is something to think about. You wanna get lunch? It's closin' in on that time."

**

GILES LAY ON HIS BACK, fresh boxers, a shower and clean sheets. He stared at the cracked plaster ceiling while equally fragmented thoughts ran around in his head. Chihuahua offered little in the way of entertainment; wasn't much of a place to begin with and why stay here? But where would he go? He needed a plan for once in his life—at least a direction. *I'm aimless. Don't know where or why I am going or if I should remain.* The one thing he did know was that things would change. They always did, and he took some small satisfaction in that—made a mental note on the ceiling. His eyes caught some movement from a crack in the plaster. A spider came out, trotted around a bit, seemed to be checking things out, and then disappeared back in the crack.

He didn't know what lay ahea; had only a hazy recollection of what was behind—Maria and Juan the clearest. He might want to compare the unknown with the partially recollected and from there find some direction, but he wasn't the analytical type. And that was another thing he knew—he was intuitive, led around by his gut or maybe his nose when his gut was otherwise busy. Well, there's the second hard revelation; he might be making some headway and he took note: things would always change, and he operated mostly on intuition. He knew it. It was familiar, but he had never before seen it written out on the ceiling.

He closed his eyes. There were people racing around in his head like bumper cars—touching and leaving: Paul and Dalton, Dennis and Nick, Izsak and Anna ... Lacey. What had become of them? He knew from Izzy's letter that things were not right with he and Anna, or at least not as he'd left them. And what of Lacey? He thought she had found success; certainly seemed so at first contact. Was she the woman for him? Probably not, at least not now.

The one he saw more clearly, and that was a surprise— Suzy. Perky, self-contained, not too serious, well put together and liked the motorcycles she sold and he bought. With her, he might find commonality. Of course, it was guesswork— something more for the ceiling.

Maria beckoned—dark-skinned, big smile, loving eyes. She wanted him to come with her and Juan to San Angelo. What he knew and saw of Texas did not favor his kind. Had she stayed at the cantina in the land of love, good food, romance, and song ... well, that could be a life ... and for a while it was.

But what was this thing with women—the longer he loved and remained with even the best, the less he liked them—eventually it all came down to the promise. It just took a while to let it come out. He wasn't ready to settle. It wasn't that he abhorred the idea ... in fact, he liked it. He liked it as an idea.

His eyes were losing their focus, the ceiling was losing it scrawls, his lids were drooping. Soon he'd be chasing his dreams, and that not a bad place right now. Tomorrow ... tomorrow would bring what it would.

THE MORNING FOUND HIM rested and fresh, not a mark on the ceiling or a distraction in his head, and with strong black coffee and a plate of hot buttered tortillas in front of him, he asked the way to Durango—about a ten-hour ride, all going well.

"You go this way for a few kilometers, señor, then you go that. Then you go the way to Durango. It is not a long distance." *Well, those directions were clear.*

He gassed up, both tanks to the top, filled his thermos with coffee, and when he arrived at the intersection, he turned toward "that." Five miles down the road he stopped and cut the engine. *Christ, it's quiet.*

He poured coffee and sipped. He looked out at the sameness of desert and brush to the horizon. He felt the mid-morning sun on his face and its promise to get hotter. And as he sat there straddling his bike and sipping his coffee, those random thoughts began again to roam through his head and the names and faces popped up. He gave them their rein for a while and then, without formality, tossed out the grounds in his cup, cranked up the engine and turned around - back to the intersection and left to "this" in place of "that," through the mountains toward Hermosillo, and then on toward LA.

**

"DO YOU, PAUL ALEXANDER SMYTHE, take this woman, Mary Frances Martinez-Torres, to be your lawful wedded wife; if so, say 'I do.'"

Jesus, did he? Did he fucking really? And he said, "I do." And he smiled while he was saying it. Well, she was beautiful, standing there at the make-believe altar with the make-believe witness of the make-believe chapel, the Wee Kirk of the Heather, in a white cocktail dress that showed plenty of leg, and her radiance would light up the Strip from the Nugget clear out to the Tropicana.

The guy with the book was a skinny fuck with a puss that would curdle chilled milk and the woman next to him, a fat little gnome, wore a smile that she must've been born with—frozen in place even when she spoke, which luckily wasn't too often. "You will never regret this, Mr. Smythe," she had said as she took his twenty bucks and asked if he wanted a recording.

And he had a job as a junior accountant at the Downtown Golden Nugget making almost twice what he made at Chevrolet, and Mary was delirious, and the kids were happy, but they always were, he reminded himself, running around the house, stoked up on various forms of sugar. *And I'll start in three weeks—three fucking weeks, and I'm married—went on a quick trip to Las Vegas to bolster my attitude, and in only a couple of days, a family man with kids and a job and a new location. "Holy shit!" as Dalton would say, "a fucking head-spinner."*

Mac shook his hand with an arm around his shoulder like they'd known one another since birth, then kissed Mary F in a manner more suited to foreplay, and Charlene did likewise to him, though he clenched his teeth to prevent her darting in.

He gave the woman another twenty bucks and bought the recording—a recording of a recording of an accordion for the most part, and they headed out to the lounge at the Sands.

"Oh, Paul, I'm so happy. I've never been happier, not ever. I love you so much," she told him in the back seat of the cab ... Mac and Charlene taking the kids in the car they all

386

came in and would drop them off with a sitter who worked at the hotel. "Are you happy too?"

"Yes ...."

"I genuinely hope so. It's been sorta quick and I'm not so sure about you."

"You can be sure," he said as he recalled the events. Arriving on Saturday, he had interviewed on Sunday and was hired that afternoon although he wasn't sure even then—when just getting started—that it would accelerate like a dragster at the sound of the starting gun. And even now, the checkered flag down, he wasn't sure if he'd won or ended up in the wall. But then recently—back home—he'd not been certain about anything, when only a month ago or so, he knew all the irregularities in the track, was at one with the car, middle of the track and confident about winning.

But somehow, he had to have a job—wherever and from whom didn't matter. *Jesus Christ! Was life just about having a job? Who I am, what I think, my values—all about pushing a pencil, running a lathe eight-to-five?* And he thought about his good friend Giles, who didn't give a shit about work, eschewed the thought of it, and certainly didn't need its confirmation. *What the fucking hell ... what is our difference?*

"I'm going to have lobster and Champagne tonight, buckets of it," she said. "Let's get the best, what is it ... Dom Perignon, and ... and we'll have caviar and truffles. I want us to celebrate, Paul. We've been working up to this, and while ... well, I guess it's been kinda sudden, these last few steps .... But we knew they were coming, and darling—can I call you darling now?—they are here, and we're happily married with a new life in Las Vegas. Oh ... I could squeal." And she moved over on top of him a little and gave him a big kiss ... and as her kiss lingered, he found he kissed her back.

**

"WHERE THE HELL'S OL' ROB? And what's this new management shit I see on that sign? Got my car out there and it needs his fixin', so where is he?"

"Hi," she said. "I'm Maxine. I can help you. Rob has sold out and we've picked up the business—Nick and me. Let me call him. I'm certain we can help you. He's an excellent mechanic."

"Can I help you?" Nick said through the door from the shop.

"Well, how the hell do I know?" he said. "It's the goddamn car. C'mon out, I guess. I'm here and you might as well have a look ... listen to the click in the engine. What happened to ol' Rob? He die?"

"No." Nick laughed. "He retired."

"About goddamn time. I thought he was attached to this place by his umbilical ... and his old man before him. Seen 'em both spend their lives here—day and night. Well, not so much the old man, mostly before my time, but Rob, ya know ... went to high school together, right here in Van Nuys. Well, that was a time ago. I see ya got the place cleaned up ... junk's all gone. Ain't never been like this before. Here, let me start her up and you can listen to the click. Name's Antoine, by the way, call me 'Tone.' Been coming here regular for years. Gonna miss ol' Rob. You any good? Don't wanna waste any money. Your missus says you're good. That true?"

Nick laughed again. "Start her up and release the hood." He pulled out a mechanic's stethoscope and put it here and there on the block and across the head, listening in to the chatter of moving parts. "Okay, that's enough. Shut it down."

"So, what's wrong? And what the hell's that thing you're prodding around with there? Looks like a water witching thingamabob. Never saw Rob usin' one of those."

"You have a sticky valve, Tone. How many miles on this engine?"

"Odo says hund'rd five thousand, there abouts. It was out for a while. Had her since new, ya know."

"Well, if you're keeping her, you'll need new valve guides, maybe a couple new valves. If you're not, we'll throw in some detergent and run it for a while, clean out the varnish. That'll cost you a lot less, last a little while, but the click won't go away for long, and it won't do the engine any good ... and at some point, new seats and valves plus the guides."

"I'm keepin' her forever so whata ya recommend and how much will it cost me? Ain't got a whole lot, ya know. Ain't nobody got a whole lot these days."

"Minor overhaul would do you for another hundred thousand miles. Check the bearings, new rings, grind the valves, replace if you need them ... new guides, clean out the sludge and the oil routes, points, plugs, rockers and springs where needed, and about $200 maybe two-fifty all told—depending on parts."

Tone laughed, slapped the fender and said, "Shit, I don't know any a that. I do know a hundered thousand though. Well, I guess ol' Rob wouldn't let his name be used by no shysters and hooligans, so's ... okay, let's do her. I'll bring her back in the morning."

"Max! We've got our first customer and damn if it isn't an overhaul," Nick almost shouted as he came into the office and gave her a hug, smudges over the back of her white blouse. "We'll get some pizza and cold beer—celebrate. This might actually work."

**

"IZZY, I WANT A DIVORCE. I've retained a lawyer. You'll be served in a couple of days. You must've seen it coming. It isn't a surprise—not a big one." Anna poured him a drink and sat down, her eyes full of tears because at the bottom, her heart wasn't in it. "I'm so sorry, honey-pops, but you must understand. I want us to be friends—more than that. I love you. You know I love you, but things have changed."

"You could have made it stronger."

"Stronger? Don't be sarcastic, Izsak. I thought you'd want it direct. You've always admired honesty."

"The fucking drink, Anna ... the drink." He looked at her, caught her wet eyes. "And I do understand, though it doesn't make it easier ... and not sure it makes any sense. I've drank stronger water; can you spice this up?"

She took his glass to the sink and dumped it, added two cubes and then to the brim with single malt scotch. All the time, Izsak was talking.

"I've been sitting here in this goddamned chair—waiting. Waiting for the axe to fall, to chop off the rest of my manhood, and not really knowing … only suspecting. It's Randle, right? The only asshole with a grinning anus."

"Izsak! That's not like you, for God's sake … and no, it's not Rory, though you're selling him short. It's the situation, and you know it. I need independence. You … if you remember, advanced the idea and we've talked about it and now it's here and I have the shot we have wanted … both wanted, Izzy. The shot that you, my dear, have worked unselfishly toward for over the years, and we know I need to be free to pursue it.

"I have a life in film, and now after years of letting it slip, of being your wife, I realize it's finally here … truly arrived. You know that. I know that you realize that I must be free to fully exploit it."

He took a strong pull on his drink, watched as she crossed her legs—marvelous legs, shapely, while his, he noted, wouldn't move. *She is a good human being, a beautiful woman, loyal, and for years a great deal of fun.* His life in the chair had been tolerable with Anna at his side, even productive, when otherwise he might have been dead—absent her, quite likely by his own hand.

She didn't bargain for any of it but nonetheless held firm to her commitment. *But why a divorce? Christ, what an ugly word.*

"Do you need a divorce to live out your life, your dream, as you say, coming true?"

"It's a piece of paper, Izzy."

"It says it's the end, Anna—the finale. It says we are through … kaput, and the credits are rolling."

"No. It says I am free to play on the field where the game is being played. It says you are not in my way. It says your associates don't need to consider *you* when dealing with me. Moreover, it says nothing about our relationship which I hope will not change. It's a business deal, Izzy, that's all ... at least from my point of view. It's legal, not personal. Please see it that way."

"Before you leave, fix me another drink, will you?"

"Izsak ..."

"Look Anna. Look at me. I'm stuck here. I'm not going anywhere. You, on the other hand, have got your ticket, packed your bags, and ..." He wiped his eyes. "You, my dear, are on your way. It's a goddamn fact. I don't like it. There are other things I don't like, but not much to do but accept them. Let me wallow, eh, swallow a bit ... and the drink please, on your way out."

He watched her pick up his tumbler and walk over to the bar, knowing it might be the last. It was a business-like stride, direct and purposeful, that he was compelled to admire. What a body she still had and now a head to go with it. He remembered, before his accident, the wonderfully joyous times they had—she whimsical and romantic, though ambitious and hopeful, he, aspiring and moving up. Concerts and parties, she liked horseback riding and hiking, and they often made love—passionate, consuming love, as if alloyed into one. Life was overflowing then when the future was a promise in hand, but this ... this was the end, the goddamned end ... and those that had anything to say, said, "You must let her go."

She put the drink on the table beside him, touched his hand gently and kissed him on the cheek.

"I will always love you, Izzy—always." She turned and went out through the large, paneled doors ... she beautiful for him despite it all, perhaps more so because of it.

He knew she was right; what else would she do? She was on her way—what he had promised a long time ago, a very long time, it seemed now. She was likely more than he deserved then and certainly more now. *What a fucking cliché, that 'deserved.' People got what they worked for or lucked into, and she was his bargain.* He knew that in his gut; what was he thinking? He needed to stand up. He needed to wish her the best. He needed to ....

He sat for a while staring at his polished paneled walls, the near endless shelves of books, the beveled glass that split the sun into colors that reflect from the Italian tiles that made the floor he rolled upon.

"Sir ... eh, Mr. Izzy ...." Arthur at the door of his study. "Rose and I are wondering ... is there anything we can do for you? Something to eat, perhaps?"

"Come in, Arthur. Sit down. I suppose we should talk."

"Yessir, if that is your wish."

"Arthur ... we've been together for a ... shit ...." He picked up his drink and drained half, putting it down with such force that the remaining spilled over on his hand. "Arthur, things are changing ... no, things have changed. Anna will not be back. We are getting a divorce; rather she is divorcing me. She—"

"We know that sir, and we are quite unsettled and sorry. You have our loyalty ... and our support. If we are to leave, that will not change ... not change at all, sir."

"No, no, that's not it. Tell me, Arthur ... you've been here for ... Christ, so many years, seen it all—our success and our setbacks. You've been privy to my personal life, and all the time, Anna has been here with me, loved me, understood me ... a part of me, and I her. In many ways, I have moved aside and given her room ... in my psyche, I mean. And that has been good for me, and I came to rely on her presence ...." *Oh, for God's sake, why am I blabbering on like this?*

"Back up ... I want you to know this change will have no effect on you and Rose. You are part of our family—Anna's and mine—and I have come to regard you highly ... to respect you, to think of you as a friend. We, you and I, don't often get into this kind of ... eh, this personal a conversation, but Arthur, man-to-man, I'm wondering: what do you think should be next; that is, what should I do? I need your opinion. With Ethan gone, you know, I have no man to talk with, no man's reflection. You understand. I'm alone now, more so than ever. So, tell me, what do you think I should do?"

Arthur was silent.

"C'mon, man, give me your thoughts."

"May I have a drink, sir?"

"Eh, yes, of course. Pour for us both."

When Arthur had brought the drinks and sat down, he sipped a bit and leaned in. "Today is Saturday, sir. I think tomorrow we, you and I, should go down to the Hut on the Boulevard and listen to jazz. After that, starting on Monday, you should sit down with your notebook and pen and write the best screenplay anyone has seen and then get it produced. I don't have to tell you that you are able. You already know that. And right now, sir, right this minute, I think we should get out the pieces and play a game of chess."

Thirty
Up is Tough

GILES WOULD TAKE THE ROAD through Cuauhtémoc, over the mountains into Hermosillo and stay that night. Next, the long haul to Mexicali, then Tecate, where he'd cross into the USA. From there a few hours into San Diego where he would sit down to a KC steak and baked potato with a Roquefort dressed salad on the side ... all served by some blonde, blue-eyed American girl with shapely tanned legs and a big smile. Somebody who'd say, "Hi-ya, how ya doin'?"

That was his plan and his mouth watered as he thought about it, never mind the desert heat, the swirling dust and rough road. Three, maybe four days, he thought ... could be longer, depending on encounters, but now that he had a plan, he was eager to get it done and to seeing ... to seeing who? The question lingered. It wasn't the Beck Street guys, though maybe Paul; not Lacey, not ... well, he'd see Izsak, and Anna, if still around, and .... Obviously. no real need to hurry. It was the blonde who'd be waiting his table who held his attention.

As he left Cuauhtémoc behind and began to climb, it was colder than he expected, then freezing as the mountain air rushed up against his torso, and the sun on its way down ceased its warming. He stopped to put on his coat. *It's going to be a long damn night.*

At about nine he stopped—too cold to go on. He pulled the bike well off the road and laid it down. No point in waving a flag. He retrieved a can of beans from his bag and debated about a fire. He'd been cautioned—a gringo in bandito country was tempting. He ate the beans cold, wrapped with chopped peppers in a tortilla.

The sky was alive with stars, so many it didn't seem dark. There weren't any nights like this in the Valley, and he felt a part of it, if starkly alone. It belonged to him, he thought, the night, the stars, the occasional nocturnal sound, and he was comfortable with it and completely at ease. He flattened the duffle under his head, pulled up a blanket and let his wanting sleep into his lazy, inviting mind.

IN HERMOSILLO the next day he replenished—filled gasoline tanks and bought food. Mexicali was about ten hours away with a couple of stops in between. He might be there by midnight.

AS HE RODE THROUGH town looking for life, any life at all, he remembered the song "Mexicali Rose" and the excitement and longing it brought on. *Where the hell was that now? Rose must be snug in bed with her lover. Wait, there's a sign: Rooms/Vacancy* and he pulled up and dismounted, relishing the freedom from his leather seat as he pulled down the crouch of his pants, jiggled a bit, and rang the bell. He was getting closer to the end and for an unknown reason, it lifted his spirits some.

"Hola!" came gruffly from inside. *"¿Quiere una habitación?"*

"Si .... One room for the night, *para la noche*"

The door opened. A very old señora stood in the light of a bare bulb. She breathed sour, looked straggly and was barely dressed in a tattered slip of a gown. "Oh, you ... gringo, three dollar for the night. You want woman?" She was missing some teeth.

He reached for his wallet.

"She young, only two dollars more."

He thought about it and wondered if it might be a daughter. He was tired, but it *had* been a while.

"One-fifty?" she said

He gave her three, hesitated, then counted out two more. *What the hell. It's customary and I don't want to offend.* She put three in the cash box and two in a pocket and smiled. "Buenas noches, señor, you will sleep with the gods."

The room was nothing to write home about—a saggy, full-sized bed draped with a tasseled white spread and a single pillow, a ceiling light that glowed a dim yellow, a window he tried but couldn't get open beyond an inch—*home was where you parked your ass.* He laughed at the thought, tossed his duffle on a chair, and flopped down on the bed that gave with a squeak and didn't rebound. The sheets were clean, no bugs crawling around, no strange nocturnal sounds—those of traffic were infrequent, seemed distant, and all-in-all a far cry up from the freezing top of a mountain.

There was a knock on the door; it opened, and she walked in ... about twenty, he judged, flowing black hair, brown eyes, a comely smile, and an old pink robe hanging loosely without a tie.

"My name is Rose," she said. "I am your woman to-night."

"Mexicali Rose," he said with a grin, and without getting up, he patted the bed. She came over, sat down, and began unbuttoning his shirt.

"The light?" he said.

"If you like," she said. "And I can be here all night."

He reached for her, took her arms. She was lovely—a quiet fragrance and soft presence, and one hell of a reward at the end of a grueling ride. *Life is good, very good, and Rose is making it better.*

**

"IZAAK, IT'S ME, LACEY," she said with a quiet energy into the phone. "How are you? Been meaning to call. Is this a good time?"

"My God, Lacey. Of course, any time with you is good. How have you been?"

"Well ... very good, in fact. And I have a need of your advice. May I come over ... share a drink and catch up?"

"You bet. Any time, Lacey."

"This afternoon be alright?"

"COME IN. COME IN. Come give me a hug. It's not been that long by the calendar, I guess, but so much has transpired." He had pulled himself together a bit, sat straight and donned a smile. "Anna has sued for divorce, you know."

"I didn't know." She bent down and gave him a kiss and a pat on the shoulder.

"Of course, you didn't. No way to know. I just recently was served myself—damnable papers. It's all I can think about."

"I'm sorry Izzy; can you talk about it? I mean, do you want to? Does it disturb you?"

"Yes, it disturbs me, and talking about it disturbs me more."

"You must've seen it coming. I mean, she's off living her dream, a lone opportunity, you can't blame her for that. She's been at it so long, the trying."

"Yes, the trying. We are all doing that. What's on your mind, Lacey, and what have you been up to?"

"Let me fix us a drink ... the usual?"

"You know where it is. That hasn't changed."

She walked to the bar as he watched. *Beautiful, that woman.* He'd got in the habit of watching his female friends, the few who visited, walk over to the bar. It might be his only pleasure, a thought he abandoned as soon as it arrived.

"Izzy, I've met a man ... a comedian. He does stand-up. He's good but not known. He works out of a coffee shop in Van Nuys. It's a small place, The Coffee Grotto. I doubt you've heard of it."

He smiled. "Not a word, Lacey. Coffee, as you know, is not my cup of tea." He chuckled. "Especially not now. Here, let me have that drink."

401

"His name is Cole Stringer, and we have struck up a sort deal. I'm to be ... well, I am his business manager—books, bookings, promotion, and the rest—and I am looking for contacts. You know ... people who know people who can give him a chance ... get him in front of an audience."

"Sorry, my dear, you have come to the wrong man. If I knew any of those sorts, it was long, long ago, unless, of course, you think he would draw at the Hut. Arthur and I get down there now—still on Sundays." He laughed out loud. "It's my one real pleasure, and big thanks to Arthur."

"Oh, Izsak." She sighed, took a sip of her drink. "Your life can't be that bad. Your scotch is as good as ever." She put her hand on his arm. "I just thought you might be able to point in some direction, a place where I might start."

"My advice, talk to Anna. She's the one in this family ... eh, that gets around ... and around and around." His eyes watered up and he stiffened.

"Look," she said, "let's talk about you. What are *you* going to do? It goes on, you know ... life. You can't sit and wallow, that doesn't work. I can personally certify. You're a talented man, Mr. P., Let it out. You like to write ... you do it well." She leaned into him. "I've read some of your work, you know. Your scripts are good. Get yourself an agent and get them out, circulated among those producers you know. For God's sake, Izzy, do it ... do it for yourself!"

He smiled, though it was tough through his anger and sadness. "Anna has an apartment in Santa Monica. I'll give you her address and her phone number. You give her a call. She can help with the contacts."

**

"COLE, WE HAVE A SPOT ... amateur night at the Derby. One night a week they hold open mic for those on the first rung. It's on Wednesday ... this coming Wednesday. We'll go together. The right people should be there ... and they know others, and word gets around. You may open some doors that we wouldn't have known were there. Pick me up about seven. I've got you on the list and if you get to the mic, we'll be on our way." He smiled and reread the message she had left with the pizzeria.

**

GILES WAS SEATED quickly at Caesar's in San Diego by a man in a tuxedo, his small round table covered with white linen and laid out with crystal and silver. He thanked the maî-tre d', looked around at his alcove of walnut-paneled walls that reminded him of Izsak, bronzed, tooled tin overhead, and set back apart from the main dining room. It was classy and this was the US of A. The only problem: the wait staff were Italian men with serious faces dressed in black with bow ties. Well, he had asked around for the best in steaks, and Caesar's it was, but no pretty young blondes with tanned legs and big smiles in sight.

He ordered a KC cut, medium rare and the famous salad, which would be made to his liking from a cart wheeled up to his table. Raw eggs in the oil-based dressing and ancho-vies tucked quietly away under garlic dipped croutons ... so much for Roquefort. But a martini first and very dry. This was living, and tomorrow he'd be in the Valley.

"Your drink, sir. Can I bring you anything else, pan-roasted oysters? They're in butter on the half-shell with a couple of drops of Disaronno ... molto deliziosa, signore."

"Thanks, I'm fine." He could hear the tinkle of dishes being handled and the murmur of conversation. Off somewhere a piano was playing. Waiters moved quickly about and the patrons were dressed to the nines. He nibbled an olive and sipped at his drink and pondered the wealth in the main room. It wasn't the cantina in Juarez.

**

"YOU THINK THE KIDS'LL BE OKAY with Mac and Charlene?" Paul asked as they sped down US 91 toward Beck Street—away from the hovel they'd rented, the casino, the Strip, the Wee Kirk of manacles and bars ... but not his marriage to Mary F, sitting there beside him and maybe too close. He felt in a vortex pulling him down ... and down, and down and helpless to do anything about it. *What if this wasn't what I would have ... no time to think, but what if ....*

"They'll have the time of their life."

"Maybe we shoulda brought them along."

"Paul ... they'll be fine. They like Charlene and they'll enjoy the baby ... and we'll have a few days to ourselves. We have a lot to do, saying good-byes, packing, and all the arranging. I'll want to call my dad, and there's the office, and ...."

Her voice drifted off with the multitude of arrangements she'd have to make while he could think of none.

"Yeah, I suppose ...."

404

"We won't be gone long. It's not that we'll need a lot, maybe three, four days. Don't ya love it ... starting again with a whole new life."

He mused. She was giddy, could hardly contain her enthusiasm, might just explode. Just a few months ago she and the kids were sitting on a curb outside the Carnation broke and destitute—their few belongings in cardboard boxes, prospects dim, and wondering what, if anything at all, might be next. And now ... now she was married to this guy with his hands on the wheel, a new life in Las Vegas, her own home close to her friends, and the kids were eating real food. It was near unbelievable, but here it was, and he was the guy, and they were on their way to finalize everything, pack up and finish the move.

"Oh Paul, darling, I am so happy." She took his arm and snuggled in next to it.

'Darling'.... He hated that. I'm no one's 'darling' ... not hers, not even my mother's—clingy, syrupy, candy sweet— it's making me sick to my stomach.

"Paul ... you seem preoccupied. Is something the matter? I mean, you just had the best sex in your life ... I'm guessing of course, but you said ...."

Why the fuck can't she leave it alone for a while? She's got what she wanted, she—

"PAUL!!"

THE CAR VEERED AND ITS TIRES SCREECHED as she grabbed the wheel just in time to avoid a head-on. They swerved back and out of the way of an oncoming big rig and abruptly onto the right-side shoulder, and when he over

405

corrected, they spun in the gravel, around a couple times and into the desert where, in a cloud of sand and dust, the car rocked and settled.

"Jesus Christ, Paul," she screamed. "You almost got us killed. Were you asleep?"

"I ... I'm sorry ... I'm really sorry."

"What is wrong with you?"

"I dunno ...." He slumped over the wheel, unable to look at her.

They sat frozen—she glaring at him, he looking straight ahead and neither one speaking. Then she opened her door and got out, walked away a dozen yards and stopped. Her mind was a jumble; she couldn't focus. *That was too close; what the fuck is going on here? That asshole almost ended my life.* She let her gaze wander. *And what a barren damned place to lose it.* She kicked at a rock, then another, spun around, and then another thought invaded her consciousness ... *was it intentional?* She returned to the car, threw herself in and sat down, leaving her door open.

"Okay, mister, let's have it. You've been moping around since before we left the Valley ... and worse now than before—not with it, not with it at all. You could hardly repeat the vows and now ... you can't even drive the goddamn car. Now, I want it and I want it all. Just what the hell is bothering you - your underwear too fucking tight? Out with it."

He couldn't escape; he knew it. He was guilty but didn't know why, at least not enough to discuss it. He had to say something, but how to begin? He stared out through the windshield, itself a huge challenge—his jaw set, his mouth silent.

406

"Out with it!" she repeated.

"It's not what I had in mind," he finally mumbled.

"Not what you had in mind! Well just what the fuck *did* you have in mind when you came here with me and said, 'I do'?"

"I dunno...."

"Look ... you snap out of it. We're going to have this conversation now ... and we need to be honest. We are beginning a new life here ... entirely new, and we need to get off on the right foot. So, spill it, mister. What is it that's disturbing you so? If I hadn't grabbed the wheel, we would be dead."

He sat, staring—the windshield was dirty. There was so much, and a lot of it was only a feeling and hard to explain.

"Paul!"

He firmed up his grip on the wheel. "Let's just go, huh? I said I was sorry."

She reached over and took the keys. "Like I said, we're going to have this out right now. What is it that you 'didn't have in mind'? It's time that we both know."

He turned to her, looking past her into the desert, the distress on his face reflecting that in his mind. He took a deep breath and let it out as a sigh, then another.

"Well, it's us. It's the kids. It's this trip, the job, that shack of a house we rented. It's Las Vegas ... and I guess it's Dalton. I took his girl, then sent him close to his death and I can't get over it. Since he and I met, he'd been taking the shit I shoveled down on him from the top of my hill—a little here and a little there until finally he'd had it and blew up. It wasn't intentional. I wasn't even aware of it, but it was there ... and not until that day did I see it so clearly, lying on the floor broken and bloody, him yelling it loudly, the pain he'd endured for years, that it finally occurred to me—the constant superiority I assumed in our interface ... and then the accident.

"He shoulda just kick the shit out of me and left satisfied, but his combination of guilt and anger at his attack nearly killed him. And here ... here I am, still on top of the fucking heap I managed to concoct with my arrogance ... my college degree, white-collar job, and the shit that goes with it. Dalton in his smudged blue shirt with his name in red over the pocket, and now with no chance at all ..." his voice trailed off to almost a mumble "... and me with you and your new life .... And I saw to it ... until you saw to it. I don't want any of this, yet I've got it. I've got it all.

"Well, there it is, and it eats at me ... all the fucking time." He pulled his watery gaze from the sand and rocks, the scrub, the heat moving into the brilliant blue sky in waves you could touch, and he looked into her eyes directly. "That's what's troubling me. And I'll say it now ... if I'd a known how to stop it, I'd a done it before this ... but I didn't ... and you're very goddamn persuasive—pushing and pushing and not letting up."

Time went by as they sat, eyes connected. They were gorgeous eyes, he thought—a richer, deeper, darker blue than the sky behind them he'd been staring at, deeper and darker than any blue he had ever seen.

"Did you purposely head for that truck?" she finally said.

"Christ, no!" He dropped his stare. "I would never do anything like that ... hurt you, or the kids."

"You've thought about it for yourself?"

He was silent for a while, re-establishing his gaze with the desert.

"Sometimes ...."

Again, they were quiet. The minutes ticked on.

"Paul ... I love you. I married you because I love you. I know you've been depressed. We all know it. Another thing we know is that Dalton's accident was not your fault. Even he has said that ... though you were probably not listening. You are not responsible for Dalton ... not now, not then, never were. He's his own man ... has his own demons.

"Yes, it's a tragedy, and we all feel his loss ... but you didn't do it; he did, and you've got to get that into your head ... chase out the other." She reached over for his hand, put it up to her cheek, then kissed it and adjusted herself in the seat, turning more toward him.

"Yes, I was pushing. I was trying to get you out of that rut ... just didn't know how deep it was, thought it was only about the job you were missing.

"Now ... you do what you want. If this whole thing is a mistake, now's the time to correct it. We can have the marriage annulled ... almost as easily as we put it together. I don't want that, but more, I don't want to continue on into a new life with half a partner. I've done that before, you know, and it *does* get worse. You decide—move ahead or turn around."

She had tears in her eyes and wiped them, then lit a cigarette. "And while you're at it, I think you need to talk to someone ... either way, you know, a priest or a counselor. And by the way, I was never his girl."

"I'm sorry," he said.

"Yes, I know. Now, let's trade places, I'm going to drive. Which way shall we go?"

Thirty-One
Acceptance

W HEN NICK AND MAXINE pulled up to the house, they met Paul and Mary carrying out boxes, the trunk of their car open, the cavity filled.

"This is the last of it," Paul said, moving to open the back door.

"Where ya goin'?" Nick said. "Wherever it is, it looks permanent."

"Big changes," Paul countered. "We're moving to Las Vegas. Got a job there ... with the mob." He laughed. "You can take over here while I work on becoming a made man."

"Hey, congratulations on that, but not me. I'm outta here too ... not yet made but working at it. Max and I just rented a place in Toluca Lake—an apartment just down the street from Bob Hope. You'll need to find someone else to close things out—maybe Dennis. He says he's here till the end, he and Wayne. Las Vegas, huh?"

"Yeah ... and we were married while we were there, in the Wee Kirk of something or other."

"Of the Heather," Mary chimed in. "Give me a kiss, Nick. I'm Mrs. Mary Smythe now."

"I heard that," Dennis yelled from inside. "What happened to the 'F'? Gone with the rest of the fun? I say we celebrate, have a big party before you leave."

"Can't do it," Paul said. "We need to get back. Got the kids farmed out but only a few days."

Dennis laughed. "Shit ... it be me and Wayne now; the adults all gone. Look out, Beck Street, the kids are gonna holler."

"Where *is* Wayne?" Nick asked.

"Yeah, where? That's a good question," Dennis said. "He met some excitement in West Hollywood, and I haven't seen him since. Nice looking gal, though ...."

"You've met her?"

"Yeah, I did, and a few others as well that I'd rather not talk about. Say, Paul, you gonna stop in and see Dalton before you leave? He's working now ... got a job sweepin' up over at Meisner's—a wood shop on Glenoaks—and probably like to say goodbye."

"Sweepin' up, eh ... I dunno ... don't think we'll have time." He glanced over at his wife, saw her reassuring smile and found it surprisingly settling. "I'll catch up with him another time."

"Let's you and me have a beer, Paul," Nick said quietly. "C'mon ... I want to hear the entire story."

"Yeah, okay ... maybe one, but there isn't much more to tell."

"You go, Mr. Smythe." Mary laughed. "I'll finish the packing."

412

THEY WENT INTO THE DEN where Nick drew a couple of drafts and gave one to Paul. "You know Max and I are setting out together and we're optimistic about everything we see—the shop, the partnership, and possibly marriage sometime down the line. We feel pretty damn good about the whole thing ... and about each other, but we both know it's only a start. There's a lot of life out there and some of it's trouble, and if we tie the knot, we wanna be damned sure about it ... or as sure as we can be.

"The thing is, we're holding hands now, and will knowingly face it together." He paused, put his hand on Paul's shoulder. "Tell me, good friend ... are you? Are you guys holding hands? I'm not throwin' a pall down here, but we've known each other for a while now—I'd say we're close—and frankly, Paul, I don't get it. She pulled you outta here the other day like she was coaxin' a mule into harness. It was obvious you weren't with it ... and at that time we're talking a lousy interview for a job. And now, for Christ's sake, you're married with kids, livin' with neon and bells, employed by somebody countin' notches on a gun and, well ... you seem to be movin' into the shallow end of the pool, buddy. That's one hell of a change over a weekend. You been smoking something, or have I got it all wrong?"

Paul started to speak but didn't know how to answer. He collapsed a little into his stool, stuck his nose in his glass. If it were possible, he'd melt into the cushion, run down the legs and out the back door—*shit*. He was trying ... what the hell was he supposed to do? He'd agreed now and had been attempting a good face ... for himself as well as the others, but

413

well, Nick was right, and he was a close friend and he supposed something like this had to come.

"Look...." He sat up, put his glass on the bar and turned to Nick, who had plopped into the wingback in the corner, crossed his legs and was waiting. "No, I'm not sure ... not sure, and not optimistic. And I'll be honest, Nick ... I'm doing this because ... well, because when I try to assemble the pieces, none of them fit. I move them around ... still nothing. I realize I haven't a lot of practice with these kind of puzzles. And later maybe a few might be fitting together ... but slow, ya know, and things out there in the desert and immediately before were and are progressing at lightning speed. And well ... I've got nothing better to do, so I might as well go with it. And in the meantime, keep working the puzzle. I'm thinking, someday a picture will come into view and maybe I'll bolt or maybe I'll like what I did. There's nothing here for me now. You've all gone ... or are going your separate ways. I can't find a job here. So, what the hell, I might as well go to Vegas ... deal with the puzzle there. I like Mary ... the kids are okay ... yeah, it's different, but well, it's something ... and I like to say, things may well work out."

"Not much of a foundation ... I mean, to grow on," Nick said without much conviction. *But what the hell, it isn't my life.*

"Not much, no ... but Mary's enthusiastic ... enough, I suppose, for us both. I'm not delirious about it but, well ... it's what there is. You see that, don't you?" He swallowed the rest of his beer in a gulp and stood up. "I gotta get out there and help with the packing. We'll stay in touch."

**

GILES CRUISED DOWN the new Ventura Freeway, past the familiar Hollywood sign on the hills to his right, and dropped into the San Fernando Valley. He thought it should look different, but it didn't. And now that he was here, what would he do, where would be go—another result of superb planning. His Triumph was still pushing along at about sixty miles per hour, but where to turn off? Not back to Beck Street; no appeal there, as he didn't want to get involved in the tangle of accusations and questions that were sure to confront him. Lacey was out for similar reasons; moreover, she probably wouldn't open the door once knowing it was him. And even though his primary interest was Izsak, he just couldn't drop in. There *was* a place though ... where a friendly environment awaited, and he could figure his next move. At The Little Brown Hut he'd be welcome.

He took the off-ramp at Lankersham, found the Boulevard and up a few blocks pulled into the parking lot in front of the Hut and parked.

"Oh, for Christ's sake," Bogey, smiling as usual behind the bar—some things wear well with time. "Look who walks in here as big as you please. Where the hell you been? You look a mess. How about one on the house, rinse off the dust?" The few at the bar turned and nodded.

Giles grinned.

"Yeah, been a while ... down in Tecate-land, but now—Pabst Blue Ribbon time." He sat at the bar.

"You bet, kid, good to see you back. I heard you been traveling, all a bit of mystery though—that man, Giles. The

415

guys stop in often ... and your sidekick—the old guy, Izsak, he's been coming in again on Sundays. Brings a long-faced guy in place of his wife." He laughed. "Miss her, I tell you— whata pair of gams."

The group at the bar all nodded. "Hear, hear," one of them said.

"Here ya go, pally, happy landings." He laughed, his robust frame jiggling with the guffaw as he slid a frosty glass of suds across the bar, poured one for himself and held it up before drinking. "Here's to good friends, more and better drinking." They touched glasses, and the others at the bar held their's up in a salute and then drained them. It was good to be among friends and Bogey would always be that.

HE RENTED A ROOM at the Rest Awhile, a dumpy little motel off Van Nuys Boulevard in front of the Valley's overflow culvert—a river they called it. The room was cheap and served his purpose—one yet to be known.

"How long ya be with us, Mr. Anderson? Weekly rate's the best."

He didn't know, but took a week as it would give him time without a push, should he need it. It had air and a hot plate, a sink and a shower—a step or two up from the road. He had looked and nodded.

"If you wanna stay another week, jus' let us know ... and ya pay ahead a time." She wasn't homely, just wore out. She turned the book around and read his name. "G. Anderson, huh. We change out the linens every other day ... and the freeway noise quiets down about eleven. No parties and no women, though I'm a little soft on the last one. Just keep the noise to an acceptable level."

What, no girls? Maybe I have to ask. He chuckled at the thought, and the difference in Mexican motels and those in the states

ON SUNDAY, after strolling around the place, checking out the 'river' only inches behind his room, he rode over to the Hut. The place was jumping—side boards up and a combo playing. A clarinet was running through the strains of "String of Pearls" in a rendition made popular by Stan Getz. Izsak was at a table, thumping his fingers to the rhythm, an empty glass in front of him. Arthur in a sport jacket and open collar white shirt was hardly recognizable without his bow tie. Giles smiled; some things do change.

He tapped Izsak on the shoulder from behind. "Can I get you a refill, Izzy … scotch, if I remember correctly?"

Izsak looked up. "Ooh, for God's sake." He laughed. "It'll be the first you ever bought. Sit down here, Giles. Grab a chair if you can find one. Jesus, Arthur, find the traveler a chair."

"You're lookin' pretty good for an old geezer," Giles said. "Hi ya, Arthur, lose your tie?"

"Arthur brings me down. We listen. We've become friends, Arthur and I, and about fucking time." He looked up at the tall, formal-looking man who had pulled over a chair and put his hand on Arthur's arm. "And he's teaching me how to lose gracefully at chess."

"Hello, Mr. Giles, nice to see you again. Are you back for a while or visiting?"

Giles laughed and shook Arthur's hand "I haven't a clue, and nice to see you too."

"Where are you staying?" Izsak said.

"Got a bed down at the Rest Awhile. Fits my wallet, and it's not as bad as you might think. In many respects it's better than some I've recently—"

"Giles, pack up and come stay with me. Anna has left. I'm batching now and could use the company ... God knows, there's plenty of room."

"Yeah, Anna ... I want to hear about that—you and Anna. You inferred there was trouble in a note long ago, but since then I've heard nothing."

He thought briefly about pursuing the story of Anna, and then the pros and cons of staying with Izzy—not many of either. It would be cheap but regulated. Living under another roof always came with some obligation, although with Izsak, probably not much—listen to tales of yesterday's glory and play chess. On the other hand, he was running low on dinero, and soon would need to supplant—job, hours, mindless response to some asshole's orders. *Ouch, back there again, the threat of eight to five.*

"And yes, Izsak, I'll be most happy and grateful to roost for a while in your ambiance of abundance. Thank you. I might help out ... but not often." He laughed. "We might cry in our beer together as we contemplate our loss of feminine company. If anyone knows about failed relationships, you've found your man, and together we might make quite a scene." Lacey appeared in his mind's eye, then Suzy flashed by on a motorcycle, Mary F in the sidecar, while Maria sang something in Spanish—a parade of women any of which seemed, at the time, to fit comfortably, but a comfort that came with that promise, sooner or later. "Yours is a generous offer ... one I shall not refuse. No need to be coy with you, I know ... and I won't. Give me a couple of days, and I'll be on your doorstep."

THE NEXT MORNING, he slept in. He would wake up, note the sun streaming in through a window, roll over and return to sleep. It was delicious. At about two, he got up, showered, and walked a block to a café for a breakfast of waffles and ham. How American was that, and life was good until "what next?" entered his mind. Why was he back? He had no ties, no draw. He might just as well be in Timbuktu.

"More coffee, sir?"

"Eh ... yes, fine." He glanced up and noticed her name tag. She was an attractive blonde and he wondered about her legs. "Thanks, Emma. Say, what do you do around here at night ... you know, for entertainment?"

"My husband picks me up at five." She smiled. "He plans the itinerary."

**

"GILES, I HAVE PLENTY OF MONEY, you probably have none ... very little in any case, and I want to put you on retainer—pocket change, you know. You can do things around here, help Arthur with the cars, etcetera. He knows nothing about mechanical things ... hardly knows how to drive. And we'll find other things to keep it all well in balance." He puffed on a cigar. "Now before you say anything, this is a done deal; it's the price, if you like, for staying here—listening to my stories and moving pieces around the board. I'll win, of course. That too is part of the deal."

After bringing Giles in, Arthur watched from the door at his master's animation and cheerfulness. Izsak seemed uplifted—a notch or two above his former disposition. Was it Giles? Did Giles offer a different interface, a youthful, more energetic challenge? Arthur seemed delighted with his observation and some relief from the constant introspection. Arthur was a "buck-it-up" kind of man, no time nor truck with the wringing of hands.

GILES WAVED A GESTURE of refusal regarding the retainer idea. "I'll tend to the cars and whatever needs my untrained hand, but I don't want your money. Taking me in is generous enough."

"Hogwash ... I won't embarrass you with huge amounts, just enough for toothpaste and beer." He reached over to the table and picked up an envelope, "Here, take this and not a word. I have plenty of this stuff; you have none. We could argue about it, of course, and I would eventually win. But let's save all that consternation for something we *both* feel is in need of it."

"I ... I don't ... dammit, old man, do you ever lose?" While Giles' first reaction appeared to be 'No', his recollection brought back Izsak's inherent generosity—it was normal for him and what's more, he was down to the change in his pocket—another inherent characteristic. He folded the envelope and slid it into his jacket.

"Alright, I'll save us the argument ... getting used to being a kept man, although I'm not very fond of it these days. As we go forward, my friend, you will need to live up to your end of the bargain and find something useful to you for me to do."

"Of course. And the keys to those cars are still on the hook in the foyer. Feel free to use them as yours. You are the only one in the house now who actually knows how to drive, and they need an occasional outing. Giles … we are both kept men. In a manner of speaking, all men are kept. We live in the shackles of choice."

**

"DENNIS, HERE'S MY RENT for the remainder of the lease and this other is our new address on Valley Spring Lane." Nick held out a check and a white slip of paper. "No phone yet but will let you know when we get one." He looked around, took the place in. "In a way, I hate to leave. In another, letting go seems timely. It's been a helluva ride and I wouldn't trade it for any other time in my life, but we're moving on, ya know. That's what we do."

"Yeah, I guess," Dennis replied. "Wayne's still here, some a the time." They were wandering slowly out the front door.

"Okay, pal, be seeing you. Drop by the shop when you get a chance and I'll show you around—tune up that heap of yours, and maybe come over for dinner sometime when we get set up." He waved as he got into his brother's Ford.

Dennis moseyed into the den, drew himself a beer and sat down … let his eyes wander. They stopped at a poster behind the bar—a blonde emerging wet from the ocean, her thin blouse clinging. He'd often gone to sleep with, maybe passed out, with her image. She was advertising Pabst Blue Ribbon and doing a right smart job of it. *I gotta figure this out ... what am I gonna do when the end of October shows up? Maybe Ray's got an idea. Might move in with Wayne, sleep on his old man's couch and help with the boat. Screw it, too early to worry, that's well over a month away; no need to worry today.* He finished the glass and drew another.

**

WELL ON THEIR WAY, Mary said, "Okay, bud, we're fully committed now. In a couple hours we'll be back in Vegas and in our new home. And you're still here, I see. So, tell me, what are your thoughts?" Mary was anxious but knew somehow things would turn out alright.

"I'm okay."

"Just okay?"

"Don't prod."

"I'm not prodding, Paul. Dammit, we have a life ahead of us and ... and not a damned thing back there. Can't you muster a little enthusiasm?"

"I'm enthused."

"You're not showing much of it."

"What do you want from me? I'm going ... It'll take time. Look ... put yourself in my shoes for a minute. I'm leaving my only friends, going to live in a distant town ... one I wouldn't have picked for myself in a hundred fucking years. I'm facing a new job with a new employer I know nothing about but is probably a gangster, and suddenly I've got a wife and kids. The only goddamn familiar thing I have is the clothes in a bag back there, and some memories ... and you want me to sing hallelujah!"

"You have me ... I'm familiar, and I'm with you, Paul, and I'll be with you always. That's something, isn't it?" She moved closer and gave him a quick kiss on his cheek.

"Yeah, I s'pose that's something."

"We'll have some tough times maybe, but we'll get through them together. Try a little optimism. It'll work much better. You're a smart guy, a good-looking man. You'll do it up brown at the casino. They'll see your skills and ambition, and you'll advance. Heck, in no time you'll be back on top of that hill ... and you belong there. You do belong there, you know." She nuzzled up next to him.

"I've had twenty years of making my own decisions and liked the results ...." He talked to the windshield while she hung onto his arm. "And now in a month a total change in every aspect of my life, and none of it the result of a decision of mine. You'll probably argue that point." He looked down. Her eyes were closed. "But I know my processes—the weighing and contrasting the pros and cons. The fact is ... all of this is yours, your planning and doing, and I haven't had time, more accurately, the focus, to think about it, much less decide if I like it. But I'm working on it ... it's here and I'm adjusting."

Did she hear him? He didn't know, but he was caving. He knew he would cave; this was the only route on his map—the road to Las Vegas and all of the rest. He wanted what was behind but knew it was no longer available. She was right; it was a matter of attitude, a matter of perspective. He must deal with what there was, and what was ahead and not what he wished had been.

"I'm sorry to be your cold water. I'll get into this, I really will. It's a great opportunity as you've said. I need some time." He turned to smile at her, but she had moved to the far side of the seat and was looking out the window. He sought out her hand and squeezed it.

Thirty-Two
Adjustments

AFTER A CUP OF ROSE'S COFFEE, Giles went for a walk, and as he moved along briskly in the cool of the En- cino morning, he thought about what he would do— what he might do for Izsak and what for himself. Not much came up on either count, but he might get back to writing. He would have time here and would feel somewhat motivated. As to Izzy, he'd let that take care of itself.

They would talk—Izsak liked to talk. They might play chess. The idea of working—a defined and scheduled rou- tine—was not appealing but the digs with Izzy were worth whatever tasks that came along. He chuckled to himself. Ar- thur would not release very much.

The valley sun moved higher and the air was warming. He turned and headed back.

Down the drive on his way to the rear door, he noted his Triumph, dirty with travel and could certainly use a good go- ing over, and he'd been thinking about Suzy. Cute, he remem- bered, straw blonde and tan, a big grin under her pale blue eyes; at the Round Up they'd had fun and he'd felt a certain communion. He saw the freckles on her nose, a kind of turned-up nose, and recalled their conversation when she said she appreciated his need to be free. "... the idea of the wind and the road just do it for me ... and some day ...." Her final comment at their only meeting still rang in his ears. *She could be my kind of lady.*

"SAY, ARTHUR, I'm taking my bike to a shop for a tune-up and wonder if you have time to pick me up. It's down on Ventura, at Laurel Canyon; Cycle Specialties is the name."

"Certainly, Mr. Giles, shall I follow you?"

"No, it's only a few minutes and I'll call when I'm ready. That okay?"

"Yes sir, that's fine."

Giles grinned. "And, Arthur, if you stop calling me Mr. Giles, I won't start calling you Mr. Pembroke. That okay? We're both hired hands, so to speak."

He laughed. "Certainly. I'll be here when you call."

HE PULLED INTO the shop's parking lot and around to the back, his heart beating a little faster than normal, and he felt a tad flushed. Maybe the heat, as he wondered if Suzy was still there.

"Hi, can I help you? Hey, I remember you, the guy who bought the Triumph. I'm Hank, you may recall. I own the place."

"Sure Hank, I remember, Dalton's friend ... and the bike's in the back. I'd like you to look it over—rejuvenate, do whatever needs to be done. It's been on the road a bit ... odo says 5,226 miles." He looked around, no sign of Suzy. Shit, that's most of the reason he came.

"That's a good distance; how's your rear end, the one in your pants?" He chuckled.

"It's toughened up some, that's certain."

"Let's have a look ... at the bike, I mean," and he laughed again.

Humm, very funny, a comedian or a mechanic? I only need the latter.

They went out to the back and Hank had his look—checked the oil, "Low and black. Distributor needs points." He pulled on this wire and pushed on that, tightened caps and checked the chain. "How's she working for you? Looks like she's had a run." He squeezed the front tire.

"Just fine. Not a complaint ... just want her cleaned and refreshed."

"Okay, let's go inside and do up a work order. What about tires? Got some good deals."

"No ... not this time. The rubber looks okay to me." His eyes traveled the desk. *That bandanna ... wonder if it's hers.*

"Deals won't last, ya know; could buy 'em and I hold 'em till you need 'em."

Giles gave him a look like, don't understand English?

"Jus' askin' ... it's the distributor's deal."

"Suzy still working here? She sold me the bike and I'd like to say hello."

"Suzy? Sure. Off for a week—her honeymoon. Let's see, I can have this ready by ... eh, say next Wednesday. That okay? Suzy'll be here then." He winked and pushed the work order across the counter to Giles. "Sign at the 'X'. Her lunch hour starts at one."

Giles nodded and signed. "Married, huh. Well, tell her congratulations. Can I use your phone? Need to call my ride." *Or maybe I'll just go across the street and have a beer, say hi to Slugger.*

"IZSAK, I GOT LITTLE ELSE TO DO while I'm here and I think I'd like to write, maybe some short stories. Had a couple published a few months back, and encouragement for more."

"Did you mention that in a letter? I don't recall, but I'm not surprised. You have a good mind, Giles, and it likes to wander. That's creatively good."

"Well, I'm wondering if I could set something up, maybe here in the library. It's quiet and references are handy ... if you wouldn't mind my poking around. And who knows, I might meet your muse. I've heard she hangs out occasionally. Left my own just south of Juarez."

Izsak looked up from a script he was putting together. "What's that you say? Of course, do what you like."

"I don't want to be a bother, Izzy, and if you'd prefer to be alone, say the word. We writers need our solitude, you've said."

"Not a bother ... absolutely not, Giles." Focusing now. "I'll enjoy the company. We might exchange ideas, another pair of eyes, you know. Yes, I like the idea. I'll ask Arthur to set it up. You tell him what you need."

In short, a small secretary from Anna's room was brought in with a chair and set against the windowed wall, to the left of Izsak's location ... a comfortable distance between them. It was perfect from both points of view. Giles picked up what he'd need from a stationery store and went right to work.

428

He had a few ideas—way more than a few—and his first would be based on his surprisingly welcome encounter with the Mexicali Rose.

**

"SO, YOU'RE MARRIED," Giles said as he entered the Cycle Specialties shop on Wednesday about 12:55 p.m. She turned in her swivel to face him and smiled ... and she was radiant. Giles saw her pretty much as he'd remembered—short blonde hair with those streaks of gray, sparkling blue eyes and the freckles around the bridge of her nose all traveling with him on his first leg out of the Valley not so long ago, but she was married, and it seemed like ages now.

"It *is* you. Hank said he thought it was you—the guy I talked about for days after our beer at the Round Up. He kidded me for weeks after you left, thought I shoulda gone with you."

"But you didn't."

"No, but maybe I shoulda."

A lump formed in his throat as he tried to think of something to say, something that would change the situation.

"But instead, you got married."

"I did. Well, the mice will play." She laughed. "This guy, the one on the license, had been bugging me since high school. He's a nice guy, not especially exciting—doesn't own a bike, but will probably make a good husband. Are we gonna have a beer? The Round Up's still pouring, you know, and I've been saving my thirst since the last time we were there."

"Of course you have." He smiled and relaxed.

"It's my treat, you know. You got the last one, and I remember." She got up and came to the counter.

"I know my place ...." *Damn, she'd be a helluva handful if not for that name on the license.*

She laughed. "C'mon, let's go. Nobody owns anybody where I come from."

"Right ... and you say it's your treat—"

"Hank," she yelled into the shop behind, "I'm going now, back in an hour." She ordered a pitcher from Slugger along with two of his grilled dogs and steered them to a booth at the front near a window.

"Looks like we're the only ones here," Giles said. "You might be at risk."

"You? Are *you* my risk? Must be you, 'cause Slugger and I are old friends. And let that be a caution... you wouldn't be the first to meet up with his watch-over-me. He's like the mafia, you know; I pay weekly with my lunch needs and bubbly personality, and he sees to my protection.

"So tell me, Giles, where have you been? I sorta thought I'd see more of you, kinda wish I had. Hank said your bike looked like it had been through some pretty serious traveling."

"Long story, and long trip into Mexico and around. Spent some time here, some there ... shedding some, gathering other ... more therapy than tourism. Good time, though, and well worth it—some great people south of the border ... and some others on our side."

"Humm, you're making me jealous. How'd the bike work out for you?"

"Not a hiccup. You did me right with that Triumph and thank you." He grinned and his eyes lit up. "You could see the match-up, that we were meant for each other and should be betrothed. I like everything about it but high on the list is the feeling of it being a part of me, my wish its intention. Even more, I guess, almost a friend."

"Well, that's more than I expected." She laughed. "Most of the guys I sell to either turn them in the next day with their wives hanging on to their ear, or they beat them to death and get pissed over the cost of repair."

"Yeah ... tell me about your marriage. I notice you're not wearing a ring."

"Well, that's another long story ... but I'm not in the mood. I'm glad you're back, Giles. I really like our repartee. I don't get that from Marvin."

"Marvin?"

"Yeah, he's the other name I was talking about."

Stories—they just keep coming. Gotta get back to my desk.

**

"HI YA, NICK ... MAXINE. You come in to buy me a beer?" Bogey laughed. "Two for the price of a couple tonight. It's a Brown Hut special."

"Well, whatta ya think, Max, can we pass up such a bargain? Do we need a coupon?" They all laughed.

"So, how's the business going? Any grease under your fingernails yet?" Bogey was dependably in a good mood.

"We're alright," Nick said. "We like what we're doing, and old Rob's customers are gradually becoming ours ... likely nowhere else they feel as comfortable. An overhaul's more affordable than a new car, and a lotta aging iron on the highway these days. Whatever the reason, business is good and picking up. You gonna draw those beers? Or are you waiting for the special to end?"

"I'm on it, Mr. Entrepreneur. Hold off the auditors."

"And I'll have one of those pickled eggs, too. Max, you want anything? Most of it's toxic, you know, and the rest of it came with the place."

"Saw your old buddy, Giles, last Sunday. Actually, dropped in a few days earlier, maybe Wednesday, lookin' kinda beat. Said he just pulled into town."

"Giles?"

"Yeah, he might be stayin' with Izsak. You know Izsak Padgett, the guy in the wheelchair? I overheard them talking last Sunday. Don't take that to the bank, though; might be a counterfeit."

"Humm, wonder why he didn't check in? Wonder if he knows about Dalton?"

Max took his hand. "Giles is his own person, Nick. I know him mostly from stories, but I'd guess he needed a change of clothes. Surely he'll make contact if he wants to."

"Yeah, you're probably right. Bogey, you got a phone number for Padgett?"

"Nope. But he's a big name in films, or he was, and is probably not hard to find ... lives in Encino, I think. Maxine, how about a hamburger? Cow walked in this morning, and for you, a free load of fries."

**

"THEY LOVED YOU, COLE. You heard the applause. It's thrilling, and you know what? A man came over as you left the stage and gave me his card. He owns a small club in Venice, close to the beach, and wants you to come down."

"Wow, Lacey, that's terrific." He sat. "I could use a drink. When does he want me?" He took the card, looked it over. "Not much here but a name—Al Leverton."

"That's his club manager, he said. I need to call him to set it up. I'll call next week, give some time for the message to settle in."

As they sat at a table toward the back of the Derby, after midnight and the room thinning out, a man sat down, signaled a waiter and said, "Drinks? And I want a word."

"Sure," Cole said. *Who is this guy?* "I'll have a stinger."

"And you, Lacey?"

"The same is just fine." *Who the hell ... how does he know my name? If Cole knew him, wouldn't he have introduced us? Humm ...."*

The man nodded at the waiter and laughed. "I'll have a stinger too, Lenny." He turned to the table. "I own this place, name's Brown," and he laughed again more heartedly. "Mind if I sit?" He pulled over a chair from an adjacent table. "I saw your shtick, Mr. Stringer, and I like it ... mostly because so did my patrons." He laughed again, slapped his leg. "And I'd like you to come back. I've talked to my booking and scheduling guy ..." more chuckles, "Yeah, Sam Doodlestein, and he'll be wanting to talk to you, sweetheart. Set you up with your own date; no more a this amateur-night stuff.

433

"You're good, Stringer; need your own show. I like the subtlety you poke through with the good laughs." He got up and pushed his chair back. "Enjoy your drinks; they're on the house. Mine will be on the bar." He laughed again as he walked away.

She leaned in toward Cole. "You think his name is really Brown?"

**

"HEY, HEY, it's the Melrose furniture man ....."

"Can it, Wayne. It coulda been the other way around, ya know."

"Yeah, but it wasn't. Beautiful Belle ... she asks about you all the time. Dreams of being Mrs. Denny, and is sorely disappointed you failed the exam, and that her almost-fiancé doesn't call ... return for another round. Says she's coming over some night and surprise you. I mean, good buddy, she's lookin' for a ring, and is eager to run off with the Valley fellow. And, from what I hear, Daddy loves his Belle, and anything she wants is his to get. So, buddy boy, be wary."

"Ha ... you tell where we live, or how to get in touch, you're dead, man. You tell her that I've ... don't tell her anything. You don't know me ... that understood?"

"Yeah, yeah ... no need to worry. If she finds you, it won't be through me, although I'd like to be around if it happens."

"You seeing Jeannie?"

"Yep ... all the time we're gettin' closer. I like her, ya know. She's hot and exciting. She likes the Bird, likes the speed, likes me or says she does, and is good for most anything that comes along. We're cruising up the freeway late the other night and she says floor it. Well, I did. Got the speedo needle buried under one-two-oh, and ya know what she yells in my ear? 'Is this all?' I mean, we're passing everything in sight, some so quick you couldn't hardly see 'em ... and she wants faster. That's the gal for me."

"Thought Joey was your true love."

"She is ... Jeannie's just fun. You know, somebody to split the sheets with till I get serious."

"How's she in the sack?"

"Not there yet, but closing in."

"What? I hear that right?"

"Well, when it comes, it comes. In the meantime, we're livin' ... and that's enough for ol' Wayne Gundersen. Sex isn't everything, Denny boy, and as you grow up, you'll discover ... it's compatibility that counts. Anyway, I heard that somewhere ... maybe I read about it."

"Didn't know you could read."

"There's a helluv a lot you don't know, my friend ... and even more you don't know about me." He laughed and punched Dennis lightly on the shoulder. "Let's have a beer, and we'll talk about it some, get you your GED."

"Always wanted a formal education."

Thirty-Three
Revelations

IZSAK'S LIBRARY, as quiet as Westminster Abbey, was an inviting place for neurons to dance to the muse's tunes. If one listened severely, a shuffle of ideas to the movement of pens filled the acoustical spectrum as both Giles and Izsak laid words to paper.

It had been this way for several days: Izsak rewriting a screenplay featuring a character the image of Anna, with a larger more visible role; Giles on a story from his Mexican experience, a scene written and scratched several times as his mixed thoughts of Maria and Juan searched vainly for the appropriate words and questions regarding their condition and displaced his literary progress

What and how are they getting along, and what would his life have been like had he went with them to Texas? It gnawed at him some, and he found her in his dreams as well, a couple of nights a week.

"Okay, I'm through for today, had enough," Izzy said. "I could use a drink. Any interest, Mr. Anderson—a scotch and cigar? And please crack a couple of those windows while you're up ... cooling off some now in the evening and a little new air will feel refreshing."

"Sure, I'll get 'em ... doing more daydreaming than writing anyway—a little trouble getting Maria off my mind."

"Maria ... you haven't told me much about her. Maybe talking will help make room for your story."

Giles laughed. "Or muddy it up. Here you go, splash of soda over two shots of Longrow. Where do you get this stuff, anyway? I been looking to replace a bottle or two and couldn't find it in any store I know about. Most didn't know what I was talking about."

"Special contacts, my friend, and I won't divulge at the risk of losing my source."

"Understood." He grinned, "I too have a source I need to protect, right here at your library bar."

"Where it comes from is of little concern; that it's here is paramount. So ... what about this Maria? You've said very little."

Giles sat down opposite Izsak, lit both their cigars. "She's in Texas now, with her son—San Angelo. If her plan worked out, she is running a small restaurant. A lovely woman, Maria Castillo ... all the good things you can say about a woman, you can say about her—solid gold. Took me in when I stopped for a beer at her cantina, outskirts south of Juarez."

"And Juan?"

"Her young son, about 10, dad skipped; I don't think they were married. She inherited the cantina from her father and, while I was there, sold it to a guy across the street, Manolito, who ran a garage and repair shop, anything from autos to wheelbarrows."

"Pretty, I suppose ... Maria, not Manolito."

"Beautiful—empathetic and tender."

"I suppose it became romantic."

"I'd say so, I guess ... sexy at least, after a while. She wanted me to come with them to Texas, but Izzy ... I didn't know. I was taken with her and Juan, but couldn't get into that decision. Big move, you know—entanglements."

"Giles, my friend, you were born to wander free from all encumbrances."

"Yeah ... s'pose you're right. I figured it out one night on a ceiling in Hermosillo. It's the commitment, the long-term promise to a particular life that slams the door on the rest of the world—adventure, the free execution of will ... you know what I mean. I just won't adjust to being tied down ... or into a particular direction."

"Oh, you're tied down, alright. You're tied to the notion of not being tied down. And let me tell you this ... that's as limiting as you perceive the commitment to be."

"Umm. You wanna elaborate?"

The promised breeze came in through the open tall windows and indeed did freshen the air, and the late afternoon sun, split by the beveled glass into its composite colors, painted some parts of the room in rainbow.

"Giles, you talk about doors. Anytime you shut a door, you are limiting your freedom—you've said no to whatever is behind that door. If you govern the speed on your motorcycle, you are limiting your riding agility. When you eschew the nine-to-five regimen, a marriage to Lacey, the Texas adventure with Maria, you are shutting those doors, not allowing yourself the experience. Add to that notion that nothing is permanent except perhaps change. With every door you walk through, several more open. Suppose, for instance, you signed up for a job, or married Lacey … you're not in a trap. As soon as you decide the pros and cons are weighted significantly in favor of cons, you may, and can, change the direction. If anyone knows that, it's me."

"Umm … what about the promises?"

"Don't promise; just do, and there may be your key."

"I get your point … never thought it that far through. Don't promise, just do."

"You don't make a secret of your interest in freedom. You wear it like a medallion, and the people who deal with you know it soon enough. Lacey certainly knew but was willing, as I saw it, to go along with you anyway … likely because of it, in my opinion. Moreover, everyone likes freedom. It's a crowd pleaser, my friend, the entire country … it's in our Declaration, and it's there because it's in our blood."

"Never saw it quite like that. Most everyone I know, including my parents, seem caught by obligation and bitched about it constantly. It formed my view." He was looking at his feet. They were bare and he wiggled his toes and noticed they were not constrained by the shoes he had decided not to wear.

"There not connected," Izzy went on. "The situation and the complaint. We like to complain—most of us—and it's no matter about what. If we feel down, rejected, things not going well, we complain. It's an emotional thing, unconnected to reality, and with some, a way of life."

"You're making a point … several."

"Think about it, and while you're running your brain, fix us another drink."

440

"Gotcha."

"So, what about this Maria?" He spoke up over his shoulder.

"Yeah, Maria ...." His mind wandered back as he uncorked the Longrow and poured. He heard her laugh, saw her sparkling eyes ... always smiling, those eyes.

He put the fresh drinks down and relit his cigar.

"Good cigars, Mr. Padgett."

"Maria?"

"Okay, Maria .... She was open. When she engaged, it was all of her ... honest and straight, no hidden agenda. She was charming and gracious with everyone, and everyone loved her—coal black hair, brown glittering eyes, and a generous mouth. Loved to laugh, came bubbling up, bold and full like an opera alto-soprano." He gazed out the windows, saw the breeze as it ran through the trees and noted the darkening sky.

"She had a serious side too, but it didn't last longer than the decision needed. I liked her from my first beer in the cantina and it grew ... every day it grew. A little on the voluptuous side considering our Valley standards, but everything fit very well." He stopped. His eyes took on a faraway look and in his mind's eye he saw her. He didn't rightly know about love, but he knew he adored her then ... perhaps even now.

"I guess the most memorable thing ... the one that sits high in my mind, is the way she treated me and others around her. We were her family ... close and accepting and without any argument. We were hers as easy as we belonged to ourselves.

"You know, Izzy ... I got off my bike after a full day's ride, dusty and ragged ... walked into her little cantina and before the damn screen door slammed shut behind me, she was opening a beer. 'Cerveza?' she said, 'Do you like a glass, se-ñor?'"

"Giles ... you speak very fondly of her, but you speak of the past. Is she dead?"

"No ... hell, I don't know. I haven't talked with her since I left."

"Maybe you could make the attempt."

Giles was stopped cold—a snap of the fingers. Even if he wanted to, he couldn't—no address, no name of a restaurant, no phone, no nothing. He had left with a bag of burritos and the name of a town.

**

DALTON FINISHED HIS SHIFT at Meisner's and punched out. He could go out through the side door and into the parking lot with the rest of the workers, but tonight chose to hobble through the reception area and out the front door. He felt good about this job and his prospects, and his old confidence was coming back ... less so the anger, and somehow, he felt relieved. As he entered the vestibule, he glanced over at the front desk. He'd been thinking about her lately.

"Hi ya Daisy ... you're still here. I thought you office types left at four." He smiled, inviting response.

"Of course you're kidding." She smiled back a bit coyly, her eyes still on her work, pen in hand.

442

"Ya know," he turned to face her, "I been thinkin' about you. And I been wondering if you're attached, and if you'd consider goin' out if you're not. Nuthin' special, you know, maybe supper ... take in a film, something like that?"

"Which answer would you like first, Mr. Dobbs?" She now looked up.

"Any will do. Take your pick."

"First, I'm usually here until after six. Some of our customers work, you know, and need time to get over here. Next, I'm not really attached, not in a permanent way, though I do date a guy sort of regular-like."

"And the other?"

"The other?"

"Yeah, would you like to go out sometime?"

"With you?" she teased.

"Well yeah ... with me." This may not be working, he thought ... bad idea, and he turned toward the door, positioned his crutches for the next step.

"Stop. Have you no drive? I heard you once were a quarterback, called the shots, carried the ball. Are you now giving up on the first play?"

He grinned; she had him, and the answer was no, he never gave up until the final whistle. He turned back.

"Well, I called the play; are you gonna line up? It's a quick pass over the scrimmage line and down the right side"

"Damn right. I'm on the team, and I am going out, a sprint around the right end." She laughed. "And yes, I'd like to go out with you sometime, take in whatever you like."

He smiled. It lit up his face. "That's great, Daisy. Maybe this Friday. We can leave from here."

"Friday's good but we won't leave from here. I like to freshen up a bit after the week ... you know, head for the locker room. I'll give you my address; you can pick me up there." She grinned now, her coyness lost to reception and maybe she liked this game.

"Okay then, it's a date."

"So, tell me, Dalton, how are you doing back there, still on the broom?"

"Nope ... didn't last. Not too effective at that and so now I'm sanding. I can sand without moving around very much. Hard to hang on to these crutches while pushing a broom."

"A little clumsy. I can see that."

"I'm getting a leg. It'll be awkward at first, no dancin' at the Savoy. Got fitted last week for a pro ... a proth ..."

"Prosthesis?"

"Yeah, one of those. And they say, given my muscles and such, I can be tossing these sticks in a coupla weeks."

"Hey, that's terrific ... and then you can get back to the broom." She laughed.

"Fat chance. I'll be playin' softball with the team. You watch my dust."

"I'm happy for you, Dalton, and from what I hear, you'll be a principal player in time, but not on the softball team as much as back in the shop."

"Well, I'm tryin'. I like it here. Nice bunch of guys, and the receptionist is very appealing ... if she just wouldn't take so long to get to the line. There's a penalty, you know, for stalling the game."

She laughed at his ribbing. "'Bye, Dalton, see you on Friday. Here's my address; shall we say about seven?"

"Yeah, about seven." He turned and pushed the door open with a crutch. Things in his life were indeed looking up, and a lightness came to his heart that was welcome.

**

"NOW WHAT CAN THIS BE?" Wayne said, rifling through the mail he'd retrieved from the box. "An official looking letter for Dennis ... no, wait, it's for *Mister Dennis M. Delaney* from some attorneys down near those hills named after Beverly. I'll bet it's old Rosenthal suing your ass for breach of promise." Wayne chuckled. "Here it is, return address: Hart, Shapiro, and Dryer, Attorneys at Law, Santa Monica."

"Lemme see that." Dennis threw a magazine aside, got up from the chair in the den and into the dining room, feeling more anxious than curious.

Lawyers? What of the many things that might tie him up in a proceeding, but hadn't yet, could this be? In his mind he began the review: unknown but probable pregnancies, citations not paid, overdue car payments he'd intentionally delayed and subsequently forgotten, surveying gear not returned to a former employer—would that be larceny? And then, the accident up on the Angeles Crest that they'd surprisingly slid though without comment from the law, but that he occasionally dreamed about and awoke in cold sweats. There were likely more, because a number of slots in the list were still open.

He hoped, of course, that none of these were the case, as there had been no change in his behavior—nothing to defend or beg with, nothing to support a plea for mercy, nothing to suggest that it all wouldn't happen again.

"Humm." He held the envelope up to the light, shook it a little and put it back on the table.

"C'mon, open the damn thing. It's not going to bite; too thin for explosives, and whatever it is, it ain't going away because you don't look inside."

"Yeah, suppose so. Nothing from a lawyer can be good." He tore the end of the envelope off, blew, and pulled out a single sheet, did a cursory glance and then, "Hey, listen to this."

> Mr. Dennis M. Delaney
> 6327 Beck Street
> North Hollywood, CA
>
> Dear Mr. Delaney
>
> You are named as a beneficiary in the final will and trust of our client, the deceased Malcolm S. Delaney. A reading will occur on the 23rd day of September, this year, 1957, at the offices above. The reading will begin at 1:00 p.m. sharp; please plan to attend. If unable to be present, call our offices and make other suitable arrangements.
>
> Sincerely,
> Salvatore Shapiro, Attorney at Law

"SALVATORE SHAPIRO!" Wayne exclaimed, "Ya gotta love that name on a lawyer—an Italian Jew shyster. And whata ya make of the invite? You're coming into some dough, says Salvatore Shapiro ... boy, that glides off your tongue like a warm buttered oyster."

"How do you know it's money; could be an old sword from a war, a hand-woven rug, or maybe a debt. I don't know any Malcolm Delaney anyway. My dad's old man was Mel and he died years ago ... and my old man, he's still kicking around somewhere back east, drinkin' Genesee and gettin' laid ... this is probably a mistake. I'm not gettin' my hopes up, least ways not yet."

"Yeah? Call 'em. Set your mind at ease. Don't want you pacing around here and thumping your fingers on the bar, worrying about the heights of your hopes."

"Ha! Yeah, that's me ... worrying."

"By the way, what's that M in your name for? I didn't know you had an M ... maybe it's for Malcontent or Missed-the-boat."

"Up yours, Wayne."

**

"HAVE A SEAT, MR. DELANEY, and we'll begin," Salvatore Shapiro, an imposing man in a pin-striped suit, squared shoulders and a superior expression on his longish face, motioned him to a chair.

"Huh, where's the others?"

"You're the only one."

"Oh ... somehow, I understood there'd be more." Dennis looked around at the rich paneled walls and contemporary furnishings, eyes wide, but the rest of him seemed to be shrinking. Santa Monica was like this ... full of uppity lawyers in plush offices wielding big sticks and if you weren't careful, you'd be quietly walloped with one of them. The pain could be lasting, he'd heard. He'd heard a lotta shit that made him uncomfortable sitting there.

"Just you, Mr. Delaney. Here's your copy," he said stiffly. "You may read along if you like. I am bound by agreement with the late M. Delaney to read the entire instrument to you." He handed a folder to Dennis that contained five sheets.

"'Being of sound mind ...'" Salvatore solemnly began.

"Hold on ... please, Mister Shapiro, if you don't mind. Who is this Malcolm Delaney? What is he to me? You know, I'm not gonna refuse if there's somthin' coming, but I'd kinda like to know where it's coming from." He was surprised at his brashness, looked around, wondering if he had a right to ask, and if one of Shapiro's enforcers might appear and extract him.

"The documents will make that clear, Mr. Delaney. I'll continue.

"'... of sound mind and possessed of my faculties, do hereby make my last will and testament. All of my assets, listed below, are to be poured into The Living Trust of Malcolm S. Delaney, also initiated this date. If not before, within 10 days of the date notarized below, and distributed upon my death or complete incapacity as described in the Trust.

1. One Land Rover Ninety, 1954

2. Three bottles of Dom Perignon brandy bottled in 1874

3. Five big-game hunting rifles, Mausers M98 .450 (2) and .458 (3)

4. All cash and securities held in my several bank accounts:

> Bank of Zurich, #45-275694-9998
>
> Nakuru Trust, Nairobi, #B783967
>
> All cash held by Bank of Nairobi, Nairobi.
>
> Account Malcolm S. Delaney - 4B44

5. One Burberry hunting jacket, leopard patches on sleeves, smoking pipe in vest pocket

Signed,

M. S. Delaney

Malcolm S. Delaney,

At the Offices of Latten and Proulx, Nairobi, Kenya

Notarized by Argua Muthengi, Dec 4, 1947

Nairobi, Kenya'

"And now, Mr. Delaney, the trust, executed that same day, December 4, 1947. I won't read the headings ... it begins, 'I Malcolm S Delaney do hereby appoint Dennis Malcolm Delaney, my nephew, last address known, Van Nuys, California, as sole trustee and beneficiary; and with assistance from Hart, Shapiro, and Dryer, Attorneys at Law, of Santa Monica, California, executor of this trust,'" He looked up. "That's us, Mr. Delaney. '...and that he be notified of this appointment

449

and benefit status upon but not sooner than my death or incapacity. That he ...'"

Dennis sat silent and dumbfounded. Kinda knew his old man had a brother; thought he was dead, but otherwise no idea of where he was or even his name. *Africa, shit, now that's really something ... and a hunter, wow! Goddamn ... Double wow!*

"...and that's the sum of it, Mr. Delaney. I've checked on the aforementioned accounts, and discovered you are now worth roughly, um, well over half a million dollars more than you arrived with today. You will need to be authorized to access, withdraw, or otherwise manage those accounts, of course, but the will and trust will do the trick; you will simply need to present them.

"Now ... if you like, Mr. Delaney, we here at the firm can act on your behalf with the paperwork ... and there's a bit of it. And, if you like, additionally, you may put us on a small retainer and we will manage your entire estate ... in any way that you prefer, of course." He smiled. "That's our specialty, you know—managing estates, and if I may say so, we do it well—averaging a growth that exceeds the S&P by well over twelve percent over the years. Of course, it's up to you, strictly up to you." He sat erect, shoulders squared, his expression flat and noncommittal.

Dennis sat stunned, as if hit full in the chest with one of his dead uncle's .458s. He couldn't breathe—his lungs without the effect of a functioning diaphragm.

"Holy shit, Mr. Shapiro ... I ... I'm not sure how to reply. Yeah, I suppose. But I really don't know ... this is one big fucking shock. Eh, excuse the language, but I had no idea ... not in

my wildest ... well, you know. I got to think on this some ...."
He took a deep breath. *What the fuck is the S&P?*

"Can I get you some water ... something stronger?"
Shapiro turned to the credenza behind him and pulled out a
decanter and two glasses.

"Yeah ... that'd be good."

Shapiro smiled now, an ingratiating smile, and his
shoulders slumped a little as he relaxed and sat forward in his
chair, sweetness overtaking his face. "Here, drink this, Mr.
Delaney, and if you don't mind, I'll join you. I can see this is a
surprise. We see some of it here from time to time, you know,
so don't be embarrassed. People don't know what life will
bring—death in this case—or how they're expected to respond. We understand, here at the firm of Hart, Shapiro, and
Dryer, and stand prepared to help, should they ... er, should
you, Mr. Delaney, desire that." He downed his drink; his thin
lips opened into a smile, perfect, implanted teeth peeking out,
and his pinky ring glittered in the light from a polished brass
lamp as he drummed his fingers lightly on his oversized desk.

*Jesus Christ, I'm rich. This guy is making me rich ... no,
no, he's only the messenger ... a courier carrying the news,
maybe seeking a tip. Dear Uncle Malcolm—the old man's
brother—he's the one making me rich. Wow, this is good
whiskey, maybe another.* He motioned ... Shapiro poured.

"Uh, yeah," Dennis grinned. "I'll sure let you know, got
your card here ... and well, yes .... Eh, yes, you see to the access
thing, and we'll be in touch. That okay, Mr. S?" *Fuck me, I'm
in charge here.*

"We'll get right to it. It may take a little time. These
things go slow at those overseas banks, and I'll have papers

for you to sign ... eh, related to our arrangement. Thank you, sir, it's a delight to serve you, and in any capacity. We have all the skills and knowledge needed for most any legal occasion—a broad array of contacts and know-how within these walls—and be pleased to serve your needs on into the future. If there is anything, Mr. Delaney, anything at all, you know where—"

"Yeah, Sal, eh ... keep your shirt tucked in, I'll let you know." *Son of a bitch ... son of a goddamn bitch. Maybe I'll go look at some cars.*

On his way out, Dennis shook Sal's hand, patted him on the back, and winked at the receptionist.

"WELL, MR. DELANEY, Mr. Dennis M. Delaney, whata you gonna do now? I mean, a rich fuck like you can do just about anything he wants," Wayne said after Dennis returned and they were celebrating with a bottle of Wild Turkey that Dennis had bought at Ernie's for the occasion.

"WILD TURKEY?" Beth exclaimed. "That's kinda rich for you guys ... somebody die?"

"Yeah, somebody died so another can live and I'm on the livin' side. Drop by when you get off if ya wanna."

"I GOTTA THINK ON IT, WAYNE ... opens some doors. I could travel ... go to Africa, buy a new car. I got a hankerin' to go down to West Hollywood and give old Rosenthal a piece of my mind. I kinda liked Annabelle."

"Forget it pal, she's engaged now and it ain't to you. Got another wide-eyed buck in the bright Rosenthal beam, and they like *him*, the family does ... and the word is, he's got more than a car." Wayne chuckled.

"Ten bucks it's not a Land Rover."

"Nope, it's not. It's a shiny new Jag, and Jeannie says he's got the job ... managing the store that you passed up." He laughed again.

"New Jaguar, huh?"

"Dammit, Mr. Dennis M. Delaney, one woulda thought a man of your stature coulda done a little better with the Rosenthals."

Thirty-Four
Again, at the Gourmet

THEY SAT IN LACEY'S LIVING ROOM mulling over success—the numbers in the ledger in front of her illustrating the fact. Not huge, but Cole was approaching the big-time—so they'd appraised it—and it did look promising. He was a success at the Brown Derby and closing in on another permanent engagement at the Bare Plank. Venice hosted a different crowd, paying less attention to his humor, more to themselves—more about poetry and navel-gazing, and not about guffaws. He was adjusting his schtick—targeted, slower, artful.

A small piece in the entertainment section of the *Times* had mentioned him favorably. "Original," it had said, and "Funny without being loud; has subtle humor returned?"

"Lacey, it's time I took you out for a good meal—celebrate. It's time for the Gourmet. Whata you say; shall I splurge? We're making money. No more dumpster nutrition or clothes from the thrift shop, and hear this, lassie, I bought a new suit—Hart Schaffner and Marx."

"Another place."

"Why? The Gourmet is fabulous—five twinkling stars from the locals, and I might have extra pull because of you. The place is grand, Lacey; it's gastronomically superior."

"It holds bad memories."

"Look, for Pete's sake—put it out with the trash, they pick up tomorrow. Memories go in the green can. C'mon, we're havin' a great time here—strong revenues, big applause, we're on our way, babe—so stow the memories and look at the now, and a peek at the out ahead. There's nothing but big in our future. We'll go to the Gourmet. You'll have a new experience. It'll displace the old and it'll be over."

"I surrender." She tried to smile.

"SURE, WE'LL HAVE A COGNAC; make it a good one," Cole said after the dessert plates were cleared and running his hand through his jumble of hair.

"Cognac?"

"Sure, we're celebrating, aren't we? And I've got something to show you."

"And what would that be?"

"When the drinks arrive."

"Must be important, such ceremony you apply—a stock that's been lingering has hit a new high?"

"Yeah, you'll see ... here he comes now."

"This, sir, is Gautier Extra XO Gold, the best we have. I certainly hope you enjoy it."

Cole nodded his appreciation and picked up his glass, a canary-eating look on his face. "Here's to us Lacey, a great team, good partners, and my fervent wish that we go on together, through life and—"

456

"Cole! What the hell is going on?"

He reached into his Hart Schaffner and Marx jacket and brought forth a small jewelry box and opened it. Resting among the gold embroidered satin was a diamond ring—a solitaire the size of a blueberry. "I want you to marry me," he gushed. "Will you ... will you make me the happiest man on the planet and be Mrs. Stringer?"

Her chin fell. Her eyes glazed up, wide with wonderment. She seemed woozy and put her hands on the seat to steady herself.

"How could ... This isn't fair, Cole—you bushwhacked me with this. We said from the start, no romance. No gender stuff .... I'm not into marriage, not now. You might as well propose to the waiter!"

"I know." He squirmed in his seat and leaned forward toward her, drops of sweat running down from his pits. "Please don't be angry. I know what you've said. And I've held to that promise ... almost. It's just that ... well, I've fallen in love with you, Lacey. I want to make us real partners. We're adults here, we spend a lot of our lives together, why not get married?"

"It's not a 'why not' proposition, Cole. It's a pretty serious contract, and dammit, it's based on mutual love, *mutual*, Cole—that means reciprocal, that I love you as you love me. It's a lifetime of living together, a union of souls. And you enter the bond because you both want nothing else at the time ... *both*, Cole. And never because there's nothing else to do. Anyway, how the hell do you know that you love me? Jesus Christ, we've never even kissed."

He was taken back, run over by one of those huge trucks that came to the dump. He slumped in his chair, took a sip of brandy. "I ... I can feel it here in my gut. It's that we do well together, enjoy the same things, think the same thoughts, and—"

"No, no! You don't know what I'm thinking, or you wouldn't have done this and ... and, Jesus Christ, I don't want you to know what I'm thinking. Can you understand that?"

He was dumbfounded, felt hollow inside, mind a blank, everything gray. There came a silence. He thanked the Gods that he knew for that. He had no out, no place to go, was certain she would say yes but he had misjudged, misjudged completely ... and none of it was funny.

"Look." She put her hand out on top of his. "It's a beautiful ring and a very sweet sentiment, but it isn't for me, at least not now ... and, Cole, please don't harbor the notion that I'll be considering it later. I have no idea what I want in a marriage these days, or even if I want one. I'm sorry, Cole, but it's not going to work."

"Can't we talk about the possibilities?"

"No. What we can talk about is this. We have a business relationship. Yes, we do see a lot of one another but it's between agent and client ... oh, I suppose we're more ... I'm not denying that. We do have similar tastes, and it makes the partnership work better.

"Here's what I'm going to do. Tomorrow I'll see a lawyer and we'll draw up an agreement—agent and client agreement. We've talked about it ... it's time." *And, I might want another client, and another. I'm ready. Maybe I'll talk to Izsak—get his perspective.*

458

"Shit, Lacey, I didn't mean to set off an explosion."

"After we've executed it, we'll know more where we stand in definitive terms. There'll be no misunderstandings. Can you take the ring back?"

"Yeah ... I told the guy it wasn't certain. Down at the bottom, I guess I knew. Sorry ... I'm really sorry. Let's drink the golden cognac, celebrate our forthcoming contract .... The price for this stuff makes the ring look like a Saturday's basement bargain."

**

"CAN I HELP YOU, SIR?" said a salesman at Frank Millard's on Ventura Boulevard at Firmament. "The Man in Red" sold Jaguars and maybe a few others, but Dennis was only interested in the English Mark. "I wanna see a roadster."

"This our newest, an XK140MC. It's a 1956 model. Beautiful, isn't it?

"What's the MC stand for?

"Well, sir, that means the engine is fitted with a C-type head and special carburetors, boosting the horsepower to 210 from the standard 190. This car gets up and goes, officially clocked at just over 140 miles per hour. See here on the dashboard, the plaque that states it's so."

"Umm." Dennis opened the door and started to get it."

"Oh, sir, you won't make it feet first. Here, sit first, then pull your legs in. This isn't a sedan."

He did as instructed. Took the wheel, felt the shifting knob, depressed the clutch pedal and checked out the transmission and the short throws. He looked over the gauges and admired the plaque on the dash. Then looking out through the windshield, he spotted another roadster—slightly different, lower to the ground, sleeker, and painted a bright, fire-engine red.

"What about that one?

"Yes, that's an earlier model—a modified XK120, clocks out at 156 mph. She's equipped for racing though never been on a track. Got heavy-duty springs and shocks, thicker torsion bars, quicker steering, and the engine's been tuned and balanced. Yes sir, goes like the wind, that one ... but she's not for sale.

That's the car I want"—*sleeker, lower, cleaner lines.*

"That one belongs to the owner ... eh, his personal car."

"I'll buy it."

"I'm afraid, sir ... as I said, it's not for sale."

Dennis got out. "Let's talk to him." He walked over to the red XK120, ran his hands over the fenders, the natural leather inside, pearlescent paint you could see into, and opened its door.

"I'm very sorry, sir, but as I said, that car is privately owned. It's just in here for detailing and Mr. Millard will be back soon to drive it away."

"Tell you what, Mr ...."

"Shultz, sir, Abe Shultz"

"Tell you what, Mr. Abe Shultz. You ask Mr. Millard how much he wants for that car, and I'll be in tomorrow with a beat-up Lincoln and a handful of cash. Now you ask him, Mr. Shiltz, what it will take?"

"Shultz, sir"

"Yeah, Shultz."

**

"SALVATORE ... THIS IS DELANEY. I need some money; call it an advance. Can you handle that?"

"How much will you be needing, Mr. Delaney"

"Oh, I don't know ... let's say, eight grand."

"Eight thousand dollars?"

"Yeah ... think that's what I said."

"Yes ... eh, it will be structured as a loan. We're not in the lending business, you understand, but in these special cases we do have a fund. There'll be a small initiation fee and of course the interest, but we can have it available tomorrow, should you want to come in then and sign the papers."

"I'll be there in the morning."

"Yes sir, eh, that'll be fine. Goodbye, Mr. Delaney."

"So long, Sal."

"HEY, WAYNE, you wanna see my new wheels? They're out front with your Bird .... Oh, hi Jeannie, didn't know you were here."

"Whadja get?" Wayne said.

"C'mon, take a look."

"Wow, Dennis, it's beautiful," Jeannie squealed. "I love the color; it looks really sleek. Does it go as fast as it looks?"

"She's clocked at 156. It's a race modified XK120, belonged to the 'Man in Red' ... that's what they call him."

"Sure is a beauty," Wayne said. "I've heard about him, up on Ventura, right?... Got those little foreign brands for sale."

"This was his personal car ... bunch of extras, tuned engine and suspension stuff. Grabbed me the minute I set eyes ... knew she was mine."

"Oh, it looks sooo fast." Jeannie said. "Can I sit in it? You don't mind, do ya, Denny? Can't wait to tell Belle."

"They took the Lincoln?" Wayne asked, walking around the Jag, dragging his fingers along the fenders, across the door "An even trade, I'll bet." He sniggered. "One thing, buddy-boy ... doin' the world a hellva favor—gettin' that pile of junk off the road."

"They weren't real eager, though money can be persuasive."

Jeannie sat in the driver's seat. She ran her hand along the leather coping across the dash, on the drop-down door and the chrome up over the windscreen. Her eyes reached the gauges and she saw the speedometer, noticed the triple digits at the bottom of the scale.

"Wayne honey, will this car go faster than the Bird?"

**

"Izzy, TAKE A MINUTE and tell me about Anna." Giles turned from his desk after pondering the elephant in the house for over a week. He had thought that Izzy would bring it up but that wasn't happening. Moreover the delay was adding to the suspense, which had now become so present it was stymieing his creative progress. "I had a warm feeling for her—never romantic, maybe a big sister. What's she doing now? And why the split so formal, and after so many years of what certainly appeared to be solid?"

"She left, Giles. It's as simple as that."

"Bullshit!"

"My, my, you are impetuous." Izsak looked up from his notebook and frowned. "Well, I could give you my side of the story, though I'm not particularly inclined. Things happen; the planet turns on its axis."

"Help me out here, Izsak. We're friends. You don't want me to make up my own story, go through the rest of my life with one that likely wouldn't resemble reality. I might make my version favor her ... leave you a cranky old asshole. On top of that, my muse is tickling my imagination these days, and who knows what devastation together we might wreak upon you."

"Oh, for Christ's sake. Alright, get us a drink. It's not a short story."

Giles felt the grin on his face as he went to the bar and retrieved the single-malt scotch from the cabinet, an appropriate elixir for pondering with Izzy. He poured out a couple of triples.

"Okay, I'm ready," he said as he placed one on Izsak's table and sat down across from him.

Izsak took a deep breath. "Anna has always been her own person, you know, and that was my initial and lasting attraction. I fell in love with her, for being that way."

He took a sip, put the glass down and pulled a cigar from his waistcoat pocket—preparing himself for a performance. He fought his loneliness these days with snippets of history— Anna and Izsak and all the good times—and verbalizing those recollections to an interested audience had a powerful advantage over the daydreaming he usually fell into.

Sometimes, before Giles' recent arrival, he would get physically sick with the emptiness—stomach churn, sour mouth, gut in spasms—he might vomit, a fucking mess that Rose would need to clean up. Awful, goddamn awful.

"Of course, I was whole back then—when we were young and poor, but ambitious—me in the thick of producing, she with promise and wanting to act—we thought, with my success in the industry, I could help. Things changed with the accident.

"She wanted me to ride. I was afraid of horses—tons of animal, ounces of brain. Anyway, I lost the edge, the one we depended on, and she settled into being my wife and caretaker—a role she hadn't planned on, and didn't care for, but, due to the obligation of serious vows ... and love, I suppose, she was locked in. A woman of talent and beauty, her destiny now confined in a mask. Then you came along; I gave you the key, and the mask came off."

"The Alexandre Dumas thing? I remember that from somewhere."

"Yes, I believe that fits."

"Go on."

"You know the rest. She found success, got parts, got in line for more and needed to be free to capitalize on the opportunities. She may have met a man ... of course she met a man ... men! Lots of fucking men in the business, and I mean that literally."

"You mean a special man, a romantic liaison?"

"Maybe. I don't fucking know, Giles, but there is one—the co-lead in *Sugarcane Blues*, Rory Randle."

"Randle? Yeah, I know a little of him ... tall, good-looking guy. Met him once at the Onion, one of the many times there with Anna. He seemed well-liked, givin' off with the smiles ... lotta teeth, but a little too smooth for me."

"I don't know him; don't need to or want to.

"She had a story—a plausible story. She was cramped here. She had big opportunities coming in. It was her time, and she needed to be free to exploit them. It went on. I knew what she was talking about, of course ... it's the business. A fine-looking woman, moving up in the studio world ... she *needed* free reign ... she needed to be single, to be completely available—without any domestic ties.

"A married woman today just won't make it, especially one married to a cripple ... a loner, now. The divorce gave her freedom, made her more attractive. There's the mystery, you know ... brings more interest from everyone, including those who can help her. The promises. The couch coercion."

Izsak's voice broke as he talked. He fidgeted, his hands moving from his chair to his face, lifting his empty glass and putting it down. He puffed on a dead cigar. Had he been able to walk, he'd be pacing.

"She's smart ... takes care of herself." His voice tailing off.

"What about you? Are you okay?"

"I was hurt, for God's sake ... hurt to the quick like never before ... my world fucking shattered. The worst of it is, I understand it; might recommend it if on the outside. I talked to Arthur a little, consoling he was, and then to Lacey once or twice. Those conversations ... surprisingly were helpful.

465

"She's got hold of it now, Giles ... her life, and she pointed the way out of my doldrums. She pushed pretty hard on me one night ... reset my compass and I caught a little wind in my sails. Riled me pretty good and what was there of that hurt turned to anger ... pissed at everyone for days, and then ... top me off here, will you, dammit; I'm running on vapor."

Giles brought the bottle from the bar and filled their glasses.

"I threw a few things around. I suppose ...." He laughed. "Had I been ambulatory, I might've done some serious damage." He laughed again. "Anyway, in time, I began to realize I was still alive, had some talent and experience and liked to write ... and I got out a bit with Arthur. We went down to the Hut on Sundays and to dinner now and then. We play chess, you know. He's damned good."

Giles sat back and considered his friend who was locating a fit, finding a place in life much as he was trying to do. Izsak had been hit hard on several fronts. He could be a pile of shards, but he wasn't. He was standing strong, facing life's headwinds, and moving on. *And that's what I need to do—get the fuck up and move on.*

"So where now?" Giles asked. "You're back on track, so where are you headed?"

"I found an agent; showed him a script I'd had around for years and recently dressed up. He liked it and damned if he didn't sign me ... thought my name might help with the peddling. Well, I was surprised ... eh, pleasantly surprised, I might say. I know a good story, you know, but he was surprised—didn't expect one from me.

466

"He tells me he's found some interest. Bob Meyer, of all people—don't think you know Bob, the president now of Star-lit Studios. Anyway, he's considering an option. It's not the money, of course, but getting back in the game ... and that I like."

"And Anna?"

"Anna is doing fine; what else would you expect? Our divorce will be final in about four months. She has a place in Santa Monica; I'll get you the address."

"Yeah, I'd like to see her."

"So, Giles, what about you? Where is the breeze taking you?"

Thirty-Five

Half a Bowl of Cherries

"DALTON MY BOY, come in and have a seat there next to the coffee table," Mel Meisner said. "I'm finished here in a minute."

Dalton sat in a wingback and looked around, and then again ... his first time here in this office and he was amazed. It looked like something out of the Victorian age, though he wasn't sure what that might be, exactly. He thought he wanted to know; he had been studying ... well, he'd been thumbing the *Architectural Digest* in his doctor's office. Well, what the fuck, it was a start—he gave himself credit, and why not.

There were beautiful carved pieces of dark wood— cherry, walnut, teak, and not a sliver of white-oak in the place. Meisner's desk was as long as his car with a matching credenza behind it; oils on the walls in ornate frames, silver around where you might expect brass, and the rug, thrown over polished fir planks, was thick and plush, probably wool, with a woven abstract design. His eyes widened as he took it all in. *Shit, this is ... well, I didn't expect this.*

"There, that's done ... can I pour you a drink? Maybe a coffee? You know your dad and me, we go way back—been good friends since ... well, far back as I can remember." He wheeled in his desk chair to a side table next to the credenza and pulled open a door. "I'm going to have a teaser of Southern Comfort ... you?"

"Yes sir, er, I guess I'll have the same."

As he poured and without looking up, Meisner said, "See you have a new leg. How's that working out for you?"

"Fine, sir, a little uncomfortable at first, but the therapy—"

"Here ... here ya go ..." as he left the swivel and came to the coffee table, "and help yourself to a smoke if you like." As he sat deep in a leather chesterfield, he removed the lid from a silver box and slid the box toward Dalton.

"Daisy's been telling me about you. Seems she's a bit smitten. Says you're ready for more responsibility, I'd call it challenge ... that true? I get other reports, you know, all of 'em good—seems you're smart ... good with the tools, and a dedicated worker."

Dalton was puzzled—didn't know why he was there or what might be coming—like a baby must feel when pushed out from its warm and cozy uterus.

"Well sir, I'm doin' my best. Don't like to blow my own horn ... not very good at it anyway."

"Yes .... Well, don't be modest, my boy, won't get you beans at the cantina. If you want more, say so! Otherwise, no one will know. Here now ..." he pushed a glass toward Dalton "...have a sip of that whiskey; it's the best on the shelf from my way a thinkin'—takes the edge, unbridles the tongue. She says you'd like to design ... that true?"

Dalton sat back. He didn't expect that and wasn't prepared ... how should he handle it? And then, like Meisner inferred, he'd just lay it out and go for it. That's what he did as quarterback, and they carried him off on their shoulders. He took a sip of the whiskey. It was sweet, went down easily and left a warm glow. He leaned toward Meisner

"Yes sir, she's right. I *would* like to design. I see what we're building here; I can do as well ... better." He warmed inside at his bravado. "I've had a little experience on my own, designed and built a few things ... a pretty nice bar where I was living that everyone thought was grand. I have a code, think form needs to serve, not follow function, and my—"

"I'm promoting you to designer. We'll see what you can do, and there'll be a nice raise. You'll report to our Chief Drafter, Lloyd Gerner. That's in the east wing. Start there tomorrow. He'll give you a board and the tools are furnished ... everything's there, you know. How's that strike you?"

"That's swell, you won't regret—"

Meisner leaned in. "Now tell me about Daisy, Daisy and you. You seriously interested in my daughter or just foolin' around? Not pushing, my boy, just like to know. Call it a father's curiosity. I know about young men; was one myself for a while.

"And..." He leaned closer, presence felt, voice lowered "...if it's just a little nookie you're after, that's okay. She knows how to handle herself. But if you're serious about her, I mean marryin' serious ... well, I can help you along. Not with her, mind you, but with your career here at Meisner's." He sat back, arms folded, big smile on his face. "So ... have another go at that tumbler, my boy, and tell me ... are you serious about Daisy? I'm her father, you know. Talk to me like that."

Fuck, he ain't much for beating around the bush "Yes! I am serious about your Daisy. I ... I like her a lot. I think we'd do well together, and from my reckoning, we'll ... well, dammit, sir, I don't know any more than that. We haven't discussed our ... our relationship, no confessions about feelin's. We have a good time together; enjoy one another, you know, but we just don't talk about it. So, you're asking me questions I don't have the answers for ... but as things go right now, I'd say there's nuthin to stop us ... at least from my point of view."

"Good boy. Now, let's keep in touch. That'll be it, my boy. Thanks for coming in."

"Yes sir, thanks for the ... your vote of confidence, sir, and the promotion and raise. I like it here at the company ... eh, your company."

"Yes .... You're excused now. You tell my secretary I need the Grant Fixtures file; goddamn hardware suppliers, always late."

*

"How'd it go with Daddy? I know he called you in," Daisy asked that night as they did Chinese in her kitchen, focusing on chopsticks and numbers 6,11, and 19.

"Seems everyone knows everything around that place."

"Well, it's family."

"And I can understand now why he's successful."

"You're avoiding the question, Dalton. Did you get the promotion?"

"Of course, I got it ... and you knew I would get it, though I would rather have gotten it on my own. You didn't need to inter ... eh ...."

"Intercede? Is that what you're looking for?

"Um, not exactly, but it'll do." *Fucking chopsticks. Why can't I use a damn fork?*

"Look, gorgeous ...." She leaned in across the table, caught his eyes. "Yes, I suppose I did hurry it along. It was going to happen anyway. I did it for you ... for us. Don't be angry when a bit of luck comes your way. It's been waiting there in the wings. I just gave it a shove."

He didn't mind a strong woman, one steering the boat, as long as the course taken was one he agreed with, might even have set.

"Are we in love, Dalton? I love you and I know that for certain. It's not a passing fancy with me."

He lost his grouch and smiled at her. How could he be angry? "I love you too." It was the first time he'd said it to her. He put down his sticks and came to her side of the table, bent down and gave her a kiss on the cheek.

"He wanted to know about us. He wanted to know if I was serious."

"What did you say?" She looked up into his eyes. She was radiant.

"I told him I was. I told him you were beautiful. I told him—"

"I do love you, Dalton Dobbs. I dream about you and about us. You are my one, now and into our future, my only one ever."

He took her face in his hands and kissed her on the lips, a long and hungry kiss that she eagerly returned. "Should I move in?"

"Yes, this weekend."

**

"HELLO ANNA, this is Giles. How are you?"

"Honey-pops! It's less than ten in the morning and your voice is clear and strong ... you must be obeying the rules. I heard you were back ... Arthur told Rose who told me. I must learn to breathe. They keep telling me that and I'm fine, dear boy, and you? You must come over and visit me. I'm close to the beach, you know, and we can dangle our feet together. So good to hear your scintillating voice."

"Yours hasn't changed."

"You have my address, don't you, dear?

"Yes, from Izsak."

"Shall we check it? He doesn't favor me these days ... did a boo-boo you know—very bad. Didn't mean to cause all the disturbance, thought he was expecting it ... pregnant with his quiet anxiety for a weeks."

"It's okay. When will you have time? I'm fairly free with mine."

"Tomorrow night. Come by about eight, a few ticks before, and I'll spring for a crab salad out on the wharf. I know a great place. We'll sit outside and watch the sun disappear ...

wait, thinking a new thought now, maybe a bit earlier; we'll be more certain to catch the rays, say seven. That okay?"

"Sure. See you at seven. Do your push-ups before."

HE KNOCKED. Nice place, he thought ... real nice, and back off the street, garden entry, Mediterranean motif. She wasn't sparing the cash, typical Padgett.

"Come in, honey-pops, and give me a hug. God, you look great. Care for a Lucky, delivered today just for you?"

"Anna, you've been shedding your years—slim, trim, fresh and curvaceous. How old are you now, about thirty ... twenty-five?"

"You're a dear; now, about that hug ..." She wrapped her arms around him and squeezed, her breasts, making their presence known. And she kissed him on his lips, sending a hint of her well-cultured message.

"Whoa ... younger and stronger ... and much more assertive. Do I see Hollywood power?" He stood back with his hands on her shoulders. "And a big girl now, no Shirley Temple curls. Doubt I can keep up; not sure I'm gonna try."

"Sit, Giles. I'll bring you a beer. We'll reacquaint for a few minutes and then down to the wharf. That okay?"

"Your script. I'm just the lot boy."

He said he'd been fishing with a kid, and cadging rice and beans, that he might've been in love with a Mexican lady, but really didn't, really didn't know.

She said she was chasing a childhood dream and was finally gaining ground, that she hated hurting Izsak, but *her* life came first for a change.

475

He said he was writing fiction that was more a biography, and that he had a new piece in *Esquire*.

She said her *Sugarcane* role was perfect and Rory Randle was really a nice guy.

They agreed they were on the right tracks, that where they would lead, they didn't know, that the beer was sufficiently cold, and that it was time to walk to the wharf.

"YOU'RE RIGHT. The salad was delicious and fresh; the crab was still moving," Giles said. "And the ocean, here from the end of the pier, extends forever. Great idea, Anna, and tell me, what's next for you after this stint with nice Mr. Randle?"

The sat together on the planks at the end of the pier, their feet dangling, but the water was six yards down. The sun had started its descent and an orange glow followed the horizon on both sides.

"Look Giles, the sun is sinking, the day almost done, but we know it'll be up tomorrow again, just as bright and as promising. That's my career, honey-pops ... promising. My agent has three pictures lined up. I've read for one and there were smiles on the listening faces. That's a good sign, you know. I feel very confident these days ... not a squealing teenybopper but there are good parts for me in celluloid-land ... and I don't need to lie on a couch with my hem up around my ass."

"I can imagine."

"So, I'm staying right here, and Mr. Randle ... don't spread this around but he's not interested in me." She put her hand on his and leaned in, talking softly. "Got *his* eyes on those wearing pants. Now, this doesn't get out, but there's a lot of those masculine hunks spend their days in a closet and their nights roaming bath houses. You'd be surprised, honey-pops."

Giles laughed. "You don't say."

"Now, about you, Mr. Anderson. What's in your future?"

"I'm not sure."

"That hasn't changed."

"Humm ... I've discovered I do like to write—stories, mostly—and I've had some success with magazines, so I think I'll stay with it for a while. Izzy and I, we're—"

"Hear me, Giles ... and I mean this." She turned toward him, put her hand on his cheek. "Follow your heart. Ethan told me that before he inhaled all that gas. For a long time, I ignored mine—trying to do it all righteously, get through the pearly gates without answering embarrassing questions, but that doesn't work in the end. It's one life, honey-pops, no re-rides available, and a person must do what he, or she, does with that foremost in mind. I didn't want to hurt anyone. Stuff ... unexpected stuff happens. I'm not saying shirk obligations; I'm saying don't make them unless they're centered on your course. Get me?

"Took me a while," she went on. "After Izzy's accident, to realize it was his and not mine. How's he doing, by the way?"

"He seems okay. Over the trauma of being left alone and he's working now. He has an agent ... and a promising script that some studio exec seems interested in."

"Well, that's great. Izzy has talent; always had talent and good that he's putting it to use. And you, honey-pops, you will continue writing?"

"Yep. I'll continue, but I might go south, maybe Texas."

"Do they read in Texas?"

A chill came in off the ocean, and they walked home in the dark holding hands. Giles left her at the front door with an eye-to-eye and a touch of their cheeks, saying goodbye and wishing the best. He could have gone in, she invited, but he had other things on his mind now, and he got in the Padgett Jag and drove slowly over the hill.

"'GOOD MORNING, IZSAK."

"Yes, it is, but almost it isn't. You're a bit late today; sleep in? You're usually in here before I roll in."

"Yeah ... didn't sleep sound, stuff on my mind. I'll be leaving on Monday."

"Humm ... Texas?"

"Yeah ... might mosey over that way." A grin evolved; his eyes lit up.

"Do you know where you're going exactly? I like to keep track of the few friends I have."

"San Angelo. Somewhere in San Angelo. I'll drop a card when I settle."

"Giles, my friend ... has it occurred to you that you're not a settler? You know, some people plant roots, acclimate, cultivate, and accumulate. Others explore ... there's the king, and there's the king's navy. One sits, the other sails, and both seem content. Maybe you're navy."

"I'll send you a bottle of something from my next port-of-call."

"Ha .... Have you seen Anna? You might do that before you leave. She'd be—"

478

"Yeah, I did. We had crab on the pier last night ... and a big helping of philosophy."

"How is she?"

"First rate, Izsak. Real fine. Got her hat on straight and seems well directed. Must've got that from you."

"Maybe. I think it was there all along and was only recently noticed. It's no matter, though, I'm glad to hear she is good. She's got something there, that lady ... a big something." Izsak's eyes watered up. "Yes ... good that she's doing well."

**

"Say, Wayne, where the hell've you been?" Dennis said. "Jesus ... you're not around anymore. It's a morgue here, like you already moved out."

"Things to do and the time's almost here, Dennis, my man. End of October the lease is up and ol' Sampson be knockin' at the door ... or knockin' it down. So, good buddy, what are your plans? Don't tell me, I know ... you don't have any."

"I'll do something when the time comes and it ain't here yet."

"What about Shelley? She gonna take you in? A waif with a couple of corrugated boxes and an easy chair wouldn't take up much room. And her daddy's got that position waitin'."

"Screw you, Wayne." He smiled. "I'll get along okay. You know there's a Halloween party at the Hut on the 31st. Bogey's promising a combo; says he'll buy a few rounds. The winner of the apple-bobbin' contest will be set for the night ... and yeah, shit-head, I'm takin' Shelley ... I guess I am. I just as soon not, but she was with me when he brought it up."

"Yeah, I heard about it. Jeannie wants to go, so I expect we'll be there. She wants me to move in with her when Belle moves on with her new fiancée. I'm not so hot on that neighborhood ... rather stay in the Valley. Be temporary, though, if I do. She wants us to find a place of our own, and I'm not so hot about that either—livin' with a broad sort of ties you down."

"What about Joey?"

"Yeah ... Joey, and that's a puzzler. If I was to get serious about some dolly, it'd be Joey. I may be in love with her, and she treats me like a king. I talk to myself, ya know, and I ask, what is it about her you don't like, Wayne, and there ain't nothing—not a word. And then I say, well then, Wayne, what do you like about Joey ... and shit, I'm there for an hour and the goddamn list keeps growing. So then I ask myself, what the fuck is holding you up? And the answer is always the same. It's just ... it's that I'm just not ready now ... and I'm not pushed by Jeannie. She's just fun, and those questions never come up."

"I getcha ... in that same spot. Still got a bag of oat seeds."

"Jeannie ...." He mused. "You know what else that crazy broad wants? She wants me to trade in the Bird on a Jaguar like yours. Shit ... fuckin' women."

"Yeah, they want ya hard until you turn, and then they want to change ya."

"So, what will you do about a pad? I mean, the dooms-day date is just around the corner. I'm packin' my stuff up to-morrow—goin' home for a while."

"Well, if nothing else shows up, I s'pose it'll be Shel' for a while. Even her parents want me there."

**

THE HUT WAS POPPING and snapping, like sprinkled wa-ter on a hot oiled skillet. Most in attendance wore masks. A few were in costume and behind the bar helping out—Slick Eddy, the previous owner. Damn, Dennis thought, and imme-diately his head filled with visions of Eddy's gorgeous wife.

"Who is that guy in that stupid white apron with the greasy black hair?" Shelley said.

"It's Eddy."

"Eddy? Who's Eddy?"

Dennis wasn't paying attention. His eyes were roaming the crowd in search of Mitzi. He'd had a fancy, earlier on, and was disappointed when Eddy had sold out. He dreamt, in mo-ments of musing , that she returned his interest, though with Eddy's tight hold, had little opportunity for reciprocal expres-sion.

"Eddy who?" Shelley repeated

"Slick Eddy, that's who. He's the jerk who sold the place to Bogey ... that's 'Eddy who'," Dennis grunted.

"What's he got his hair like that? Looks like he stepped out of the twenties... and from under a rock."

"Well ... he's got *something*. See that platinum blonde over there, the one in the black mask that looks like a model for Vargas? The one sittin' in that guy's lap. That's Mitzi, Slick Eddy's wife."

"Humm, she *is* pretty."

"Yeah, pretty hot. Hey, there's Nick and Maxine. Two platinum blondes at the Hut. Gonna be confusing; gonna be some kind of party. Let's mosey over and yell out hello"

The combo was playing a jazz rendition of Cole Porter's "Abracadabra," filling ears and blocking the remainder of sounds. People were using hand signals to communicate and so many dancing so close it was impossible to tell whose partner was who's. The Pabst Blue Ribbon flowed from the tap continuously, glass after glass, and shots were thrown down like popcorn at a Hitchcock movie. 'Mosey' was out of the question as they grabbed a beer and threaded their way through the crowd to where Nick sat with Maxine and four or five others.

"Hey Nick! Nick and Maxine! I see you managed to get out from under the cars and spend a little a that cash you been earnin'," Dennis yelled out as they attempted an approach.

"Hey ... and who's that cute blonde you got taggin' along. Shelley, nice to see you again. Where did you find that troll on your arm?"

"Oh him," she said, "found him straddling a broom down under a bridge ... said he was going to wing it up here, but the broom wouldn't cooperate." She laughed.

"So, you gave him a lift?"

"Yeah, in a red Jaguar," Dennis said. "And just maybe it was the other way around ... you know, with the broom."

"Yeah," Nick said, "heard you got a new car, and from the 'Man in Red' ... congratulations."

482

There was no place to sit, and they stood at the end of the table and yelled at each other as the combo blared on. "I've never seen this place so crowded." Dennis said.

"You got Slick Eddy's stalwarts on top of Bogey's friends—that's a big bunch of people, and as I recall, the former a bit rowdier than Bogey's 'Blue Ribbon' crowd. Remember how Slick Eddy kept a sawed-off behind the bar; showed it off now and then when things got explosive," Nick talking history to the girls.

Two of the group across from Nick looked at each other, eyed the bar and nodded, and when they got up they motioned Dennis and Shelley to sit down.

"Think we'll see Dalton tonight?" Nick said.

"Dunno," Dennis said, "though Wayne said he'd drop in with a friend named Jeannie."

"Oh boy, a homecoming," Maxine said.

They drank and laughed; Dennis won the apple bobbing event—free beer for the night—and about ten a loud argument broke out near the pool table and stopped the band and the vocalist in the middle of "Stormy Weather." A couple of guys from Slick Eddy's crowd.

"Screw you, fuck-head, who made you the beer-tasting expert?" And the "expert," feeling challenged, shoved the challenging mouth against the pool table, causing the one in position for his final shot to lose concentration and scratch on the eight-ball.

"There was twenty bucks on that game, you asshole." And the offended player felt obliged to respond and offered the butt-end of his cue to the mid-section of the cause of his misfortune. This brought the friends of the one doubled over into the debate. Several who'd been watching engaged as well and the ensuing discussion heated up as more entered in. A ruffled few were soon moaning on the floor while others stood off to the side holding pain-riddled jaws and dabbing at blood from their noses, but the scuffle went on and cue sticks were flying.

Slick Eddy, seeing need, pulled out his twelve-gauge and blew a hole in the ceiling, bringing an immediate stop-action to the scene.

Bogey thought this a bit too dramatic and admonished his help for creating the damage, but things quieted after that. Some of Slick Eddy's crowd were shown a speedy exit and the combo began again with slow and soothing tunes. The vocalist packed up and left.

Dalton didn't show but Wayne came in with Jeannie on his arm about eleven. "Hey everybody, happy Halloween to all you goblins. I want ya to meet Jeannie." They all nodded awareness and bid them sit down, there being a bit more room now that the injured and friends had exited.

The apple-bobbing long over, Dennis had taken full advantage of his prize. Free beer was unusual at the Hut, and he was loath to pass up a good deal. They all talked about old times while he drank his two or three to their one.

"S'was wonderin' what old Giles is doin' these days; anybody heard?" Dennis said.

"Not me," said Nick, "not a word. Though Bogey said he's in town."

"Guess he's jus' fuckin' sig ... ignorin' us," Dennis muttered. "Som-a-bitch wasn't never a close friend ... get me a refill here, save my seat, will ya Shel?"

484

"You've had enough," Shelley said.

"Nope … yer wrong, Shelley girl, never enough till yer on the damn floor," and he shoved her too hard on the shoulder and into Nick's lap.

"Cool it, Dennis," Nick said. "She's right, you know. You oughta slow down."

"I'll do what I wanna do; no one's business. Anyway, I'm goin' to Africa," Dennis blurted.

"You're going to Africa alright, in your dreams, and there'll be pink elephants and polka-dot hippos floating around on the savanna."

"Let him go, Nick. Maybe he'll pass out," Wayne said.

Mitzi sauntered over, tapped Dennis on the shoulder. "Hey sweetie, you too drunk to dance with me?"

"Naw. Not me. I can dance with you okay … anytime ya wanna. C'mon." And he got up and took her hand. "Some party, eh, and I like this song."

"Harbor Lights" was drifting through the room, and a girl with a smoky voice was singing from the jukebox, *"I saw those harbor lights … they only told me we were parting …"* Shelley seethed as she watched the two dance, belly-to-belly.

"Damn, she's better'n the Platters," Dennis whispered in platinum blonde Mitzi's ear as he nibbled a bit and she moved her undulating body along with his.

"Blow if you wanna, darlin', but no nibbling."

"Screw him," Shelley grumbled. "I'm calling a cab," and stomped over to the bar and Bogey's phone while the object of her anger sort-of-danced, sort-of-stumbled, and the suggestive voice kept singing. *"…For all the while my heart is whisp'ring, some other harbor lights will steal your love from me."*

Shelley remained at the bar until her taxi arrived, and without a word to Dennis, bid the others good night, "and tell that asshole to call me, if he wakes up in the morning."

"What's a matter wid her?" Dennis grumbled. "She pissed? Jus' a little dance wiff ol' Mitz?"

Mitzi sat at the bar with one foot on the railing, the other on a rung, with her dress hiked up above her knees. Dennis watched her for a while, then went over.

"Shay, ya wana dance again?"

"She's finished for the night, buster." Slick Eddy responded. "Go back to your table and take a nap."

"S'okay, but I didn't ask you." And he retreated back to the group, plopped into his chair and dropped his head onto his arms on the table.

"We're gonna go now," Nick said. "We'll drop him off. He can't drive."

"Ask him," Jeannie said to Wayne. "Ask him before he passes out."

"Yeah ... right. Dennis ... Dennis, can I use your Jag tomorrow? Do you hear me, pal? Jeannie and I are off to a family picnic and she wants to show 'em your car. That okay?"

"Uh? Ya know I am ... am the winner ahhh the bobbin con ... con ... race?"

"Your car ... can I use your car?"

"Sozz I'm fux ... fuckin' goin' ... go shoot me a Lyon ... jus like munkle Nal-come."

"Your Jag, Dennis, can I use your Jag?"

"Suit your-slef ... don't care. I'm goin' to Africa."

"Okay, the keys, buddy boy. I need the keys."

"What will you do with the Bird?" Nick said.

"Leave it here, I guess."

"Better I take it," Nick said. "I'll drop Dennis off; Max here can take the Bird with her to the apartment ... be a lot safer there."

"Yeah, s'good idea," muttered Dennis. "Ke-eeep ever-ry body safe."

"C'mon, Wayne, let's go," Jeannie said. "This is over for me."

"Yeah, yeah, let me help Nick get this lunk-head into his car."

Thirty-Six
A Lasting Explosion

A T SEVEN THE NEXT MORNING, NOVEMBER ONE, Victor Sampson and three of his muscled-up buddies came in through the front door of the Beck Street house like a caravan of Mack trucks late for a delivery; Horace Blunt left, shuffling papers in their van. They came to reoccupy his house and it was "about fucking time," according to Sampson. He had been seething over this misbegotten deal for "damned near a year" and was ready to "clean out the shit and restore it to a livable condition, then move in with my friends."

A part of that "shit" turned out to be Dennis, still under the apple-bobbing influence, and curled up in a fetal position, asleep on his bed in the sunroom. The sunroom was the last of the "deplorably disarrayed" scenes in the house Sampson and his trucks came rolling through and there they stopped—jake brakes bellowing.

"Get the fuck up and out, you piece of shit. You got one-half hour before you turn into dust."

Dennis, still fully dressed, had an empty Pabst bottle clutched in his hand and was contentedly snoring when

489

Sampson's blood pressure blew the top of the barometer, his well-developed muscles filling out while an extra helping of red rushed into his shaved head. His adrenaline screamed for action; his testosterone vaporized with heat.

"Get your lousy, stupid, ass up and outta my house," he squeezed out of his bulging throat. And he reached down to a semi-conscious Dennis, grabbed his belt with on monstrous paw, the other on his shirt at the collar, and lifted him off the bed, swiveled him to vertical and pushed him hard against the wall, his feet dangling. The Pabst bottle dropped to the floor.

"Your stay here is over, you aimless son-of-a-bitch. You got exactly thirty minutes to get your belongin's together and exit before I fuckin' pulverize you. You're overdue, asshole, and I've a mind to stomp a little a the shit outta you right now ... do me some good." and he bounced Dennis again, roughly against the wall, still holding with his white-knuckled grips.

"Let 'im go Victor, he can't 'exit' with you holding 'im there," one of his Vic Tanny's buddies said.

Horace arrived with the lease in hand and safely back behind the trucks, he spoke. "It says here," as he waved the papers above the heads of the entourage, "that the occupants are liable for double the daily amortization of rent for each day overstayed from October 31. That would be—"

"Can it, Blunt. I don't want his goddamn money. I want 'im outta here and the sooner the better."

He released Dennis, who took his first deep breath since being rousted, and said, "I'm goin' ... I'm goin' now. Gotta find a box."

"Twenty-five minutes now, or I'll tear your head off," Sampson growled. "You assholes ... destroyed my property, and I'll have you in court, squeeze your wallets so dry they'll look like the Mojave. Everything you got ... every fucking Abe-Lincoln in your pocket, hear me? Now get to it, the clock's a-tickin'."

"Yes sir ... I'm doin' it." Dennis shook his head. He needed an aspirin; a bicarb wouldn't hurt, another four hours of sleep ... and he stumbled into the bathroom, doused his face, chewed a couple whites and followed with a drink from his hands under the faucet. *Shit, where is a box ... maybe the garage.*

He part ran, part stumbled, once fell, on his way to the garage and, under the leering eyes of Sampson and his brigade, found and packed a couple of boxes. With help from Blunt, he managed to get his emerald-green easy chair, the two overfilled boxes, and a table lamp out to the sidewalk in front. *Where the fuck is my car?* And after a few minutes of desperate wondering, it came to him. His Jaguar was at a family picnic.

He couldn't wait here. It would be dangerous, he thought. *Shit, what now? God, whata headache.*

That space between his ears ... it felt like the tympani drumhead during the 1812 Overture coda, and in the pounding, he couldn't think of an immediate answer but one ... and he walked, trying hard not to stagger.

"What the goddamn hell?" he heard Sampson yelling. "What's this junker Plymouth doing here in my garage? Damn those hooligans ... there ain't no end of it."

Dennis wanted to smile but his immediate problem wouldn't allow it. At the Teagarden house, half a block away, he rang the bell.

491

"Eh, hi, Mr. Teagarden. John here?"

"No, he'll be back this afternoon. Can I help you?" Mr. Teagarden, in his swimming trunks, cropped white hair and one hell of a tan over his sun-wrinkled body, rubbed his white stubbled chin in a questioning way.

"I'm Dennis Delaney ... a friend of John's. You know, from up on—"

"Yeah, yeah, I know about you guys. I can hear you most weekends all the way down here ... rowdy damn bunch. What can I do for you?"

"Well, I'm in a ... a sort of a bind. You see, I ... eh, I was wondering if I could stow a few things here. Just a chair and a couple of boxes and ... and only for a few hours till Wayne ... you know Wayne Gundersen?"

"Yes."

"He's got my car and ... well, he should be back in a couple hours and then I'll be gone."

"Humm. Wel, okay, was young mysel, a few years back. Put it here in the driveway, eh, up near the house. You look a mess. Could you use a beer?"

"Gee, thanks, Mr. Teagarden. I'll bring my stuff right down. Thanks again, a lifesaver ... and you're on target with that beer"

"I'll leave it here on the porch, and if you need anything else, I'll be out back. I'm cleaning the pool. Every Sunday, I clean the pool."

With enormous effort, Dennis shoved his chair and boxes down over each crack in the walk. He thought about counting them, but the challenge of numbers was great. Once the chair was in place, in front of the Teagarden garage, he sat out of breath and tackled the beer. It had been a rough morning so far, but he didn't care to think about it more, and his hands soon relaxed; the bottle dropped, rolled into the grass, and he fell asleep.

The Teagarden neighbors, as they entered their cars on their way to church, cocked their eyebrows over curious stares directed at Dennis and whispered to one another through cupped hands about that Teagarden bunch and those outrageous young men up the street.

AT THREE THAT AFTERNOON, John nudged Dennis on the shoulder. "What the hell are you doing out here?"

Dennis woke, shook his head. "You're back." He felt some better, if a little bit stupid, as he related his ejection from the Beck Street house while John held a laugh.

"So little effort brings you so much trouble. So whata you going to do now? You can't stay here; the neighbors are already calling. The ol' man laughs, but Mom doesn't know what to say."

"Yeah, I'm sorry about that. Maybe take me over to Nick's. I think Wayne's Bird is there. And if he goes to the house, he'll know right away I'm not there." He chuckled. "His next stop's bound to be Nick's. I'll pick up my stuff later."

"Let's shove it into the garage."

DENNIS KNOCKED. The radio was on, maybe the TV; there was talk. He knocked again louder. Nick pulled open the door and nodded them in.

"You seen Wayne? He's got my Jag, right?"

"Huh ... you haven't heard? It's on the radio, local news."

493

"Heard what?" Dennis said.

"There was an accident. Wayne is dead. The woman ... they aren't saying a name, but it must be Jeannie. She's in the Valley Med ICU, and they say she may not make it."

"What!? What the hell are you saying?"

"I'm sayin' they're over ... I mean fucking over. That's like ... in no more. And your Jag is dust. Seems they were out on the freeway last night, report says goin' well over a hundred ... lost control and sideways, they say ... flipped over and over—maybe six or seven times, threw both of 'em out after a while and the car slammed into an abutment. Wayne DOA, Jeannie, I'm guessin' it was her ... pretty much looks like your car. They're not giving out details yet."

Dennis sat down, dropped his head into his hands and mumbled, "Jesus Christ, Jesus H fucking Christ." John steadied himself on the door frame. Wayne was a close friend.

"Yeah, it's been on the news, couple times this morning," Nick went on. "I mean, where ya been? The TV at noon. Pictures of the Jag ... unrecognizable. I'm thinkin' they hit something small on the pavement ... at that speed, you know, anything can happen. Once when I—"

"Okay, Nick, that's probably enough for now," Maxine said. "You guys may as well sit down; the next news is coming on at three ... I'll pour you some coffee."

"Wayne," Dennis mumbled, his head still in his hands. "I can't believe it, just can't believe it."

**

GILES LEFT EARLY, FOR HIM, and on a more direct route than before. He headed straight across the Central Valley, Indio and Phoenix about a hundred miles ahead. He'd drop down into Tucson, spend the night. If he got that far, the trip to San Angelo about 1,300 miles from there. It wasn't adventure this time, nor was he out to find himself—it was getting to San Angelo, plain and simple. And now that he'd decided, and he thought that he had, he was eager to see Maria and Juan and get on with his life with them.

His mind wandered as he cruised along about 70 on a highway all but deserted ... up over a rise and down, again and again, with nothing but sky and scrub as far as he could see. He thought about San Angelo. Was it a big place, and how hard would it be to find them. And he questioned too if Maria had opened her restaurant yet. These thoughts, and the wonder he always got from the ride, filled his head.

His energy high, his interest peaked as he imagined a life with Maria. He certainly found her attractive, and Juan a delight. Maybe he could help out, scrub the floors, something. Shit, he might even learn to cook, and he smiled at the thought.

He'd want time to write, of course. Izsak had graciously set up an account and advanced him a few bucks. He would see that his checks from the stories he sold, when he sold them, would be deposited there

"Listen, Giles. Since you don't know where you're going to be, my accountant says we can set up a system with the bank. You'll give me a limited power-of-attorney and as checks come in, I'll sign and deposit them. Of course, you'll have access through all normal channels. There's a branch in San Angelo."

Smart man, that Izsak. A check from *Esquire* for a few hundred bucks was due at the Padgett address.

In Tucson, he got a room, had the special, a meatloaf dinner, and realized he was bushed—nothing left for fooling around. It didn't matter. He'd read a little and get some sleep, another big day tomorrow.

AT DAWN he awoke rested, and in less than an hour, had finished his breakfast in a café next to the motel. Bacon and eggs with home fries, salsa on the side and a full decanter of coffee. He noticed the waitress was cute. *Damn, what a life.*

Another clear day and temperatures warming as he headed east, next stop, or stop over, El Paso. From there, less than a day to San Angelo. He gassed up at a station out of Tucson and checked the oil, tires, and saw that his duffel was tight. His Triumph had become an old friend. He kissed his hand and patted the tank.

"Hey buddy, got room on that thing for another? Just me, no luggage." A voice came from in front, a ragged looking man attached—glassy-eyed, scuffed coat, no socks.

Humm, he didn't want company. "Can't say that I do, sorry pal. Best you find somebody with four wheels."

"C'mon, Mac, I won't be a bother. Just lookin' to go to Juarez."

Giles cranked the engine, which came alive. Put on his helmet and shook his head. "Can't do it my man, no room for a rider. Already loaded down."

496

The man jumped in front of the bike. "Bullshit! You got room; you're being an asshole. Maybe I slash a tire, maybe teach you 'ow to be neighborly-like." He pulled out the switchblade and pressed on the button, click. A long blade, looking sharp, swung out and the man began waving it back and forth.

The man was thin and raw looking, the kind of raw that comes from not eating regular and sleeping outdoors. He had a mean gleam in his eyes. The knife kept waving.

"So, what now, muthafuck, you gonna give me a ride? I'll be nice, you know, settle down, but I need to get to Juarez. It ain't much I'm askin'." The knife kept waving.

Giles pulled on the clutch lever slowly and ratcheted the transmission into first with an audible clunk. The man sneered, more maliciously, and the red around his eyes brightened up. A guttural sound escaped his mouth, and he dropped a muscled hand with the knife toward the front tire. "You fu-ucker," he yelled at the identical time that Giles revved the Thunderbird engine, ducked his head and let out the clutch.

The tire was saved. The man with the knife went sprawling, and as Giles checked out the mirrors, he could see him flat on the macadam, likely breathing in the heavier fumes from the station. There are those occasions when you just haven't got time to bother.

GILES BREATHED EASIER. The fucking guy had it coming. Las Cruces was his next major stop and then down into Texas, five hours and about two in the afternoon, then lunch. He'd be later than planned, he mused; plans weren't his strong suit. From there, a fat 400 into to San Angelo on roads that

497

wouldn't be pleasant. He might as well spend the night in El Paso, across the river from Cuidad de Juarez. He thought about these things in some detail as he rode.

Jackrabbits looked up, watched him pass by, twitched their big ears and cocked their heads. It was desolate country, brush and rock, a tree in the distance and a lot of that between stops. He imagined the sound of his engine was the only one within hundreds of miles, should anyone be listening. He took it all in for a while and then his thoughts turned again to Maria, and the life with her he'd enjoyed. The fishing with Juan on the river, the afternoon snoozes he'd had. The hammock he enjoyed, and the beers Juan brought out, the cantina itself and the warmth from her patrons given freely to him ... the solace it all brought. And of course, Maria ... beautiful, voluptuous, giving Maria. What more could any man want? What more could he imagine as he fantasized the good life—and with her he would write good stories.

He wondered a little about Manolito. He was good with his hands, had a knack for repair, but he'd never run a cantina. In Las Cruces he spotted a Mexican café, pulled in and sat at the counter.

"Bueno, señor, can I help you? A big man with a locomotive girth, large eyes and a smile that stretched ear to ear stood in front of him wearing a clean white apron still carrying the creases of folds.

"You have a menu?"

"Si, on the wall, señor, you would like a beer?"

"Humm, good idea ... a Pacifico, and two beef enchiladas," Giles said without looking up.

498

"No beef today; maybe you will have cheese, maybe chicken?"

"Chicken."

The man shouted the order to the back and opened a beer, no glass. "You come a long way? Your motorcycle is dirty; you look like the road."

Giles chuckled. "Yep, a long way ... and more to go." There were four men in back smoking and through a window he saw two others eyeing his bike.

"We don't get so many travelers in here ... on the motor-cycles," the man said as he grinned. "You have money to pay?"

Giles looked at him quizzically. His antennae, had he had any, would have gone up as he remembered his earlier encounter in just such a place.

"Yeah, I have enough to pay for enchiladas," he said.

The man laughed. "I am only asking. They will be here soon in one moment." And he looked at the four in the back of the room who had put their cigarettes out, were standing now, eyeing Giles and chuckling ... gesturing toward the door.

"Shit," Giles mumbled, following his look, and turned on his stool and started to get up when in through the door came three men dressed in tan with ranger hats and badges. They sat at a table in front, removed their hats, yelled out an order to the man in the apron, now absent his grin.

The four in the back sat down and lit up. "Coffee," they yelled at the apron.

Giles finished his enchiladas. They seemed especially good. And while he was eating, he wondered why the Mexi-cans he'd encountered south of the border were friendly and warm, and those on this side were shit.

Once on his bike and out of Las Cruces, he reconsidered. He realized he didn't know many on either side, and that there was 'shit' in small number most anywhere you looked. A smile sauntered in and came to rest behind his eyes.

**

DENNIS RENTED A CAR. He bought a six-pack of Pabst and took a room with a fridge at the Venetian Inn, a couple blocks from the Hut. He called Sal to inquire about progress and then settled in as best he could, his mind in turmoil—a lot of thinking bouncing around on unfamiliar ground. In a day or two he would call Shelley to apologize for his Halloween rudeness and to make amends if he could, though he hadn't much hope. He felt non compos mentis, or whatever it's called, and preferred to remain that way for a while, gathering his wits slowly, catching his balance, and trying to figure what was next.

"HI SHELLEY, It's Dennis."

"Dennis who?"

"C'mon, don't make this more than it is. I just want to apologize. Yes, I was an ass, drank too much, and ... well, I'm sorry."

"Oh, that Dennis."

"Please ...."

"Look ... I've had enough. I fell for you at first 'cause I thought you were a sweet guy ... someone I could spend a long time with, maybe marry, but now I know better. You drink too much, you do reckless things, you cheat, you ... you *kill* people. You'll kill yourself sooner or later, it seems. Everything you touch turns sour and others get hurt and now it's a funeral. No, I'm finished, period. Do me a big favor and don't call anymore." She hung up.

Mmm, I guess she's serious.

NICK CALLED AT THE INN. "You going to the services?"

"Yeah, I guess, hadn't thought about it. You going?"

"Yeah. Max's going too. I got ahold of Dalton, who said he'd probably attend. No church service or anything at the mortuary … only graveside at the cemetery—Mountain View in Pasadena."

"Yeah, probably not much to look at."

"You hear anything about Jeannie, the girl he was with?"

"Nothing."

"You know how to get hold of her folks?"

"No … maybe … I don't know. I could check into it."

"Be good to know."

"Yeah. I'll give it a try,"

DENNIS DROVE OVER THE HILL into West Hollywood, down Hollywood Boulevard and left on Melrose to 3945 and parked behind a new Jaguar coupe. *Must be the fiancé is here.*

He wasn't excited about this visit, but it would be short if not very sweet. He rang the bell at 503, Anabelle Rosenthal's apartment, heard voices and waited. The voices got louder and then he heard, "Well, get the damn door, then." It was her.

"Hello, can I help you?" A tall handsome guy, slim with shiny black hair and blue eyes, stood in the frame.

"Is Anabelle here?"

"Maybe, whata you want?"

"I want to talk to her."

"Well, maybe she is and maybe she isn't, so who the hell are you?"

"Tell her it's Dennis Delaney. She'll see me."

He shut the door. Dennis waited. He could here disagreement in low voices and then he heard clearly, "You're not my keeper so back off." The door opened again. Belle poked her head through a small opening.

"Hi, Dennis. I'd ask you in but you wouldn't like it inside. It's about Jeannie, right? Jesus, what a calamity. She's ruined Dennis ... even if she pulls through, she'll be a total wreck."

"She's alive?"

"Yes, but you can't see her ... intensive care at the Cedars."

"You got a room number? Maybe an address for her parents?"

"Her parents are dead. You won't believe this ... they died in a car accident about six years ago on the Hollywood Freeway."

"Boy, that *is* strange."

"She has an aunt that's close, her mother's sister. She lives over in the Sliver Lake district. I'll get you the address."

"Belle! Knock it off. Get him what he wants and finish it," a voice came from inside and she moved the door closer to closed.

"That your fiancé ... Freddy?"

"Yeah, a jerk sometimes, but ... well, Daddy likes him, and I guess he's okay"

"Gotta nice car, huh?" Dennis laughed. "You know there's a service for Wayne. Graveside this Sunday at the Mountain View in Pasadena."

"Yes, I know. I won't be going. Freddy doesn't see the point. Wait a minute." She left the door open a crack while she went for the address.

**

DENNIS RODE OVER WITH NICK AND MAXINE. The service was at ten. Dennis had sent a wreath to the mortuary and a note with a small spray of lilies to Gladys Bentley, Jeannie's aunt: '*I am very sorry, Dennis Delaney, a friend of Wayne and Jeannie.*'" He had no idea if lilies were appropriate but the girl at the shop said everyone liked lilies.

Pasadena was socked in when they arrived at a few minutes to ten ... part smog, part fog from a lingering overcast, and the place showed a deep green with the moisture and carried a late-night quiet. They parked and walked over to a small gathering. Most were silent with heads bowed down, a few whispering.

"Hi, Dalton. Good to see you again ... not since the hospital." Nick extended his hand.

"Nick. Dennis. This is Daisy." They nodded and shook hands.

"You remember Maxine," Nick said.

"Sure. Hi Maxine, meet Daisy."

"Nice to meet you," Maxine said to Daisy. "Tough times, here. We might get together later."

Daisy nodded. "I'd like that, Dalton speaks well of you guys."

A hearse pulled up, followed by two limousines. From the first, an older man, graying hair, rimless glasses, and a tall woman got out ... she in a black veil and sobbing, he holding her up and consoling. From the second limousine, five men emerged as the gate at the rear of the hearse opened and a mahogany coffin rolled partially out. The men gathered at the gate, began whispering to one another.

Another man from a third car joined their discussion, then turned and approached the gathering. "I'm pastor Bergström, and I'm wondering if I could prevail upon one of you men to be the sixth pall bearer. We seem to be missing one."

Nick looked at Dennis, "You, Dennis, you were his closest friend."

Dennis hesitated. "Gee, I dunno, I—"

"Yes, you'll do. Thank you." Pastor Bergström said, and he took Dennis's hand and shook it. "You are?"

"Dennis Delaney."

"Yes, Mr. Delaney. Please come with me."

Five men in black, and Dennis in a navy-blue blazer, carried Wayne slowly and in step to the lift that would lower the coffin, hoisted it into position and moved away. Flowers were carried up, placed near the gave opening, and the service began.

Bergström's voice was low and melodic as he read through his ritual. Women wept, men stood silent and glum.

When he finished, he closed his book and turned to the gathering, "Would anyone here like to say a word?"

Dennis's mind raced. Yes, he'd like a word. He felt compelled, a personal bond with Wayne, and some with the 'Man in Red' ... but what would he say? Words hid out as this obligation propelled him to the front of the gathering where he hoped something fitting would find its way to his brain.

"Yes, uh ... I'd like to say something. I'm Dennis Delaney. Wayne was a good friend. We partied together sometimes, and sometimes we just talked about our lives, what we might do as our time coming up went by." He paused; his legs trembled a bit. "I ... I loved Wayne ... like a brother ... didn't have one, you know. We supported one another, talked over our problems, and shared good times. And we had a few laughs along the way, you know." He put his hands in his pockets and looked to the ground. "I'm gonna miss Wayne ... miss him terrible." His voice broke, and he had some trouble with words. "... but well ... maybe he'll stay with me like I'm gonna stay with him ... in my thoughts ... most every day. And ..." He glanced over at Bergström, "...well, thanks for letting me talk here. Bon voyage, Wayne, I won't be forgettin' you ever."

Mrs. Gundersen let out a wail and began sobbing again.

"A warm sentiment," Bergström said, "from the heart of a friend. Anyone else like to speak, to remember Wayne?"

People shuffled and whispered but no one spoke up, and Pastor Bergström continued with his eulogy—praising Wayne and introducing him to God—as the coffin was lowered. When in place, Mr. Gundersen threw some dirt on the lid and mumbled, "Christ be with you, my son."

Some woman in black threw a bunch of lilies.

The gathering slowly broke up and folks dispersed to their cars. Mr. Gundersen came over to Dennis and extended his hand. "Wayne spoke of you often ... your roadster he was in that night?"

"Yes sir."

"I hope you'll be alright, Dennis. Maybe you'd like to visit us sometime, when Grace ... eh, Mrs. Gundersen ... is feeling better. She doesn't blame you, but this loss has been tough ... tough on us both, but hit her the hardest."

"Yes sir, I understand, and I might do that sometime ... visit you folks. Thank you."

The sun was peeking through the haze from directly overhead when they reached their cars. The grass was drying out and the earlier rich colors were fading. Daisy said, "That was a very nice speech, Dennis. You should be proud."

"Yeah," Nick said.

"I agree," Dalton said.

"Gotta be a bar around here somewhere," Dennis said.

Thirty-Seven
Things Just Are

NICK, DENNIS, AND DALTON went to dinner that night at Haley's ... for old time's sake, they said.

"So, Paul and Mary F got married," Dalton said. "I thought I was in love with her once. I wasn't, you know. I suppose I wanted to be for a while. Anyone heard how they're doing?"

"Not a word," Dennis said.

"Big mistake," Nick added. "I don't think it'll last, not wishin', ya know, but ... well, they just don't seem like a pair. Paul, pretty depressed after your accident, and the loss of his job ... might've stepped in without lookin' ... shit, might've stepped anywhere, and she was pulling hard, If you were to ask me—"

"It wasn't his fault," Dalton said. "The accident. It was mine, flying off the handle and stuff. I told him that after. I was angry back then ... at most everything. Daisy says I was trying to keep up, be someone else, and feeling I couldn't ... she's probably right."

"Steaks here are great," Dennis said.

"And the salads," Nick added, "and best Roquefort in town. I've never ...."

"Too bad about Wayne," Dalton said. "Way too bad. I couldn't believe it. Always thought him a good driver, and he didn't hit anything, they say ... I mean, to cause the crash."

"It was Jeannie," Dennis said. "Hard to blame her ... I mean the mess she's in, but we don't know who was driving; easily could have been her. Now think about that. That would explain a lot of things. She was a speed freak, could never go fast enough."

"There must've been something in the road," Nick said, "dark night, didn't see it. Maybe a two-by-four fell off a truck ... something. I mean I know that car ... it's steady and roadable."

"Yeah, tuned for racing," Dennis said. "Special suspension—springs, shocks, torsion bar all set up for competitive handling. And doncha think, Nick, they would've found something in the road, something that caused it? No-o. I bettin' on Jeannie."

"Jeannie? Never met her," Dalton said. "What about her and Wayne ... serious?"

"Humm," Dennis said. "He said he liked her because she was exciting, never said no, ready for whatever came up, but down deep, I think it was Joey. Shit ... I guess I'll have to talk to her."

"Daisy and me ... we're getting serious. She's a great girl. And I'm designing furniture now at Meisner's. He's her old man, you know, interested in her future, he says, and mine, of course." Dalton laughed. "Things are working out good,

508

though. We're sharing a roof now, moved in with her a week and some back."

"Say, that's swell," Nick said.

"Hey, there's the waiter," Dennis said. "Sir, eh, waiter, another round here, please."

"So, Dennis, what are you going to do?" Dalton said. "You're the odd man out; the rest of us moving steadily on course into responsibility." He chuckled. "You seem the only one free."

"There's Giles," Dennis said.

"Doesn't count anymore," Nick said. "Not for much."

"Dennis?" Dalton said. "C'mon, what about you?"

"I'm going to Africa. Got my tickets, leaving on Thursday."

"You're shittin' us," Dalton said.

"Nope, not at all. First leg is to New York, then Lisbon, then Nairobi ... that's in Kenya."

"Can you swallow all that, Dalton?" Nick said. "He told me about it the other day; damn near keeled me over."

"Kenya!" Dalton said. "What the hell will you do there?"

"Pick up some Mausers and a Land Rover that's mine, get a guide, cruise around ... I don't know. Turns out I got ... had ... an uncle lived there. He died, left me some money and such, and I thought, why not. Maybe a new life for me. This one's not working out so well."

"Mausers! Jesus, Dennis, you could be hunting wild game instead of pussy." Dalton laughed. "And I'll bet you'll score higher."

"Take a bible," Nick said. "If the huntin' doesn't work out, you can minister for a church. Seems you'd be good at it.

Ol' Bergström can give you a recommendation. I hear Cole is doing stand-up, Lacey is managing ... putting the ring in, I'm guessin', but doing pretty good, had a run at the Brown Derby—six weeks, I heard."

"I liked Cole," Dennis said. "Lightened things up. Can't see the ring, though; thought he was his own man."

"Okay, let's see," Dalton said, splaying a hand and touching each finger. "Paul married with family—geez." He shook his head. "Still can't get over that ... Nick in business—his own garage, Dennis off to Africa, Cole's on stage, Wayne's off to a different place, and I'm gonna get hitched, I imagine, soon ... so back to Giles. Nobody's heard? Nothin' at all?"

**

"HI, DALTON, thanks for meeting me here," Paul said as took off his jacket and scooted into a booth across the table from Dalton. "See you have a beer, though low in the glass; hang on a minute, I'll get us a fresh start."

"Sure. No hurry, though, I took the afternoon."

"You're working?"

"Yeah but got all the time we need. Hey Bogey," he yelled out, "draw two."

"I'll bring 'em over. Always happy to see old friends," Bogey said, wiping his hands on his apron. "Anything to eat?"

Paul looked at Dalton, raised a brow.

"Yeah, I'll have a burger," Dalton said. "Cut the onions."

"Make it two, onion on mine."

"Missed you at the service," Dalton said. "Tragic thing, that accident ... fucking pulverized the car, same for Wayne.

Closed coffin, you know; I doubt there was anything recognizable left. I didn't know the girl."

"Yeah ... meant to be there; got the message too late. The guy I'm working for ... he's not big on sudden departures. Casinos ... what a hell of a business."

But he wasn't there to talk about Wayne, his boss, or the casinos. He wanted to go back, to assuage his guilt, deserved or not, to change the things that happened and his involvement in them. It was holding him hostage, idle moments, an empty glance, all immediately filled with the Paul he was but no longer wanted to be. He wasn't hopeful because he had tried—back to the beginning, he tried to erase the posturing and pronouncements, but of course he couldn't. All he could do now was confess and Dalton would be his confessor. It seemed the only way to get back, rid himself of the thing that was pulling him down—his history. He wanted to be absolved ... to be forgiven. He wanted to change his history—to destroy the earlier Paul—the Paul who invited Dalton to join him at the Paradise Apartments and then proceeded to belittle ... to advise and correct, not intentionally, but because he felt he knew better.

"Tell me, D, how are you doing?" Paul looked up, catching Dalton's eyes. "I suppose you know I'm here on an errand. Not sure how to start but ... well, here goes. I apologize. I can't tell you how sorry I am about all that ... that stuff that precipitated the fight." He crossed his arms over his chest, then quickly dropped them down to the table. "Your accident ... your leg. I feel ... well, I feel responsible and can't seem to shake it ... don't know that I want to just yet, or even if I can, but I'd like a re-do, even as I know it's not possible."

He leaned back in the booth, a jumble of thoughts if nothing coherent. He'd rehearsed his speech, gone through this session with Dalton over and over if not word for word, at least the high points. He had to confess, to seek absolution, get this fucking weight off his mind. No, it wasn't for Dalton he'd made this trip, it was for him—to cleanse himself, to correct his past even as he knew it impossible. It all seemed a difficult chore with failure most likely, and the thing that he feared the worst was the most likely to come—Dalton's dismissal.

"I've thought a lot about it," Paul continued. "I need something I guess, and it might come from you. It wasn't the fight so much ... the culmination, you know ... but that arrogance of mine leading up to it, and I imagine the anger you must've felt as it was grinding ... every day for years, you must've felt it grinding." He raised his hands as if in surrender, pushed his arms against the back of the booth then let them fall. "I am sorry, Dalton. I am sorry for my stupid, ignorant behavior. I didn't realize at the time ... that I was being so presumptuous, pompous, and overbearing—that only I had it right, and you needed to follow."

Dalton chuckled and leaned in toward Paul across the table. "Paul, we're friends. I'm over it. Sure, you were a first-class ass, and I carried a big chip for a while, but I've moved on, and suggest you do the same." He smiled; an open, generous look came over his face. "We live and we learn, they say ... and they're right, ya know. You thought you were king, and I gave you the crown. I participated too, played my part. But I'm a good student now and since I have learned ... though it took a big wallop aside this thick skull." He laughed as he patted his head. "So, let's forget it, huh, at least put it behind. That's where it belongs, you know."

"You're a good man, Dalton. If only I'd realized it then. Things could have been different. Maybe you'd have it in your heart ... you know, could you forgive me."

"No ... I don't need to forgive you. You did, I enabled, it's history. You have no idea how pissed I was ... looking back, time to time, anger building and not letting go." He smiled— big grin, ear-to-ear. "No idea, Paul. Sure, things could've been different, but they weren't. Let's take it from here; that's what I wanna do. Okay with you? Shall we shake?" He reached across the table and Paul met him tentatively in a solid and comfortable handshake. Not what he had come for but seemed it would have to do.

"As it turns out," Dalton said, "my life looks good. I've met a girl; we're living together and have plans for the future. I'm working again, designing furniture. The shop belongs to her dad, and we get along just fine. So, there you go, Paul ... without the accident and the rest, I'd still be servicing cold boxes, my name on my chest, and paying those union dues. So, my friend, let it go. I may decide, someday you've done me a favor."

Paul smiled, a painful smile ... not satisfied and wasn't sure why. What did he need from Dalton? What more could Dalton give and why was he so okay with all this? He didn't know, but it wasn't finished, and he pondered the reason why. And then it occurred to him, the problem wasn't Dalton's to solve.

"Here ya go guys, Bogey's best, fresh from the pasture ... fat and juicy half-pound burgers with the Hut's secret sauce.

The one with the pick has the onion ... and the fresh frosty Pabst is on the house."

"So," Dalton said, "tell me about you. Who are you working for and what are you doing? How is Mary? I hear she's your wife now."

"Yeah ... well, I'm counting money at the Nugget downtown ... the golden one. And there is glitter and noise, shuffling and dealing, clicks of the wheels, and bells that keep ringing. The money goes only one way, into the coffers of those that own—likely the mob. I find it distasteful at best, counterproductive, and more than that, I likely won't last."

"Whoa, that's a lot to digest. Why do you stay?"

"Nowhere to go, I guess."

"And Mary ... the kids?"

"We see each other for breakfast."

"Breakfast?"

"Yeah ... I'm off at six in the morning, home about the time the others are getting up. I fix coffee, she cooks, we eat, and they're off to school as I go to sleep. At about three I wake up, shower, have something to eat. Mary will be out to pick up the kids. Sometimes they're back before I leave, sometimes they shop or visit with friends."

"Doesn't sound like much of a life. The money's good, I suppose."

"It's okay. We're saving for a house, maybe a business."

"Well, there's a bright light."

"Yeah, I guess, but there's a long dark tunnel ahead of it."

"Humm ... how is she doing with all of this? Not working I guess."

"Nope. She has some good friends there, Mac and Charlene, spends most days with Charlene ... school chums and all that. Mac runs a gas station, maybe two—more time at the station than me at the Nugget. They ... well, I'm not too happy with all of it. Don't see much of either Mary or the kids. Might have been better to stay in the Valley ... Umm, gonna miss these burgers."

PAUL LEFT AFTER THE BURGERS. He'd got as much as there was of what he had come for and if there was more, it wasn't with Dalton. On the drive back he thought about his life and gave it a "65." It sure as hell wasn't what he bargained for when he left the University of Kansas.

He wouldn't last at the Nugget, the 112-degree heat lasting most of the night. He didn't like Las Vegas, even when visiting on weekends, and now he was a resident.

It was the whole damn package including Mac and Charlene—ordinary people, but Mac's idea of a "great weekend" was a backyard portable grill and a tub full of beer, followed inevitably with pleading faces from hungry kids, righteously angry wives, and little nasty quarrels necessarily forgotten the next day. He was caught, and he knew it—a one-time happy fox in a bear trap.

Maybe Dalton was right. Things are what they are; best to let the past go and turn fully to the future. It looked ugly, but what else could be do?

**

GILES PULLED INTO EL PASO in the early afternoon, a little late to start the long leg to San Angelo, but not too late for a run over to Juarez and the few miles south to the cantina—maybe just cruise by and have a look, maybe stop for a beer and a "bueno" for Manolito ... see how things were going for him.

He located a place by the river to spend the night. The Starlight featured a café-bar and club off the lobby, a promising diversion, should he be interested later.

"You want single, suite, view, cook privileges—all comes with kitchenette—one, two beds? You want room service? You want girl later—$15 for an hour and must reserve now. My name Hui. I here till midnight. What? You tell me now."

He grinned, wondered if there might be a list he could study. Hui, a little woman wearing a black Nehru and enough gold to supply Fort Knox, looked up at him with large piercing eyes set prominently in a stern, angular face. She wanted his answer now, he thought, right fucking now.

"Let's see, single ... one bed, no cooking, no girl, no view. That work for you?"

"View only left."

"Okay, view."

"That be $25. You pay now."

"Twenty-five dollars, wow. That's kinda stiff."

"You want?" She pushed the registration book toward him and smiled for the first time. "You sign."

What the fuck, I'm here and that make me committed. He chuckled.

The view, down a cobblestone alley leading to the street, allowed him a small piece of the Rio Grande. He could see it when standing in just the right place. He laughed, brought in his packs, brushed his teeth and left his fine view through the window for the real one. He drove across the street to a gas station and filled up—the bridge just ahead and Juarez.

An hour later, he pulled up to the cantina and sat, engine idling. "Humm ...." The sign hadn't changed. The corner was the same. Manolito's repair shop was just as it was the last time he stopped here. He killed the engine and opened the same screen door and listen to the same squeak. The same little bell rang as he walked in and the same smells filled his nostrils. A woman, behind the bar washing glasses, turned. His eyes needed to adjust but ....

"Giles! *Mi amigo bueno* ... what a wonderful surprise. I think about you often and Juan, he talks all the time."

"Maria?"

"*Si. Por supuesto*, it is me. What are you doing here? Come, *mi novio*, give me a hug." She ran from around the bar with her arms extended.

"Why...?" He didn't have an opportunity to finish his question as she took his surprise in her hands and gave him a long kiss, then her arms wrapped warmly around him for her "abrazo." "*Dios mina*, it is good to see you. I will get you the beer ... un cervaza." She laughed, her face beaming.

Several patrons laughed as well. "*Bien venido!*"they said.

"Sit, Giles. I will bring the beers and we will reacquaint. I want to hear ... where did you go? Why did you return? And then I will tell you."

He took a chair—confused and curious. She brought Pacificos and cold mugs. "Your favorite, do I remember?"

He smiled. "You remember."

He related his last couple months, though briefly. "And now, you. Why are you here? I thought San Angelo...."

"The bank," she said seriously. "El presidente ... he did not approve the loan ... in its entirety. And Manolito so disappointed, he wept. He went to hiding in his garage, turned the business away. I too felt very sad. Juan would not go to school in the USA. I was very disappointed, almost as Manny.

"Then, Giles, I had the dream. Manolito and I would become partners. He would give me a little cash, whatever was fair, and half of the garage, and I would give him half of the cantina. We would be partners, in business together. It would be good, a complementary arrangement. I spoke to him the next day. He was still very sad when I found him but when I told him my dream, he became happy. And Giles, it worked. And now with a little money Manolito got from the bank to purchase only a part of me, Juan would still go to school on the Texas side, the USA, and all would be fine. Juan ... he takes the bus. He is in school now, in El Paso. Isn't it wonderful?"

Giles' mind trembled with confusion—a kaleidoscope of questions. *What now for me? How would I fit in? Partners? What did that mean? Maybe business? Maybe more? Why is it all so different? Change ... there is always change.*

She was beautiful, as lovely as ever—"*in her presence, the flowers blossomed, bees buzzed, and the sun shone brighter than before*"—a tribute he gave to her when last he was here came back to rest in his head.

"So, Giles ... You must tell me, why are you here now? Where are you going?" she asked, her brown eyes twinkling.

The bell rang and Manolito came in. He paused a minute, then sauntered over to their table, bent down and gave Maria a kiss on her cheek, his hands on her shoulders.

"*Hola, muje de las minas* ... and Señor Giles ..." He extended his hand, which Giles took.

"Hi Manny."

"*Bueno verte*," he said. "I will get a beer ... should I join you?" He directed at Maria.

"In a little time," she said. "*Giles y yo familiarization de nuevo.*"

"*Bueno*," he said with a big smile, kissed her on her neck and walked over behind the bar where he put on an apron and sat.

Giles watched. So, Manolito was that kind of partner. His wondering stopped.

"So, my beautiful Giles, what will you do now? Will you stay with us for a while, *por favor*? See Juan? He would like that. And the hammock, it is still there."

Giles' head was whirling—it hadn't stopped, and he waited for an answer he knew was there somewhere amidst the swirl.

"Giles...?"

"No ... eh, no, I won't stay. No."He shook his head. "Just passing through .... You know these feet, no moss on these soles." He pushed back his chair, and with difficulty he couldn't articulate in his mind, brought up a grin. "I'll go now. Seems you are doing fine; have what you need ... and I guess what you wanted. I'll be on my way." He pushed his chair back and with some effort, got up. He looked around, kissed her lightly on her forehead and waved to the others. The screen door squeaked; the little bell rang.

She ran after him.

"You ... You could have said .... I wanted you to say, but you left, my beautiful man ... as you go now. So go again this last time, this very last time and *ve con los dioses*. Now, this day, there is nothing for us."

He sat on his bike for a few minutes, watched her as she went back through the cantina door. His eyes clouded up, and a tear escaped down his cheek ... fell to make a small bit of mud in the dust. Then, in the dry hot air he kicked on the crank and turned left to El Paso and the Starlight Motel.

Fini

D.L. has traveled a good part of the northern hemisphere: earlier on a wind-parched thumb, then in an old ford coupe  won in a poker game, and later, four chrome-spoked British wheels occasionally on a track somewhere in the Midwest.

He's had three squares, a uniform and billet from the USAF, gone church-mouse hungry for months in LA where he shopped dented cans in Watts, and with a friend of similar means charmed wealthy women at clubs—maybe a breakfast, at least a drink.

D.L. has weathered the storms of romantic love, spent wonder-filled summers sailing Georgian Bay with Canadian friends of life-long acquaintance, skied the slopes at Tahoe and Mammoth, and when sufficiently seasoned, settled into the quiet life of family and job.

Adventure his companion, risk an associate, he has explored most opportunities encountered. and today entertains us with some of what he has learned.

Dave, as he is otherwise known, is a long-time member of the California Writers Club, the founding chair of its regional association, the NorCal Group, past president of the South Bay Branch, and ran a critique group ten years in operation. He is also founding and seven-year editor of the California Writers Club's Literary Review

www.ingramcontent.com/pod-product-compliance
Lightning Source LLC
Chambersburg PA
CBHW021835010726
47493CB00005B/1407